THE
DEVIL'S
BANSHEE

The Devil's Intern Series

BOOK III

Donna Hosie

Holiday House / New York

For Kathleen Welch

Text copyright © 2016 by Donna Hosie

All Rights Reserved

HOLIDAY HOUSE is registered in the U.S. Patent and Trademark Office.

Printed and Bound in June 2016 at Maple Press, York, PA, USA

www.holidayhouse.com

First Edition

1 3 5 7 9 10 8 6 4 2

Library of Congress Cataloging-in-Publication Data

Names: Hosie, Donna, author.

Title: The Devil's banshee / by Donna Hosie.

Description: First edition. | New York : Holiday House, [2016] | Sequel
to:

The Devil's dreamcatcher. | Summary: Team DEVIL is back—this time, led by
the indomitable Viking prince Alfarin to wrest a banshee from her hiding
place in the Nine Circles of Hell.

Identifiers: LCCN 2016001254 | ISBN 9780823436507 (hardcover)

Subjects: | CYAC: Hell—Fiction. | Future life—Fiction. | Death—Fiction.
| Vikings—Fiction. | Banshees—Fiction.

Classification: LCC PZ7.H79325 Dam 2015 | DDC [Fic]—dc23 LC record available at https://lccn.loc.

gov/2016001254

THE DEVIL'S INTERN SERIES

by Donna Hosie

CONTENTS

ACKNOWLEDGMENTS

I've always wanted to incorporate elements of the imaginative *Divine Comedy* by Dante Alighieri into a manuscript. With *The Devil's Banshee*, I finally have my chance.

I relied on the Oxford University Press edition of his work, translated by C. H. Sisson, to guide me through the Nine Circles of my version of Hell. Variances from the original are intentional. *The Divine Comedy* is a joy to read but even more fun to study, and I am indebted to those who have spent years examining and interpreting the text for future generations of readers and scholars.

Much love and thanks also go to the following:

Kelly Loughman, editor and Alfarin fanatic: Thank you for making me laugh all the way through the months of editing by constantly proclaiming your love for my bighearted Viking.

Beth Phelan, agent and Team DEVIL's first advocate. Thank you for your ever-present critical eye and hard work.

Aubrey Churchward, publicist and fellow Raven Boys fan: Thank you for the Maggie Stiefvater photo. And the publicity stuff. But mainly that photo!

Sabrina Abballe, coconspirator on the photo mentioned above and so much more: Once Team DEVIL, always Team DEVIL.

Everyone at Holiday House, publisher: They also have cake!

Harry, my dog(!): Why am I thanking my dog? Because I left him out of the acknowledgments for books one and two and my kids have given me so much grief I was made to promise to dedicate book three to him! The dedication is going to my beloved Granma, but Harry is mentioned now. Look, kids, he's getting more lines than my editor!

Steve, my husband: Stop telling me I got Septimus's accent wrong. He isn't Idris Elba!

Emily, Daniel, Joshua, my kids: The best teens EVER. Love you.

Reviewers, bloggers, friends and Team DEVIL readers who review and share the love: You rock. Our Circle of Hell has Mars bars, books and air-conditioning!

From a little spark
may burst a flame.

—Dante Alighieri

Ein

Alfarin and Elinor

"How did ye die?"

It was the way she asked the question that caught my attention. As if she already knew me. The strange girl was like a floating, ghostly goddess, dressed in a long white gown with cotton slippers on her feet. Her red hair flamed, as if Lord Loki himself had chosen her to be his angel of fire in Hell. Her almond-shaped eyes were dark pink. A maiden who had been dead for at least a century, I surmised.

And the expression on her beautiful face as she looked at me was so glorious; it was as if she had been waiting her entire existence to find me.

My stomach felt strange. Had I accidentally eaten some of Cousin Loof's nut roast? That always disagreed with my manly constitution. My insides felt as if a den of snakes were slithering where my intestines should be.

I had seen intestines before, spilling from the gut of a wolf-hound. It was one of the last earthly images I remembered, before the great Odin claimed me for Valhalla....

But no. This was not the time to think upon my death—and captivating as this lovely maiden was, I had more important matters to attend to than impressing her with the details of my demise. "Out of my way, wench!" I cried. "I do not have time to dally with women. I have Saxon skulls to pulverize. Go find a kitchen and make yourself useful."

Saxons were my quarry this day. In Hell, fighting was glorious sport, and Saxons' dead blood was especially thick and lumpy. When we Vikings fought them, we sprayed the halls of Valhalla crimson with it.

But the beautiful-yet-troublesome wench refused to move, and at my words, her demeanor quickly changed from delight to annoyance.

"I *will* go find a kitchen—then a mallet to hit you over the head with!" retorted the red-haired goddess. "Ye big oaf."

She glanced disparagingly at the two Saxons I held by the scruff of their necks. I clunked their heads together and they dropped to the ground. My Viking kin and I had been ambushed by their clan in the corridors of Hell as we were on our way to my cousin's watering hole. Normally, Saxons were no contest for strong Vikings with eager fists and a thirst for ale, but if I wasn't careful, this ghostly girl was going to throw me off my game.

"What do you want with me, woman?" I roared. "Can you not see I am in the midst of battle?"

"This is not a battle, Alfarin, son of Hlif, son of Dobin," she replied. "This is five ugly brutes against five even uglier ones. And my name is Elinor Powell, so ye can stop calling me *woman* right this instant."

She knew my name. This pleased me. My reputation was spreading across the abyss of Hell.

"Alfarin has got himself a wench," sang my father brother Magnus. He had a Saxon held high above his head and was twirling him around and around. "About time. And she's a beauty for sure. Although not much of a rump on her to slap."

"Ye slap my rump and I will play marbles with yer balls," replied the maiden called Elinor Powell. My kin laughed. This woman was not of the Valkyries, but she had a fire in her soul that matched the color of her hair.

A wily Saxon had procured a length of wood whilst I was distracted. My legs gave way as he smacked it against my calves.

"Leave me be, woman!" I cried, embarrassed to have fallen in front of my kin. "Go and plague another." I punched the wily Saxon in the nose. The pain in my knuckles was magnificent, and I immediately felt better.

Elinor Powell sighed. She seemed disappointed.

"I have been searching for ye for a hundred years. So when ye are ready to be the devil I know ye will one day become, Alfarin, son of Hlif, son of Dobin, ye come and find me," she said. And without so much as a backward glance, Elinor Powell disappeared into the shadows.

My intestines were still squirming.

———

It took me a further three hundred years to realize just how special a day that had been. For Elinor Powell would become my closest woman companion, in heart and mind and soul.

But then she was taken from me. Ripped from the heart of Team DEVIL by the Overlord of Hell himself. He took her to be his Dreamcatcher. To stand at his bedside and filter his most ghastly thoughts as he slept. It was a torturous ordeal, and I do not know if my princess will ever fully recover.

The Devil eventually allowed her release, on the condition that Team DEVIL complete a near-impossible task.

As I sit here now, I know that by Thor's fury, The Devil will not be getting her back.

But I also know that I may meet my true and final end in ensuring that.

So that is why I am writing down our story in this diary. To make certain that whatever happens to me, wherever I am cast by The Devil when this is all over, there will be a record, somewhere, of my love for Elinor Powell, who has made my dead heart feel more alive than it ever did in life.

1. Bót

My name is Alfarin, son of Hlif, son of Dobin. I have been dead for over one thousand years, and Hell is the domain where I have dwelled during that time. Up There and Hell are not the places the living imagine. The living foolishly believe that their eternal existence is determined by the way they choose to live their lives while their hearts still beat. The living are so very wrong. The eternal domains are governed, and a person's final destination is determined by a simple checkmark in a box on a piece of paper—and the whim of the Grim Reaper who wields the pen like a weapon.

This is but one thing that *most* of the newly dead will find unfair in the Afterlife.

Not me. I always knew Valhalla was my final destination, and I found it in the dark, hot, crowded confines of Hell.

Here, I am many things to many people. A Viking. A man. A devil. The possessor of great hair. A friend.

And of all those parts of my identity, I now value being a friend above all else.

Elinor was my first true friend in the Afterlife. Mitchell Johnson and Medusa Pallister are my other best friends, though I met them much later. Mitchell has been dead for less than a decade. It was Elinor who found him. She said we needed another companion. At first, her choice made me jealous. Was I not man enough for my princess? Yet Elinor treated Mitchell like a brother and nothing else. I quickly came to respect his friendship, his honesty and work ethic. It is because of Mitchell that Elinor found me in Hell, and I will never forget the sacrifice he made to bring us together.

If Mitchell is a brother-in-arms to me, then Medusa is like a sister to Elinor. She came to us only recently, rounding out the group as if she had always been there. At times, when I am on the cusp of slipping into the dreams of the mighty Norse god Hoth, I see Medusa in memories that I know were accidentally erased when we played with time. She's with us now—and then. A shadow in thoughts past.

The four of us, Elinor, Mitchell, Medusa and I, are Team DEVIL.

Lately, Team DEVIL has been pushed to its limits. We have traveled through the fabric of time itself. We have been ripped apart physically and mentally, and still we endure.

Now we have a new test. We must venture into the darkest pits of Hell. The Nine Circles. The dwelling of the Skin-Walkers. For there, hidden among the very worst of the Underworld, hides the original Dreamcatcher of The Devil, a Banshee by the name of Beatrice Morrigan. She is The Devil's wife. Returning her to him is the only way to save our Elinor from a permanent horror that even my learned mind cannot fully understand.

We do not have long before we must leave for our perilous journey. While Elinor rests after her ordeal of filtering the dreams of The Devil, and Mitchell and Medusa make preparations for the test to come, it is to Hell's library that I have retreated. Recently I have spent every waking moment—and even those moments of half-sleep, when I'm not quite aware of who or what I am—here, in this mausoleum where everything but learning is dead.

I'm relying on this place to help me in my quest to find out anything and everything I can about The Devil's Banshee. So today I am reading in the bowels of the library, away from the hive of activity by the main entrance. The air in these dark, dank aisles swirls with decay and dust. Very few of the librarians come down this far. It scares them. They say there are creatures here, watching in the impenetrable darkness. I understand their fear, for I have seen the most fearsome of these beings. She is Fabulara, the Higher who controls Hell. Her head sits on an elongated neck that stems from the shoulders of a grotesque statue. Six other heads sit beside hers, but they are dormant, for Hell is Fabulara's domain. Her yellow eyes blink as she watches over the realm from behind the shelves of cracked spines and aging parchment. She reeks of death, and her shadow alone would cause most devils to quail in their boots.

But not I. I am afraid of nothing—except losing Team DEVIL to those whose nefarious ways are beyond the comprehension of most of the dead.

They should be thankful for that ignorance.

———

The only devil I have seen down this way is the buxom wench Patricia Lloyd. I dare not say it aloud, but I have been grateful for her company—though it is sometimes distracting. Patricia likes walking up and down the aisles, moving in a manner I am unaccustomed to. Is she hurt? It is as if her hips have dislocated from her spine. Her strange stride makes her rear end protrude and swish from left to right to left, like a pair of melons wrapped in a muslin hammock, rocking to and fro in the breeze. I try not to observe, but my eyes are drawn to her in the same manner that they are drawn to my second cousin Odd whenever he leans down to speak to his wife. The sight is grotesque, yet amusing—and therefore, impossible to avoid watching.

Odd is married to a banana. We do not talk of it.

———

Patricia is doing that walk now. It looks painful. Often, when we encounter each other, Patricia will ask me if her bottom looks big in whatever cloth she is wearing. I say no, because it is the truth, and because I sense this is the answer that will satisfy her. But the question perplexes me. It seems that some women, like Patricia Lloyd, prefer having a small rump. Yet other women want their rears to be big enough to place a tankard on. Viking women certainly do. So Mitchell and I get very confused. We wish to compliment the fairer sex, but we always say the wrong words. My father has no such problems with women. He would spank any rear within a longship's distance, but I know better. Women no longer expect their rears to be slapped as a sign of courtship. I learned that from Elinor Powell, and had that knowledge reinforced in the great city of New York not long ago when Team DEVIL ventured back to the land of the living.

"Alfarin, I've found another book on Banshee countermeasures," calls Patricia. I snap out of my reverie of rump-slapping and behold her wardrobe selection of the day. She is wearing tight red pants that Medusa calls *skinny jeans*, and a piece of elastic cloth over her upper body that is no bigger than the dish towel I use to wipe the glasses in Thomason's, my kin's watering hole.

How can Patricia move in such constricting garments? It's just as well she doesn't need to breathe in Hell. In the land of the living, she would not be able to do so.

"I am thankful for your help, Patricia Lloyd," I reply. "But I do not need to know how to scare Banshees away. I wish to know how to get one to accompany me. You need not trouble yourself looking through the books here. I still haven't found what I am looking for, but I will know it when I do."

"That's the title of a song, you know," replies Patricia. "Or close to it. Speaking of, I can't wait for Bono to get down here. You know they're creating a special suite for him? It'll play 'Do They Know It's Christmas?' on a loop twenty-four seven for the rest of eternity." At this, Patricia smirks, but my eyebrows knit, betraying my confusion. Patricia looks frustrated. "You know…he recorded it with a bunch of other musicians a million years ago? They used to play it on the radio nonstop?" She searches my eyes for a hint of recognition. When she finds none, she leans over and starts twirling a wisp of my beard around her finger. "So I'm thinking I should wear my sexy Santa costume when I meet him. The pants are kind of like the ones I'm wearing now, except—"

"I am a Viking prince," I interrupt, shutting a heavy tome titled *The Origins of Hell.* "We do not understand Santa."

Now it is Patricia who is confused. I remove her finger from my beard and explain.

"If a fat stranger with a long white beard were to enter earthly dwellings, uninvited, on any day other than the twenty-fourth of December, people would call the law enforcers. If such a man came to my hearth, I would run him through with my axe."

My axe. My beloved blade has been with me since my tenth winter. It lies here now, on the gritty rock floor. The blade glints red in the firelight, a reminder of the blood of foes—and friends—it has spilled.

"Do you have a name for your axe?" asks Patricia, bending down to pick up the books I have already discarded. "I once dated a Saxon who worked in the furnaces. He was so hot. He had a javelin that he called *Irwin.* Something to do with a boar or whatever—I wasn't that interested. I didn't even like the way he talked, but man, he kissed like he was licking chocolate off my lips."

Why would Patricia have chocolate *on* her lips? Don't girls like to *eat* chocolate? Do they now use it as lipstick, too? No wonder my friend Mitchell gets pains of the stomach when it comes to women. They are as complex as they are beautiful.

"My axe has no name," I reply. "Other than *axe.*"

Blades are named for the great battles they have fought in. I did not live long enough to name mine. It was never a concern after that. Yet now it has a purpose, and when I have found The Devil's Banshee and returned her to the embrace of the master of Hell, thus saving my Elinor for eternity, my axe will have a name.

Bót.

In the language of my kin, it means "atonement."

Only then will it—and I—be truly worthy.

Patricia has left me; I did not notice when. I have set aside two books that may be useful on our quest, but otherwise, I have found no further information to help me snare or entice a Banshee. I stand up and stretch. It takes a while to work out the kinks, and I revel in each crackle of my spine. I am not built like Mitchell, with the girth of an eight-year-old, nor am I bendy like a drinking straw. There must be times when it is helpful not to possess bulging muscles and a powerful gait…and one day I may think of such an occasion, but not today.

For today, Team DEVIL is gathering back in the office of the great Lord Septimus. He will see us to the entrance where the Nine Circles await us.

Limbo.

Lust.

Gluttony.

Greed.

Anger.

Heresy.

Violence.

Fraud.

Treachery.

One Skin-Walker is responsible for maintaining order within each circle, or so it is written. *Maintaining order*…that phrase is a bad joke. The Skin-Walkers thrive on disorder and hatred and pain.

In one of these Circles of Hell, we will find Beatrice Morrigan, The Devil's Banshee. If we are lucky, we will find her in the First Circle and quickly put this whole affair behind us.

But judging from past adventures, Team DEVIL does not appear to have much luck on its side.

As I leave the darkness of the inner corridors of the library, I hear shuffling behind me. A rotten smell, worse than one of Cousin Thomason's bodily emissions, washes over me. I know that stench.

"What do you want, Fabulara?" I call. My words echo with many voices, not one of them mine.

"So you are determined to go through with this, Viking?" The voice is cold and harsh, like the scraping of a blade on ice.

"If I must enter the Nine Circles of Hell to save my princess, then that is what I will do," I reply. "And every second of every minute of every hour of every day in that putrid landscape, I will have a smile on my face. For I will find The Devil's Banshee, and I will bring her back with me."

"Or die trying?" sneers Fabulara.

"I am already dead."

"There are worse things than death, as you will discover if you and your friends enter the domain of the Skin-Walkers. They were the first evil, as you well know, and are therefore the purest form. You believe you are learned, that you know what to expect. But the horror that awaits you cannot be gleaned from books. You and your friends will not return."

"You created Hell, Fabulara, but I am not afraid of you or your words. Unlike you, I do not skulk about in the darkness. I must embrace my task. And if it leads to my doom, then so be it. I will face it head-on, like a Viking. A man. A devil."

I stand in the flickering light of a flaming torch, waiting for Fabulara's response, but there is nothing. I want to believe that her desire to frighten me has been sated, but as I reach the express elevators, her words echo in my mind.

You and your friends will not return.

Tveir

Alfarin and Elinor

It was weeks before I saw Elinor Powell again. I did not seek her out. Vikings do not go looking for women—women flock to us.

It was a mere coincidence that I stumbled across her in the library in the section reserved for hair care.

My mane was like that of a lion steeped in honey. It needed attention.

"Are ye following me, Alfarin?" she asked as I turned into the aisle.

"I do not follow, woman," I replied. "I am a Viking prince. I *lead*."

Elinor Powell shook her head and sighed. Since she did not have to breathe, I suspected this was for my benefit, not hers.

"I have told ye my name, and it is not *woman*," she said.

"I have forgotten your name," I lied. "I have many important things to remember. I do not retain inconsequential details that mean nothing to me."

"That's a big word," replied Elinor sarcastically, her eyes narrowing. "Almost as big as yer stomach."

I instinctively rested my beloved axe against my shoulder and jiggled my belly with my spare hand.

"A real Viking should have meat on his bones," I said.

"Well, ye certainly have that," replied Elinor. "Why, the kitchens could roast ye on a spit and ye could feed Hell for a month."

"When you have quite finished mocking my person, wench," I

said, slowly and quite deliberately, "kindly remove your worthless, interfering carcass from this aisle. I am busy, and time is of the essence."

"We have nothing but time, Alfarin, son of Hlif, son of Dobin," replied Elinor Powell. "And I am not going anywhere until ye have remembered my name."

"Vikings do not play games."

"Ye have to remember my name. It is important."

Beautiful and troublesome. Those were the adjectives I associated with women, dead or alive. I had passed over into Valhalla in my sixteenth winter—too early to have taken on a mate to bear my sons. But after watching the Viking pairs square off in the halls of my fathers during my lifetime, I was grateful to have been spared a wife. I had witnessed womenfolk kicking, slapping and even head-butting their menfolk. The truly tormented males even had their dinner fed to the dogs.

In death, womenfolk were just as bewildering, and Elinor Powell was turning out to be the most confounding of all. I had met her only the once before, and she was already getting under my skin.

Which was difficult because, as she had pointed out, there was a lot of it.

"I do not remember your name," I lied again. "Now begone and let me have some infernal peace."

"As ye wish," replied Elinor Powell, pulling a book from the shelf. A thin plume of dust cascaded to the ground as the sleeve of her white dress dragged back along the shelf. Her shoulders slumped slightly.

She was displaying the same sense of disappointment she had when I first met her. I did not like this. I wanted devils to be overawed by my impressive stature.

She slipped past me, leaving me and my unruly mane to the dust and the books on hair care in Hell. It was a popular section, as the heat of the Underworld was not a friend or ally to anyone's follicles, but today the aisle was deserted.

I was glad to be alone. For I knew what I wanted, but it would be difficult to find—and I needed peace and quiet.

A librarian had written the words down, so I laboriously traced the outline of each letter on the paper against the letters on the spines of the books. It was dull and repetitive work, and it was not long before my arms were aching from being held in the same position.

"Alfarin," called a soft voice. I jumped back, scrunching the paper into a tight ball.

It was Elinor Powell again, already come to return her book. Curse this woman and her glorious red hair and silent feet.

"What do you want?" I snapped.

But her face softened. She looked at me like my father, King Hlif, looked at his hunting dogs.

"Can ye not read?" she whispered.

"I am a warrior," I replied. "I fight and bathe in the cooked brains of my enemies. I do not need to read in order to send Vikings into battle."

Elinor held out her hand.

"I couldn't read, either, when I arrived in Hell, but I am slowly learning," she said. "I know my letters and many words now. I can help ye find what it is ye are looking for. And then ye can be on yer way to fight some Saxons even quicker."

I scratched my beard. Elinor Powell's proposition had merit. She was cunning and strategic. These were not the traits of most peasants. I handed her the piece of paper with the title of the book I was hoping to find.

"Ye see this letter here," she said, pointing to a symbol that had two upright lines and one across the middle. "This is the letter *H*. I imagine it to look like a house without a roof. That is how I remember it. And this is the letter *S*. It looks like a snake, don't ye think?"

I knew all about snakes. They were wriggling around in my stomach again.

———

I was a quick learner, which was no surprise, for I was born into greatness and died that way, too. Everything came naturally to those gifted by the Allfather Odin. Satisfied that I had learned enough of the alphabet for one day, Elinor guided me back to the shelves, and together we found the book I required.

It was a picture book with no words. I felt ashamed that my options were so limited because I could not yet read.

"If ye want to take it with ye, don't forget to check it out at the front counter," said Elinor. "It is the year 1771 and we must act civilized and proper and follow the rules."

Elinor and I walked through the library. I had my axe in one hand and the book in the other. I checked the book out and passed a librarian whipping someone who had been late returning a tome.

"Well, it was nice seeing ye again, Alfarin, son of Hlif, son of Dobin," said Elinor Powell sweetly. "Good-bye."

She did not wait for me to return the gesture. She just turned and left. Perhaps she did not want to hear me call her wench or woman again.

"Perhaps we could meet here again?" I called.

"Perhaps," she replied without looking back.

"Thank you!" I shouted as devils started to swarm into the space between us. "Thank you . . . Elinor Powell."

She did not turn around or reply. Elinor Powell had been swallowed by the dead.

2. Into Battle

Lord Septimus is a great man. Few in Hell are as revered and respected as he. A Roman general in life, Lord Septimus is now in charge of the finances of Hell, an undertaking that is fraught with more danger than leading any Roman legion. He is a man of many titles: his Roman acquaintances call him General; the Vikings call him Lord; my sweet Elinor uses the title Mr. Septimus when speaking to him; while the woman who serves up fries in the burger bar calls him Sex-on-Legs.

He used to smile at this last description.

Used to.

I am not the only devil who sees a change in The Devil's accountant, but I am one of the very few who know the reason for it. Recently, Lord Septimus was betrayed, right along with Team DEVIL, by the master of Hell. An Unspeakable was let loose from the bowels of the Underworld with The Devil's stolen Dreamcatcher in tow. In the wrong hands, the Dreamcatcher could unleash unspeakable horrors.

At first it seemed as if the Unspeakable had pulled off an impossible theft and escape. But in fact, his heist and liberation were instigated by The Devil himself, in complete secret. He never even consulted his number one ally about the wisdom of his hotheaded plan.

So Lord Septimus was as stunned as the rest of us when The

Devil's grand scheme was painfully revealed: *he* had freed the Unspeakable, and through him, had used the Dreamcatcher to test the effects of a Hell-made virus on a small group of angels.

The virus worked, and not just on the heavenly ones. I still have the scars to prove it. So do my friends on Team DEVIL. We were caught in the crossfire when it happened. We will not soon forget it.

Since then, I have been thinking that the Devil's betrayal could prove to be the greatest mistake of his existence, for I sense a storm brewing in Lord Septimus's heart. His waking hours are now filled with secret messages and flimsy lies to explain sudden absences. Sealed memos and communiqués are delivered at all hours. My good friend Mitchell has witnessed all this as he works alongside Septimus in the accounting chamber, and he has told me everything.

I pass one of Lord Septimus's former servants on my way to level 1. Aegidius is a strange fellow. He wears a toga and walks everywhere barefoot. His feet are hairier than my father mother's back, and she has been mistaken for an escaped gorilla. Aegidius's toga is smoking. To anyone not in the know, this would not be suspicious—many a devil has tried to set himself on fire in Hell before—but I know better. Aegidius is carrying another mysterious smoking message for Lord Septimus; these messages burst into flame the moment they're read. Lord Septimus and Aegidius are working together, and according to Mitchell, there are many others, too, who are in near-constant consultation with the former Roman general.

I am a warrior. A fighter. I was readying for battle from the age of seven, so I know the signs.

Lord Septimus is preparing for war.

I take the elevator to level 1. There are several devils rocketing along in the metal compartment with me, including Aegidius. I also recognize Sir Richard Baumwither, former head of the HBI. He is a bulbous fellow with red cheeks and a white beard. His head wobbles, like the small toy that my friend Mitchell has on his desk. The movement is hypnotic. I long to tap him on the cheek to make him wobble more, but instead I stay as far away from him as possible, because Sir Richard does not like devil-to-devil contact anymore. He has avoided it ever since he was ripped apart by the Skin-Walkers and scattered amongst the levels of the central business district of Hell. He has healed well, for someone whose head was found floating in a toilet.

Only Aegidius and I are left in the elevator by the time we reach level 1. The doors open and Aegidius departs first. His hairy feet squelch along the rock floor. The sound reminds me of my cousin Thomason eating soup. A strange sickness invades my stomach. I did not say good-bye to my kin, but I will think of them on this journey into the unknown.

Except for Second Cousin Odd. He should not be thought of by anyone who does not wish to regurgitate his last meal.

Mitchell and Medusa were charged with making all of the supply preparations, so I have only brought with me my faithful axe and two tomes: *The Divine Comedy* by Dante Alighieri and *The Origins of Hell* by an unknown author, which I checked out of the library. Both books are first editions and falling to pieces. I do not expect them to survive the entire journey through the Nine Circles of Hell, but they may be useful as long as they last.

Ahead of me, I see Aegidius disappear into the accounting chamber, but my eyes are drawn to the door next to it: the main entrance to The Devil's Oval Office. I can sense the fire and anger building up inside me. I will not be able to immolate in Hell—no devil can—but if I could...Oh, for just one, glorious instant I wish I could. I know exactly where I would erupt with the force of Mount Vesuvius, and I know who would be cindered to a crisp with my hatred.

If Lord Septimus is starting a war, I hope it is a mutiny. When our quest in the Nine Circles is over, I will gladly stand shoulder to shoulder with one of the greatest generals I have ever known to—as Mitchell would say—slam-dunk The Devil's sorry ass. I wonder what The Devil's head would look like floating in a toilet....

I never had these kinds of thoughts before Elinor was taken. Love is a terrifying emotion. That is why Vikings do not display it. We fight, we make merry, and we fight some more. My father says love makes men weak.

Team DEVIL is about to prove him very wrong.

"May I enter?" I ask, peering around the entrance to the accounting chamber. Mitchell and Medusa are in there, speaking to Aegidius. Lord Septimus is not, and neither is Elinor.

"Hey, Alfarin," calls Mitchell. "Look, four backpacks. And there's actually useful stuff in them. For once, we're gonna be prepared. Go Team DEVIL." He pumps his fist.

"As long as we don't leave any of the bags behind," says Medusa. "And as long as we don't erase ourselves in a paradox. Or fall into one of the Circles of Hell. Or—"

"Yeah, yeah, we get the point," says Mitchell. "Vortex of doom and all that. I was trying to cheer Alfarin up. Make it look like this adventure won't actually go wrong."

"Where is Elinor?" I ask.

"She went to see Johnny," replies Medusa.

"Has she told him what we plan to do?" I ask.

"No—she's going to tell him that devil resources needs her for a special project," says Mitchell. "But she wanted to say good-bye, without actually saying it."

Elinor's brother Johnny is not a devil. He is one of four angels who have been exiled from Up There. The other three are Private Owen Jones, who was killed on the first day of the Battle of the Somme; Miss Angela Jackson, a pretty female from the beautiful land of Aotearoa; and an angel who is more fearsome than any devil I have ever met: Jeanne d'Arc—better known to English speakers as Joan of Arc. I have known the French maiden for just a short while, and already she stands behind only Elinor and Medusa in my estimation of greatness. I do not tell her this, of course. She would almost certainly want to cause me pain for placing her third and not first. Yet a more capable female warrior I have never known. The great goddess Freya would find her match in Jeanne.

I certainly did.

The four angels have been exiled because they were the unwitting victims of the Hell-made virus unleashed by The Devil's Dreamcatcher. Jeanne is so angry with the fate that has been forced upon her that she has almost managed immolation here in Hell.

Not for the first time, I wish I could take the French warrior with us into the realm of the Skin-Walkers and the Unspeakables.

But it cannot be. She is not a devil; she is a misplaced angel. It will be dangerous enough, entering the Circles of Hell. To add to our burden with an untested Jeanne, however brave, could be a disaster. I must lead this quest with a strong heart and a strategic mind.

And a full stomach. Is that pizza I smell?

"Food's up," calls the sweetest voice of all, and Elinor tiptoes into the accounting chamber, balancing four pizza boxes in her hands.

"Elinor, you are an angel!" cries Mitchell. "I tried to get Medusa to go down to the kitchens for food, but she refused."

"I've got better things to do than be a slave to your stomach, Mitchell Johnson," replies Medusa, flicking an elastic band at his head.

"Ow!"

"Bull's-eye!" crows Medusa triumphantly.

"I got ye a quadruple meat feast, Alfarin," says Elinor, handing me a cardboard box that is dripping with glorious grease.

"My princess," I reply, although my fervent rapture is drowned out by my intestinal tract, which is making the noise of a goat bleating in pain.

"Hello, Aegidius," says Elinor. "I am very sorry. I did not know ye would be here, or I would have brought ye pizza, too."

"I am here for General Septimus, not to eat food that falsely proclaims to be from my homeland," replies the Roman.

"Huh?" asks Mitchell, a slice of pepperoni pizza hovering inches from his open mouth.

"I think Aegidius is saying our pizza isn't really Italian," replies Medusa thickly. She has just placed an entire slice of Hawaiian pizza in her mouth. I do not know whether to be impressed or appalled.

Who am I fooling? I am impressed.

Another devil enters the accounting chamber. Five becomes six, but Lord Septimus has the aura of ten devils. One day, I hope my magnificence will press people against the walls of Hell, instead of just my stomach.

"I'm glad to see that there are some things about Team DEVIL that do not change," says Lord Septimus, in a drawling voice that is akin to those who arrive from the American state of Texas. "I thought I could smell pizza."

"Can't think on an empty stomach, boss," says Mitchell. "And this might be my last meal." He takes a swig of Coke from a can and burps loudly.

I know my friend is trying to keep the intense atmosphere jovial for Elinor's sake, and I silently thank him for it. Intentional humor has never been my forte, although I seem to make other devils laugh. Intimidation and an impressive beard are my personal strengths.

"I take it you have something for me, Aegidius?" asks Lord Septimus. "Unless you have decided to join my interns and their two friends, of course?"

"Another letter arrived this past hour, General," replies Aegidius, taking the smoking letter out from the folds of his toga. "And I have personally ensured that another has taken up the position vacated by the deserter."

"Do not call him that," replies Lord Septimus sharply, opening the letter. "Sometimes it takes a braver man to flee."

Mitchell and Medusa are watching Lord Septimus with open mouths. It is rare to hear him speak with such an edge to his voice.

"Who deserted, boss?" asks Mitchell. "Don't tell me another Unspeakable's escaped Hell!"

"No…no," says Lord Septimus. "It's…it's nothing, Mitchell. My apologies, Aegidius. I did not mean to speak harshly. I just feel responsible for the fate of…our informer."

"Your men understand fate, General," says Aegidius. "And your men embrace war. We are ready."

"That is good news, Aegidius, for our time is coming," replies Septimus. "But let us speak no more of it now. I will be out of commission for the rest of the afternoon, for I must see Team DEVIL to their destination."

Four gulps echo around the accounting chamber. The quadruple meat feast pizza that I just finished devouring is suddenly sitting uncomfortably in my stomach. I want to start this journey so badly, and yet I feel a sense of prickling cold invading my skin. I am ashamed to know that it is fear. I have felt it before, just seconds before a peasant's rusty hatchet blade was swung through snow and blood to end me.

Aegidius bows and leaves the accounting chamber without a word to us. Lord Septimus closes the door behind him.

"Does Aegidius know what we're doing, Septimus?" asks Mitchell.

"No, he does not," replies Lord Septimus. "But he will not question me. My soldiers were—*are*—accustomed to sending and receiving only the information that is relevant to them. And he is very loyal."

As Lord Septimus speaks, I do not imagine the quick curl of the lip and penetrating glare he gives the door that connects the accounting chamber with the Oval Office. If looks could kill, then Lord Septimus would be a weapon to rival the Dreamcatcher.

Hell hath no fury like a devil scorned.

"When did ye wish to leave, Mr. Septimus, sir?" asks Elinor. She rubs her neck twice, but stops when she realizes we are all watching her.

"We will depart for the Nine Circles only when all four of you are ready," replies Lord Septimus, and the softness in his voice is the antithesis to the hatred that flamed in his red eyes just seconds ago. "And Prince Alfarin, I will need to debrief you once you are ready."

"I am your servant, Lord Septimus."

"And in you I am placing my greatest trust," he replies. "I know you will not let us down."

"Medusa, how are the provisions?" I ask, wiping my greasy fingers on my tunic, keen to show Lord Septimus that I am worthy of his trust.

"I've packed food, water, clothes for everyone, and several changes of underwear...."

"You and clean underwear, Medusa!" exclaims Mitchell. "I've told you before, me and Alfarin can just turn ours inside out."

"No you haven't," she replies. "And that's disgusting."

A frown crosses Mitchell's face. "Was that paradox Medusa, then? I can't remember."

Medusa digs Mitchell in the ribs with her elbow. Her aim is lethal.

"It doesn't matter if that *was* paradox me who said it. Turning your underwear inside out to get out of washing it is disgusting in any timeline."

I cross the floor to Elinor. She is watching their bickering with a faint smile.

"I will be ready when you are, Elinor," I say.

She slips her hand into mine and squeezes. "I am ready, Alfarin, because I have my friends with me."

Suddenly an electric-blue flash zaps across the ceiling of the chamber. Medusa squeals and ducks down with her hands pressed against her snakelike hair.

The connecting door opens.

And in walks The Devil.

Prir

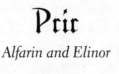

Alfarin and Elinor

A companionship had been forged in the heat and fire and written words of Hell. It was not an effortless friendship. It required much thinking on my part. This I found exhausting, and as a result I often drifted off during my work at Thomason's, and just as often, was awoken with a bucket of cold water to the face. My kin believed I was being tired out from *other* activities, and I did not correct them. I did not wish to be mocked. I was a proud prince.

Elinor Powell and I would meet in the library every day. She would teach me how to read, and I would impress her with my rapid understanding. Elinor Powell did not know that after we said our good-byes, I would go back to the labyrinth of books and continue by myself. The words she had spoken when she first encountered me often repeated in my head.

"I have been searching for ye for a hundred years. So when ye are ready to be the devil I know ye will one day become, Alfarin, son of Hlif, son of Dobin, ye come and find me."

What did Elinor Powell know about me? I wanted to ask her, but my arrogance kept me aloof.

That did not change the fact, however, that I was developing an aching desire to make her proud of me.

Elinor Powell was accepted by my kin. She held her own and did not swoon in the company of such male magnificence. Indeed, she did not seem to be very impressed by bulging muscles and sweaty armpits at all. So, after reading a tome on the female of the species, I wondered if I should impress her with my nurturing side.

It did not go according to my plan.

"Will ye stop yer fussing, Alfarin!" exclaimed Elinor. "If I tell ye nothing is the matter, then ye just have to trust me."

"If you will not allow me, then at least permit one of my kin to have a look, Elinor," I replied.

Why was this proving to be so difficult? Had the book lied to me? Did women not want men to take an interest in their grooming habits?

"I am telling ye, there is nothing to see," said Elinor. "And yer kin are not going foraging through my hair like monkeys on the hunt for lice, either."

"But if it is lice…"

"Will ye keep yer voice down!" cried Elinor. "And for the fiftieth time, I do not have head lice."

I had chosen the anniversary of Elinor's death to show my nurturing side. Most devils took their death anniversary in one of two ways: they gloried in the majesty of their passing, or they sank into the blackest of depressions and attempted to kill themselves. The latter was an exercise in futility, as they were already dead. The former was the way of the Vikings. We did not need a reason to celebrate; we just needed a location.

Elinor Powell was unlike other devils. She had accepted her passing with stoicism and grace. It was a quality I much admired in any devil. Elinor had told me she was meant to pass on at that moment in time. Elinor spoke of fate as if it was of comfort to her.

But as the fourth of September had drawn closer, I noticed that Elinor had started to rub and scratch at the back of her neck more and more. Even my kin had noticed. My father brother, Magnus, believed Elinor to be infected with the bubonic plague—but then

Magnus believed every devil was infected with some kind of pustular affliction.

"It is not lice. I do not have the plague, the pox or scabies, Alfarin," chided Elinor. "We have only known each other a few months. One day...one day...I will be able..." Then her red eyes filled with tears, and I felt a strange sensation in my chest. It was the same sensation I felt when I was served only ten dumplings at dinner instead of fifteen.

It was a feeling of being bereft.

But I had not meant to make Elinor Powell cry. I had only wanted her to like me. I had wanted to show her I cared.

I needed a different book.

"I am sorry, Elinor," I said remorsefully. "Forgive my inquisitive nature. What can I do to make it up to you? Would you like my serving of beef stew at dinner tonight? Or would you like to braid my hair? Shall I score my skin with one thousand strokes of penitence?"

"Oh, shush now, ye big oaf," replied Elinor, sniffing. "It is just me being silly."

But Elinor did not strike me as silly or foolish, and later that night, when I found her brushing her long red hair before we left the library, I saw her silently weeping over the usual congratulatory deathday message from The Devil.

I said nothing.

And I did not tell her I saw the long pink scar on the back of her neck.

3. The Devil's Farewell

As The Devil walks into the accounting chamber, Elinor and Medusa fall back against the stone wall. Both of Elinor's hands are on the back of her neck. It is the position she takes when she is frightened or worried, and it pains me, for I know now that I am the cause of her obsessive behavior.

I place myself in front of Elinor and Medusa with my axe raised. Let them come, I think to myself, expecting an army of ghouls to bleed out of the walls once more. Let The Devil's guards come. He is in *our* domain now, and I will strike my blade through anyone who tries to take our girls away from us again.

At the same time as I take a stance to protect Elinor and Medusa, Lord Septimus strides across the room and places a warning hand on Mitchell's arm. They could not be more different, in appearance and history, and yet I am often reminded of a father and son when they are together. The anger on my friend's face is majestic to behold. It is hatred and a burning desire to see a face with a black goatee floating in a toilet on level 666.

Mitchell's hatred of The Devil matches my own. We are brothers joined by death and love and loyalty.

"Team DEVIL!" exclaims The Devil in his high-pitched voice. Some would say he sounds like a girl, but I believe that is insulting to the female of the species.

"Sir," says Lord Septimus calmly. "I thought you had a meeting with Florence Nightingale. Aren't you due for your shots?"

"Yes, yes, yes," replies The Devil, twisting his black goatee around his index finger. "Septimus is a worrier, isn't he, Mitchell? Always looking out for those he cares about."

The Devil smiles. Behind me I hear Elinor make a noise. I cannot tell if she is sobbing or gagging. Neither sound is one I welcome. I can feel the heat starting to burn inside my chest; my hands are shaking. The flaming torches around the accounting chamber are reflecting off the silver blade I sharpened with loving care this morning. It is a color that is permanently tattooed on many of my earthly memories—and the moment of my passing—because the fire in this room is also the color of blood.

What color does The Devil bleed, I wonder? If it's as black as his mind and heart, it will be darker than the shadows that are now swarming across the walls. Watching. Waiting.

"Don't look at him, El," whispers Medusa. "Look at me. Hold my hand. That's it, look at me."

"Medusa Pallister always knows what to say," says The Devil, leaning to his right to peer around my body. "Such a smart young lady."

"You stay away—" Mitchell starts.

"Mitchell, be quiet," says Lord Septimus; his voice is so low I can feel the vibrations of it against my own chest. It's like a heartbeat. How strange it is to feel that after one thousand years of death.

"And Mitchell Johnson, or should I call you M.J.?" The Devil's top lip curls. He is enjoying this. "The one who would give everything up for a brother he's never even known."

"Sir, with the greatest of respect, is there a point to this visit?" asks Lord Septimus. "I would be happy to call back Aegidius to assist you if you are in need of something to calm you before your shots."

"I just wanted to wish Team DEVIL bon voyage," replies The Devil. "That is the tradition in the land of the living, is it not? Then again, you are about to embark into the Circles of Hell and not Disney World, so perhaps bon voyage was the wrong phrase. Such a frightful place. *It's a Small World* is my idea of Hell on earth."

The master of Hell starts laughing at his own joke. I can feel Elinor trembling behind me.

"I'm certain Team DEVIL is thankful for your kind words, sir," says Lord Septimus; his bloodred eyes flash a warning to all of us to maintain our silence. Mitchell is not struggling in Lord Septimus's arms, but I can see him shaking with rage. My friend was the first of us all to immolate. I know that, like me, if he could complete such a transition now, together we would blow level 1 of the central business district apart.

"So, who is to lead this adventure?" says The Devil. He sweeps a pile of papers from one of the desks onto the floor and perches on the edge. "All expeditions need a leader. Someone brave. Someone prepared to sacrifice themselves when the going gets tough."

"I will be leading," I say. "I am not afraid of the Circles of Hell."

"Why, Alfarin, son of Hlif, son of Dobin," says The Devil. "I approve. You're going to have lots of fun, especially if you make it to the Seventh Circle. I would imagine a Viking will have lots to think about in there. I believe that's Visolentiae's domain, is it not, Septimus? You've already met that particular Skin-Walker. And I know Cupidore is looking forward to seeing Medusa once more. He liked the smell of you, girl."

"Maybe he likes the smell of Beatrice Morrigan more," says Medusa sharply.

The Devil's black eyes narrow at the mention of his wife's name. "You had better hope for the lovely Elinor's sake that he does not," he replies. "And remember what I told you in *my* domain, Medusa Pallister." He flashes me a look with his ink-black eyes, and for a moment I wonder if The Devil can read my mind. "I don't cope well without sleep, and the longer I am made to wait for a Dreamcatcher, the worse it will be. For everyone."

The flaming torches on the wall are starting to lower and dim, as if the fires of Hell are cowering in the presence of such despotic evil. Then with a sudden clap of his hands, The Devil jumps to his feet.

"I feel the need to break into song!" he cries. "What about 'So Long, Farewell'? I do love *The Sound of Music*."

"I will ensure that the film is streamed to you once you have recovered from your shots, sir," says Lord Septimus. His voice is so calm, so steady. "But you should head down to the medical center. Miss Nightingale's needles get larger the longer she waits."

"They do, don't they! Why, last time I swear that woman stuck a needle the size of a Toblerone bar into my backside. I couldn't sit down for a week. Oh, Septimus, what would I do without you?" asks The Devil, sighing dramatically. "Well, bon voyage it is, then, Team DEVIL. And to you, Alfarin, son of Hlif, son of Dobin, do not forget what is at stake here if you fail."

"We will not fail," I reply. I know my irises are red after one thousand years in Hell, but they are now infused with so much anger I feel as if I could burn holes in The Devil's face just by looking at him.

"That's the spirit," replies The Devil. As he reaches the interconnecting door, he turns and addresses the one devil he has not yet spoken to.

"Sleep tight, pretty Elinor."

Mitchell and I react at the same time. Medusa is not far behind, but The Devil is gone before we reach the door. Our three hands grab the handle, and our flesh sizzles upon contact.

"Fall back, Team DEVIL," booms Lord Septimus. "You are filled with anger, but you will face far worse than the master's baiting once you have entered the Nine Circles. You must learn to control yourselves. This is not New York or New Zealand. This is far more dangerous, and you will fail in the very First Circle if you do not get a grip on your emotions, however hard that may be."

"H-how can you...I don't know...," stammers Mitchell, his face screwed up with rage. "How can you stand it, Septimus? The Devil doesn't even have to speak and I want to rip him apart. He's worse than the Skin-Walkers. How can you be so...so...*civil* toward him?"

"Mitchell, I will not warn you again," says Lord Septimus. "For your own preservation, never, ever speak ill of The Devil, especially in this office."

"But he's a monster!" cries Medusa. "He deserves every word!"

"He is The Devil," says a voice behind me. "And he enjoys the game. Mr. Septimus is right. Ye should not speak ill of him. I have seen The Devil's dreams, and he's just itching for an excuse to wreak havoc."

"Listen to Miss Powell," says Septimus, his gaze softening. "Your emotions are about to be pulled apart. Do not lose control before you have started."

"Sorry, Septimus," mumbles Medusa.

"Yeah, sorry, boss," adds Mitchell. "Sorry, Elinor. And you, too, Alfarin. You two kept your heads—"

"Mitchell," I growl.

"It's just an expression, Alfarin!" says Mitchell, throwing his hands in the air. "I can't keep checking myself every time I mention heads."

"*Try.*"

"It is all right, Alfarin," says my princess. She steps out from my shadow. "When I was in there, with The Devil, I never lost hope. I knew ye would all come for me, even if it took a thousand years. Ye are all the greatest friends a devil could have, and I love each and every one of ye, jokes and all. I do not need protecting, from words or deeds. Not anymore."

"The Devil is not reclaiming you, Elinor," I say, going down on one knee. "For you were never his to take in the first place. And I swear it now, in front of those who mean the most to me, that by my blood, I will not fail. I will lead us all into the Circles of Hell, and moreover, I will lead us all out again once we have found our quarry."

The sound of my blade slicing across my forearm is glorious. A quick yet tuneful whistle. Steel on skin.

"Do it to me," says Mitchell, striding forward, pulling up the long sleeve of his green shirt. "I want to do a blood oath, too, Alfarin. Quick, before I change my mind."

I do not wait to be asked again. Mitchell's blood mixes with mine on the blade of my axe as I score his forearm with a single cut.

"Argh! Oh, *shit* that hurts!" Mitchell pales at the sight of his arm.

"Perhaps you ought to lie down, my friend," I say.

"What? No!" Mitchell glares at me and then closes his eyes. "Okay. Okay, here goes. I swear by this Viking blood oath that this quest—ow, holy shit—hang on, no, that's a swear, but that's not my real swear. I mean, my real oath. Okay. I swear that we're going to get The Devil's wife back and Elinor will be safe—ow, ow, ow. Septimus, I need a Band-Aid."

While Lord Septimus pulls out a red first-aid kit and tends to a swooning Mitchell, Medusa steps forward and silently offers me her arm. Scars from our time in New Zealand, where The Devil's awful virus was unleashed upon us, have pockmarked her body, but the one I am about to inflict is one she will not shudder from.

She flinches slightly, but I know brave Medusa has suffered worse, and she absorbs the pain like a true Viking goddess.

"I swear a blood oath that Team DEVIL will not fail. We will not leave the Circles of Hell without Beatrice Morrigan, and the Overlord of Hell will not take Elinor from her best friends again," she says quietly.

"And now me, Alfarin," says Elinor, stepping forward. Her pale arms are freckled like her face, but the remnants of the virus unleashed from the Devil's Dreamcatcher are worse on her skin than on Medusa's. Pink swellings, like small coins, have scarred her body.

But I will slight Elinor's honor if the mark I make on her now is smaller than those I scored onto Mitchell and Medusa. So with a quick sleight of hand, I draw my blade across Elinor's arm.

"And I swear, as an honorary Viking, that no harm will come to those I love," says Elinor.

"Gather your belongings, Team DEVIL," says Lord Septimus. "It is time to leave. Prince Alfarin, I take it you have formulated a plan?"

"I am a Viking warrior, Lord Septimus," I reply. "I have been preparing for this moment my entire death, whether I knew it or not."

"Excellent. We will discuss this further as we walk. But first, I have a gift for you." From his inside pocket, Lord Septimus draws a small bundle wrapped in a purple silk handkerchief. He places it gently in my enormous palm. I do not need to open it to know what it is.

"For the journey home," says Lord Septimus. "Make a note of the date and time right now. The quest you are about to embark on will be your most dangerous yet. I hope you have been listening to my advice over the years, Prince Alfarin, for my words are never in vain, and I do not waste them." He looks at me steadily. "I will expect to find you back here waiting for me."

He winks, and I bow. Elinor rubs her neck. Mitchell and Medusa look at each other with confused expressions, but now is not the time for explanations.

"Mr. Septimus, sir," says Elinor as Medusa starts handing out the backpacks. "May I add one last statement to the oath I just swore?"

"It was your oath, Miss Powell," replies Lord Septimus. "You may add and subtract as you see fit."

"It's just... it involves ye," says Elinor. "I have seen his dreams, ye see, and I wish to swear, as an honorary Viking, that when this is over, I will help ye."

"Help me with what, Miss Powell?"

"I wish to help ye unleash Hell."

Fjórir

Alfarin and Elinor

War. For the Vikings, in our era, it was a glorious state. Yet as the centuries passed in the land of the living, conflicts between men became larger and bloodier and longer.

The Great War was to be the war that ended all wars, and for four brutal years, mankind fought for territory and rights. As a result, by 1916, the war's midpoint, the Deceased Dominion—the landmass where the HalfWay House stood—was rumored to be on the verge of anarchy. Soldiers, obliterated by bullets and shrapnel, were arriving by the tens of thousands. They were healed before the Grim Reapers sorted them to Hell or Up There, but the stench of their blood made its way to the Underworld anyway. After a time, the overworked Grim Reapers could not cope with so many, so they started sending the dead to Hell without assessing them.

By this time, thanks to Elinor, I was the most learned amongst my kin, but I remained a warrior first and foremost. So Lord Septimus had taken to calling on me to assist with the processing of newcomers, and the quick disarming of anyone who caused trouble in the reception area.

It was there that I learned that Up There had reneged on its promise to take its share of the glorious dead from the war, and that broken vow became more apparent than ever on the first of July, when the Somme in France became a river of blood as sixty thousand British men fell.

The dead, with wounds still dripping, came in droves. The long, rocky tunnels from the HalfWay House to Hell's reception room were filled to capacity. The reception room itself bulged with the sheer volume of new devils.

Elinor was enlisted to assist with the processing, too. The two of us worked until we could not move for exhaustion. Her shining hair ran even redder with the blood of the new arrivals. Carnage was everywhere.

Even so, we were efficient. We became a team. Lord Septimus said I was the brawn, Elinor was the brains. As we worked in tandem—processing more of the dead than any other devils, Grim Reaper or otherwise—we were called into a side chamber to assist with "special cases"—those devils that were to be taken away for "projects."

I knew from their paperwork that these devils were deserters: soldiers who had fled the field of battle in fear, or refused to advance when ordered.

I wanted to call them cowards. It was a man's birthright and duty to protect his people. Yet these young men before me did not look like witless chickens. And I knew enough now from my own reading and experience that there was more to bravery than facing death with a roar.

These devils had answered a call to serve while living. They had left family and hearth and faced the most horrendous terror like men. My heart may not have been beating, but it was still touched by these boys wilting with fear before us.

"You two get to assign this sorry lot for the special jobs," said the Grim Reaper on duty. "Feel free to make it as gruesome as you can for them."

The Grim Reaper left Elinor and me in the anteroom with fifteen of the young men. All but one were still shaking. Their eyes had already started to change to the color of foamy milk, but several pairs were so white, they were clearly still rolling in their sockets.

"They are all younger than me, Alfarin," whispered Elinor as she flicked through the processing forms. "I will not do this. I will not make death harder for them."

"We have our orders, Elinor," I said.

"Alfarin," said Elinor, and she touched my hand. I could not remember her doing so before. "Can ye honestly tell me ye have no compassion in yer heart for these boys? Not all orders are the right ones. Sometimes ye need to do what is right, not that which was told to ye."

I was truly conflicted. I had been brought up to listen to authority. My death came about because I did not. I had gone on alone into the village, believing I was invincible.

I took a step toward the soldiers, and all but one brave soul took a step back. I remember he wore a brown uniform, though his face was quickly lost to me.

"We will find you safe jobs and warm beds. You will never escape death, but you can make a safe existence for yourselves here," I said to the new devils.

Elinor was still touching my hand, and she gave it a quick squeeze before she started to give them their assignments.

I had made her proud. It was a good feeling to earn respect instead of demanding it.

But defying orders did not come easily, and I did not sleep well for many nights.

By the end, Elinor and I had seen so many of the glorious dead that they all became one in our minds. There were too many names to remember. Too many bloodied faces to recall. We found jobs for everyone who came our way to be processed. Jobs of importance. Even the great Lord Septimus took one of the soldiers, the one in the brown uniform who had not quailed at the sight of my axe.

But the living did not learn. The Great War became just another war. And twenty years later, it happened again.

And again... and again... and again...

4. Swagger and Secrets

Lord Septimus allows me to lead Team DEVIL away from the accounting chamber. The burden of expectation—and potential failure—rests heavily on my shoulders. It is a weight I bear willingly. I have my axe. I have my friends. I have the written word of knowledge in my backpack.

Mitchell and I are sharing the last pizza, but my friend is not happy.

"Urgh, gross!" he exclaims as we reach the express elevators. "There are anchovies on this slice. Who in their right mind puts stinky little fishies on a pizza?"

"Stinky little fishies!" exclaims Medusa. "Stinky little *fishies*? Are you three years old, Mitchell?"

Elinor is smiling. It gladdens my heart to see it. Mitchell and Medusa are very amusing, especially when they are arguing. Me, I do not like to fight with words. I find my fist does a quicker job. It means I can multitask by fighting and eating at the same time.

These are important traits in a warrior. My father, King Hlif, once went into battle swinging an axe in one hand and a whole roasted hog in the other. As the hog had been cooked—or I should say overcooked—by the bowman of my father's longship, who was not known for his culinary skills, I'm not sure which caused more damage as they were swung into the noses of our enemies.

"How far will you be able to accompany us, Lord Septimus?" I ask as we all crowd into the elevator.

"I will take you out of the reception area and into the tunnels," he replies. "The entrance to the dwelling of the Skin-Walkers is in there. You will have to find the guide yourselves, I'm afraid. For you must abandon that which we all cling to before you can enter, and that is something I cannot reveal, not now."

"Uh, boss," says Mitchell, still picking flakes of *stinky little fishies* from his pizza slice. "You know I think you're awesome and all that, but just for once, could you *not* be cryptic and instead tell us exactly what it is we're supposed to do? Just once. Consider it an early death-day present to us all."

"Oh, for Pete's sake, Mitchell," snaps Medusa. "You're flicking bits of anchovy into my hair." She grabs the pizza slice from him and stuffs the whole thing into her mouth. "Ver. No vor anhovyz vor roo," she says thickly, grease dribbling down her chin.

"You are gross, Medusa," says Mitchell. "What do you have to say to that?"

"Han't talk. Eatin' pissa."

Elinor is laughing so hard she gets hiccups. Dead hiccups are very painful because the diaphragm goes into spasms, but a devil cannot hold his or her breath to stop them.

Despite Elinor's affliction, the atmosphere is so jovial that I do not press Septimus for a better explanation of his enigmatic words, even though they weigh heavily upon me.

The doors of the elevator part and we push our way out. Many more devils are trying to push their way in. A flash of familiar red catches my eye before it is swallowed in the crowd. I look behind me, and Elinor is right there, holding on to my tunic as I plow a way through the corridor.

I say nothing, but I could have sworn to the Norse god of truth, Forseti, that I just saw young Johnny, Elinor's brother, in the throng.

"Where is Team ANGEL, Lord Septimus?" I ask.

"Private Owen, Miss Jackson and Mr. Powell are still getting settled into their new quarters," he replies.

"What about crazy Jeanne?" asks Mitchell.

"Mitchell, don't be mean," says Elinor. "She was very brave, and saved all of ye from a horrible fate in Aotearoa."

"That choice of word is ill-advised, Mitchell," adds Lord Septimus. "Mademoiselle d'Arc is to be transported to Hell's asylum later on today."

"What?" cry Elinor and Medusa together.

"Keep walking, all of you," instructs Lord Septimus. "If you lose momentum now you'll become gridlocked. The asylum is the safest place for Mademoiselle d'Arc at this time."

"But the French maiden is a warrior, Lord Septimus," I say. "She does not deserve such a fate."

But Lord Septimus does not reply. He has taken over the lead and is carving a way through the crowd with his mere presence.

It has always been this way. Everyone stops in their tracks when The Devil's accountant is around. Men quail and women swoon. Lord Septimus is the monster under the bed that modern-day children fear, and he is the one devil everyone in Hell wishes to get close to. He has power, influence and an astonishing number of pinstripe suits.

Elinor, Mitchell and Medusa sink into the shadows in his wake, not wishing to draw attention to themselves. But I puff out my chest, clasp my blade and attempt a swagger, drinking in the gaze of the throng that comes to me simply because of my association with The Devil's right-hand man.

Mitchell once showed me how to swagger. It is all about attitude. My friend is better at it than me, though. Elinor thought I had been afflicted by gout as I strutted around my cousin Thomason's bar, trying to follow Mitchell's instructions. I also managed to upend my great-aunt Dagmar's tankard of ale in the process, which is a dangerous mistake on any day, but especially when Great-Aunt Dagmar happens to be holding a carving knife. My own hide almost ended up in the house stew that night.

Today, my swagger has not improved. It is hard to move with attitude when your thighs meet at the knees.

We reach the reception area of Hell. This is as sorry a place now as it was when I worked here during the Great War, and many years later, when I passed through with Team DEVIL on our way to the land of the living. Sobbing and wails have always drowned out the music. It is like that now, although we cannot see who is making the noise because there are fluorescent green drapes pulled across the processing booths.

"Mitchell, is that another recording of ye over the speakers?" asks Elinor.

"Yeah," replies Mitchell, looking embarrassed. "It's the piano version of 'Relight My Fire.' The Devil thought—well, you can guess what he thought."

"Septimus," calls a woman from behind a glass screen. She has a flabby neck that reminds me of a turkey. "I'm not falling for this again. Do you know how much trouble I got into last time these … these kids …"

But she trails off with a confused look on her face. The receptionist is staring at Medusa.

"But as I am here this time, Josephine, there shouldn't be a problem, should there?" replies Lord Septimus, leaning against the counter. "Is that a new blouse? It brings out the color of your eyes."

The receptionist giggles and touches her earlobe. I find these interactions interesting. Vikings are not known for their subtle ways with women. We grab them, carry them over our shoulder and bury our faces in their ample bosoms. But I do not know why this is so, especially nowadays. To me, it is not worth the risk. Women have knees, and from my observations, they are pretty lethal shots, especially when it comes to aiming between the legs of a Viking.

Elinor, Mitchell and Medusa are getting restless. Naturally, my princess's hands are clasping the back of her neck, while Mitchell and Medusa are playing a game of who can flick the other's forehead the hardest. It is a game they have taken to playing often recently. The first one to cry out loses. I believe Medusa has a perfect record.

I turn around and scan the crush of devils who are waiting just beyond the glass doors to the reception area. Black-suited HBI patrol the area. If the vault doors open, they are there to stop devils from running back out to the tunnel that leads to the HalfWay House.

And then I see it again. In the sea of panicking devils, there is that same flash of vivid red hair I saw earlier. I would recognize it anywhere because it is exactly the same as Elinor's. When I am meeting my friends, it is always the color I look out for. It makes my stomach dance with happiness.

Should I tell Elinor of my suspicions? I do not make a habit of keeping secrets from my friends, but a little voice is telling me to keep quiet. The great lord Loki is the god of mischief, and I know it is his slippery tones that are speaking to me now. But for once, he is right. I do not wish to cause more distress to Elinor. She has already said her farewells...hasn't she? As far as I know, she has informed her brother she is going to work in devil resources on a special project for a time.

Did Johnny not believe her, or did he just want to keep his sister in his sights until the very last moment? I hope he does not intend to rush the reception area when Lord Septimus and Team DEVIL pass through.

The receptionist is still giggling, Lord Septimus is still flattering, Elinor is still hiccupping, and Mitchell and Medusa are now trying to arm-wrestle without a table to rest their elbows upon. Two HBI agents by the doors shift their positions, and another three charge the increasingly distressed crowd outside. A blue-and-white light starts to flash and people start crying and shoving in a futile attempt to get away from the reception area now that alarms are sounding.

And now it is not just Johnny I see in the crowd. For standing next to him, watching me watching them, is Angela Jackson. An angel who saw eighteen winters on earth before an insidious disease called cancer claimed her life. When I first met her not long ago, it was back in the land of the living. She and Johnny and two other angels had been dispatched from Up There to intercept the Unspeakable and The Devil's Dreamcatcher. At that time, she still had turquoise eyes, as beautiful as alpine lakes. Now her pupils are white with a hint of pink, already reflecting the heat of Hell, the eternal domain she has been banished to.

A third member of Team ANGEL has sidled up to them. The change in appearance that has affected Private Owen Jones, Team ANGEL's leader, is even greater. His eyes are already pale pink.

What are they doing here? All around them, devils are pushing and shoving. Yet Team ANGEL does not move. I look around for their fourth teammate, Jeanne d'Arc, but she is not there. She must have already been moved to the asylum.

Death is cruel.

Then, as quickly as they appeared, the three angels—now devils—are swallowed by the crowd. I turn to Elinor, but she is watching Lord Septimus.

I know now that Johnny knows the truth, that Team DEVIL is leaving once more.

It will stay my secret—for now.

Fimm

Alfarin and Elinor

My father, King Hlif, son of Dobin, wanted to talk. Viking to Viking. Man to man. Devil to Devil.

In that order.

I knew what this was about. My father believed it was time I took a female devil companion. The majority of my kin were married. Some more than once, but only because the women they took often ran away.

It was not hard to run away and hide in Hell.

"My son," said my father, sitting on his throne in the hall of Valhalla. "It is time for you to marry. Negotiations will be opened with the family of Elinor Powell for her hand. It would be better if she agreed, but that didn't stop me with your mother when we were alive."

His laughter boomed around the eaves. I said not a word. My father was missing his right ear, sliced off on his wedding night by my mother. She was aiming to chop off something else, accordingly to legend, but was so drunk she missed entirely.

From what I had seen among my kin, marriage did not seem to be a happy state. Besides, Elinor Powell and I had become friends. I enjoyed her company, and it was refreshing to see the Underworld beyond the eyes of dead Vikings. This peasant girl had brought understanding, compassion, the gift of words and learning and the art of hair braiding into my death. If we married, then Elinor and I would have to fight and throw plates at each other and she would slap my face and I would have to drag her down the corridors by her hair, and that would be us in a civilized state.

I left my father's hall not knowing what to do.

When I met Elinor later that day in Hell's library, she knew I was troubled, but I did not want to tell her why. It would scare her. It scared me. I had arrived in Hell with all of my manly body parts. They could most likely be reattached by the healers, but I did not want to take the chance that they could not.

"Will ye please tell me what is troubling ye, Alfarin?" asked Elinor. We had never ventured this far into the depths of the library before and we were alone, save for a naked old man who was walking up and down the aisles with a ball and chain hanging from his—

Oh, in the name of the goddess Eli, there are some things that should not be described.

"My father wishes me to take a wife," I said glumly.

"Oh," replied Elinor, tugging at the back of her neck. "Who?"

"My father intends to open discussions with your family," I replied.

"My family?" replied Elinor. "And do I not get a say in this?"

"You are a chattel, a possession of your dead brothers, Elinor," I replied. "This is how it is done. It is how it has always been done."

"I am no devil's possession to give away like a piece of meat. And my brothers in Hell have never given a rat's arse about me anyway," snapped Elinor. "*I* will decide who I marry, not any other devil."

"If you decline, you will be seen to have brought dishonor on me and my kin," I replied.

"I have become yer friend, Alfarin," said Elinor. "For now and for always. And perhaps one day it might become more, but I will not marry ye just because some Viking says so, even if he is a king. And if that means I am no longer welcome in yer halls of Valhalla, then so be it."

Elinor said no more, and, for once, I was grateful for her taciturnity. I knew what I had to do, as a Viking, a man, a devil.

———

"I will not marry Elinor Powell."

My statement to the council of Vikings was met with uproar. I was disobeying the wishes of my kin and king. Their angry voices were drowned out by the thumping of their fists and feet on wood. I stood my ground. Elinor did not wish to become my possession. And it would be wrong to try to take her as such. No woman was a possession of a man. Nobody should be the possession of anyone. I knew this, and I also knew that I could not allow Elinor to take the heat of Hell for this decision. I would fall on my blade first.

"You must take a wife, Alfarin, son of mine!" roared King Hlif. "Saxons, Normans—why, even the Romans are beginning to talk! They speak of my son as if he is soft in the head. All that time spent in the library, consorting with a peasant girl. It isn't the Viking way."

"We are a learned people, Father," I replied. "Maybe not in the world of words retained in a library, but we are clever nonetheless. You are respected as a wise and benevolent ruler in Hell. I will not marry Elinor Powell, and you cannot force upon me a union which I do not desire. This is my last word on the subject."

"Then be gone from my sight!" roared my father. "And I will deal with you later."

I knew I had displeased him deeply, and a Viking who displeases his king does not escape punishment easily, even if he happens to be the king's kin.

But I would not force Elinor into a marriage she did not want. I did not wish to pull Elinor's hair. I wanted to place flowers in it.

———

Later that evening, Elinor gave me her serving of lemon pie, even though it was her favorite. I think she thought she knew what had happened.

She did not know the half of it.

My father did not speak to me for three hundred and sixty-five days. And a mark for each day of his silent judgment was scored into my arms with my own blade.

The wounds themselves did not cause me pain. Nor did my having to wear a long-sleeved tunic to conceal my powerful arms from Elinor for a full year.

What truly hurt was the knowledge that this was the first time anyone else, dead or alive, had ever dared to use my axe. And it was used against me.

5. Plan B

The thick metal vault doors within the reception area open, and as feared, the devils outside the reception area attempt to storm the HBI barricade, which is trying to keep them from escaping Hell.

"Alfarin, hurry!" cries Elinor as Lord Septimus pushes Mitchell and Medusa through the only entrance to—and exit from—Hell.

"What is going *on*?" cries Mitchell. "This didn't happen last time. There was hardly anyone around last time we tried to leave."

Lights are still flashing and sirens are screaming. The sound is not the torturous noise a devil hears when Hell's lockdown alarm is activated, but it is true screaming. High-pitched and terrible.

"That's a Banshee!" cries Medusa. "It has to be! Nothing living makes that sound."

"But we are not living, M," replies Elinor, pulling at my arm. "And ye don't know what a Banshee sounds like. This screaming could be anyone or anything. Quickly, Alfarin. Ye must hurry."

The glass doors to the reception area shatter, and a flash of golden light illuminates the cleaved rock corridor beyond the metal vaults as Lord Septimus, Elinor, Mitchell, Medusa and I run through. My axe is vibrating in my hand, but it was not I who broke the glass. There is another sensation, too. A pulsing from the backpack on my shoulder. It is the Viciseometer, the device that has allowed Team DEVIL to travel through time and through realms. It's letting me know it's there, waiting, ready to be used.

The doors shut with a heavy clang, blocking out all sound and light from behind. Red flame bursts forth as Lord Septimus ignites a torch fixed to an iron bracket on the rock wall. The smell of soot lingers.

"Were you expecting that, Lord Septimus?" I ask. "Mitchell was correct. When we passed through the last time we departed Hell, there were no revolting peasants prepared to storm the reception area."

"I was expecting it," replies Lord Septimus quietly. He has stopped walking, and he seems distracted by the tunnel ahead. It is as if he is searching for something in the darkness.

Skin-Walkers?

No one moves. They are waiting for me. My axe is no longer vibrating and the Viciseometer is still once more. I hold out my hand for the flaming torch and Lord Septimus hands it to me.

We are in for a long walk. I hope Mitchell and Medusa packed ointment for possible chafing.

"Ye will tell us when ye are going to leave us, Mr. Septimus?" asks Elinor. "So we are prepared?"

"I will," he replies in his deep, soothing drawl. "But that will not be for a little while. In fact, if you could indulge some of your time, Miss Powell, would you fall back a little with me? There is something I wish to discuss with you."

I cannot help but turn around. Three pale faces light up in the firelight, and Lord Septimus's shines with a black glow, like a precious opal. He had said he wanted to talk to me—so why is he singling out Elinor?

"What do you think that's all about?" whispers Mitchell as we continue onward.

"Shhh," hisses Medusa. "I'm trying to listen."

"If Lord Septimus wanted us to be party to the conversation, he would have asked," I say indignantly. "Privacy is a sacred state."

And then I stop talking, for I wish to hear, too. Alas, Lord Septimus and Elinor keep their voices low. A heavy foreboding beaches itself on my shoulders. I can sense a change in the air, and I do not like it. Team DEVIL is different since our journeys to the land of the living.

And Elinor is different since The Devil took her to filter his dreams. I sense that I am losing her all over again, and I do not know how to get her back. We have been friends for so long, but it feels to me as if the bonds of trust and loyalty that took us hundreds of years to forge were crushed in one fell swoop by The Devil. I understand that she may not be able to share with me everything she witnessed in the mind of that blackhearted monster, but she never used to be *secretive*. And there is something else, too, that I've only been able to identify now. Elinor is…distant. I can see it in her eyes. They still betray the red heat of over three centuries of death, but the glow that once danced there has gone.

The windows of her soul have died. The Devil has done what the Great Fire of London in 1666 could not. He has destroyed her spirit.

My father once wanted me to take Elinor as my wife. I refused and I was punished. Every day, for three hundred and sixty-five days, my father scored a line of penance into my skin with my own axe. In spite of the humiliation, my soul was never broken. It never even came close. What horrors did Elinor see in The Devil's dreams? What degradation was she dragged through as his Dreamcatcher?

"Alfarin?"

"Yes, my friend?"

"You have a Plan B, don't you? In case something goes wrong in there…?"

"Mitchell, I will not fail."

"I know. I'm just saying—"

"I will not fail."

"No, Alfarin. Listen. What I'm saying is, you have the Viciseometer. So if you need to, use it. Get Elinor away. The two of you can go anywhere in time."

The meaning of Mitchell's words washes over me and I am

nearly overcome with emotion. I pat him on the shoulder and his knees buckle. For someone so tall, he has the muscle mass of an old lady. If he had been a Viking, Mitchell would have been used as a spare oar on the longship.

Yet his heart is ten times the size of mine. I would not be surprised to find life in it still. Mitchell forsook his chance to change his death in order to do right by Team DEVIL. Very few would have been so selfless. He is doing the same now, and it comes to him as easily as breathing comes to the living. Mitchell is the most honorable, decent man—and friend—I know.

"Mitchell, I will not fail," I repeat for the third time. If I say it often enough, I might believe it.

"Okay, man. Okay," Mitchell whispers. "It's just that, if things go wrong—and let's face it, Team DEVIL does have a reputation for screwing up—I want you to promise me something."

"Anything for you, my friend."

"Get Elinor out of Hell, and go find my brother. Keep him hidden until he's too old to be taken."

"Mitchell," gasps Medusa.

"He'll still be on the list of future Dreamcatchers, Medusa," says Mitchell. "I'm not having him put back in danger because we messed up."

"I wasn't disagreeing," replies Medusa gently. "I think it's a great idea."

"A Plan B," I say, frowning.

"Promise me, Alfarin?" asks Mitchell, and the urgency in his voice gnaws at me. "We need to have a Plan B. The Devil can't take me or Medusa as his Dreamcatcher because we aren't pure enough, but he could take back Elinor. And he will—we all know that's what he's planning on doing if we fail in there. I bet anything that's what Septimus is talking to her about now. So we don't give him the chance, okay? If we fail to convince Beatrice Morrigan to return with us, then you don't think twice. You and Elinor go back to Washington, DC, to that first time we saw my brother, and you take him."

"But your lady mother—"

"My mom will get him back eventually. You just take care of him until he's past the age of five and too old to be used as a Dream-catcher. I'm begging you, Alfarin. Please."

"Oh, Mitchell," whispers Medusa. She wraps her bony arms around his waist and hugs him while we are still walking.

"But Plan B means leaving the two of you to the fate of the Skin-Walkers," I say.

"Septimus will look out for us," says Medusa.

But she cannot see the sideways glance of Mitchell's pink eyes, nor the fact that he is biting down on his bottom lip. He wraps his arms around Medusa and quickly kisses the crown of her head. Her curls smother his face. Mitchell subtly shakes his head from left to right to left, and I understand the wordless gesture.

We cannot rely on Lord Septimus to put us first. Not now. We are pawns in a much bigger game. The Devil has made his number one general look foolish. There will be no forgiveness by the servant of the master once Lord Septimus decides to strike back.

"I promise, my friend, to do as you ask," I say. "Let us prepare for the blood oath."

"*Again?*" asks Mitchell. "Um. Okay. Can I do it? I know you don't like anyone touching your axe, but . . . I don't know, it just seems like it should come from me this time. Because of M.J."

Lord Septimus and Elinor have drawn level with us once more. Mitchell takes my axe from my hands. It does not feel natural to see someone else bear its mighty weight, and yet what Mitchell is about to do makes perfect sense. I am proud he has asked me for this honor.

"Across the palm," I say, holding my scarred hand flat. "Straight and true."

The cut that Mitchell inflicts on me is not as deep as I would have done to myself, but thick blood still seeps through the opening in my skin.

"Yer axe has seen more of Team DEVIL's blood than it should," says Elinor. The tone of her voice carries the full weight of her displeasure. "Are ye sure this is necessary?"

"It'll be the last time, Elinor," replies Mitchell, holding my axe between his knees. "Trust me. But this is important."

Mitchell swipes his hand down over the edge of the curved blade. He makes a noise like a baby being force-fed root vegetables. I take his hand in mine and our dead blood mixes once more.

"Plan B," we both say.

"And what is Plan B?" asks Elinor.

"Something that will not be necessary, my princess," I reply, letting go of Mitchell's hand. Medusa is already pulling a strip of cloth out of her backpack and winding it around Mitchell's hand.

"No more blood," she whispers to him. "Okay?"

"I'm afraid he can't promise that," says a wheezing voice from the shadows. My axe clatters to the ground as Mitchell drops it. Elinor and Medusa cry out in fright.

"Who's there?" I shout. "Show yourself."

An old man steps out of the darkness. He's wearing a long red robe that falls to the ground. His head is covered by a red skullcap. With a long, hooked nose, pointed chin, and cloudy eyes, he isn't the most pleasing of fellows to look upon.

"So it has come to pass once more," says the old man. "It has been many centuries since I was last required."

"Who are you?" asks Medusa. "What did you mean, Mitchell can't promise no more blood? You have no idea who we are or where we're going."

"Oh, but I do know where you're going. And there, child, you'll find nothing *but* blood," replies the old man. "Septimus, old friend. Aren't you going to introduce me?"

"Miss Powell, you asked that I tell you when I am leaving," says Lord Septimus softly. "That time has come sooner than I expected. This is Virgil, and he is your guide into the Circles of Hell."

Sex

Alfarin and Elinor

Employment was a way of death in Hell. Hard work and toil came naturally to Vikings, but many other devils were desperately unhappy about having to exist in the Afterlife in the same manner that they had lived. Most factions stayed within their own groups: Vikings worked in establishments that provided food, ale, weapons, ale, brawling services, woodwork and ale; Romans were the bureaucrats; and any royalty was responsible for what little entertainment was on offer in the oppressive, hot darkness of Hell.

Peasants were given the jobs no other devil wanted, such as cleaning toilets. This continued for many centuries until those who were called reality television stars arrived. I did not understand this phenomenon, but they all appeared to suffer artificial browning of the flesh and oddly shaped lips.

I had employment in my cousin Thomason's bar. I collected glasses and cleaned them. My father, King Hlif, made me take on the job as a way of further punishing my insolence in refusing to marry Elinor Powell. My kin were still unaware that it was Elinor who had refused me, and that I had taken the blame to ensure she was not banished from the halls of Valhalla.

It would stay that way. Not all secrets were an ill.

———

By this time, Elinor's reading and writing were so good, she did not clean out toilets like the other peasants. Instead, she was employed as a records clerk for the Grim Reapers: a role she had continued after the influx of soldiers during the Great War.

Elinor and I were growing ever closer. I found myself searching for red hair amongst the sea of bodies that swarmed around the corridors of Hell. I found myself craving that first smile of hers as she spotted me. I would even occasionally resort to deliberately dropping food on my tunic, because I knew Elinor would be the one to wipe it off.

It was hard to hide my true feelings around my kin. During feasts it was customary to slap any delightfully big bottom that happened to pass our way—and I had done so many times. But the longer I spent with Elinor, the less I felt inclined to behave like that. Was I ailing? Could a Viking lose his Vikingness? There were times when I thought I knew myself around Elinor, but there were other moments when I believed she was changing me into a man I did not recognize.

"I have been searching for ye for a hundred years. So when ye are ready to be the devil I know ye will one day become, Alfarin, son of Hlif, son of Dobin, ye come and find me."

I knew Elinor and I had never met before in the land of the living, so why did these words from our very first conversation keep haunting me? Elinor refused to talk about many things, like her death, and her family in Hell. But the one that caused me the most frustration was her steadfast determination not to discuss why she had come looking for me in Hell.

It was as if I were being prepared like a hog for slaughter.

I did not welcome the unknown. But I trusted her.

———

Elinor and I had settled into an easy existence; a cycle of something that could be described as domesticity—without the hair-pulling, rump-slapping and kneeing of private manly parts. We worked, we read, we learned, and I ate enough for the both of us to be satisfied. At the end of the day, I returned to the hearth of my kin, but I did not always feel at home there.

My Valhalla was becoming two separate worlds.

Our comfortable routine changed one day when Elinor received a letter. It had been left on her bed.

I did not make a habit of entering the sleeping quarters of the peasant girls, as they tended to swoon in my magnificent presence, but I made an exception this day, as Elinor's hand had covered her mouth while she read the neat script. I thought it could be bad news. I knew I would have to be ready to offer a broad shoulder or a clean handkerchief for her to weep into.

I did not have a clean handkerchief. The sleeve of my tunic would have to do.

"I got a job in devil resources, Alfarin," whispered Elinor as I finally reached her. "The flu pandemic amongst those left after the war has killed so many, they are taking on more staff. I got the job, Alfarin. I did it."

"I was unaware you had applied, Elinor," I replied. "My axe and I pay tribute to your tenacity and filing skills."

"I'm getting closer, Alfarin," said Elinor. "I'll be able to check on every devil in existence now. I'm going to find the other one—I just know it. It's fate. Fate."

And she kissed me briefly on the lips.

It was the first time Elinor had shown me such physical affection. My heart was unaccustomed to the sudden rush of emotions that followed, and my head was spinning with her cryptic words.

Who was the other one? What was fate?

And were my lips too chapped?

I never found out the answer to the last question, for it would be nearly one hundred years before Elinor showed me such physical affection again.

6. Virgil

Virgil. I know that name. It was mentioned over and over again in *The Divine Comedy* by Dante Alighieri. I had read that tome during my lonely sojourn in the library, and brought it with me for our journey. The language in the epic poem would be archaic to some, but for me, it was a welcome return to the speech of old. Virgil was a Roman poet, which explains his acquaintance with Lord Septimus. Virgil was the one who guided Dante through the Circles of Hell, on to Purgatory and eventually into Paradise. He was a mentor, protector and guide.

My Viking reserve is overtaken by relief. If Virgil is to be our guide, we are saved, for he will know the way.

"It is an honor to meet you, Virgil!" I cry, going down on bended knee.

"This is Prince Alfarin, son of Hlif, son of Dobin," says Lord Septimus. "On this quest, he is the leader of the four devils before you, Virgil."

Virgil massages his pointed chin and seems to appraise me. He offers no greeting in reply. Instead, he turns his attention to Elinor and Medusa. His large nose sniffs the air like a dog's.

"These two smell slightly less of meat and tomatoes and sweat," says Virgil. "The inclusion of women is unwise, Septimus."

"Medusa Pallister, one of The Devil's two interns," says Lord Septimus. "And Elinor Powell—"

"Yes, I know who these two young women are," interrupts Virgil. "As I said, unwise."

"We're a team. We stick together," says Mitchell.

"Virgil? Weren't you the guide Dante wrote about?" asks Medusa warily. "I read the *Divine Comedy* in school. You showed Dante the way."

"He was a dreamer, Dante," says Virgil. "Blinded by love, like most fools."

"Team DEVIL intends to find Beatrice Morrigan," says Lord Septimus. "They are returning her to The Devil."

The roughly hewn rock corridor starts to shake as Virgil laughs. It is a horrible sound. Whistling and gasping and hacking and screaming echo up and down the darkness. Elinor trembles and reaches out for Medusa. Mitchell backs into the wall and is showered in black crystals that fall from the roof. The torch in my hand extinguishes so quickly it is as if a blanket has smothered it.

"Lasciate ogne speranza, voi ch'intrate," booms a deep voice in the darkness. Hot fingers grope at my skin. Elinor loses all composure and screams, but I cannot reach her. My body is frozen in ice. A stench, worse than that which follows Fabulara, rolls over us in waves. I hear Mitchell gagging and then Medusa cries out for help. She screams that she is drowning.

"Enough, Virgil," bellows Lord Septimus, and the crushing weight of ice leaves me. The torch illuminates once more. I catch a glimpse of Virgil; he is momentarily transformed from a man into a gargoyle-like creature. His face is contorted by anger and hate, but his eyes linger upon Elinor. They have changed from opaque white to a fierce, burning red. A forked black tongue flickers between pointed black teeth. He is a snake in a man's skin.

"Lasciate ogne speranza, voi ch'intrate," repeats Virgil, and he is the man once more.

"What does that mean?" asks Mitchell, the bulge in his throat bobbing furiously. "What did you just do to us?"

"Abandon all hope, ye who enter here," says Virgil quietly. "That's what those words mean. You are foolish to do this. You are but children. Go back. I implore you. Go back."

"We can't!" cries Medusa. "I promised The Devil—"

"Foolish girl," growls Virgil. "Whatever you promised The Devil is not worth this risk. Septimus, I will not do it. Look at them. They are young, but whatever it is they've done, whatever it is they've experienced, is going to complicate things. My journey with Dante Alighieri was a comparative cakewalk to what this passage will be. His soul may have been lost, but it was not forsaken. Can you say the same for them? Take this one—" Virgil sniffs at the air again and jerks his head toward me. "I can tell already that he is in grave peril. His feelings for that quiet one beside you will be his undoing. The odds are good that he will not make it out the other side."

"I am not afraid," I say loudly. "And if I am in grave danger, then I will be destroyed trying to do the right thing. For I will not allow Elinor to be taken back as The Devil's Dreamcatcher. I will not. *I. Will. Not.*" My axe slams into the rock with each word, and I am surprised to feel the heat of immolation rising inside me.

"The Devil's Dreamcatcher," gasps Virgil. "What do you mean?"

"Alfarin—" says Elinor quietly.

"No," I interrupt, unable to look at her. If I do not say this now, I may never be able to say it. The weight of words is so crushing, I am the Norse god Tyr, holding up the world with one hand. "The shame I felt, Elinor, at not being able to protect you. The dishonor that still bleeds from my wretched soul...I would die a thousand deaths to protect Mitchell and Medusa, but for you, for you there is no number. And if I cannot stop The Devil in his nefarious ways, then I will cease to exist. My soul will rot for the carrion birds to scavenge. You have to let me do this. For you, but for me also."

"Oh, Alfarin," says Medusa softly. Mitchell whispers something into her ear, and she falls into his chest.

I am still unable to look at Elinor. My princess, my world. Will she think me a lovestruck fool for laying my heart open to the decay of Hell? My status as a Viking, a man, a devil, has been built on my reputation as a fearless fighter, with brute strength and a weapon that looks like a comet streaking through the air when I wield it. But Elinor has made me more.

I like the Viking, the man, the devil that Elinor has made me become—but does she?

It as if I have spoken the question aloud. Her warm, slim arms embrace me around my neck. The kiss is glancing, and yet I know I will remember every fold of skin in her lips as she presses her mouth gently to mine.

"Ye mean more to me than life itself," whispers Elinor. "If I could give ye my beating heart from centuries ago, I would."

"Where do they get these lines from?" wonders Mitchell aloud. Elinor blushes as red as her eyes and backs away.

"Don't ruin the moment," says Medusa, but the moment is gone. Still, Elinor does not take her eyes from mine, and the rest of Hell melts into a blurred shadow, frothy at the edges like a tankard of beer.

With a roar, I grab Virgil by the folds of his long red robe. He is slightly smaller than me in height, but I have more muscle mass in one bulging bicep than he has in his entire body.

"You are the guide, yes?" I roar. "Speak, man. Every second in this tunnel is a second wasted."

"I am, I am …," replies Virgil. "Now unhand me, you brute."

I bring his pointed face to within an inch of mine. Virgil smells salty.

"You will take us into the Nine Circles of Hell. I do not ask you to help us remove the Banshee, and I will not ask you to fight whatever heinous creatures we find in there, but by the blade of my axe, you will show us where Beatrice Morrigan is."

I can feel Virgil's feet poking at my shins; I have lifted him clean off the ground.

"You think you can get what you want with threats and violence?" asks Virgil, saliva pooling at the side of his mouth. "You will not last past the Seventh Circle, Viking."

"Where is the entrance?" I say slowly, elongating my vowels. If I have to drag Virgil by his hooked nose, then by Thor's fury, I will. He called me *Viking* as an insult. I claim the title with pride. Team DEVIL has never truly seen me in the mind-set of a warrior. Even on my deathday, it was self-preservation that they saw from that rickety shed that smelled of piss. What I am now, is truly a prince among devils. Determination and deliverance are my allies on this quest.

And my axe is getting hungry for some real action.

"I will be your guide," mutters Virgil. "But do not say, when you are face to face with the worst that Hell can throw at you, that I did not warn you. *Lasciate ogne speranza, voi ch'intrate.* These are words that will haunt you all for the rest of your existence. Limbo, lust, gluttony, greed, anger, heresy, violence, fraud and treachery . . . you will see, taste, smell, hear and feel the evil of man, and in the face of all this, you will find yourself wanting, Viking."

I turn to Lord Septimus. His red eyes gleam in the darkness.

"You may return to the Underworld," I say. "I will lead on from here."

"Your father would be proud of you, Prince Alfarin, son of Hlif, son of Dobin," says Lord Septimus. "As am I."

He turns to Mitchell and Medusa.

"Don't say good-bye," whispers Medusa. She is shaking.

"Stay true to one another, and accept help where it is offered," says Lord Septimus.

"We'll be back, boss," says Mitchell. Medusa is not the only one shaking. My friend is having a vertical seizure.

"Miss Powell," says Lord Septimus. "You are the calm in the center of the storm, and the heart that binds the four of you together. Do not doubt yourself, or your friends. Use whatever information you have at your disposal."

"Thank ye, Mr. Septimus," replies Elinor. She holds out a slim hand, which The Devil's accountant shakes; then, after a slight hesitation, Lord Septimus bends and kisses it.

"You never cease to amaze me, Team DEVIL," says Lord Septimus. "And Virgil"—he turns to the old man—"if you betray my charges, then know that I will search every inch of the Skin-Walkers' domain for you, and I will not rest until I have scattered your remains within the Nine Circles and beyond."

"Your threats might scare everyone else in the Underworld, Septimus," replies Virgil, "but I have experienced too much down here to be fearful of mere words."

Lord Septimus does not touch the guide, but the look he gives the old man would make even the Skin-Walkers quail. It is anger and contempt and a warning rolled into one. I immediately vow to perfect such an expression myself, but I am distracted by a subtle movement to my right. For a brief moment, the shadows of Team DEVIL are not of two males and two females. They are taller, wider. Four figures mounted on animals.

Then the shadows bleed away like dissolving ice, filling the crevices of rock with darkness.

"*Mere words* can incite an army, Virgil. Both Prince Alfarin and I have gone into battle on less. Remember that, when the time comes to choose a side." Lord Septimus turns to me. "See it through to the very end, Prince Alfarin. Do not waver in your commitment. To the very end, do you understand?"

And then, with a blast of hot air that crackles like electricity, Lord Septimus disappears.

Sjau

Alfarin and Elinor

I was born a Viking prince. The first son of King Hlif, son of Dobin. As soon as I could understand the language of my fathers, I knew I was destined for greatness...or so I was told. My father mother, Queen Tabitha, called me the *mestr*, which means "the greatest" in the English tongue. My father had sired several children with other wives after I was born, but all had died in their first year.

I did not know the love of a mother. Mine passed over when I was a babe in arms. Her name was Valencia, which means "strength."

I was never told how she died, and she was rarely mentioned by my father or our kin. I was forbidden to ask questions because that was not the Viking way. Our women were tough. I was always left feeling that despite her name, she wasn't strong enough for whatever fate befell her. I once overheard Queen Tabitha say my mother had deserted her place. That she had brought shame on the line and that her blood was bad. This confused me. My father's next sons had all perished, too—was his blood not bad? I once questioned this aloud, and Queen Tabitha boxed my ears. Questioning the king's bloodline was tantamount to treason. Fault always lay with the women. Always.

But my mother's blood ran through me, and now, even though I was dead, that connection would always remain. Did this mean my blood was bad, too? Even in death? My thirst for knowledge about my mother's demise was increasing, and the irony that I could not ask my kin for information was not lost on me. I needed to know more—but the information had to come from elsewhere.

When Elinor started her employ in devil resources, I saw an opportunity. When she wasn't on the clock, Elinor would often busy herself with side projects, first researching her family, and then, she told me, researching someone else. She said she was looking for a friend whom she had met late in her life. I did not question her further, thinking only that if Elinor could comb millions and millions of devil resources files for answers, then perhaps I could, too. This could be my chance to discover more information about my mother, and perhaps learn why she wasn't strong enough to stay with me. And of course, it would give me a chance to spend even more time with Elinor, if she would allow my company.

———

Elinor was one of six children. She had two brothers in Hell: Michael and Phillip. Neither paid her any attention. Perhaps that was why Elinor was so at home in the company of Vikings. We fought hard, with words and the occasional swinging of goats, but our family stuck together, and outside the halls of Valhalla, we were feared and admired in equal measure. Queen Tabitha adored Elinor, and my friend appreciated the attention.

Still, I knew Elinor craved the connection to blood family.

Elinor was happy to smuggle me into devil resources so I could look through the files. Her mother had abandoned her during the Great Fire of London, so she understood what it was like to have no knowledge or memory of a maternal bond. Alas, I quickly discovered that there were many thousands of Valencias in Hell, and with no family name to distinguish the bloodline, I realized it would be an almost impossible task to find her—if she had even come to Hell.

It was different for Elinor. She discovered—through a process of elimination with the family name Powell—that the three kin she was searching for had gone Up There: John, William and Alice. She became emotional when talking of John and William especially. They were her younger brothers.

"They were there, in the fire with me," she whispered. "They were saved."

"If I had been there, I would have saved you," I replied.

It was the right thing to say, because Elinor wrapped her arms around me and placed her head on my shoulder.

"We were fated to meet, ye know that, don't ye?" she said. "But I wish I could see our John and William one more time. We were very close. I loved them very much."

Love. Such a cruel four-letter word. Did Valencia not love me enough to hold on? Or did she die because of it?

I would never know, because I never did find my mother amongst the billions of names in Hell.

7. Love and Treachery

No one moves. Five sets of eyes, ranging from foamy white to pale pink to the deepest red, are fixed on the spot where just moments ago, Lord Septimus was standing.

"How did he do that?" asks Medusa. "He didn't have a Viciseometer. He just...he just disappeared."

"Just because you are close to the man, do not fool yourself into believing you know everything about him, girl," says Virgil. He straightens himself up and tilts his head arrogantly.

But his shaking hands betray his fearfulness.

"Her name is Medusa," says Mitchell. His back straightens, too, and I am pleased to see it has a more impressive effect than Virgil's stance—and not only because his length nearly matches that of a longship. My friend in death has a proud streak when it comes to defending his woman.

"As in the woman of many snakes," sneers Virgil.

"We have no time for idle talk, Virgil," I say, stepping in front of Mitchell, who has a face like thunder. "Lead on."

"You mean to go through with this folly?" asks Virgil. His question is sincere, as is my reply.

"Yes."

We walk on in silence. It is not a comfortable quietude. Elinor is deep in thought; one hand is massaging her neck, the other is in her mouth as she chews on her fingernails. Mitchell is now bringing up the rear of Team DEVIL with the torch. Every time I turn to check on everyone, his pink eyes meet mine. Mitchell is biting down on the inside of his cheek, which distorts his jaw. It reminds me of when Elinor punched him the first time we left Hell.

What journeys we have been on since then. When I first arrived at the HalfWay House in 970 AD, death seemed simple. It has proven to be anything but.

"Alfarin, do you still have the book by Dante in your backpack?" whispers Medusa.

"I do."

"Can I have it?"

"Of course."

Medusa would make a good thief. Her sleight of hand is subtle as she unzips my backpack and pulls out the tome. Then she sidles up to Virgil, who is leading the procession with another torch procured from the tunnel wall. His long fingers glide along the rough stone, presumably to balance his frail frame.

"Virgil, you said he—Dante—was a poet and a dreamer," says Medusa. "So how much of this book is actually true?"

"What does it matter?" replies Virgil. "You will find out soon enough."

"It matters because we need to be prepared," I reply. "To start, I want to know the location of each Skin-Walker."

"The Skin-Walkers are not contained creatures," replies Virgil, with another hacking laugh. "Do you not move around your own dwelling, even in a place as crowded and confined as Hell? To them, their own circle is...is a banquet hall. They feed off the wretched souls' terror, but the same meal day in and day out would bore anyone. The Skin-Walkers often leave for fresh meat, and as we all know, there is never a shortage of evil souls out there."

Virgil's words are not entirely surprising. Team DEVIL has seen the Skin-Walkers outside the Circles of Hell before. We passed eight of them on our first journey from Hell. We have met Perfidious, their leader, in the secret level of the CBD, and all nine accosted us in the land of the living after we joined with Team ANGEL. But never in all my reading did I come across any information about the frequency of the Skin-Walkers' departures from the Circles.

"Alfarin," says Medusa. "Are you thinking what I'm thinking?"

"Almost certainly, wise Medusa."

"Any chance of letting those of us almost certainly not thinking what you're thinking know what the Hell you're thinking?" calls Mitchell from the back.

Elinor giggles. It is my favorite sound in the world, other than the frying of bacon.

"Ye make me laugh, Mitchell," she says. "If Mr. Septimus heard ye saying the word *thinking* three times in a single sentence, he would make ye do lines a thousand times over before making ye read a thesaurus to improve yer vocabulary."

"Don't mock me, Elinor," replies Mitchell. "I'm thinking about thinking here."

Now it's Medusa's turn to laugh. Virgil snorts with derision, clearly indisposed to the easy way we on Team DEVIL interact with one another. He will learn that our camaraderie is not to our detriment, but rather, what brings us closer. We have been through things in life and death that many others have never had to endure. Humor is food for *our* souls.

Not that I will ever give up the true joy of food, of course. It was a metaphor. I take a furtive look around, and hope the shadows that are tracking us cannot read minds. I do not wish to replace cheeseburgers and fries with one of Mitchell's jokes.

"Alfarin," says Medusa. "Do you want to explain our train of thought to Mitchell, or shall I?"

I smile. "My friend. We already know the Skin-Walkers do not watch their circles continuously," I say. "We have seen them ourselves on multiple occasions. But Virgil has now confirmed that these vile creatures abandon their posts on a regular basis. We can use this information to ease our passage through the Circles. We will simply wait for each Skin-Walker to depart, and then we will enter."

"But what about time, Alfarin?" asks Mitchell. "You heard that psychopath earlier—"

"Shhhhh, Mitchell," chides Elinor. "Not even here, away from the confines of *our* Underworld, should such words be spoken about the master."

"Fine, the definitely-not-psychopathic nutbag called The Devil, then," says Mitchell, his voice dripping with sarcasm. "You heard him. He's going without sleep while we do this. We can't wait around forever, believing the Skin-Walkers will leave."

Virgil has slowed down; he is listening.

"Then we will just have to hope that enough evil is busy in the land of the living to warrant their attention," I reply.

But my nonchalance is noted, especially by Medusa, who stops walking suddenly and turns to me with her hands on her hips.

"Alfarin!" she exclaims. "How can you say something like that?"

Another laugh escapes Virgil's lips. "An early death was a fortunate escape for you, Viking," he sneers. "Your eagerness to wish ill on others would have seen you end up with some of your more vicious kin in the Circles."

"I—I did not mean I wished…that was not what I meant," I stammer.

Medusa's face has fallen with disappointment. I am embarrassed, not just by my words, but by the ease with which they came.

I am not evil. I am *not*.

But I am in Hell, and I am angry, and one thousand years of death can corrupt the purest of souls.

I wish to ask Virgil more questions, and I want to confer with my friends, but I am too ashamed to open my mouth. I do not wish for the kind of evil that befell Medusa to happen to anyone. She endured much suffering at the hands of her stepfather, Rory Hunter, when she was alive. And in death, too, as Rory was the very Unspeakable who stole The Devil's Dreamcatcher not long ago. But now, as we embark on a new quest, I am facing up to the inevitable fact that the Skin-Walkers will need the distraction of those like Rory Hunter to remove them from the Circles.

"It is not as easy as you thought, is it, Viking?" Virgil whispers. "Good and evil are not always separable like black and white."

Our guide is now walking by my side. We are the two least able on this part of the journey. The tunnels are narrowing as we walk, and I am burdened by my impressive size; he is hampered by feebleness because he died in old age.

"I never thought it would be easy," I reply. "But I take comfort in knowing that while my heart may be dead, it is true."

"And does she still think that?" Virgil sniffs and nods toward Elinor, who is walking arm in arm with Medusa. "I hear the wretched affection you have for her in every word you utter. Dante spoke of his woman with the same doleful voice."

"I am doing this for her," I reply.

"You think this journey will bring out the best in you, Viking," says Virgil. "But it could also bring out the worst. In all of you. Friend will betray friend. Love will be unfaithful to love. It is inevitable. All of your masks will slip and you each will be revealed for who you really are."

"We just want Beatrice Morrigan."

Virgil laughs. "Yes, as did Dante."

"They are the same woman?" I exclaim.

"Does that mean you know her?" cries Medusa. "You know what she looks like?"

"I know...of her," says Virgil.

"This is excellent! You can lead us straight to her!" cries Mitchell. "Virgil, I gotta know. With all these crazy dead dudes after her... is she hot?"

Medusa aims her elbow at Mitchell's ribs. Because the tunnel is so narrow, she doesn't miss.

"Beatrice is an extraordinary woman. Did you think The Devil was the only one ever to fall in love with her, even if he did let her go?"

"I would have thought the fact that she was The Devil's wife would be enough reason to stop anyone else from falling in love with her," I reply.

"Love is the most corrupt and terrifying force of nature there is, Viking," says Virgil. "Man cannot control it."

"Or woman," says Elinor, turning around to smile at me. "Yet love is also the most beautiful force there is. It makes people selfless. We cannot control it, but we can choose how to let it into our lives, and deaths."

"Alfarin, what's the Viking word for love?" asks Medusa.

"In old Norse, it is *elska*," I reply.

"I would elska a pizza right now," says Mitchell, grinning at me. I cannot help laughing.

"Ye had a pizza earlier, Mitchell," scolds Elinor. "Ye boys are always thinking with yer stomachs."

"And Alfarin elskas his axe, and Mitchell elskas his girly pink eyes," quips Medusa.

"You are very strange," says Virgil. "All of you. I should not be your guide on this journey."

"Why?" asks Mitchell. "I elska this group. We're awesome."

Suddenly a scream pierces the air in the narrow corridor. We all cry out in surprise. The pitch is so high the blade of my axe vibrates.

The scream is quickly followed by a blast of hot wind that smells of burning flesh.

I should not know that smell, but I do.

"Skin-Walkers," groans Virgil. "They will be coming this way with an Unspeakable. We would be wise to circumvent them. Quickly, we must enter from the other end!"

"The other end of what?" cries Medusa.

I understand immediately. "The other end of the Skin-Walkers' domain," I explain calmly. The mind of a warrior has no time for panic. Self-preservation is only accomplished by thinking ahead, and the old man seems to comprehend this. "Virgil, what do I need to do?"

The old man is tracing circles on the rock with outstretched hands, one clockwise, one counterclockwise. "Do you trust me?" he asks.

"Yes," I lie.

"Then give the blade to me," replies Virgil. His body twists as he reaches back with his right arm. His fingers grope at the air.

"Get us in first," I say. "And then I'll give you my blade."

"Alfarin!" exclaims Elinor. "What are ye doing?"

"Trust me, I know what I am doing," I reply. And I do. I am a learned Viking. I have read *The Divine Comedy*. I know what we're about to face.

Virgil places both hands back on the rock wall. He starts to mutter in a language that I think is a rudimentary form of Latin. The screaming is getting louder, and Medusa's face has been completely engulfed by her snakelike hair as the scorching wind gathers momentum.

"Hurry up, Virgil!" cries Mitchell as his torch extinguishes.

Then the rock wall is suddenly illuminated with the outline of an arch. It is a doorway, covered in gargoyle-like etchings.

This is it. We are going through. I turn to my friends, who, I can see in the dim light, are gripping one another tightly.

"Stay close to me, and do not look at its three faces," I say.

"Oh, Hell!" cries Medusa. "You've got to be kidding me! We're starting off in the Ninth?"

"You have a choice, girl," snaps Virgil. "Stay and be consumed by the approaching Skin-Walkers, or enter with me now."

"Wait," I say. "Before we go any farther, we must be clear on our task. We must be thorough in each circle, leaving no stone unturned, in our hunt for the Banshee. Only when we are certain we have looked everywhere can we move to the next circle."

"Alfarin!" shouts Mitchell. "The Circles of Hell won't matter if we don't get out of the way of the Skin-Walkers. Get us out of here."

Virgil and I join forces to push the rock door open. Immediately, the scorching stench of evil is replaced by a blast of freezing cold wind.

"In—now!" cries Virgil. The four of us acquiesce, but before the door closes behind us, a streak of golden light flies past us, almost knocking Elinor off balance. My princess places a hand on Virgil's arm to steady herself, and the old man jumps as if he has been given an electric shock.

"That cannot be," he whispers, staring at his arm and then at Elinor, but he quickly recovers his composure and holds out his gnarled fingers.

"You promised me the axe, Viking," says Virgil. "Give it to me."

"No," I reply, tightening my grasp.

"I will need the blade to make a passage through. You gave me your word."

"I will not part with it."

Virgil snorts. "You really are going to fit in here, Viking. Be careful. With your scheming ways, I expect now that more than one circle will attempt to claim you."

"Alfarin," calls Elinor. "What is going on? Ye must tell us."

"I am matching Virgil at his own game, Elinor," I reply. "Now prepare yourselves, Team DEVIL. Our journey through the Circles has started in the Ninth, the final resting place of the truly treacherous."

Átta

Alfarin and Elinor

I was sixteen when I died. In the modern world, a male of that age is barely considered to have reached adulthood. To a Viking, the man had already arrived.

Yet while my father and kin considered us to be Viking first and men second, there were traits that all of us shared, sometimes to the detriment of others.

It was called being human.

I was not a duplicitous person by nature. Lying did not come easily to me, and that was just as well, for I generally did not require a silver tongue to get my way, or to convince someone I was right. A well-aimed fist to the stomach worked far quicker.

But sometimes words that go *unspoken* achieve the same effect as lies. That is what happened on the night I betrayed Elinor.

We had fallen into an exhausted sleep along a dusty row of cabinets in devil resources. It was 1935, and the Great Depression—a catastrophe of epic proportions—had brought on another enormous influx. Starvation is such a tragic way to pass over, especially for the young. Emotions amongst the dead in Hell were running very high, as many parents had been separated from their young at the Half-Way House, where their children began the journey to Up There. For the first time since our original meeting, Elinor and I were truly bickering.

It got so bad between us, I was even considering marrying her.

As we slept on the hard ground of Row S, I was abruptly awoken by Elinor's voice—it had become my personal alarm clock—but I was still pained by lack of food and fatigue, and my red eyes were sore and itchy.

Elinor was speaking in her sleep, but her words did not make sense to me. She was lying on her stomach and crying out.

I considered comforting her, but I was irritated. She had disturbed my slumber. A Viking who is tired and armed should not be in the company of others.

A shadow flickered on the wall, but for once, it was the silhouette of an actual devil, and not the insidious darkness that manifests itself in shapes along the corridors of Hell.

I soon realized that the approaching figure was one of the young soldiers we had sorted after the Battle of the Somme. I recognized him by his brown uniform, which I could make out in the dimness. But I could not see his face. Most of the torches had long burned out, and the firelighters had yet to arrive to replenish the flame.

"What do you want?" I asked. My deep voice was intimidating to almost everyone, in life and death, and when it took on a grumpy edge, it was known to loosen a devil's bowels.

But the soldier was calm. "I have a message for Miss Powell," he said quietly, his English accent echoing in the hall. "I was not aware she was sleeping, or had company."

"Give the message to me. I will pass it on."

"Very well. Tell her, 1967 and 2009."

"1967 and 2009? That is not a message. Those are answers to a math equation," I replied, annoyed that I would have to remember numbers while my stomach and legs were cramping. "Go away, or I will run you through with my blade."

Without another word, the soldier melted into the shadows. I was not even sure I had not imagined the episode. I once came down with a sickness in Hell that resulted in a high fever that lasted many days. During that malady, I swore my cousin Loof's roasted hog started singing "The Star-Spangled Banner"—with the apple still in its mouth.

Elinor awoke.

"Who were ye talking to, Alfarin?" she asked. Then, before I could answer, a clock chimed the hour. "Oh, look at the time!" Elinor exclaimed. "I have barely had time to shut my eyes, Alfarin, and here ye are, talking away in the middle of the night. I cannot do my job if ye are here under my feet all the time and making noise. Ye need to give me room to...room to breathe."

To this day, I am ashamed of my disloyalty. But the truth of the matter seemed important at the time: it was her fault that I had awoken in the first place. So, without a word, I picked up my axe, clambered to my feet and left Elinor with enough room to try to be the only devil in the history of Hell to actually breathe.

I never delivered the message.

Only decades later did I come to understand the numbers.

1967 and 2009 were the years Medusa and Mitchell passed over. Which raised more questions: How did the voice in the shadows know that Mitchell and Medusa would be important to us, years before their deaths even occurred? Or did he know nothing at all, and was he just a messenger, a conduit? And if he *was* just a messenger, who was the message really from?

But these were questions that I could never ponder with Elinor, because then she would have discovered that I had been deliberately deceitful that night.

8. The Ninth Circle

The Ninth Circle of Hell. It was the last circle I had read about and therefore the one I recalled best. In the tome written by Dante, it is the last place the treacherous-in-life will ever see. In four concentric zones, a different kind of treachery is punished, and in the center of this pit of doom resides a three-headed, winged beast. It is written that the beast is forever devouring three traitors, while all along the beast itself is trapped in a huge block of ice, which prevents it from flying away.

"Keep close...to me," I say, shivering. "We are starting at the bottom of the Circles...and so we must work...our way to the top. This Ninth Circle...is a narrow cave...like a funnel...it will wind around and around...four times in a continuous loop...that will get smaller...and smaller...as we ascend."

"No one...is going anywhere...until...until we all have... more layers on," Medusa says, teeth chattering. "Ice in Hell," she muses. "H-how does it not melt?"

She slips off her backpack, unzips it and pulls out two sweaters and a knitted beanie. The hat immediately plumps up like a pillow as she places it on her head, such is the incredible mass of hair contained within it.

We all follow suit. Clever Medusa packed the bags for all extremities, even in the depths of Hell.

"I haven't got anything for you to wear, I'm afraid, Virgil," says Medusa. "I thought we were doing this alone."

The old man is shivering. Now that we are in the Ninth Circle, I understand why he wanted my axe so badly. We are treading not on rock, but on thick crusts of pale-blue ice. My blade could mean the difference between escaping to the Eighth Circle and plummeting into the chasms that surround us.

"Does anyone have any rope?" asks Mitchell, looking around. "If we have to climb *up* to get to the Eighth Circle, then we'll have more chance of making it if we're all tied together. You know, like mountaineers."

"That's in Elinor's bag," replies Medusa. "And in case it's not long enough, there's also rope in Alfarin's."

"You're amazing, Medusa," says Mitchell.

"She most certainly is," I say, placing a knitted hat on my head. It is small and barely reaches my eyebrows. "You must have been a Viking in a previous life."

"Existing and knowing about one paradox is enough for me," replies Medusa, patting my arm. "But thanks for the compliment, Alfarin."

Mitchell sidles up to me. He is so tall and long in body that his new sweater barely reaches his waist.

"Dude, do you have a book on women or something?" he whispers. "You kick ass at compliments."

I slap my friend on the back, and then quickly grab him when it becomes obvious he is about to stumble over the ledge of ice we are standing on.

"There is no book on being a Viking," I reply. "We just are. But I will gladly give you tips on how to keep your woman happy in the Viking way."

"Bury your face in my chest, or slap my ass, Mitchell Johnson, and you'll be begging for the Skin-Walkers to take you away by the time I've finished with you," growls Medusa.

I give Mitchell the thumbs-up: another modern tradition of the more newly dead, although I've noticed that only a few of them actually use it. He gives me a confused look.

"Dude, she just threatened me," he whispers. "That's not a thumbs-up thing."

"But she did not deny that she was your woman, and that's a start," I reply.

The upper half of Virgil's face is hidden by shadows that are reflecting the blue glow of the ice, but I can see that the lower half is contorted into a perverse smile. It is not the look of a devil who is happy to see joviality in the midst of the Underworld. It is the smile of someone who is keeping a secret.

"Are ye scared?" asks Elinor. "I am."

I take her hand in mine and kiss her knuckles. "I am only scared of losing you again, my princess."

"If it helps, El," says Medusa, feeding rope through her hands, "I'm as terrified as I've ever been. There's so much adrenaline coating my tongue, I think it's been replaced by a steel bar."

"Then let us get it over with. We are prepared for this circle," I say to our guide as Medusa finishes tying a length of orange rope around my stomach. "Lead on."

"Watch your feet," calls Virgil. "You don't want to step where you shouldn't."

An icy wind beats down on us in waves as we inch our way across the ledge that will take us into the main cavern. It is not wide, and it is our only path. As we come out into the circular opening, a towering black rock appears in front of us. It glistens with a blue, shimmering light. If this were not the foulest part of Hell, a devil could wonder at the beauty of it.

"What is that noise?" asks Elinor. She is right behind me in the line.

I strain my ears. Elinor is right. There is something beyond the howling of the wind. A continuous, high-pitched noise. It is unmistakable.

"It is screaming, Elinor," I reply. "We are reaching the center of the Ninth Circle. If Dante's words were true, then that sound will be a constant accompaniment as we ascend to the Eighth Circle. Stay strong. We are all here with you."

"There was so much screaming...when I was his!" cries Elinor. "His dreams...are filled with screaming. He enjoys it."

Out of the corner of my eye, I see Virgil reach out for Elinor, and then just as quickly, he retracts his hand. Does the guide feel empathy for Elinor? Perhaps that is something we could use to our advantage.

"Remember we are searching for Beatrice Morrigan," I shout back to the others. "Do not dwell on what you see and hear in this cursed place."

Mitchell is starting to swear. The wind is picking up. It is biting at our dead forms with sharpened teeth. The wails are getting louder. It is the sound of relentless suffering and torment. Elinor had previously said that all victims of the Skin-Walkers had their tongues removed, but there are some here who clearly did not.

"As we get to the other side of the rock, we will approach the creature that is trapped here," calls Virgil from the front. "Do not look at its three faces."

But the moment we finish the loop of the first zone, I look.

I am a brave warrior. There is little in death or life that has truly frightened me. Yet the colossal hybrid beast in front of me, covered in fur, with thrashing wings and three flailing scaly heads, is a monster that cannot be ignored by the command of someone so puny as Virgil.

Elinor screams, and immediately one of the beast's three heads snaps toward us. It is the red face. The two others are yellow and black. The monster's skin is cracked and weeping with pus that's oozing from volcano-shaped sores. In each of its jagged, tooth-filled mouths is a figure, stripped bare of flesh.

Dante claimed that Brutus, Cassius and Judas were the victims of the three-headed beast, but how could he tell? From where I am standing, there is nothing left of the figures to ascertain if they were man or woman, let alone to know who they once were in life. It is a grotesque sight of flesh stripped to moving bone, each body flailing with desperation as it tries to escape the torment of razor-sharp teeth and claw. Is it their agony we've been hearing on the wind?

"Keep walking," calls Virgil. "And watch your feet."

"That…that thing won't grab us, will it?" cries Mitchell. "Oh, Hell, I'm going to be sick."

A shower of blood is dripping from the beast's mouth. As it falls onto the ice, steam rises up in the form of a wolf on two legs.

"This is Perfidious's domain," I call as we start along a slow incline to the second concentric zone. "We need to watch out for him, as well as look for Beatrice."

"And watch your feet," adds Virgil for the third time.

"Why does he keep saying that?" asks Elinor, her voice shaking with fear. "We know it is slippery. It is ice. We are not stupid."

Mitchell is the first to realize why. As we start to wind our way from the second circular zone into the third, he cries out in terror.

"They're watching us!"

Unlike the footsteps of my featherlight friend, my tread is so heavy, I did not sense what was protruding out of the ice.

Faces. Faces attached to bodies that are lying supine in the ice. All are totally encased, with the exception of their eyes, mouth and nose, which are left open to the biting wind. Their bodies are twisted into shapes that are inconceivable. Arms bent backward at ninety-degree angles; necks snapped in two; legs splayed under spines.

"Those who knowingly killed kin are brought here," says Virgil. "For betrayal of one's family is the most heinous act of treachery there is."

"We are treading on *people*, Alfarin!" cries Elinor.

"No," I reply quickly. "Do not see them as people, Elinor. They are the condemned dead. Not fit to be devils. Remember what you know about the Skin-Walkers and the Unspeakables. They are here because they corrupted and defiled the honor and privilege of living."

But there is little conviction to my speech. The pale-blue ice is lighting up all around us, mocking and tormenting Team DEVIL with sights we cannot escape. And to my left, the three-headed beast continues to twist its black, furry body, as if it, too, is in pain from its icy containment.

"How do we get out of this circle, Virgil?" I ask. Upward, I can see the fourth circular zone winding around perilously close to the back of the beast.

"You have read the book, have you not, Viking?" mocks Virgil. "How did Dante and I get down to the bottom of the abyss? Remember, we have to undertake this journey now in reverse."

But I am unable to recall. The higher in the cave we climb, the closer we get to the continuous screaming from the three forms being devoured in the mouths of the beast. My ears are ringing with a pain that cannot be dislodged.

"What if it tries to get us, Alfarin?" yells Medusa. "We're fresh meat, and that monster is going to be close enough to try to grab us soon."

"Alfarin," calls Mitchell. "Give Virgil your axe. He's guiding us. We have to trust him. If that beast tries to take us, then we have to fight it off, and the guy in front may as well be armed."

They are turning against you, whispers a voice. It is neither male nor female. It is the whisper of the wind. *You should leave them while you still have the chance.*

Elinor gasps behind me. I hear her cry, "No!" I turn around and Mitchell is staring at Medusa with a look of horror on his face. The wind must be speaking to them, too.

"Get us out of here, Virgil!" I shout. I have seen no sign of Beatrice Morrigan—only terror. There is no way anyone could conceal themselves on these ice paths. They may be filled with death, but their surfaces are barren, save for the frozen faces staring up at us. There are no crevices in the cave walls, either. There is no place to hide—unless she's chosen to imprison herself within the ice. And something tells me that a Banshee headstrong enough to leave The Devil would not opt for a shelter so confining and miserable.

We need to leave before we turn on one another.

"There is only one way to the next circle," replies Virgil. "And it is up there." He points to a red glow, just above the beast's shoulder.

"And how do we get up there?" I shout. "The fourth zone ends with solid rock. There is no passage."

"Dante and I climbed down the beast to get here, Viking," replies our guide. "You will have to climb up."

Nĭu

Alfarin and Elinor

𝕿rustworthiness was a trait that Vikings held very dear.
A clan, a group of brethren, was only as strong as its will to stay
together and believe in one another. My death came about because I
failed at being trustworthy. I had foolishly wandered off alone, placing not only myself in mortal danger, but also the other Vikings I had
arrived with in the longships. I laid no blame for my demise on the
villagers who attacked me with blades and dogs. It was my fault, and
my fault alone.

I should have obeyed my leader and stayed close. I did not. I
believed I knew better, that I could handle myself alone in enemy
territory, and it cost me my life.

But the question of my trustworthiness—and my ability to trust
others—would haunt me well after my death. A truly awful occur-
rence happened in the year 1942 that had me pondering the notion
of trust until I was nearly sick. I was so stricken by the horror of it all,
I almost handed over my axe and relinquished my Viking ancestry.

It all started when I was given a ticket to the Masquerade Ball.

Oh, the shame, the degradation! I had not applied. Vikings do
not go to balls. Dancing is for the womenfolk. Men drink beer and
fight.

Or so I thought.

It was my third cousin Magna's fault. Jealous of the giggling girls in her overcrowded dormitory, Magna had applied to the lottery and had won two tickets.

And I was forced into being her companion for the night.

I pleaded within the halls of our fathers to be excused from this most vile of tasks, but the decree was made. I was to wear a suit and accompany Magna to defend her honor. If Saxon scum attempted to carry her away, I was to strike them down with my axe.

Carry her away? She was four hundred pounds when she died. I would like to see the Saxon heathens try.

Yet my biggest concern was for Elinor. How would she react when I told her I was going to be spending an evening with another woman? Spending time with Elinor had opened my eyes and forced me to acknowledge that other devils had feelings, and that these feelings should be considered. So I placed myself in her shoes, and knew immediately that if Elinor had told me she was attending the Masquerade Ball with another devil, I would have sabotaged the whole affair with my axe and, failing that, with a copious supply of laxatives slipped into my rival's beef stew. It wasn't that I wouldn't trust Elinor, I told myself. It was that I wouldn't trust the *situation*.

Yet Elinor was a better devil than I. When I told her of the duty being forced upon me, she merely smiled and soothed my concerns about the Masquerade Ball's surely being the worst night of my death. Elinor even came with me to choose my mask.

"There will be mead, and there will be women," I said as we took up our regular seat in Thomason's. "Temptations galore in such a den of sin."

My cousin and his friends were jeering. They had told me that Magna was intending to sit on me and kiss me.

I could not take much more of the stress.

"Oh, Alfarin," said Elinor. "I admit I was a little jealous when ye told me ye were going to be surrounded by pretty girls all night, but I am at peace with it now. Indeed, I want to hear all about it tomorrow."

"Then you are in a place I do not think I could be in, if the roles were reversed," I admitted.

"Then ye must learn to trust me, as I trust ye," she said.

"What if I am not very good at trusting?"

"Then ye must learn, Alfarin. It will make ye a better devil, a more content devil."

"I am a Viking before a devil."

"Viking, devil, man, big ol' oaf with soup in his beard," replied Elinor, pulling out a comb from her apron pocket. "One day, ye may have to place yer trust in others, and doing so may save ye from an awful fate. Now put on yer mask while I brush yer hair."

Yes, Elinor was always the better devil.

9. Malevolence on the Wind

"Climb up the monster?" screams Medusa. "Are you insane?"

"I'm not climbing that freaking thing!" cries Mitchell. He doesn't realize it, but he has backed into the wall and his sneakers are pressing down on the face of a screaming, twisted body. Because the tongue has been removed and the vocal cords ripped out, we cannot hear its cries, and that's just as well, because the shrieks coming from the three victims in the beast's mouths are enough to chill the blood of the undead. It is hard to imagine how the screams of all the condemned combined within the Nine Circles would sound. But I suspect the noise would bring Hell down to its very foundations, and it suddenly makes sense why the Unspeakables' ability to make noise is removed.

The monster is enormous. Medusa and Mitchell are right. Climbing it will be an impossible task.

"Elinor, I will go on alone," I say. "I will not blame or condemn you for leaving now."

"Leave? And go back to what?" replies Elinor. Her flaming red eyes are not blinking. The beating of the beast's wings has hypnotized her. "If I return to Hell, I return to his dreams. I am scared, Alfarin. I am so very scared. But I trust ye, and I will go with ye into every circle of torment to find the Banshee if I have to."

She lies, whispers the voice of the wind again. *The redhead has darkness in her. He has corrupted her mind and taken her soul. She will betray you to your doom.*

The beast is keeping a constant watch on Team DEVIL. Its three pairs of black eyes roll around in its heads as its brutally sharp talons swipe at the air. I can hear the sound of replenished flesh being torn from the bodies in its three mouths, like a wet zipper being relentlessly dragged up and down, up and down.

Before I lead my friends into the worst danger we've ever faced, I look around one last time to confirm what I already know.

"She is not in this Circle of Hell, is she?" Medusa whispers.

"You did not expect it to be that easy, did you?" replies Virgil. "Beatrice is not simply going to leap out from wherever she's hiding and reveal herself. But even if she were inclined to do so, where could she possibly conceal herself in here?" Medusa gives him an annoyed look, which he ignores. "Now, are you going to continue to the Eighth, or is your quest going to wither and cease to exist right now?"

"Lead on," I reply. I tighten the rope that links me to Elinor around my stomach. "Mitchell, Medusa, my friends. We will untie you from these bonds so you can return to Hell, if that is what your hearts desire. Elinor and I will continue with Virgil, even if it means climbing the back of the beast itself."

Mitchell swears, and I look at him in admiration. His ability to create new curse words and use them in the most interesting of ways is impressive, although I don't think The Devil's lady mother would be too happy to hear her name taken in vain like that.

"We're coming with you, Alfarin," he replies, once he has stopped cursing. "But can we please plan this out before we do it?" My friend is pale of face, while both Elinor and Medusa are pawing at their own skin, as if they fear it will be stripped just by the wind in this cursed place. Virgil is standing just behind Elinor; he slowly raises his hand once more, as if he wants to touch her hair. I tighten my hold on the axe. No one touches Elinor or Medusa without their permission.

But Virgil slowly drops his hand and shakes his head. There is something sorrowful about his movements.

"We must aim for the area where the beast cannot touch us," I say, pointing with my axe to the joint between the creature's wings. "The beast is encased in ice up to its stomach. It will not break free. We can get to its back if we continue around to the end of this path. It will take us in another loop around the creature. We must jump from above to its shoulders and climb up to the base of its neck. It is a short ascent, and from there we can jump across, back onto the path of the upper concentric loop, to reach the doorway that will lead us into the next circle."

"The one reserved for the fraudulent," says Medusa.

"Medusa, I know you are the smartest person in the Underworld," says Mitchell through gritted teeth. "But can we get the Hell out of this circle before we start thinking about the next one?"

"I was just saying—"

"Just for once, please, don't say anything," snaps Mitchell.

Elinor takes my hand. "Can ye hear voices in the wind, Alfarin?"

"Yes."

"What are they saying to ye?"

Do not trust her, or the one with snakes for hair. All three will see the beast claim you for its own. Their bodies should be stripped of flesh with the other betrayers.

The pull of the voice is physical, and it hurts. It is not just the biting of teeth on the wind. There is a corporeal pull, deep inside my chest. Something wants to guide me away from my friends.

The beast with three heads swipes a long arm toward our group. Medusa, who is nearest the edge, screams and ducks, but her sneakers slip on the ice. Shards break away beneath her as she falls.

"Medusa!" cries Mitchell, and he catches her hand as her legs slide over the edge. But momentum and the icy ground betray

Mitchell. He starts to slip, too, and Elinor and I are jerked forward as the rope connecting us pulls us all toward the edge.

"Let go of my hand, Elinor!" I cry. "Trust me."

And my princess does so without comment or question. With my full weight and the power of both my arms behind it, I slam my axe into the ice. Medusa screams as she falls over the edge. The beast's razor-sharp claws are just a few feet away from us. It is flailing and flapping furiously in an attempt to capture new prey. I can smell the rancid stench of toxic blood on its breath, and amongst the wretched whispers of the wind is a new sound: the howling of wolves.

But Team DEVIL remains above the fray as my axe stays true. My feet find firm ground, and slowly, with pain coursing through my stomach as the weight of the rope digs in, I start to climb. Progress is slow and laborious, but with every yard of new ground reached, I am able to remove my axe and plant it farther up the ice. Elinor is soon freed from her terror of plunging, but as she ascends with me, she cries out in pain as she bears the weight of Mitchell and Medusa.

Untie them. They will drag you to your doom.

With a sonorous roar that comes from the depths of my chest, I stop climbing and manage to push Elinor behind me. Then I grasp the rope and haul it upward. Mitchell's head and body appear over the ledge. As I take on his and Medusa's weight, I notice that the rope is rubbing on the ice and starting to fray. I fear it will not hold much longer. Beneath the snapping rope I can make out the mangled legs of a victim of the Ninth Circle. They are twisted in the wrong direction, and my disgust at the sight momentarily makes me lose concentration.

The rope slips through my fingers.

"*Alfarin!*" cries Mitchell. "I can't hold on for much longer! Medusa, use me to climb up and save yourself!"

Medusa, dangling below Mitchell, looks horrified.

Use the axe. Cut through the rope. Let them go.

The wind's voice stops biting and instead starts to caress my cheek. My axe is still embedded in the ice. I pull it out and stagger over to the edge. The extra give in the rope causes Mitchell and Medusa to slip farther down into the icy abyss.

Use the axe. Cut through the rope. You do not need them. They will betray you before the end . . . my son.

Mother? Is that my mother's voice, and her fingers on my face? Ice and wind combine to swirl up into the ghostly outline of a woman. Her hair is flowing in the wind. Her slender arms are reaching out for me.

Then I look down and see a waterfall of blood land on the ice below. It rises up into the shape of a Skin-Walker, Perfidious. *Use the axe, my beloved son. Cut them loose.*

In war, perfidy is the act of deception. Suddenly, I comprehend his treachery. He is trying to trick us with words and whispers, but I will not be deceived. My mother's voice dies on the wind as I call on the strength of the mightiest god, Thor. He does not desert me as I slam my sacred blade into the ice.

"Hold on to the handle, my friend!" I call. "Pull yourself up as far as you can go, and I will do the rest."

Mitchell emits a guttural cry as he clasps his two hands around the handle. His fingers are long—piano-playing fingers—and his hold is steady. Elinor joins me, and together we pull Mitchell and Medusa over the ice and toward safer ground.

"Whose idea was it to use rope again?" gasps Medusa. "That was inspired."

"It was mine," replies Mitchell. He is lying supine on the ice with his left hand over his dead heart. He moves quickly when he realizes that a silent, openmouthed face, with missing teeth and bloody lips, is inches from his.

"I could kiss you," says Medusa.

"Don't—I think I'm about to puke," replies Mitchell, scrabbling away from the Unspeakable that has locked desperate, pleading eyes with my friend.

"Yer axe," says Elinor. "Do not forget it, Alfarin."

I pull my blade out of the ice, and a large section cracks and falls away. From the darkness below, we hear it crash and splinter into a million segments.

"Climbing the beast will be easy after that," says Virgil, smirking.

I am so conflicted. I do not care for this fellow, and his sneaky countenance is unsettling. I wish to ease my suffering by punching him in the face. Yet he is our guide, and if I am to lead this quest, I must place my trust in him, as the others have placed their trust in me.

Once Mitchell has recovered, we continue to walk. I have a longing to hear my mother's voice again, but the wind no longer speaks to me. It has searched my soul for treachery and has been left wanting. Earlier, I could tell from my friends' countenances that they faced their own tests. This circle is for the treacherous. And Team DEVIL does not belong here, for we are true of heart.

I turn to look at the hybrid monster. Its lumpy spine is clearly visible, but now that we are closer, I can see spikes and small ridges sticking out of its short fur. Virgil stands apart from the four of us, but it is more than just rope that separates us.

"On the count of three, we jump," says Virgil.

"Can't we go one at a time?" asks Elinor.

"One movement will be less disruptive to the beast, rather than five singular movements," I reply, understanding Virgil's logic. "We do this quickly. It is not far to the next level. Hold on to the beast's fur and use the spikes for your feet."

"Making sure we don't impale ourselves as we jump," mumbles Mitchell.

"You are quite correct, Mitchell."

"I think he was being sarcastic," says Elinor.

"Okay, Alfarin," calls Medusa. "On your count of three."

"One."

"Of all the batshit mental things we've ever done, this tops it all," says Mitchell, readying himself into a back stance.

"Two."

The beast knows something is about to happen. Its huge leathery wings are flapping in a frenzy. The icy wind is sending a tornado-like vortex swirling through the chamber.

"Three."

Even Virgil cries out as we all land on the beast's back. Our movements are quick and methodical. It reminds me of powering the oars of a longship. Virgil and I take turns to call "Climb, climb," and though the beast thrashes and twists, it is unable to remove the five irritants from its fur. The hairs are sticky to the touch, and while the stench is grotesque, the adhesive aids our ascent.

Mitchell and Medusa reach the upper ledge of rock first. They assist Virgil and then Elinor. All four hold the rope tight as I throw myself toward them. We are in the roof of the Ninth Circle, and the ice here is barely a rumor on the black rock. We run, not looking down or back until we are high above the three-headed beast. It has already gone back to clawing at the bodies in its mouth.

From high above, the four concentric zones look like pretty, stacked circles of blue light. The bodies trapped within the ice are mere shadows. I know, though, that the sounds and smells I have been assaulted with here will stay with me for the rest of my existence.

"Ye have icicles in yer beard, Alfarin," says Elinor, gently brushing at my face with her fingers.

"You don't," says Medusa to Mitchell. "Because you can't grow a beard."

"But you do," retorts Mitchell.

"Frozen albino hedgehog."

"Frozen albino snake-lady."

"Ignore them, Virgil," says Elinor, wisely preempting the condemnation that will inevitably come from the old man at such a flirtatious exchange. "The fact that a strange, cold tundra can exist within such oppressive heat has addled their minds. They will thaw."

"We should go through the next door," says Medusa, blushing slightly and stepping away from Mitchell, or at least as far as the connecting rope will permit.

"Hang on," says Mitchell. "Just one last thing. I know it's dumb, but it'll make me feel like we tried everything we could in here. " He steps toward the edge, and instinctively we all hold on to our segment of rope.

"*Beatrice Morrigan!*" shouts Mitchell. "*Beatrice Morrigan—are you in here?*"

An unpleasant sound escapes Virgil that can only be described as part hacking cough, part muffled scream and part contemptuous laugh. It does little to inspire my confidence in him as a supportive guide.

Below us, the yellow head of the beast snaps up; blood runs down its chin.

"I don't think the Banshee is here," says Elinor, pulling at Medusa. "Come, let us get out of this infernal place."

But when we turn, we find that the doorway to the next circle is blocked.

Perfidious, the leader of the Skin-Walkers, has found us once more.

Tiu

Alfarin and Elinor

"Ye cannot sign yer name on something that is not yers, Alfarin," scolded Elinor. "It is fraud."

"But I am helping the infirm, Elinor," I replied. "And besides, I am not doing this for personal gain, and that is what makes fraud... well...fraud."

"Ye *are* doing this for personal gain, Alfarin, and ye know it." Elinor seemed to grow taller when she was being overly righteous.

Or perhaps it was just when she was right, which was most of the time.

My father, King Hlif, son of Dobin, had had an accident. It was the annual Viking beer fest, and he had slipped on spilled mead. He ended up in Hell's casualty unit in traction, with his arms at an angle to his body that suggested they had been stuck there in a game of Pin-the-Appendage-on-the-Viking. He was healing well, but only because the healers had tranquilized him with a new veterinary drug that had been developed in the land of the living for rendering large animals unconscious. It had taken so much to knock my father out, it was rumored that the introduction of the drug on earth had been delayed because the stock had been depleted.

So I had been charged with taking over my father's business affairs in the halls of Valhalla while he healed. A task I was more than worthy of owning.

Until Elinor got involved.

My closest and most trusted friend in Hell was an honest devil. I had often wondered how she ended up in Hell at all. If ever there was an angel with red eyes, it was Elinor.

Yet she could nag like a housewife on washday.

All I wanted to do was lower the age of drinking for my Viking kin who were unlucky enough to die before the age of eighteen winters. Some years ago, the HBI forced the proprietors of Hell's drinking establishments—including my cousin Thomason—to adopt the modern earthly custom of imposing a minimum drinking age. They decided upon eighteen, and my father, being a king, officially declared it law with an oath at Thomason's.

The HBI claimed the change was made for the well-being of the young. But I know the real reason: the fewer inebriated souls they had to deal with, the easier their existences were. Also, they hated it when young devils made merry.

I'd never been particularly interested in drinking; ale quickly went to my head, and thus I'd spent several hundred years in Hell not giving it a second thought, even as I dried thousands of glasses a day at Thomason's. But that changed the moment the HBI told me I *couldn't*. We can hardly drink ourselves to *death*, I reasoned. And I worked hard, dammit, so why shouldn't I be permitted to partake? I wanted to drink like a man—or, better yet, like my great-aunt Dagmar, who could drink like ten men.

After giving it some more thought, I decided that adjusting the minimum drinking age to sixteen winters seemed fair. Vikings died young. We should not be penalized for that. The fact that sixteen winters was also my age was irrelevant. A mere coincidence.

"I will tell the Grim Reapers if ye do this, Alfarin," hissed Elinor. We were making our way along the crowded corridors after Elinor had had a hard day at work. I'd had a hard day, too—listening to her telling me I was committing fraud by rewriting the oath on the drinking age, sealing it with the king's ring and claiming it was my father's will.

"We are Vikings," I replied. "And I want to drink a tankard or four of mead after a hard day's work."

"Alfarin, ye get drunk on the fumes from Thomason's empty barrels," snapped Elinor. "Four tankards and ye will be on the floor. And I am not dragging ye back to yer dormitory, or holding back yer hair when ye are emptying the contents of yer stomach into a bowl."

"You are only making a fuss because beer makes you sleepy, Elinor."

"At least I can hold my ale, which is more than ye can."

Our passionate conversation continued all the while it took us to get to Valhalla, far away from the CBD. My ears were ringing, my stomach paining and my feet throbbing. Neither of us was going to be victorious, so Elinor tried a different tack. One she knew would win me over.

Oh, that peasant and her beautiful hair and her scrupulous morals.

"Alfarin, ye are the most honest Viking I know," she said sweetly, looping her arm through mine. "Ye do not wish to ruin that impression, do ye? Ye are brave and true and decent. Ye do not have to drink beer to be a real man. Signing the oaths and marking them with the seal of the king, as if it were yer father's will, is dishonest. Ye know he does not want the younger Vikings drinking for the same reason the HBI doesn't want any young person drinking. They might have had some fun, but there were more fights, and more of that yucky dead blood everywhere. Ye are creating more work, and for what? Yer cousin Thomason's beer tastes of dirty dishwater anyway."

I sighed. The noise was strange, as there was no air in my lungs to expel. I sounded as if I had farted.

"You are always right, Elinor," I replied. "Thomason's beer does taste like dirty dishwater. Indeed, I am not certain that it isn't. Your will is mine. I will not sign the oaths."

She gave my arm a squeeze and smiled. It had become my favorite sight.

"We are in Hell, Alfarin," said Elinor. "But that does not mean we have to be devious or corrupt. Once we lose our decency, we lose what made us human in the first place. Ye must always remember that."

10. The Eighth Circle

The last time I saw Perfidious was in Washington, DC. I was invisible to his eyes, hidden with Teams DEVIL and ANGEL by the power of the two Viciseometers joining together. Perfidious was conversing with Lord Septimus, who wanted the Skin-Walkers to free Medusa and return to the Nine Circles.

The Skin-Walkers' leader is taller than his brethren, and he once had an entire room of HBI agents quailing at his mere presence back in Hell. Now, here, in his own domain, Perfidious appears even larger than before, even though there is some distance between us. His body is covered in the pelt of a single wolf, but everything about him seems engorged, from his bloody, clawed fingers to his black, unblinking eyes.

And suddenly the winged monster behind us seems so very distant and small.

Team DEVIL is still bound together by our rope. Mitchell and I instinctively put ourselves in front of the girls, but they swipe us aside. Their fear is real, but their bravery is stronger. Elinor and Medusa will not cower in the face of evil. So the four of us form a horizontal line. I am nearest to the ledge and the sheer drop beyond it; Elinor is next to me, and she holds hands with Medusa on her right; and Mitchell takes the far end.

Virgil is much closer to Perfidious, and the Skin-Walker doesn't seem to like that. His wolf pelt is bristling with visible tension. For the first time I wonder where Virgil lives. Does he dwell in the Circles of Hell, and if so, is it by choice? Does Virgil have daily dealings with the Skin-Walkers? What a pitiful existence that must be.

There is an aura around Perfidious, like a haze in the heat of summer. It is black, but with swirls of crimson swimming around the edges. He licks his lips with a long black tongue, all the while leering at Medusa, as if she is a piece of meat to be devoured.

"What are you doing here?" demands Perfidious, taking a step toward us. Shadowy hands claw out from the aura surrounding him. My stomach feels so tight and knotted it is causing stabbing pains to spasm into my chest.

"We are seeking The Devil's Banshee," I reply, taking several strides toward Perfidious, which inadvertently drags the others closer, too. "Beatrice Morrigan. We are here with the master of Hell's knowledge and consent."

"The Devil has no authority here," growls Perfidious. His voice is deep and unnatural. Every word is forced, as if it is being uttered by something that does not find speech easy.

"And we are also here with Fabulara's knowledge," I add, holding my ground. Perfidious's black eyes bore into me; they are dark and unyielding, reflecting none of the glittering, pale-blue color of the Ninth Circle. There is no soul behind those eyes, but it does not make me afraid. I feel pity. In spite of all the horrors we have just witnessed, and all that are surely yet to come, I suddenly wonder if existence as a Skin-Walker, who has nothing but treachery and hate in its heart, might be the worst of fates.

"You are Septimus's pawn once more, Virgil," says Perfidious, turning his attention to the old man, although Perfidious makes no attempt to intimidate our guide by getting closer to him. "You always were a sheep, blindly doing the bidding of others."

"We seek passage to the next circle," I say. "We will not trouble you with anything else."

"Trouble me?" sneers Perfidious. "You forget who you are speaking to, Viking. But I will let you all pass, if only to enjoy the sport of watching what is to come."

Perfidious does not stand aside, and we must inch around him, one by one. He seems to ignore us as we begin to pass him, but then his wolf head suddenly jerks toward us, snapping at Medusa with razor-sharp teeth. She is so brave, she does not even cry out—although she does lurch back into Mitchell. Mitchell immediately puts himself between her and Perfidious. All the while, he keeps his terrified face fixed on the black eyes of the wolf, who pays him no heed. Instead, he is leering at Elinor and Virgil as they approach. But when my princess and our guide reach Perfidious, he yelps as if he has been kicked. The sound is so painful to my ears, I sense something pop inside my head. But Team DEVIL does not stop, and the others keep their eyes straight and true on the path ahead once they are past him. I am the only one who sees the look of puzzlement on Perfidious's face as he slinks back against the rock.

I do not stop to wonder or ask about his reaction. Right now, we must place one foot in front of the other. For a few moments, our only companion is the echo of our feet on thin ice and rock.

"We did it, guys," says Mitchell in a shaking voice. "We passed through one of the Circles."

"Hopefully we'll find Beatrice Morrigan in this next one and we can leave," adds Medusa as we pass through the doorway into a blast of heat. As we leave the Ninth Circle, the howl of a lone wolf causes my hair to stand on end. Then I see a movement in the corner of my eye that appears out of place in this monstrous setting.

We are being watched—by more than just shadows and wolves.

––––––––––

We are in a narrow tunnel, much like the underground passage that leads from Hell to the HalfWay House. I have a feeling that each circle is connected by some kind of passageway. After the icy torment of the Ninth, the heat of the approaching Eighth Circle quickly prompts Team DEVIL to strip off our extra layers of clothes. We do not touch the rope that binds us to one another. That stays. Elinor and Medusa are wearing short-sleeved green shirts over loose black pants; Mitchell is wearing a T-shirt that bears the image of a crown and the words DON'T PANIC, JUST EAT PIZZA. It is advice that would have been helpful earlier. My own tunic is pale blue and has the remnants of pizza all over it, because I *did* panic. I feared Medusa would eat it all, so I ate my manly fill as quickly as possible. My friend with the snaky hair has an appetite that could frighten a Viking cook.

"A quick rundown on what we can expect in here would be helpful," says Mitchell, stowing his sweater in his backpack. "This circle is fraud, right? Seems a little excessive to put someone in eternal torment for counterfeiting money or whatever, don't you think?"

"That is not why someone would be dragged to this level, Mitchell," replies Medusa. Both she and Elinor have wrinkled their noses up in disgust at the smell. "Here, fraud doesn't mean a fake ID."

"Thank Hell for that," replies Mitchell. "Otherwise they might not let me out the other side."

"Still joking, you four," mutters Virgil. "At least Dante was contrite during his passage."

"It will be a sad day indeed the day Mitchell loses his humor," replies Elinor.

"His jokes are so bad, how would we know?" retorts Medusa, playfully punching Mitchell in the ribs.

"Shut up, short-ass," says Mitchell, ruffling Medusa's hair. "I'm not the one who's been going by a different name since day one in Hell. If that's not fraud, I don't know what is. They might not let you out of this circle, either!"

The relief of having passed through the Ninth unscathed has raised our spirits. I do not wish to be the harbinger of doom, but to keep us on course, I see I must be a leader first, a friend second for now. Preparation and strategy must always be foremost in my mind.

"Medusa, may I have the *Divine Comedy* back?" I ask. "I made notes in the margins when I was in the library."

"You wrote in the book?" exclaims Mitchell as Medusa hands me the tome from her backpack. "Dude, Patty Lloyd is gonna kick your *ass*! Then she's gonna whip your ass. In fact, you will be in so much ass pain that—"

"I think we get the idea, Mitchell," interrupts Medusa. "But a potential ass-kicking is worth it if it means Alfarin can lead us through this...right, Alfarin?"

"What notes did ye make, Alfarin?" asks Elinor, getting us back on track.

"The tormented souls in this circle are those who benefited personally by murdering others," I say, thumbing through the well-worn pages, "whether it was done for riches or title. It is written that the Eighth Circle is divided into ten ditches of stone. My friends, we will have to cross the ditches via bridges." I hard the tome back to Medusa.

"Which Skin-Walker resides here?" asks Elinor. She's looking at Virgil, but it's Medusa who answers.

"Frausneet," she says in a distant voice. "I remember him."

Medusa was taken by the Skin-Walkers, albeit for a short while, when we were tasked with finding The Devil's Dreamcatcher. She has never really spoken about what she endured in their grasp. We know they encircled her in a dome that lifted her clean off the ground. It was a circle of hate that clawed at her soul. I was just thankful that Mitchell had the presence of mind to call Lord Septimus for help. Private Owen knew what to do as well. If it had not been for their quick thinking and the two Viciseometers, I cannot bear to think of what would have happened to Medusa that day.

Remembering the potential of the Viciseometer, I find myself regretting the technical complications of our current plight. If only I had been able to envision these Circles of Hell before this moment, I could have used the Viciseometer to move within them. I have the Viciseometer in my bag, but it is useless if the bearer cannot visualize his or her destination. I could employ its powers to travel *out* of Hell, to anywhere my mind can picture—back to Septimus's office, to the place where wenches sell fried chicken from a bucket in the magnificent city of New York, to an island surrounded by crystal-blue waters that I once saw in a book of photographs...but I cannot travel through the Circles of Hell with it. So we must walk through this unknown territory unaided. We don't even have a second Viciseometer to help us become invisible.

"What are ye thinking about, Alfarin?" asks Elinor.

"Lord Septimus gave us Hell's Viciseometer," I reply. "But our journey through this cesspit would have been easier if he had also given us the other. We could have moved in secret. Invisible to all. When the Skin-Walkers took Medusa, even they did not see us when we were joined with Team ANGEL."

"The boss had to give it back to Up There," says Mitchell. "He didn't have a choice."

"Up There was happy to take back the Viciseometer, but not to take back the angels," says Medusa unhappily. "It's so unfair."

"We're lucky we have someone like Septimus looking out for us," says Mitchell. "But sometimes I do wonder how much easier my Afterlife would have been if I had applied for a job cleaning toilets."

"Are you going to continue this journey, or am I to stay here listening to your ceaseless blather for all eternity?" asks Virgil suddenly.

"Virgil is correct," I say, and his wrinkled jaw drops in surprise at my accordance. "We must move on through the Eighth Circle with no more delays. There will truly be Hell to pay if we do not find Beatrice Morrigan soon."

I did not mean to extinguish Mitchell's good mood, but we must all keep in mind what is at stake if we do not make hasty passage. That includes his brother's life.

I start the procession with Virgil alongside me. The intense heat is quickly joined by other sensations that assault my senses. First, the stench. It is excrement, but mixed with something else. A vile, oppressive sweetness that finds its way into my nostrils, even though I am not breathing.

"Whatever is in those ditches, do not look upon them," I say to the others as the tunnel widens. We are entering the Eighth Circle. "Close your eyes and I will lead the way. We are still held together by the rope."

"You okay, El?" calls Medusa.

But my princess does not answer, because we have stepped into the burning light of the Eighth Circle of Hell, and the sight is something so horrific, I am also rendered speechless.

Ten deep ditches, stretching as far as the eye can see. Whereas those taken by the Skin-Walkers for the Ninth Circle were encased in ice, these cursed devils are tortured in the open. Some are being devoured by flames, others are being whipped. One ditch is filled with men and women clearly in the grip of madness, and another is filled with biting snakes and lizards that are wrapped around the bodies of writhing individuals.

All of the ditches contain devils that are clawing at the sides, climbing on top of one another in a frenzy to escape, only to be beaten back again and again by supervising entities that control each ditch with whips. The demons look like the twisted gargoyles I briefly saw Virgil morph into when we first met him. They do not heed our presence. Their sole focus is to keep the Unspeakables contained.

"Was this in Dante's poem?" gasps Mitchell, gazing around. "How did you guys get through this, Virgil?"

"We walked," replies Virgil. "And then we flew."

"On what?" asks Medusa.

"You will see," says Virgil. "Now I suggest you do as the Viking tells you. Do not look. Keep your eyes fixed on your feet. If you fall from the bridges, the bodies contained therein will claim you."

The bridges have no handrails. They are narrow and made of crudely stacked stone. Their stability is tenuous, and as I follow Virgil across the first one, it shakes beneath my feet.

"How often have you crossed these bridges, Virgil?" I ask. Blood-ied fingers grope blindly through gaps in the stone. Elinor holds fast to my waist, and I squeeze her fingers for reassurance.

"There have not been many who have trodden these forsaken paths, and fewer who have made it all the way through," replies Virgil cryptically.

An idea suddenly occurs to me. Brilliant in its simplicity. Why did I not think of it sooner?

"You have seen all nine circles." It is a statement, not a question. "Virgil, *you* could guide us through with the Viciseometer!" Behind me, I can hear Elinor whispering excitedly to Medusa.

"I am surprised it has taken you this long to ask, Viking," replies Virgil, "but—"

"Let us go back," I interrupt, filled with euphoria at my most excellent plan. "We do not need to cross the other bridges. You can see into the Viciseometer for us. We can search for the Banshee at a distance!"

"I cannot use the Viciseometer," says Virgil. He stops walking. We are three-quarters across the first bridge. More fingers inch up from beneath us to grip our feet, desperate for a pathetic salvation from torment.

"You cannot, or you *will* not use the Viciseometer?" I growl.

"I cannot, Viking," replies Virgil. He turns to stare at me with his opaque eyes. "These old eyes are blind. They have never seen the Circles of Hell."

Ellifu

Alfarin and Elinor

"It'll be fun, Alfarin," said Elinor, gazing at me through her long, fluttering eyelashes. "I thought ye Vikings were the party animals of Hell."

"I am very happy with the thought of a party to celebrate my glorious deathday," I replied. "But I am not at ease with the idea of Cousin Odd assisting with the organization of such an event. I do not wish to wake up tomorrow and find I have been entered into a binding agreement with a root vegetable."

I could not precisely recall my birthday. It happened sometime in the year 954 AD. But my deathday was imprinted on my soul: the ninth day of Harpa, 970 AD. Harpa was now known as the month of April. I still called it Harpa, though. The noun had more musicality.

The year in the land of the living was 1970, and to celebrate one thousand glorious years of death, my kin were throwing me a party. Every Viking in Hell was invited. All had accepted. Summonses had also gone out to the Saxon contingent. We knew they would not reply, but it would have been rude not to extend the offer. We did not wish to engage in revelry with them. Oh, no. It was customary to invite the Saxons as entertainment. My Viking kin would make merry with food and wine, and then spend the night playing Lodge the Axe—a Saxon skull being the preferred location.

Alas, the Saxon scum had gotten wise to our intentions many years earlier and no longer sent anyone along to our parties. So Elinor had taken it upon herself to organize entertainment. With the express thanks of my father, who wanted Odd included, she had also invited my cousin to assist.

Elinor felt pity for him, but she seemed to change her mind once it became obvious that Cousin Odd was more interested in eating the invitations than sending them out.

"This is starting to feel like a chore, not a delight, Alfarin," she said to me. "I have read many books on the customs and traditions of the Vikings, but words on a page, especially from a secondary source, do not always mean the truth. For a start, yer cousin Odd seems to think that it is customary to expel gas into a balloon from his nether regions. If they start popping, yer guests will start collapsing from the smell. It is not at all pleasant, and I do not wish to be associated with such antics."

Elinor was clawing at her neck while she spoke. A sure sign she was getting distressed.

"How many books do you think we have read from the library, Elinor?" I asked. "We have known each other two hundred years now and have been reading together nearly as long. Do you think there are many left that we haven't opened?"

Elinor smiled. Talking about books was my way of distracting her. She loved to read, and the thought of books would take her mind off toxic balloons and Cousin Odd.

"There are so many books in Hell's library, Alfarin," said Elinor. "I cannot imagine ever arriving at a point in this existence where we had read them all. And there are still many in the deepest parts of the library that we have yet to even see. Books about the history of Hell and Up There, and even about the Highers."

"Knowledge is a powerful gift, Elinor."

She leaned her head against my shoulder. There were moments

when I wanted our friendship to last forever. Then there were moments when I wanted our friendship to change into something even closer. Elinor smelled of apples and mint.

I loved apples and mint.

I loved Elinor Powell.

"If knowledge is a powerful gift, then I know exactly what to get a clever, strong Viking for his birthday," she replied.

———

A week later I unwrapped my deathday gift from Elinor: *The Divine Comedy* by Dante Alighieri.

Cousin Odd ate the pages before I had the chance to read it.

11. Looking Without Seeing

"Virgil, how can you be blind?" I cry. "We have not traveled much distance, I know, but the terrain has not been easy and you have shown us the way thus far!"

"A person can be guided by more than just sight, Viking," replies Virgil. "A human has five senses, and the Highers decreed that those classified as devils keep those senses in the Afterlife. To compensate for the loss of one, my aging body has a heightened sense of hearing, smell, taste and touch. These are all I require to guide you."

More hands are now coming up through the gaps in the stone as we continue crossing. I notice that fingers are missing from some of them. We cannot hear the screaming torment of the Unspeakables contained within the ditches, but there is now a heavy pressure bearing down on us that is more than just the heat. I believe it is the aura of unspoken screams, of the Unspeakables' pain, and it is colossal.

"But you can be healed of your blindness, Virgil," I say. "Whilst the dead cannot be cured of old age, all who arrive at the HalfWay House are mended in practically every other way. Body parts can be renewed and restored."

I do not wish to say how I know this, or what I know of Elinor's death. It is not my story to share.

"What makes you think I want to see all of this?" replies Virgil, waving a hand. "There has always been a guide here, in the same way there has always been a Dreamcatcher for The Devil. Guides for the Nine Circles are chosen from a group of the righteous and indignant dead who feel strongly that those who led unsavory lives deserved a terrible Afterlife and should be truly punished there. The Grim Reapers take a guide's eyes, and darkness is the only friend the guide ever has. For that, most of us are grateful."

The lightness in my chest is replaced by a sickening sense of doom. For one glorious moment I believed that we would not have to travel on foot through the Nine Circles. But it is not to be. We are looking without seeing. Team DEVIL will have to keep our wits about us even more now.

Virgil and I have crossed the first ditch and my friends, still connected to me by our fraying rope, join us at the entrance to the second bridge. Our presence has been noticed by the Unspeakables in this next ditch, and already I can see their groping hands, snatching at the air through the gaps in the bridge's floor.

"Alfarin," says Elinor. "I overheard your conversation with Virgil."

"It was just a thought, Elinor," I reply. "Nothing has changed."

"But look at these cursed souls," she says. I do not want her to look in the next pit, but Elinor cannot take her ruby-red eyes off the sword-wielding demon on the other side as he beats them back. "There are so many of them. What if Beatrice Morrigan is here? Virgil is blind. He may know of Beatrice Morrigan, but we do not know what she looks like, and neither will he."

"I don't believe it," says Mitchell. He wipes away the sweat from his brow, and a lumpy red streak replaces it. His hands are bleeding, probably from being cut by the ice in the Ninth Circle. "Elinor is right. We don't know what she looks like. Did anyone think to get a picture of The Devil's wife?"

"By anyone, you mean me or El, don't you?" snaps Medusa.

"Well, now that you mention it—yes," replies Mitchell. "You two were the ones who came up with this plan, and you were the ones who had the best chance of figuring out what the Banshee looks like. And before you start yelling and hitting me, I'm good with this journey. I'm here by choice. But you've sent us off to find someone in a place filled with evil scum who can't speak, and we have no idea what this person looks like. We could be *standing* on The Devil's wife and we wouldn't know it."

"Oh, so during my time in the Oval Office, while I was trying to *save* Elinor with The Devil himself barring my way, I was also supposed to be poking around his creepy, crappy desk, trying to find a picture of his *wife*?" Medusa hollers.

"Well, you could have tried to—"

"For your information, *Mitchell*, I'm pretty observant, even under duress. And I'll have you know that the only thing I saw in there, from what I was *able* to see in there with all the perverse mind tricks he was playing on me, was a door knocker cast into the shape of a beautiful woman. But it was a *cast*. Way too generic to help us, even if it *was* a likeness of the Banshee!"

Medusa keeps yelling at Mitchell. Elinor turns to me and takes my hand.

"Ye were right, Alfarin. I should go back to the Oval Office," says Elinor quietly. "We were fools to believe we could do this. We will never find the Banshee in here."

"There is doubt in your mind, too, Viking," says Virgil. "I do not need to see it to know this is true."

Our paths are determined by our choices. In life, and in death. Elinor used to say that it was fate that we met. Two souls from very different times, destined to meet. And I believe her. If our travels through time have taught us one thing, it is that the past, present and future are linked. Sometimes those ways are revealed to us over the course of time, and other times they remain inexplicable.

I cannot go back to Hell to watch Elinor return to The Devil. I will not go back. There is something larger at play here. I need to see this to the very end.

My sudden resolve makes the hairs on the back of my neck stand to attention. Alfarin, son of Hlif, son of Dobin, was meant for greatness. So, too, were Elinor Powell, Mitchell Johnson and Medusa Pallister. But we cannot realize our potential if we fall apart at the seams now.

"Stop!" I bellow. "All of you. We cannot have these moments of self-doubt at every turn. Have we not faced adversaries before and found ourselves more than equal to the challenge? Medusa, when we went back in time to your homestead to find that which was being used as The Devil's Dreamcatcher, did you wilt and give up because we did not know what it looked like? No, you did not.

"Mitchell, when faced with your own death and with the power to stop it in your hands, did you forsake those whom you care about? No—you made a choice for the greater good. We do that now. Team DEVIL has found itself slipping into the abyss many times before today, and we have always triumphed. We must not lose hope."

"*Lasciate ogne speranza, voi ch'intrate,*" says Medusa.

"Abandon all hope, ye who enter here," I reply. "Have we already reached that juncture, my friends? Or could it be that those words are meant for lesser devils than we?"

Mitchell has his head tilted back. He's gazing at the cavernous ceiling with his fists clenched to his forehead. Medusa has taken a stance that is the opposite of her best friend's. She is bent double with her hands on her knees. Virgil is chuckling too loudly for my liking. Why did Lord Septimus send us on this journey with a blind man? Am I to be his eyes as well as everyone else's?

I turn and start to cross the next bridge. I am a Viking and I have my pride. I will not beg them to follow me. This was my quest, and I will see it through to the end, wherever that may take me.

"Wait, Alfarin," calls Mitchell.

A sharp tug on my waist halts my procession. We are still joined together. I fumble with the rope. Medusa has tied a good knot, but what I cannot undo with my bare hands, my blade can. I will let Team DEVIL return with the Viciseometer. They can use it to protect themselves and Mitchell's little brother. I will go on—and I will return when I have found the Banshee.

I am immediately at peace with this decision, but I will not allow them to see the hurt and disappointment in my soul.

Three swipes and the frayed rope falls to the ground. Almost immediately, bent and bloodied fingers, some stripped to the bone, grab for it. Just as I am reaching for the Viciseometer to give it to Mitchell, a large, booming voice echoes around the cavern. It isn't screaming, but it reminds me of the cry the bowman would make when shouting out a warning to the oarsmen on a longship.

Then a sharp pain digs into my shoulders. At first I fear I am being whipped by one of the gargoyle demons, but the stabbing is continuous. Without time to ready myself, I am lifted from the bridge. Elinor is on her knees, trying to pull back the rope. She is being dragged into the ditch by Unspeakables who have taken hold of the frayed end I discarded in my ill-thought-out haste. Mitchell and Medusa are crying out, not at what is happening to them, but with horror at what is happening to me. In seconds, I am at least twenty feet in the air, flying through the heat and toxicity of the Eighth Circle of Hell.

It is difficult to see what has me contained within its clawed grip. My eyes are already streaming as the acrid air blows against my face. I can make out two large front legs covered in golden fur, like the paws of a lion, yet the hair above the paws is gray and curly.

Then the smiling face of an old man peers down at me, and I cannot help but cry out in fear. The face softens, as if it is trying to reassure me.

It fails. I am in the claws of a hideous chimera. This one appears to be part lion, part man, part reptile.

I have my axe, and the warrior within is crying out at me to stick it deep into the chest of the beast. Yet the learned devil within fights back. If I kill the beast at this height, I will plummet into the cursed depths below. The writhing figures below look like bloodied worms, squirming over one another as fiery whips crack to keep them at bay.

My friends and Virgil are mere outlines on the ground now, although I can hear their voices crying out in fear for themselves and me. What torment have I condemned my beloved Elinor to? Can Mitchell and Medusa hold on to her until I find a way of getting back down to them?

The monster rears and flicks its long tail underneath my dangling legs. The tail has a large, stinging barb on its tip. The chimera hovers above a narrow ledge and then releases me from its grip. I drop down and land in a crouch. My axe is ready to decapitate the beast, but its agility is greater than mine, and it springs back to hover in the air. Its black reptilian wings beat slowly, sending a heavy yet invisible toxic cloud toward me.

"I will be back," growls the old man's face, and the winged beast dives toward the ground.

The next sound I hear chills the marrow in my bones. It is Elinor, and she is screaming.

Tólf

Alfarin and Elinor

Elinor and I had a favorite game. We would delve into the dusty, labyrinthine library, find a new book, take turns in reading it, and then we would test each other on what we had learned.

I now adored Elinor Powell with every fiber of my being, but when it came to competing, I had to be king. While the rules of being a gentleman in these modern times were a constant source of confusion to me, I did try my best. I would happily hold a door open for a lady (although my own strength was often my greatest enemy and I frequently found myself barred from establishments after damaging the woodwork); I would gladly assist a lady if she required help putting on a cloak (although my large fingers had a habit of poking holes through flimsy fabric); and I would eagerly taste a lady's food if she was unsure of its quality (although for a Viking, a "taste" often ended up constituting a normal devil's entire meal).

I will say it again: I did my best to be civil and courtly at all times.

But woe betide the devil who tried to stop my princely self from winning a game—or ten. Even Elinor would have to capitulate to what my friend Mitchell would later call my "pure awesomeness."

Because I did not lose. Ever.

Elinor had chosen a more modern tome for us to read. It was titled *Jane Eyre*, and the author was a woman called Charlotte Brontë. It had been published nearly one hundred and fifty years earlier, so it was more recent than many of the books Elinor and I had read. Elinor had said she wanted a more modern read because she was distressed with getting dust in her beautiful long red hair from the shelves farther back. I thought she simply wanted to read a woman's novel because I had—metaphorically—slapped her rump in the last three competitions between us.

I would never slap Elinor's real rump. She would not like that.

A book about a woman called Jane...I did not hide my disappointment. No doubt it would involve chaste glances across moonlit meadows, and corsets that were cinched so tight that they would cause the female protagonist to gasp on every page.

And needlework. Oh, prayers and apologies to the goddess Frigga, but how I hated reading about needlework.

Yet my pride was on the line. I would not let Elinor beat me simply because it was a woman's tome. I decided to embrace Miss Eyre with the same enthusiasm I had shown for *Beowulf*. My mood also improved greatly when Elinor explained that this was a new literary genre for us: Gothic fiction.

As far as I could fathom, Gothic meant darkness...and fear... and hopefully some blood, too.

I settled down to read....

"Alfarin, what is wrong with ye?" cried Elinor. The next afternoon she had found me alone, huddled in a corner with nothing but my axe to provide cold comfort to my destroyed soul.

"Helen died," I sniffed.

"Helen who?" asked Elinor, dropping to the ground beside me. "I have been working in devil resources all day. I cannot recall someone called Helen joining Hell today, although it is possible there was—"

"Not here!" I cry, stifling another sob. "In here."

"In where?"

"Jane, Helen..."

"Alfarin, have ye been eating more of yer great-aunt Dagmar's turnip soup? Ye know that disagrees with ye."

I was sitting on the book. It was only a slim tome. It barely registered under my left buttock. I pulled it out and showed Elinor.

She patted my arm.

"Ye are not even halfway through it, Alfarin," she said, repressing a smile. "Perhaps we should change our competition to something else?"

"No," I replied. "I am waiting for the Gothic horror you promised me."

"Okay," replied Elinor. "But just to warn you, Jane leaves Mr. Rochester and he goes blind in a fire."

"*What?!*"

———

The next day we started reading A *Christmas Carol*.

And I won the game of Twenty Questions that followed.

12. Geryon

I am as helpless as an abandoned baby. I cannot get down to my friends in the bowels of the Eighth Circle. If only I had not forsaken them and removed myself from the physical bond that kept us joined. Without my weapon, they have nothing with which to defend themselves from that winged beast.

Scenarios start running through my mind. I am dead—I cannot die again. I could jump from this ledge and take my chances in the condemned pits below, although I would likely shatter every bone in my body doing so. It is clear that the Circles of Hell have no casualty unit to heal and mend like the more *civilized* area of Hell. Pain and suffering are the desired results here.

Then I see a movement, a streak of blinding golden light. It is to my right, following along a path that has been cleaved through the rock. It moved too quickly to see what it was, but when I blink, the image becomes more defined on my closed eyelids.

It is the outline of a person.

Elinor screams again, and the sound tears at my heart. I again look past the narrow ledge to see what is happening to my friends below. My panic is rising. I am powerless and weak. The stench of death is getting closer and closer. Suddenly, the face of the old man looms into my line of sight. The normal head is attached to a body that is dragon-like: scaly and crimson red. Elinor is clenched between its long claws, which glint like slivers of gold. I think about throwing my axe at the beast's neck, but then Elinor would be the one to plummet into the abyss. The monster flies above me and drops Elinor. My axe clatters to the ground as I catch her in my arms.

"Are you hurt, my princess?" I cry desperately. Rope is still attached to her waist, but it is frayed at both ends, one of which is coated in thick blood that steams and crackles. I quickly untie it and throw it over the edge before it contaminates her.

"I am fine, Alfarin," gasps Elinor, rubbing at her shoulders. "I thought I was done for. Yet that creature spoke to me. He told me not to be afraid. I think it is the Geryon. Do ye remember? We read about him when we were studying all those books about mythical creatures."

Then Elinor's head whips to the right and I see a blaze of light reflected back from her bloodred eyes.

"There is something over there, Alfarin," she says, grabbing at me. "I fear we have been brought up here for something else in the darkness. What can we do? We are blind without Virgil to guide us."

"I think it might be the Skin-Walker Frausneet," I say. "For I saw it, too."

Elinor is about to reply when another caustic wave of filth-ridden wind washes over us. Virgil is the next devil to be dropped. Elinor and I each take one of the old guide's arms, but he shakes us off, Elinor more vehemently than me.

"I am blind, but I still know my way around these circles better than either of you," he says. "Do not touch me."

"That creature pulling us from the bridge," says Elinor. "The chimera of man, lion and dragon. Is it the Geryon?"

"You are learned for your kind, girl," replies Virgil. "Most peasants can barely remember their own name."

"And men of the cloth are meant to be penitent and humble,"

snaps Elinor. "And ye are clearly neither. Or is your cloth red because ye are not worthy to wear the color of virtue?"

The insult may sting Virgil, but it bites me even more. The viciousness and quickness of Elinor's tongue are so unlike her.

Virgil does not respond. He seems to take pleasure in Elinor's sharp words. He cocks his head toward me and a sly smile spreads over his thin, chapped lips.

"Are you shocked by her words, Viking?" he asks. "I did warn you, this place will change all of you."

I still find it hard to believe the guide is blind. His white eyes are staring directly at me. Suddenly they shine, as if a light has been switched on behind them. It is the bright golden light I have seen several times now. It is reflecting back at me once more. Yet when I turn around, it extinguishes in the darkness beyond.

Mitchell and Medusa are deposited onto the ledge next. They are clinging to each other, so it is impossible to say who was picked up by the monster first. Mitchell's dirty white sneakers are streaked with blood. Medusa's backpack has been lost.

"The creatures, the Unspeakables in those pits, started to go nuts," says Mitchell, gasping. "Even more than they already were. I think they realized we were being taken out of the circle. I couldn't leave Medusa alone, so I grabbed her."

"I tried to see if Beatrice Morrigan was in those pits," gasps Medusa. "I screamed her name, but it just made the Unspeakables even crazier. They could see us getting a way out."

Medusa falls to her stomach and wriggles to the edge. "*Beatrice Morrigan!*" she cries. "Are you in here?"

"Medusa, get back," says Mitchell, dragging Medusa from the edge by her T-shirt. "What if you fall?" He turns to the man-headed creature—the Geryon.

"Thanks for saving us," he says; his voice is so high he could shatter glass. "I thought we were about to be dragged in."

"You are welcome," answers a deep, wise voice. The creature

stretches its unnaturally long neck and sways it from side to side. Is it friend or foe? We must be prepared for either.

"I'm having a conversation with a monster," whispers Mitchell to himself, wiping his brow. "This can't be real. I'm gonna wake up in a minute and realize that I've been The Devil's Dreamcatcher all along."

"It has been a long time, Virgil," says the Geryon. "You've changed."

"It's not been long enough," replies our guide.

"So, you're a good guy?" asks Medusa.

"I am what I am," replies the Geryon. "Your coming was fore-told, girl. I intended to take you away somewhere else to question you further. You share a name with someone in my bloodline. I was intrigued."

"Medusa, the monster?" asks Elinor. "Our M is no behemoth. M, ye stay connected to Mitchell. He will not forsake ye."

The brief flash of red in Elinor's eyes is like a brand on my soul. She stares at me with utter contempt. Never, in nearly three hundred years of friendship, has she looked at me in that way.

"I was not forsaking you, Elinor," I say. "I wanted to protect you. I was going to give the three of you the Viciseometer so you could go anywhere in time to be safe."

"And ye were just going to let me go?" cries Elinor. "Away from ye?"

"Yes—no... I only wanted—"

"It's all about ye, isn't it!" she yells. "Yer pride and yer honor. Even now, it is about what ye wanted, not me. Not M or Mitchell."

"El, you need to calm d—" starts Medusa, but she is interrupted by Elinor, who has completely lost her head.

No. Why am I thinking of that phrase? Those are Mitchell's words when he is not thinking clearly. Not mine. Never mine. Never around Elinor.

"I have seen inside The Devil's thoughts!" she cries. "I know his pleasures and his temptations. Ye all think what is in these Nine Circles is worse, and that I cannot cope, but I have existed in his mind, and *that* is worse. I am not scared of what we'll find in the Skin-Walkers' domain. I am scared that when we find her, Beatrice Morrigan will prefer this Hell to the one she left!"

"Rather more vocal than Dante, are they not, Virgil?" says the Geryon. "Although this circle appears to be affecting the redhead more than the others."

"Do you know where Beatrice Morrigan is?" asks Medusa. "She's The Devil's wife, and his original Dreamcatcher. We're trying to find her."

"She *was* here," replies the Geryon.

Virgil is cackling again. Then he sniffs the air and I hear a deep, resigned sigh escape the Geryon's lungs.

"Look down below, devils," says Virgil. "You should see what is about to happen."

Medusa slips her hand into Elinor's. My princess has moved away from me; she is so angry her spare hand is clenched in a tight fist. Medusa and Mitchell glance at me with pity before we peer over the edge. I do not understand why Elinor is behaving in this manner toward me and only me. This circle is for the fraudulent. Those who kill for personal gain. I have never done that. I would never do that. Vikings marauded for food and weapons, but I never intentionally killed…

Then realization hits me and it sears my dead heart. I know why Elinor is behaving more harshly toward me the longer we spend in here. It is because she is reliving her death. Yet the toxicity of this place is making her remember things differently. I did not kill her for personal gain. I wanted to end her suffering.

"What are we supposed to be looking at?" asks Medusa. "This circle doesn't look any better from up here than down there, and we need to move to the Seventh."

"Patience," replies the Geryon. "You are safe up here, but you need to see how the Skin-Walkers control each domain. Virgil is your guide, and what he wants you to see now might help you on your journey."

"Is a Skin-Walker coming?" asks Mitchell.

"Yes!" cries Elinor. "Look, down there. And he has someone with him!"

Way down below, crossing the stone bridge at the far end of the cavern, is Frausneet. The dense black haze around him is like a moving cloak. He is dragging a bloodied figure, but I cannot tell if it is a man or woman. Frausneet howls and the figures in the pits cower with their hands over their ears. It has an unnerving resonance, because, while Team DEVIL watches in silent horror, there is no sound apart from the crackle of fire and the snapping of whips within this circle.

"What is that?" whispers Medusa. She points to a river of brown sludge that is oozing toward the pits. Everyone, including Virgil and the Geryon, gags as the stench rises. Medusa is the first to vomit; I am not the last. We do not see the latest Unspeakable thrown into a pit because the river of excrement covers all, including the stone bridges we were crossing just moments before. With pain stabbing at every muscle and tendon, I retch until there is nothing left in my stomach but bile.

"We have seen enough," I choke. "We must leave this circle now."

"Thank you again for saving us down there," says Mitchell to the Geryon. "I don't suppose there's any chance you could help us through the other circles?"

The old face laughs. The reptilian wings are already starting to flap.

"Alas, this is my existence," it replies. "I do not participate in the torment of the Unspeakables, but I serve as a guardian to stop any who are foolish enough to get past the demons and the Skin-Walker. And then, occasionally, I am lucky enough to come across a traveler or two—or four. So if you are ever traveling this way again, be sure to call for me. Especially you, Medusa. There is something different that marks you, young devil. Until next time… Virgil."

The Geryon bows its head and takes off. Elinor does not wait and walks in the direction of the blinding flash we saw earlier.

"You aren't coming back here ever again," Mitchell says to Medusa.

"We all know I'm different," she replies. "And he seemed pretty nice, for a monster."

"Well, in that case, come back for a cup of tea and cake," says Mitchell sarcastically. "Medusa is just a nickname. That beast is not your long-lost uncle ten times removed, and the only reason you're different is because you're an amazing person. Not because of some stupid paradox."

Mitchell's loving words make me want to call after Elinor, to make her stop and face me. Her death was not for my gain. She must understand that. We were fated to meet.

"Mitchell doesn't need that book on girls as much as he thinks," whispers Medusa, patting my back. "And Elinor doesn't mean to be nasty, Alfarin. I don't know why this circle affected her worse than the rest of us, but she'll be okay once we're out of it."

I nod and try to smile. I fail. Regardless of the reasons why, I know that my actions that day on September 4, 1666, are now twisting into something more nefarious because of Elinor's ordeal at the hands of The Devil.

The fear I have now is that Elinor can see darkness in me beyond death, and I am no longer certain I can pull her back to the light of her former self.

Prettán

Alfarin and Elinor

Ͳhe HBI was a source of great amusement to Vikings in the Underworld, and I was no exception. Apart from baiting Saxons, fighting the law enforcers of Hell was my favorite way to pass the time. My body was dead, not inactive. My bulging biceps required regular workout maintenance. I had heard of a place called a gymnasium, which was a new concept for giving love to one's muscles in Hell, but my kin and I avoided these cesspits of exercise like the plague. First, the ripe stench of dead sweat could strip skin right off your face, just like the real plague. Second, why would someone want to lift a weighted bar up and down one hundred times in front of a mirror, when a good manly wrestle, ending in a body being thrown through a window, was far more fun and just as effective?

Modern-day devils had missed out on so much by not being born before the invention of a rowing machine. Also, toilet paper.

Yet even I would admit that there had been times during our glorious lives when the fun wasn't...funny. Vikings were a feisty, special race. We fought, we ate, we drank and we made merry with women. This continued for those of us in Valhalla. A successful day did not necessarily mean a visit to Hell's casualty unit, although more often than not, that was where many of us ended up. So much so, that when the healers opened a new recovery wing, it was dedicated to Thomason—a source of great pride to him.

Elinor was fascinated by my stories of Viking lore and legend from the land of the living, but even I would wince at some of the tales. Recounting them aloud made them more real. Some of my brethren were extreme in their practices. It took Elinor's horrified countenance as I shared the stories to make me realize this. So I decided to stick to the tamer tales when I regaled my princess with accounts of our conquests.

I sometimes wondered what kind of Viking, man, devil I would have stayed if I had not met Elinor that day when I was fighting Saxons. It sometimes felt as if knowing her had made me more... human. A state that required me to be dead in order to embrace it.

———

"Are ye sure these other Vikings went Up There when they died?" asked Elinor. "I know ye and yer kin are very nice, but some of the others were so violent, Alfarin. They went looking for trouble like it was sport."

"A punch to the gut or chin is sport, Elinor. I believe it is now called boxing in the land of the living."

"I didn't mean that," she replied, fishing something that looked like an eyeball out of her potato soup. "I'm talking about the ones who didn't go marauding for food. I'm talking about the Vikings who... well, the Vikings who liked to kill."

Elinor shuddered. It *was* an eyeball in her soup.

I understood what she meant. My father, King Hlif, son of Dobin, said those Vikings not in Hell had brought dishonor on the brethren. The only place we were aware of for them was Up There. I always assumed not joining the rest of us in Valhalla was their punishment.

It had never occurred to me that there was somewhere else for the truly insidious to exist in the Afterlife.

13. Monster of the Labyrinth

"We have had a long day," I say as we leave the noxious fumes of the Eighth Circle behind. "Is anyone in need of rest?"

Mitchell and Medusa immediately cry out in the affirmative. Or, as Mitchell puts it, "Hell yes," before he flops to the stone path beneath our feet. Elinor remains quiet, but she does nod. Virgil says nothing, but he leans against a stone wall and closes his eyes. He is muttering, but I cannot hear his words.

"Will we be safe in a space between two circles?" asks Medusa. "I don't want any Skin-Walkers creeping up on us."

"I will take the first watch," I reply, clenching my axe in my hands. "We are not safe anywhere in this insidious place, but we have no choice. The Highers decreed that devils keep the traits of sleep and eating. We are slaves to the rules of our never-ending existence."

"Uh, thanks, Alfarin," says Mitchell. He turns to Medusa and whispers loudly, "I think that's Viking-speak for have some food and get some shut-eye." He calls to me from the floor. "Alfarin, wake me and Medusa up in a few hours and we'll take the second watch so you can rest."

Elinor and Virgil do not eat. Mitchell and Medusa snack on some wafers. Mitchell offers me a chocolate bar, but it has melted and the brown sticky mess oozing out of it reminds me of the circle we just left.

No one eats it.

———————

I do not wake Mitchell for the second watch. I have gone days without sleep before, in life and in death, and there is too much spinning in my head for me to embrace slumber in the Circles of Hell.

Elinor is not snoring. Nor is she talking in her sleep. I do not approach her. I do not know how to anymore.

———————

"What wonders await us in the Seventh Circle?" asks Mitchell. The five of us are leaving the stench of filth and blood after a restless few hours of sleep for some, and more uncertainty for the others. We slowly make our way down a narrow stone tunnel.

"I think—" starts Medusa.

"No, don't tell me," interrupts Mitchell. "I'm going to guess. This is Marshmallowland. We'll be buried up to our necks in candy before an angry swarm of three-breasted harpies swoops down to lick it all off."

"Not sure harpies would be licking, Mitchell," says Medusa tersely. "They'd be more likely to gnaw your face off, but enjoy their three breasts while you can."

"The Seventh Circle has a Minotaur in it, if I remember correctly," says Elinor quietly. She is tearing at the skin around her nails instead of pulling on the back of her neck. I do not know if that is a good thing or bad thing. It isn't an *Elinor* thing, I know that.

"How is it that the uneducated peasant girl is more literate than the modern-day son?" says Virgil. "Or did The Devil teach you these things?"

"Mitchell is not illiterate," snaps Medusa. "He was joking—even I knew that. And he's only been dead for four years. How is he supposed to know about the inner workings of Hell? Especially this part of Hell. Hardly anyone knows about it. We didn't even know about *our* Hell until we died."

"I know about the Nine Circles because I have had time in death to learn to read, Virgil," adds Elinor. "As has Alfarin."

Elinor says my name with no anger in her voice, no condemnation. Yet I am confused. Is she requesting conversation by including me, or is this another slight to my character? The change in her has caused a change in me. My confidence has given way to wariness—wariness of Elinor's feelings and wariness of my own mind. I have been dead for over one thousand years. I should know more about Hell than the rest of my friends put together. But in my heart, I fear it is clear that I do not. And we are about to enter the circle that I am certain will terrify me the most.

For the Seventh Circle is the place that contains those who killed with nothing but savagery and violence in their souls. They are here for no other reason than that they enjoyed the kill.

In here I may meet my kin. In here I may meet my true doom.

You're going to have lots of fun, especially if you make it to the Seventh Circle. I would imagine a Viking will have lots to think about in there.

The Devil's prophetic words before we left the accounting office ring in my ears. The two circles thus far have drained my soul in every way. Mental strength is a power I have learned to display since Elinor unlocked the door to my heart, but physical strength is something I was born to wield. And yet here, even my beloved axe feels heavier in my hands. I would rather take on a line of hulking Saxons single-handed than revisit the Ninth and Eighth Circles again. My energy and emotional strength are being sapped. If this continues, there will be nothing left of me by the time we reach the end of our journey in the First Circle. So much hate and death. This place may claim the souls of us all before the end.

"Why would The Devil's Banshee come to such an accursed place as this?" I ask Mitchell. "I am truly struggling to understand this."

"The girls said she wanted to *find herself*," replies my friend, making quote signs in the air with his long fingers.

"What does that even mean?"

"You're asking *me*?" asks Mitchell. "Dude, I would sooner give advice to The Devil about matching fabric colors than try to understand the mind of his wife. I'll say one thing, though. If his wife was crazy before, what do you think she's going to be like after thousands of years in this place? A few hours here and my brain's already shot to pieces."

My friend has made an excellent observation. He certainly has Virgil's attention. The guide is listening to our conversation keenly, although he has nothing to offer in the way of enlightenment.

"The Banshee is likely to be deranged," I reply. "Savage."

"Exactly. I know we've done some pretty dangerous shit before, Alfarin," says Mitchell, lowering his voice. "But this is way beyond any amount of crazy I've witnessed in the past four years."

"I thought you handled the Geryon very stoically, my friend."

"That's because I didn't believe it was real," replies Mitchell. "I wasn't joking when I said I thought I was in a nightmare. I can hear stuff—voices in my head. I see shadows and flashing lights in my peripheral vision. This place is way beyond what we can actually see and smell and hear. That's just surface evil. There's something else here, something invisible that I feel like...I dunno...it sounds stupid."

"Nothing you say is stupid to me." I pat him on the back to show camaraderie. Mitchell is propelled forward into a jutting piece of black rock.

"Alfarin, I'm not built like you!" snaps Mitchell. "When are you going to remember that?"

"I am sorry, my friend," I reply, brushing fragments of stone from his shoulders. "When we return to our Hell, you should visit that place called the gymnasium. The stench of feet will not be as bad as this place."

"I'll keep that in mind," says Mitchell through gritted teeth. "Anyway, as I was saying, that invisible thing I feel, it's like, when I was in the heart of those two circles, I felt like I was absorbing something bad, something evil. I knew the voices were a bad influence, but I was starting to lose my conscience. Arguing with Medusa on the stone bridges seemed like fun. I actually *wanted* to do it. It was horrible and fun at the same time."

"I have felt the same," I reply. "Voices whisper to me, too. My doubts and fears are being used to taunt me."

"I think that's why Elinor freaked out at you back there," says Mitchell, lowering his voice even further. "Because she would never do that normally. And I'm starting to get scared for Medusa when we get to the circle where her stepfather is."

"Yet it seems to dissipate when we are in the connecting tunnels between circles...," I muse.

"Meaning we have got to get through these circles even quicker," replies Mitchell. "Because the longer we're here, the worse it's going to get."

"Then you must watch for me now, Mitchell," I reply. "For I am about to enter the circle that The Devil taunted me about. It is the final dwelling of the violent. I am a Viking. I was born in blood and I died in blood."

"You didn't actually *listen* to that maniac, did you?" says Mitchell. "Of course The Devil was going to taunt you. He wants you to fail! You have to fight it, Alfarin. We all do."

"Can I interrupt this tête-à-tête, or are you two having a bonding moment?" asks Medusa, shuffling her little body between the two of us. I am immediately assaulted by a mass of curls that invades my nose and mouth.

"Do we have a choice?" replies Mitchell, swiping away hair.

"No," says Medusa. "I was just going to bring something to the discussion—about Beatrice Morrigan."

I glance back toward Elinor and Virgil. They are walking side by side, but Elinor seems oblivious to everything around her. She is looking without seeing. Virgil, on the other hand, is blind but keenly conscious of everything, from the rock wall beneath his fingertips, to the conversation ahead of him, to the goddess floating at his side. His entire body is twitching with alertness.

"What did you wish to say, Medusa?" I ask, hefting my axe onto my shoulder. I allow the edge to drag against my shirt, threatening to cut my skin. I deserve the discomfiture. It will remind me of what I am.

"You read Dante's book in the library, Alfarin," says Medusa. "I've been trying to work out why The Devil's Banshee would come here to the Nine Circles to find herself. I know she's probably crazy, but this place is filled with so much evil, I can't understand her motive at all."

"You and us," replies Mitchell.

"I know," says Medusa. "That's why I thought we should discuss it now, because I heard you mention *finding herself*. It's just I had a thought, so I've been going over the book in my head. More specifically, the end of the book."

The ending. Of course. Wise Medusa would not have preoccupied herself with just the circles of torment for the cursed. She would have wanted to see the hope at the end.

"There were more than just the Nine Circles in Dante's tome," I say slowly.

"There are more than Nine Circles?" exclaims Mitchell. "Are you kidding me?"

"There are no more circles," I say. "But beyond the nine are Purgatory and then Paradise."

"Purgatory is a state of purification to get you ready for Paradise," says Medusa. "I would be able to explain more of it if I had the book, but I lost it back in the Eighth Circle when I dropped my backpack."

Suddenly a roar, as loud as a pride of lions, sweeps through the ever-narrowing tunnel and stops Medusa from saying whatever it is that's occurred to her. We are getting closer to that which I am not sure I am able to face. I am clenching my back teeth and the pain is already juddering down my jaw.

"What was that?" shrieks Medusa.

"The Minotaur," replies Elinor, finally breaking her silence. "I told ye."

Mitchell, Medusa and I swap anxious looks, but not because of a Minotaur. I am not imagining the distance that is expanding between us three and Elinor. Her voice is flat. There is no musicality at all. She is no longer angry, but she seems to be nothing at all. In the previous two circles, the aura of hate and despair left us once we were making the journey to the next ring, but if Mitchell is correct, and I believe he is, about us absorbing evil when we are in there, why is Elinor not reverting to her normal, warm, loving self between circles?

"She's been through one Hell of an ordeal," whispers Medusa. "We need to remember that."

"I did think she recovered way too quickly in Septimus's office," adds Mitchell, again in hushed tones. "Is there any more of that rope left?"

"No, why?" asks Medusa.

"Because you and I are still connected, but Alfarin and Elinor aren't. I think it would be a good idea to tie Elinor to someone."

"She will not leave us," I say.

"These circles affect you, Alfarin, just as much as the rest of us," says Mitchell. "You've already said once that you should do this by yourself. What if Elinor stops arguing and does decide to go back? With the three of us here, who's going to stop her giving herself back to The Devil? She's not thinking straight."

The corridor shakes as another roar, even louder and longer than before, rocks the tunnel, which has been twisting and turning with no obvious exit. We slow our ascent. I know of the myth. The Minotaur guarded the labyrinth. What if the monster is not in the open like the other creatures we have come across thus far? We could turn a corner and come face to face with it.

I ready my axe to meet any foe head-on—even one as large as a Minotaur.

"A rundown on the Seventh Circle would be real good right about now," says Mitchell. The tunnel is becoming narrower with every step. Mitchell has already fallen behind me with Medusa. Virgil is behind Elinor; his cloudy white eyes are blinking rapidly.

"The Seventh Circle has three rings," calls Virgil. "Here you will find flaming sand and burning flakes that fall from the darkness."

"There is also a river of boiling blood and fire, and harpies," I add. "Is that the rundown you require, my friend?"

A steady stream of curses flows from Mitchell's mouth. He is becoming ever more inventive with the uses of reproductive organs.

"The head of a bull on the body of a man . . . ," says Medusa. "You can take that on, Alfarin, if you have to, right? We believe in you."

The handle of my axe is slipping through my fingers. I am so incapacitated by weariness, I can hardly keep my grip. I glance behind to find that we are now in single file. The tunnel is closing in around us. It is lit by flaming torches, but they only fire up when we are within two strides of the sconce.

I can hear heavy snorting. My senses are stretching with fear, but I need to embrace that emotion. It will keep me alert.

Then I turn another corner and a looming black figure charges at us. The metallic smell of fresh blood washes over me as I am knocked to the ground. Callused hands clasp either side of my face, scratching, tearing. Medusa is screaming. I feel a thump as brave Mitchell collides with the beast that is now pressing down on me with its yellow teeth bared. Mitchell is trying to push the Minotaur away from my body. Medusa jumps onto the naked back of the beast, but he flings her off with a muscular shake.

Then I hear sobbing and wailing. It is my princess. I cannot see Elinor, but the sound of her panic is enough. It transports me through time. I am no longer on the ground with a beast at my throat. I am in a burning building and an angel in white is on the floor, trapped by fallen beams that cannot be moved.

Anger overwhelms me. Why me? Why was it decided that I should die in order for fate to deal me this hand? If I had not died, then I would not have the guilt of Elinor's passing on my conscience. I would not have to feel my soul breaking apart now as she pulls away from us.

But now I am lying in the snow. It runs red with a river of blood. Canine jaws are straining for my throat. I hear the bloodlust of the growling hound at my neck.

The Minotaur bares his teeth, and bites down.

Fjórtán

Alfarin and Elinor

In the land of the living, my home was a village on the edge of the Scandinavian coastline. Our settlement was more civilized than most, and my father, King Hlif, son of Dobin, maintained order with authority and the threat of decapitation. History has remembered Vikings for marauding and pillaging, but we were great tradesmen and explorers, too. Many a settlement in the modern world owes its birth and dignified ancestry to the Vikings, as well as exceptional seafaring skills and great hair.

Yet for all the goodness that we brought to the land of the living, all Vikings spent a great deal of time thinking of the Afterlife and longing for one of its two great destinations: Fólkvangr—a meadow of great beauty; or Valhalla—a majestic hall ruled over by Odin, the Allfather.

For me, there was no contest. I needed to be in Valhalla. I wished to spend the Afterlife gazing at the golden shields that thatched the Hall's roof, in the company of the Valkyries, the bravest and most beautiful of Viking maidens, who died in combat. They would feed me grapes and rub ointment into my aching muscles.

I was also allergic to grass pollen, and the very thought of spending my existence in a meadow, however glorious to behold, brought me out in hives.

When I arrived at the HalfWay House on 9 Harpa 970, I knew

I did not need to be processed by witless Grim Reapers. I merely required directions to Valhalla. This was my birthright, my destiny. I got one Grim Reaper around the throat and demanded to know the route. He pointed to an expanse of darkness yonder. I was not afraid, and once I had been healed and my shredded throat and split skull restored, I ran into the darkness without looking back.

Valhalla in Hell became my second home. It was more crowded than I thought it would be. Fólkvangr was rumored to be Up There, with its expanse of light and green space, and as the centuries passed, it came to be thought of as a cursed place. The greatest warriors all came to Valhalla, and the most despicable examples of Viking did not. Fólkvangr must have claimed the heinous ones who, in their excessive warring and desire for bloodshed, had brought dishonor to the name of Viking, we thought. Paintings were commissioned for Valhalla, depicting these shameful Fólkvangr Vikings with wings and harps. These Vikings, who would never know the glory of Valhalla, were mocked. And yet there were those in Valhalla who were still too scared to say the names of the Fólkvangr Vikings aloud, as if their evil deeds in life would curse the decent in death. Eventually the paintings were destroyed and the dishonorable Vikings who claimed glory in their unnecessary bloodlust were never spoken of again.

———

Elinor found our Valhalla comforting, although she once wondered where Odin was.

"We are waiting for his great return," I replied. "One day, Odin will lead us into the battle to end all battles, and it will be called Ragnarök. Only then will the worlds arise renewed."

"So ye Vikings believe there is a battle still to come?" asked Elinor. "Even though ye are dead?"

"There will always be war, Elinor," I replied solemnly. "If I have learned one thing here in Hell, it is that man's capacity for conflict does not end with death."

"Aren't ye scared of being called upon?" she asked.

"Scared? No. Vikings are frightened of nothing. I will take my place at my father's side as he stands next to Odin and the mighty Thor, and Ragnarök will be our final destiny. Until then, Valhalla is the place where we plan for that glorious moment."

"Then I will join ye," said Elinor. "Ye will need someone to watch over ye, and make sure ye eat yer greens."

Valhalla and Elinor Powell. Could a devil want anything more?

14. Valhalla

A golden light is trying to infiltrate my closed eyelids. The destructive agony of the Minotaur's clamped jaws around my throat has gone. At first I feel nothing; I sense nothing. I am floating with no sense of self.

"Where am I?" I ask. I do not know to whom I refer the question, but I am aware that I will get an answer. I feel the presence of another. I smell something in the air. Some*one*. The scent is perfumed, with a hint of earth and blood.

A Valkyrie.

I open my eyes. My friends are gone—as is the beast with the body of a man and the head of a bull. I am lying on the stone floor of a magnificent building. It is golden in color, but not so dazzling that my eyes hurt. Instead, the color projects warmth, wealth and privilege. Enormous, dark wolf pelts drape the walls, and above every open window, a live eagle stands atop a golden perch, surveying the hall majestically with haughty black eyes. Through the open windows I see green fields and wispy white clouds. Vines trailing purple flowers cling to the stonework surrounding the windows, and the only sound I hear is the whistle of a willow warbler. So much peace in one place. I could lie down and sleep for a century in such a setting. The truly blessed must reside here.

It is when I take in the magnificent roof that I know where I am.

Golden shields thatch the vaulted cavity, which is held up by arches made of spears.

This hall is fifty times larger than the Valhalla I know and love in Hell, yet I know that this is the true embodiment of all we Vikings have been taught to revere and covet.

"Do you still need me to answer your question, Prince Alfarin, son of Hlif, son of Dobin?" It is a woman's voice, resonating with gentleness and strength.

"This is the real and true Valhalla."

"Indeed."

"Where are my friends?"

"They are here. Where else would they be?" asks the voice.

But I cannot see them. I look around for Elinor, Mitchell and Medusa, but there is only me in the cavernous hall.

A woman then steps out from behind a golden pillar. She is very tall, perhaps the same height as Mitchell. Her long dark hair is similar to the color of a raven's plumage; her eyes as black. At first I think she is winged, but it is just a cloak around her shoulders that is made of long, tightly packed white feathers. She is wearing a silken blue gown that clings to her body in a way that makes me avert my eyes.

I try to imagine the sporting game of baseball. It is what my friend, Mitchell, does when he is trying to regain control of his hormones and bodily parts. It is a dull sport and will take the sensuality out of any situation.

The Valkyrie glides toward me; her glorious body moves gracefully, like slow water through a curving riverbed. Patricia Lloyd could learn the ways of walking from this woman.

It is no good, thinking of baseball is not going to work. I may need to gouge my eyes out with my blade before I start salivating on the floor.

"Do you know why you are here?" she asks, and immediately her cloth changes. Gone is the pale-blue gown, thankfully replaced by a maroon leather cuirass and skirt. The cloak of feathers remains.

My desire for her is not sated; it has only increased.

Only then, with the maiden in front of me dressed for battle, do I realize my axe is not here. I am alone and unarmed, and I have never felt more naked and exposed.

"I am here because you have chosen me for battle," I reply. "As is the way of the Valkyries. Half of the dead go to Valhalla, the others go to Fólkvangr."

"Ragnarök is coming, son of Hlif. You will need to make a choice."

"Ragnarök is not my quarry this day, fair warrior-maiden. I am on a quest to find The Devil's Banshee."

The Valkyrie stretches out an arm, clad in protective maroon leather with golden stitching. Her slim fingers caress my face, but as she draws away, her long nails, filed to a point, scratch my face. My beard offers no protection, and my skin sears with a burning pain.

"The peasant girl has already forsaken you," says the Valkyrie. "You could stay here with me. I would teach you to be the greatest Viking warrior who ever existed. A birthright that was yours, Prince Alfarin, son of King Hlif, before the mutated ancestors of the Skin-Walkers ripped your throat out. I would love you like no other by night, and train you to destroy by day."

Her words are like honey down my throat. I feel the healing balm working from within, lighting a fire I have not felt since I—

—immolated.

Elinor, Mitchell, Medusa! My friends are alone in the Circles of Hell with a Minotaur bearing down on them and nothing more than a blind guide to see them to safety.

"Noooooooooo!"

———

I am hit by a wall of pain and heat. Screams echo through the Seventh Circle. The Minotaur has released its jaws from my neck, but we are struggling, joined as one chimera of bull and Viking. I am still supine on the ground; my boots are sliding on hot liquid. It burns my legs.

The golden palace of Valhalla has been replaced by a cavern through which runs a river of boiling blood. Bodies, the heads and arms and torsos and legs of the Unspeakables, thrash about in the inferno, skin bubbling and shredding and dissolving.

I am in the outer ring of the Seventh Circle.

The Minotaur throws back a muscular arm and I see Mitchell hurled to the stone floor. Medusa has once more jumped onto the Minotaur and is again clinging to the beast's back. I cannot see Elinor, and my fear is replaced by a thirst for violence. If the beast has harmed her, I will remove its limbs one by one and throw them into the bloody torrent—

The Valkyrie has pulled me away from my friends again. An unnatural sense of peace floods my soul. I want to scratch it out with my fingers. My thirst for violence has not been sated.

My beloved axe clatters to the ground. I do not know where it came from. The Valkyrie takes a step back and draws a long silver blade from behind her body.

"I will not permit you to leave, Viking."

"I did not ask to be brought here!" I cry. "Take me back to my friends—*now!*"

I have been dead for over one thousand years, yet my reflexes are as sharp as the blade of my axe. Centuries of battling Saxons in Hell will keep anyone in prime fighting form. The Valkyrie swings first, but my axe sweeps high to meet her sword. The faint outlines of Vikings past start to materialize in the hall of Valhalla. The Valkyrie and I battle amongst the spirits now watching us, and silver sparks rain down each time our weapons clash.

"Your place is here!" cries the Valkyrie. She crouches low and brings her sword around in a curve. I have to jump to avoid it. "I have chosen you."

"My place is with Elinor, Mitchell and Medusa!" I bellow back. I can feel the anger rising inside my chest once more. I have no idea if time here is in sync with time for those left behind in the Mino-taur's path. Seconds could be hours. Minutes could be days. That bull-headed beast could be bearing down on Elinor right now.

With a roar, I throw myself at the Valkyrie, wielding my axe in every direction as it clatters and sings against her blade. The ghosts of past Vikings are mocking and tormenting me. They say I am not worthy.

"Send me back!" I cry. Fire and pain are rising in my throat. Pressure is building behind my eyes and in my skull. My entire soul is going to ignite with the violence of the anger within me, which is begging to be unleashed.

Elinor is the first devil I see as I am returned to the Seventh Circle of Hell. She is flailing her arms at a grotesque, squawking feathered body that has the face of a haggard female. Blood is dripping from its chapped, flaking lips.

"Alfarin!" cries Medusa. "Watch out!"

I make it out of the way of the charging Minotaur just in time. The lumbering beast appears in my peripheral vision as Medusa screams. I roll to my left and land in a thorny bush that flinches away from me as if it has senses. The river of blood and fire has gone and has been replaced by decaying trees and fauna that is cov-ered in spikes. The Minotaur clamps its jaws down on my arm, but I release myself from the pain by punching the monster repeatedly on the snout. Somehow, as I've been struggling and fighting in two realms, I've been progressing through the Seventh Circle. And Team DEVIL has been with me, battling, the whole time. They have not forsaken me and I have not forsaken them, although it is clear I am now existing in two conscious states.

"Where is Virgil?" I cry.

"Cowering!" cries Mitchell as a harpy dives at him. He snaps off a slim branch to defend himself, but he drops it as the branch starts to bleed over his hands.

"Beatrice Morrigan! Do not forget to look for Beatrice Morrigan!" I yell, punching the Minotaur again.

"Kinda busy, dude!" shouts Mitchell as the harpy sinks its claws into his shoulder.

For a third time I am dragged back to Valhalla. How is she doing this? Is this a trick of my mind or devilry from the Circles? I can see my kin more clearly now, but one more so than the others. A woman. She has long blond hair and an angular face that looks cruel and harsh.

"You bring dishonor on your brethren, Alfarin, son of Hlif, son of Dobin," she says. Her back is straight. She is small, but her haughtiness adds height. "I made the right decision to leave you. I could not have borne it if I'd lived to see the disgrace you would have brought upon me."

"Mother?"

"You are no son of mine," replies the ghost. "I have no son. I chose a higher purpose."

"You abandoned me!" I cry.

"A decision easily made."

"Choose now!" screams the Valkyrie, raising her blade again. "Your ancestry or your friends? Your blood or your soul? Choose... choose... choose..."

Her beautiful face is twisting into something grotesque. The cloak of feathers is expanding outward, but her raven-black hair is growing and smothering the white. The Valkyrie now has wings. The long, lithe body that I admired is shrinking into deformity. Her fingernails are now talons.

"I have chosen!" I cry, taking one last look at my mother. My words, my choice, come from the depth of my soul. "This is not *my* true Valhalla. You defile it with anger. None of you are what you claim to be. My Valhalla will have three others in its heart. My friends, my true brethren. And I will face the end of days with them."

The mesmerizing voice that wanted to love me has been replaced by a shrieking scream. It sounds like glass across stone, and my teeth vibrate with the searing pain of the pitch. I can taste dead blood, thick and salty, and I realize that the area on my face where the Valkyrie scratched her nails down my skin is bleeding.

But the creature now flapping several feet off the ground is no longer a Valkyrie warrior. It is a harpy.

"I will devour your treacherous eyes!" screams the creature. "And then I will wait for the Minotaur to finish his share of the peasant girl, and I'll scavenge her skin!"

"*You will not touch Elinor!*" I roar, and I run and jump toward the harpy. For once in my existence, I do not think of my axe. The bloodlust of the Seventh Circle has contaminated my soul with a toxicity that is both glorious and sickening. I grab hold of the throat of the she-beast and bite down hard. Her scream becomes a gurgle, and then becomes silence. I remove my mouth and spit the bitterness of the harpy's blood onto the ground. Although she is well and truly gone, I snap what is left of her neck. The ghosts of my kin, my mother, start to swirl into smoke. The ground is dissolving, too, into minuscule particles that float up and sear my skin like burning sand. The golden shields that form the roof of Valhalla are disintegrating into flaming flakes.

Fiery flakes and flaming sand . . . just as Dante describes the third ring of the Seventh Circle. We are nearly through, even if I cannot actually see it. I want to tear down the walls of this terrible Valhalla with my bare hands. Everything has become a blur of fiery fragments in a twisted illusion. Anger courses through me. How dare the creatures of this circle mock me so! Threaten and hurt my friends!

I had forgotten the pain of immolation. There is a sensation of muscle and tissue burning, and then tearing from bone. Yet in this instant, the pain is glorious, for I know, as the corrupted vision of Valhalla disappears behind a wall of orange flame, I will soon be reunited with the friends I would tear apart the eternal worlds to find.

Immolation is caused by true, undiluted anger, but it will cleanse my soul of the filth that has corrupted it.

"Yesssssssss!"

I cannot see. The fire has been quenched, but darkness, so heavy and suffocating, has replaced it. The sensation of being contained and buried overwhelms me.

"*Alfarin!*" scream Elinor and Medusa. Mitchell is there, too, in the darkness. I can hear him yelling instructions, taking control of my death.

My mouth is filled with thick liquid. It is anger and hate. It is acidic and vile-tasting. I remember where I was before I was pulled away into a dream state. The Seventh Circle. The last place of the violent.

"We have to get the friggin' Minotaur off him!" cries Mitchell. "Virgil, don't just stand there. Help us!"

"It's all my fault," sobs Elinor. "I made him angry. I didn't mean to—I didn't want to. I don't know what's happening to me."

"I think Alfarin being angry is what probably saved him, El," replies Medusa. Even in the darkness, I know she is soothing Elinor with her words and a comforting embrace.

I spit the liquid out of my mouth. Despite my efforts, some has trickled down my gullet. It burns. It is blood, but not mine.

My friends are now coming into focus. Their forms are so distinctive to me at this point, I could find them in a crowd of thousands of silhouettes. Mitchell, tall and thin, with spiky hair; Medusa, tiny, topped with a mass of curly hair that has a life of its own; and Elinor, slim and delicate with long hair that falls down her back like a waterfall.

They are pulling a large body by its two thick, muscular legs. The fallen Minotaur.

"Did I kill the beast?" I ask, wiping my mouth with the sleeve of my tunic.

"I'm not sure," replies Mitchell. "But it stopped fighting once you took a chunk out of its throat and snapped its neck, Alfarin. You were in a frenzy, dude. It was all we could do to keep up with you both. The two of you were fighting like . . . like . . ."

"Monsters?" I ask quietly.

"I was going to say lions," says Mitchell. "On steroids. With clamps attached to their balls."

I do not have the strength to commend Mitchell for his colorful simile. Instead, I look past my friends at the scene beyond. We are no longer surrounded by a river of blood, or flaming sand. The foul smell of the Seventh Circle has dissipated slightly, but the heat, oh, dear Odin, the heat is already baking me from the inside out. Medusa seems to read my mind.

"You took us through the Seventh, Alfarin," she says. "All the way through. You held off the Minotaur. Mitchell, Elinor and I took on the harpies in the middle circle—although those thorny bushes . . . they were the Unspeakables. Did you see them? They kept switching shapes. It was the most grotesque thing I've ever seen. "

"You were freaking amazing, dude," says Mitchell, patting me on the back; his face bears the scars of deep scratches. "It's like you were in this different place. Totally in the zone."

Suddenly I am enveloped by the scent of Elinor: apples and mint. She rushes toward me and throws her arms around my neck.

"I am so sorry, Alfarin!" she cries. "I was not myself in the Eighth Circle. I could see and hear The Devil's dreams again. He is planning something awful. I could taste his hate and his desire for violence on my tongue."

"I went to Valhalla, Elinor," I whisper. "Yet I returned for you, for all of you."

"Ye thought ye were in Valhalla?"

"No, I *was* there."

"Ye just imagined it, Alfarin," says Elinor. "Ye did not leave us for a second. Ye were so brave, and so strong."

"What of Beatrice Morrigan?" I ask. "Did you see any sign of her? Anything at all?"

"Nothing," replies Mitchell. "And considering we all had to fight like crazy just to keep *standing* in there, I'm pretty sure she wouldn't have picked the Seventh Circle to hang out in for all eternity. Even if she *is* nuts."

My friends help me to my feet and the four of us collapse into one another. Medusa's clothes are ripped, as are Mitchell's. Both are covered in cuts that ooze thick, lumpy blood. Elinor has a large vertical gash down the center of her head where her hair parts. I am smothered in kisses. As much as I admire Mitchell, I hope his lips are not among those making rapid contact with my cheeks.

But as we walk on toward the Sixth Circle of Hell, Virgil pulls me aside.

"You might end up wishing you had stayed in Valhalla, Viking," he says. "War is coming, and you don't want to be in here when it arrives."

Fimtán

Alfarin and Elinor

Déjà vu is not a state of mind that often afflicts Vikings. We tend to exist in the here and now, and if we believe we are repeating an experience, or reliving a moment, that is probably because we are. For instance, if I sneak the dregs of ale from my cousin Thomason's bar, and experience déjà vu in so doing, that is probably because I did the very same thing two minutes before, and, most likely, will do the very same thing two minutes hence. Also, Vikings try to avoid using French phrases. We do not like complications.

Déjà vu was one of the many French phrases that was adopted far and wide by those in the land of the living, presumably to appear more intelligent. I did not pay it much heed until Elinor brought it up one day.

Elinor was always a great believer in fate. She told me she suspected that déjà vu had other, deeper, meanings. That déjà vu was our subconscious telling us that the facts were not always correct, and that we should trust our gut instincts more.

Blessed Elinor was always clinging to those traits that made us human. It was one of the many things I admired in her, as well as her ability to weave beads into my beard and still make me look more manly than Great-Aunt Dagmar—a truly miraculous feat.

Yet as the end of the twentieth century approached, and Hell became more and more crowded, and the earthly population was expanding at a frightening pace, Elinor and I found ourselves in a strange situation that made me question whether déjà vu was indeed a memory jog from our subconscious.

We were in the devil resources office. We now spent more time here than in our dormitories. As we researched, I had often suspected that someone was watching us. It was more than just the presence of shadows, of which there were many. This was a different sensation. A prickling on the neck. A tingle in my fingertips. Sometimes Elinor would quickly look up from a cabinet and cock her head like a quizzical dog.

The same sensation of being watched was with me on the night Elinor was filing new admittance records for those with the surname of Pallister.

Elinor was more nervous than usual. It seemed that she stopped filing to pull at the back of her neck, or whip her head around to stare at the shadows, every few seconds. The shadows had taken on a strange form this night. Instead of one moving mass, they had separated into four black figures. Only two appeared to match Elinor's and my silhouettes. Of the other two, one was tall and thin; the other was small with what appeared to be snakes surrounding its head. It was unnerving. The shadowy outlines of Elinor's and my bodies matched our movements, and then stretched up and out, as if we had mounted large beasts. Then they crept back into one large mass that inched into the darkness and left us with no shadows at all.

"Elinor, you should stop for food," I said. "You will work yourself into the ground if you do not rest."

"I cannot leave now. Someone has been messing with the *Ps*," she replied. "They are all out of order."

"Then I will procure a meal for you, my diligent friend," I said. "What would you like?"

Elinor looked up from a drawer crowded with files and raised a slim red eyebrow.

"Ye will procure food?" she asked. "Is this the same kind of procurement as last night, when ye went to find potatoes baked in their jackets, and ye came back with a slice of wilted lettuce for me?"

"The crush in the corridors was relentless," I replied sheepishly. "If I had not eaten your food as well as my own, my strength would have faded before I reached the elevators."

"Why don't ye call it quits for today, Alfarin?" said Elinor. "I will be fine here for a few more hours, and ye know it is yer shift at yer cousin's bar tonight."

I considered this. I would rather be with my princess than dry glasses in Thomason's, but perhaps I would break fewer of them if I took a brief rest.

"If you are certain…"

"Go. And anyway, I have to sort through this drawer again. I know I've seen this file before, several times now. Why do I keep finding it out of place? It doesn't make sense."

I left Elinor muttering to herself. She mentioned déjà vu and pretty, curly hair. I made a mental note to have food delivered to her. Talking to oneself is an early sign of madness—and Hell was full of it.

On the way out I passed Lord Septimus, The Devil's accountant and right-hand man. We bowed to each other and exchanged other respectful formalities, but then Lord Septimus surprised me by asking where Elinor was.

"She is filing the dead Pallisters," I replied.

"And how does she seem to you this evening, Prince Alfarin?" asked Lord Septimus.

"Elinor is tired and hungry," I replied. "But still as glorious as the sunset after battle."

Lord Septimus smiled. "And how are *you*, Prince Alfarin? You are a changed Viking from the devil who appeared in Hell all those centuries ago. And changed for the better, if I am not mistaken?"

"I am very well, Lord Septimus," I replied, honored that the great Roman was taking time from his busy day to talk to me—let alone notice any changes in my person. "I would even go so far as to say I have never been happier."

"Death is not an easy state to exist in, but I much admire your stoicism, Prince Alfarin," said Lord Septimus. "Your willingness to adapt to change is a quality to which we should all aspire."

I laughed. "Little changes in Hell, Lord Septimus. Routine is a gift of the gods. Those not fortunate enough to be Viking would say the gift of routine was a present from the Highers."

"Don't dismiss change so easily. For our existences are in more hands than just the gods, and especially the Highers."

"You are a Roman, I am a Viking," I replied. "We worship different gods."

"And yet it is in the souls of women and men that I truly believe," said Lord Septimus with a wink. "It won't be long now...," he muttered.

Lord Septimus turned away and was swallowed by the darkness before I had a chance to reply.

Madness.

Yes, Hell was full of it.

15. Elinor's Bane

Exhaustion has totally claimed me: mind, body and what is left of my soul. Virgil appears to be the only devil in our group who is not suffering after the torment of the Seventh Circle. We stop for food and rest in the passageway to the Sixth Circle, but I barely have the energy to chew before my eyelids betray me.

I do not know who takes the watch, and I am relieved beyond measure when I awake to discover that none of the group has been harmed. I must not allow my exhaustion to overcome me again. We are moving through the Circles steadily, but if they continue to be this physically demanding, we will need to factor in more rest breaks. Time is not on our side—we all know that with each passing second The Devil grows more impatient. Yet we cannot rush, for if we do, our quarry might pass right beneath our noses without our knowledge. I *must* ensure that we do not miss Beatrice Morrigan. The pace of this journey is a delicate balance.

I look to my friends. Mitchell and Medusa are curled up together like spoons. Elinor has her head on my lap.

Apparently, I slept where I slumped.

From here on, though, I will have a renewed burst of vigor in my step. We may have started this quest at the wrong end of the Circles, but we have already traversed the horrors of the Ninth, Eighth and Seventh. We are a third of the way through, and while our souls have been tested to the extreme, Team DEVIL has endured.

It is time to carry on with our quest to find Beatrice Morrigan. It seems that my friends feel the same way, because they are starting to stir.

"So, next up is the Sixth Circle," says Mitchell, stretching. "And in here is...?" He trails off, but his pink eyes are wide and expectant. He's looking at me, Medusa and Elinor, as if he doesn't care which of us answers, as long as we prepare him.

"The Sixth Circle is for heresy," replies Elinor nervously, grabbing at the back of her delicate neck. "Those who murder with righteousness in their black hearts after denying others the right to choose their own path of worship."

"That is why it is getting even hotter," says Virgil. "The murderous heretics are trapped in flaming tombs."

Mitchell immediately puts a comforting arm around Elinor and gives her a quick squeeze before letting go.

"We'll get you through this one. I'll even sing to you if you want. You'll be so appalled it'll take your mind off where you are."

My princess laughs, and I slap Mitchell on the back to show my appreciation. Elinor will not relive The Devil's dreams in this circle, but it will surely bring back memories of her own entombment, before Mitchell and I...

I still cannot bear to think of it.

"Virgil," calls Medusa. "Before we're faced with the awful prospect of Mitchell singing, do you know which Skin-Walker looks after this circle?"

"Its name is Haeresilion," replies Virgil; his opaque eyes are fixed on the roof of the tunnel. He sticks out his tongue and licks his chapped lips. "Why does it matter?"

"I like to know what I'm facing," replies Medusa. "And giving it a name makes it less of a monster. I've learned that one the hard way."

"Does anyone else find it weird that apart from Perfidious, we haven't run into a single Skin-Walker yet?" asks Mitchell. "Not that I want to or anything. It's just I thought they were going to be our biggest problem in here."

"Maybe they're busy," replies Medusa. "*Their* kind of busy."

"I do not want to think about how those monsters get busy," says Elinor, hugging herself. "They are so evil."

"You still do not understand what you have in your possession, do you?" calls Virgil. His voice is slightly higher than the mocking tone I have become accustomed to. It is almost as ladylike as the tone Mitchell sometimes adopts when he is agitated. I am compelled to tease him, as I do Mitchell in those situations, but Virgil is old and feeble and it does not seem fair to insult his manhood when he has so little of it to cling to. Instead, I just answer his question.

"We are aware that we have a Viciseometer, Virgil," I reply. "And we have already acknowledged that we cannot use it until we have found the Banshee, for none of us has seen every circle, and we cannot travel to and fro without a destination to visualize."

"You are not *seeing* what is under your nose, Viking," snaps Virgil. "You have a weapon of war in your midst that you haven't even begun to comprehend! Sheer luck has seen you through the Circles thus far. Nothing more."

"Are you saying we have a weapon against the Skin-Walkers?" I ask. I stop walking to ponder this, and as I do, I am briefly distracted by a dense shadow behind us. Team DEVIL appears to now be in the center of two very different atmospheres. We have occasionally seen a bright light igniting a path before us, but behind us is nothing but darkness.

Virgil's cracked lips rise up at one end. His sallow skin twitches. I hold my hand up to silence the others and they acquiesce without a word. Not for the first time, I wonder if Virgil has another sense he has not told us about. A sixth sense that can read minds. I do not doubt this ability exists. Elinor has often been able to read mine.

Elinor. Her name appears like a printed word across my field of vision, and once again, the blind guide reacts with a smirk.

Then I remember how Perfidious reacted when Elinor passed him on the way out of the Ninth. He yelped. Perfidious has been in her presence on a number of occasions, and even held her captive for a brief moment in the cemetery in Washington, DC, without fear.

But that was before…

"They are afraid of Elinor," I say, my voice an awed whisper. "The Skin-Walkers now sense she was used as a Dreamcatcher. They cannot and will not touch her."

"Those monsters cannot be afraid of me," says Elinor. "I am nothing."

"You are not," says Medusa crossly. "You are everything, El, and you are amazing—brave, loyal and true."

"You're one of the smartest devils I know," replies Mitchell. "And you're self-taught. Do you realize the discipline that takes, Elinor? For you to teach yourself how to read, and then to go and read most of the books in Hell's library? Other devils fall to pieces when they realize Hell is what they've got for all eternity, but you just go right on with existing. Septimus calls Alfarin and me stoic, but you're even more stoical than—wait, is that a word? It doesn't sound right. Stoical."

"Elinor, we turned ourselves into weapons in the land of the living when we learned to immolate, but The Devil has turned you something into something far more powerful in Hell, perhaps without even realizing it," I say. "You saw the effect that little boy had on the Skin-Walkers when we were seeking the Dreamcatcher."

"But I do not want to be anything that The Devil made me!" cries Elinor. "Especially not a weapon! And doesn't that put ye all at greater risk? The Skin-Walkers need only separate us and they can take ye."

"Time for the rope again," says Medusa. She and Mitchell are no longer connected. I cannot recall them untying it, but then, as Mitchell would say, I was not completely with it during our ordeal in the last circle—whatever *it* is.

"I bet that's why Beatrice Morrigan has been able to go through the Circles," says Mitchell. "She's the original Dreamcatcher. By the time she ditched The Devil, she'd probably absorbed so many dreams that she was practically a weapon of mass destruction. The

Skin-Walkers have probably built her her own private lodge down here, just so she'll stay away from them."

"Finally, the new boy shows some brains," cackles Virgil. Mitchell shoots him a filthy look, although not as mutinous as the one Medusa gives the guide. Her teeth are clenched so hard she looks as if she would love to pummel Virgil's hooked nose across his cheeks.

"This is what I was trying to tell you all before that Minotaur• creature came bearing down on Alfarin," says Medusa.

"What?" asks Mitchell.

"I just couldn't understand why the Banshee would come down here to find herself," replies Medusa. "But it now makes sense. If you need some time and space to figure yourself out, you don't need to be distracted by the one person who's driving you crazy. So what do you do if you're The Devil's Banshee? You come to the Nine Circles. Because this is the one place in Hell I bet The Devil wouldn't come."

We all look at her quizzically.

"When I was bargaining with him to get Elinor back," Medusa continues patiently, "he told me he couldn't just leave his office to go traipsing around the Nine Circles looking for his wife. He said there'd be anarchy with him gone. So it makes perfect sense that Beatrice would come here. In a way, it was a test of The Devil's love. Would he risk anarchy in Hell to come and find her? So far, he hasn't taken that risk. So here she's been, in the worst place in Hell, safe and sound. It wouldn't be safe for anyone else, but it is for Beatrice Morrigan because she's the original Dreamcatcher. Your analogy, Mitchell, of a weapon of mass destruction is a good one—"

"Why, thank you."

Medusa rolls her pretty pink eyes and continues as if she hasn't been interrupted. "—because I bet you anything she could tear this place apart if she wanted."

"And yet I remember what you were saying, wise Medusa, about Purgatory and Paradise," I say. "What if, after all this time, Beatrice Morrigan is satisfied with her time in the Nine Circles, and she's given up on The Devil coming after her? What if she's looking for an escape? A different existence entirely? What if she wanted to get to some kind of Paradise—like Up There, for example? What if she's found a way?"

"Judging from what the angels have said, I don't think Up There is the Paradise the living think it is," says Mitchell.

"It is just a thought," I say.

"But are ye saying she might not be here?" asks Elinor, a note of panic rising in her voice.

"I think we are definitely on the path *to* Beatrice Morrigan," I reply. "But what if we don't find her in the Circles? Are we to try to enter another realm entirely?"

"Either way, we don't have a choice," says Mitchell. "We have to go through all nine to get anywhere."

"Hang on, though," says Medusa. "Virgil, we need you in this conversation, and for once in your existence, save the insults, please. When you took Dante through to Paradise, you entered it via the Ninth. Why can't we just go back to where we started and find the entrance to Purgatory that way? If she's there, it'd be a lot better for us to find her without having to suffer through the rest of the Circles. And if she's not, then at least we can cross it off the list of possibilities."

"Because this is true Hell, child," replies Virgil, massaging his wrinkled temples. "And to be worthy of leaving it for Paradise, one *must* suffer the torment of the nine."

"Whoever built this place is seriously crazy. How can anyone be that sick?" wonders Mitchell.

"The Skin-Walkers were the first evil, Mitchell," Elinor reminds him. "The hate and wickedness they must have been feeding on since man developed consciousness is something we cannot even comprehend."

Medusa's little nostrils are flaring. I know she is not truly breathing, but I have noticed that she—like Mitchell—spends more time using that natural reflex than Elinor and I.

"We have come a long way, Medusa," I say. "We may have lost

the book, but amongst us, it is clear that we have enough knowledge to continue."

"Well, I don't," says Mitchell morosely.

"Perhaps not, Mitchell," says Elinor. "Yet ye are the one who asks the important questions to start the discussion in the first place. Without ye, the rest of us would be silent with our thoughts for company."

And she reciprocates the hug that he gives her.

"Perhaps you do not need me at all," says Virgil hopefully. "I would be happy to part ways now."

"Lord Septimus said you were to be our guide," I reply. "So that is what you'll do. You also test us with questions, although my friend's manner is far more pleasing on the ear. Your mockery makes me want to throttle your stringy neck."

Virgil hacks up phlegm as he laughs. He spits it on the ground, and Medusa yells as some of the green mucus makes contact with her sneakers.

"We're clearly not far enough away from the Seventh Circle yet, are we, Viking?" he sneers. "But then again, perhaps this appetite for violence is simply your natural state."

"Ignore him, Alfarin," says Elinor.

"I will find that very easy to do," I reply, but Virgil sidles up to me and whispers in my ear.

"How was Valhalla?"

I push him away. Virgil is weak, old and blind, but he is a snake in a penitent man's cloth of red robes.

Red is the color of danger.

"You know nothing about me," I growl. "Nothing about any of us."

"Keep telling yourself that," sneers Virgil, twisting his head toward Elinor. "But you are forgetting, I know this realm, and I know yours. I know The Devil and Septimus. And I know five ritual offerings when I smell them."

"Five?" asks Mitchell. "That's where you're totally wrong, man."

"Virgil is blind, Mitchell," Elinor reminds him. "And ye have many intonations of voice. He could have mistaken ye for a girl."

Medusa's and my laughter is cut short by Virgil.

"There are five of you being sacrificed by Septimus," repeats Virgil. "There is another here, ordered to stay out of sight unless absolutely necessary. The smell of burning flesh is but a rumor with the peasant, but with the fifth one, the stench is as strong as that of the burning heretics."

"What the Hell is he talking about?" asks Medusa.

"He's nuts," whispers Mitchell, although his face betrays his genuine hurt. "Septimus would never sacrifice us."

But Virgil has managed to take away the renewed energy from Team DEVIL with one sentence. We continue in silence through the passageway to the Sixth Circle.

We reach a wall with steep stone steps. The haze from the heat gathering above has distorted everything into an orange-tinged blur.

"After you, Virgil," I say. "You are the guide, you go first."

Virgil starts to climb; Elinor and Medusa follow. I stop to tuck my axe into my backpack, blade first with the handle protruding, as I cannot hope to climb such a steep incline one-handed, but Mitchell pulls me aside as I am fastening it.

"Virgil said there were five of us here," whispers Mitchell.

"Ignore the old fool," I reply. "Elinor was right. There are times when you sound like the female of the species, my friend."

"But he said the fifth smelled like burning flesh. That's what the Skin-Walkers said, when we were at Stinson Beach, remember?"

"But there are only four of us," I say.

But Mitchell is shaking his head. His grip on my arm intensifies.

"I think Virgil's right. I think Septimus has sent someone else into the Circles. You know that bright light we keep seeing streaking past us? What if it's someone immolating? Someone who's *always* angry?"

"You cannot mean . . . ?"

Mitchell nods furiously.

"Yes. I think Jeanne is here."

Sextán

Alfarin and Elinor

The central business district was known as the hub of Hell and was where many of us worked. Elinor's workplace, devil resources, was located on floors 211 to 277. By the end of the year 1980, another floor was added to accommodate the teeming personnel files of the dead. No one understood why. No one read them. Yet in some way or another, bureaucracy has a way of infiltrating the heart of all civilizations, living or dead, over time. Why, even the Vikings had started taking minutes at meetings, though it was a bit pointless. There are only so many variations of the words *fight, challenge* and *beer* a Viking scribe could record on a scroll.

The higher up the CBD you worked, the more important the office. This tradition, like everything else, was dictated by The Devil's whims. For instance, over the years his love for plush furnishings intensified. As a result, the floor where his drapes were embroidered and his cushions tasseled and his couches upholstered had been steadily climbing the levels of the CBD. When I arrived in Hell they were on floor 578. By 1980, they were on level 4, and rumor was that they were about to move higher.

Level 1, of course, was reserved for the Oval Office and The Devil's most senior staff. Elinor and I never ventured that high. I did not have dreams of advancement within the ranks of any workplace, let alone The Devil's, and neither did she. But we did like to step out onto the balcony of devil resources and gaze down upon those devils on the lower floors who were also venturing out. We did not suffer from vertigo. Indeed, we found the ever-expanding facade of the CBD rather special. With thousands of tiny flaming torches burning as far as the eye could see, we often thought it was as if the sky had been turned onto its side, and as we looked over the balconies, we could almost convince ourselves that we were looking out across the stars.

Elinor said it was romantic. Romance made me think of food. It was a good state to be in.

The only time the special ambience was ruined was when a devil threw himself over the balcony in a vain attempt to die—again. Ah, the foolish newly dead. Rumors occasionally swept among the recent arrivals that if their souls were vanquished in Hell, they would be returned to the HalfWay House once more and could be sorted into Up There. It was a cruel lie, but some devils tried it repeatedly until the healers got fed up with putting the same broken corporeal souls back together and setting the same broken limbs. It was then that the healers started refusing repeat customers. Seeing devils scuttling around like spiders, with arms and legs bent double, was an effective message for the rest of us. Elinor remarked that a few nets under the balconies would have worked just as effectively as a deterrent, but then, Elinor always was what The Devil was not:

Kind.

"Alfarin," she said to me one day. We were eating a picnic after a particularly long shift of mine in Thomason's. "Do ye think we'll ever see the real stars again?"

"Perhaps, one day," I replied vaguely; I was concentrating on devouring an especially delicious steak and kidney pie—made, I hoped, from the internal organs of a pulverized Saxon. "Death is a continual surprise," I said once I had swallowed a particularly large bite. "And perhaps, one day we may feel the wind on our skin and the warmth of the sun on the crowns of our heads."

"I still cannot believe that man is on the moon and flying in the stars," said Elinor wistfully. "I know many devils do not like getting news of the living from the recently deceased, but I do."

"Flying in the stars is too close to angels for my liking," I replied. "I am happy in Hell."

"What would ye do if ye saw an angel flying?" asked Elinor, taking a delicate bite out of a piece of cheese.

"It depends on whether they were playing a harp," I replied. "I cannot abide harp music. They now play it in the toilets on level 666. I cannot do my business when I am thinking of simpering angels."

"Ye don't know if angels simper, Alfarin. They could be brave warriors like ye."

Elinor spent the next fifteen minutes slapping my back as I coughed and spluttered at the thought. Strong, courageous, battle-ready angels? The very idea was preposterous.

16. Face of Evil

Mitchell and I start to climb the steep steps to the Sixth Circle. I am bent forward like an ape, using my hands to steady my body as we ascend. Mitchell and I have stopped talking as we concentrate on the climb, but his words are running through my head nonetheless.

What if it *is* someone immolating? Someone who is *always* angry?

Lord Septimus said no one had ever learned how to immolate in the Underworld before, not even a great warrior like him, yet I believe Mitchell's suspicions are correct. I immolated in the Seventh Circle, and while I was existing in two conscious states and may not have immolated in the true sense, if there was ever a dead soul who could twist the boundaries of death, it would be the fearsome Maid of Orléans. Plus, as we discovered on our recent journey back to the land of the living, her immolation is different from ours. Unlike devils, she does not have any heat buildup within her to allow her to explode into a fireball of rage. Instead, she was an angel, gifted with the strength of movement. But anger is still the trigger, and Jeanne would not have lost that. On the contrary, I think the desperation of her forced confinement would be fuel to the fire . . . or wind, in her case.

Silence is a virtue. As Team DEVIL and Virgil continue to scale the searing steps that will take us to the Sixth Circle, I replay the events that took place in the reception area, just before Lord Septimus took us through the doors.

I suspect that what we witnessed there was no ordinary unruly gathering of devils. It was a diversion to allow Jeanne to escape Hell. That was why we saw Owen, Angela and Johnny there, too. They were probably the ones who started the riot, almost certainly on Lord Septimus's orders.

Oh, that cunning Roman, with his Machiavellian ways and his ability to keep his shirts crisp and free of sweat stains, even in Hell...

But he should have told me, and I am annoyed that Lord Septimus did not see fit to include me in his plans. I deserve to know why Jeanne is here. I am the leader of this mission to find Beatrice Morrigan, and if I am to guide us through, am I supposed to ensure her safety, or is she answerable to no one? And now another concern weighs upon me. If Jeanne is in these circles with us, then she is going to find the next circle the hardest of all. For inside the Sixth, she may well find her tormentors and accusers—those very men who put her living body to the flame because her faith was different than theirs.

If she is here, we are going to have to find her. Jeanne is brave, but she is not as learned as we in matters of Hell, or as prepared. And if there is one thing I am discovering on this hateful journey, it is that one cannot get by on bravery alone.

Lord Septimus should have trusted me with the whole truth.

"Do not look down," calls Virgil from the front of our procession. "We are approaching the entrance to the Sixth, but one false step, and you will be lost to the deep."

I have no intention of looking down, but a small rockfall is now cascading down the steps. The stone, already worn by time and intense heat, is coming loose as each devil treads upon it. My fingers are being scorched as the foundations start to come away. I am at the end of our line, and we are no longer joined by rope. If one above me should fall, then we all shall topple like trees.

Mitchell is no longer climbing. I peer around his sticklike form and see that Medusa has also stopped. She is patting Elinor's legs, but my princess has not been stalled by Virgil. I can see his red cloth continuing to billow in the heat, which is hitching up in strength and intensity, as he continues to climb the last of the steps ahead of us.

Mitchell turns around and looks down at me. He sways as he unwittingly catches sight of the drop below us.

"I think Elinor has vertigo. She says she can't go on," he says.

"Elinor does not suffer from vertigo," I shout back.

Medusa's words of encouragement to Elinor are becoming louder and more fretful in tone. I climb a few more steps and am soon almost level with Mitchell. The stairs are not wide enough for the two of us, but my intentions are clear to my friend. He dips down and manages to maneuver himself like a snake between my legs.

"It's a sheer drop on either side," I say. "Do not fall, Mitchell."

"You don't say," he snaps, with slight hysteria in his tone. "And here I was about to throw myself off."

I am now behind Medusa, and I can see that Elinor is bent forward, clawing at the roughly hewn steps with her fingers. The heat is unforgiving. Just climbing those few steps has increased my body core to that of a volcano about to blow. I feel as if I am being cooked . . .

Oh, no. The burning heat. I was so preoccupied with the thought of Jeanne possibly reliving her death by fire that I forgot Elinor's own torment before my blade released her from the agony of her final moments on earth.

But now another sight has caught my eye, and that of Medusa, too, for she is the first to exclaim in horror. Blood. Two small pools of thick, lumpy blood are oozing down from Elinor's head. It is sizzling as it makes contact with the rock beneath her body.

"Alfarin!" cries Medusa.

"Let me pass!" I shout. "Crouch down and slip through my legs,

Medusa. I will carry Elinor on my back if I have to. We will get her through this next circle."

Suddenly, Elinor stands upright and flings her arms out to the side. She screams a primal shriek that doesn't sound human. Her head snaps back, and I can actually see the force of her scream vibrating as a black distortion expels from her mouth. Blood is slowly inching its way down her red hair.

"It's coming from her eyes!" screams Medusa. "Just like the little boy—the Dreamcatcher. Alfarin, we have to get Elinor out of here."

Medusa drops through my legs, but in her haste, her sneakers skid on loose stone. As Elinor continues to scream, Medusa slides past Mitchell, grappling and flailing desperately as she loses her hold on the steep steps.

Mitchell slides down after Medusa and stops her descent by grabbing hold of her green T-shirt. It rips, but Mitchell manages to wrap his legs around Medusa before she tumbles farther. They cling to each other, too scared to move for fear of slipping. I have a choice, and a decision to make based upon those choices. Do I pull Mitchell and Medusa to safer ground, or do I try to placate my bleeding Elinor?

"Go to her!" cries Mitchell. I nod to him, grateful for the affirmation of the only choice I could make.

I am about to climb up onto the step where Elinor is screaming when she turns to me with her arms still outstretched.

The face of The Devil stares back at me. His pale skin, so thin it is almost transparent, is covered in blood that is pouring from his black eyes. His goatee is curled into a neat point. Then his open mouth stops screaming and starts to laugh. Soon the sickening high-pitched giggle is shaking and rattling the entire cavern. Rocks dislodge and drop from the roof, shattering like glass as they make contact with the stone floor far below us. I see Virgil, now at the top of the steps, throw himself to the right to escape being crushed by a huge, cone-shaped piece of rock that plummets from the roof. The guide is blind, but The Devil's voice is unmistakable to those in Hell, even Virgil. The old man is pounding at the ground with clenched fists.

"I need to see…I need to see!" he cries. He then claws at his face, dragging down the loose skin around his white eyes.

Elinor gasps, and her face becomes her own once more. I know she knows what has happened because her expression is one of pure terror. Her lips are spread so thin in a silent scream they have all but disappeared from her face.

"He's gone, Elinor!" I cry, reaching out for her. "You have beaten him back."

Elinor's ruby-red eyes are swimming with tears now instead of blood. Her face and T-shirt are streaked with the remnants of the possession.

The cave shakes violently one last time. The step Elinor is standing on dissolves into dust. In slow motion, she slips past me and falls into the abyss.

Sjaután

Alfarin and Elinor

How did you die?

It was the most popular question within our immortal domain. For some of us, it was an icebreaker: a way to instantly bond with another devil. For others, it was a constant reminder that they were dead, and therefore as unwelcome as Second Cousin Odd at family gatherings, Viking social events and...well, anything, really.

For me, it was not a question I asked of any devil, ever, with the exception of one. That is because the knowledge of how someone died had never really concerned me before I became close to Elinor Powell. I was dead. Everyone around me was dead. Did the journey to this destination really matter? I might have felt different if devils asked each other, "How did you *live?*" Because what better measure of a person was there than the facts of how they spent their lives? I would have been heartened to learn that the devil next to me was a professional ale brewer in life, or a fashioner of tools, or weaponry or longships. Perhaps he was victorious on the battlefields of his life, or perhaps he knew the bitterness of defeat. Perhaps he was an inventor of great things that contributed to the progress of mankind, such as fried chicken served in a bucket.

But no. Devils were far more interested in how it all ended—and the more dramatic, the better. I had heard of every way to die during my one thousand years of death, but I had learned that the dead can lie just as convincingly as the living.

Some even wore their demise with pride, especially those who wished to impress devils like the buxom wench, Patricia Lloyd, who started working in the library in 2001. Many a devil would regale her with tales of his bravery in his final moments of living in order to get an extreme close-up of her tattoos and piercings. It was astonishing how many males found themselves gored to death by unicorns or half-eaten by dragons.

Vikings were proud in life and prouder in death. Our weapons were big, and our tankards even bigger, for we had much to toast in death. And it mattered not if we arrived in Valhalla by axe, spear or bow—the cause of our deaths had no effect on how we existed in the Afterlife.

But Elinor was not a Viking. She shied away from violence and pain. And I noticed she had a particular nervousness about her when it came to fire. She avoided the torches that lined the hallways. She joined us at our hearth, but never too close.

I knew she had died in the year 1666. Some of my kin would put two and two together and get seven, but Elinor had given me the gift of being learned. So it was not difficult for me to guess what had happened to her. Still, I sought out information in the library to learn more about her life and times—and, of course, the year of her demise. The year 1666 was a celebrated date in Hell. And for me, Elinor's unease around fire was an arrow that pointed straight to the month of September.

I did not need to ask her if she died in the Great Fire of London. I just knew. But the tomes in the library spoke of horrors in that catastrophe that I could never have fathomed.

Armed with this knowledge, one day I decided to ask her *exactly* how she died. If I heard the cause confirmed, from her own lips, then I could take steps to ensure that she was never reminded of her death again. My axe; my massive upper-body strength; and my impressive beard, which she was constantly grooming, would keep her safe—or distracted—from anything that might bring back heinous memories.

We had settled for the evening in Thomason's Bar. My cousin was trying a new concept called Cocktail Night. I think someone should have explained that the words *cock* and *tail* should not have been taken literally. I was most definitely not drinking what was being served up.

Being underage for drinking was most definitely working in my favor this evening.

In spite of the unfortunate beverages surrounding us, Elinor was in a good mood. She was relaxed. Her neck did not seem to be paining her as much as usual. It seemed like a good moment to ask the question that everyone else asks.

"Elinor," I said, clearing my throat. "May I ask you something?"

"Ye do not need to ask permission, Alfarin. Ye can ask anything of me, ye know that."

"How did you die?" I asked, taking care to keep my deep voice quiet.

Elinor bit down on her bottom lip. "Ye know how I died."

"I know you died in the Great Fire of London," I said. "But how? Was it flame, smoke, the collapse of your building or some other nefarious incident?"

"I cannot tell ye now, Alfarin," she whispered.

"But I am your closest friend," I replied. "I want to help ensure you never have to relive it."

"Ye are my closest friend, it's true. So...so just know that one day...one day, I will tell ye. But not now."

Straightaway I knew my mistake in pushing the question. Elinor's deep-red eyes were darting left and right. Both hands were on her neck. It pained me to see her in such distress. I wanted to tell her that I would have suffered in the fire for her. That I would have inhaled the smoke if it meant keeping her alive longer.

I wanted to tell her that I loved her and that even though I couldn't save her in life, I would do anything to protect her in death.

I spent the rest of the evening in a state of deep penitence for my inquisitive folly. I even sneaked one of Cousin Thomason's cocktails and slugged it down, just to make Elinor laugh, which she did.

Then she helped my uncle Magnus perform the Heimlich maneuver when the tail of a rat became lodged in my throat.

———

Fire was said to be one of the worst ways to pass over. Many a brave devil would quail in the presence of flame.

I would not ask Elinor again, not ever. She would tell me when she was ready.

17. Four of Nine

"*Elinor!*"

The sight of my princess slipping into the vast darkness below me is too much. I do not stop to think. I throw myself down after her. In the rush of hot wind whistling by my ears, I can hear Mitchell and Medusa screaming, too. My clothes start to tear from my body as I plummet into the abyss after Elinor. I can just see her limp body below me, twisting and turning as she falls.

Then a blinding flash engulfs me. My flight is brought to a quick end, and I am pulled upright. The suddenness of it causes my neck to snap back, and I bite my tongue.

I can sense a freezing cold hand gripping my right arm. A fragile, hot body is then pressed against mine in the blinding light—the angel has Elinor, too. My princess and I are quickly pulled upward and deposited next to the shaking Virgil.

"You!" I gasp, turning to my rescuer. "That is not the first time you have saved my magnificent hide, Jeanne."

"And I doubt it will be the last time, Viking," snaps the fearsome outcast from Up There.

"You saved Elinor, too," I say. "Maid of Orléans, know that from this day forth, my axe will honor your—"

"What were you thinking?" snarls Jeanne. "*Vous êtes un idiot!* Did you think you would catch the peasant and bounce back up to the top? You are in the Circles of Hell! Start thinking and acting like a leader. I have been watching you from afar, and I have not been impressed. You have been as witless as Owen."

"Good to see you, Jeanne," says Mitchell, clambering up the last of the steps with Medusa on his back. "I'm glad to see Hell hasn't diluted your charm."

"You can put me down now, Mitchell," says Medusa. "Thank Hell you have long legs. I don't think I would have been able to stretch over those crumbled steps."

Jeanne gives Mitchell a look of utter contempt.

"Jokes and foolish gestures will be your undoing, Mitchell Johnson."

"And not learning how to take an occasional break to smell the coffee will be yours, Jeanne," replies Mitchell as Medusa slides off him and heads straight for Elinor. "I bet if there's one dead person who could still have a stroke or heart attack, it would be you. I can feel your dead blood pressure rising from here. But since I'm a gentleman, I won't say any more, except thanks for saving Elinor and Alfarin back there." Then he turns to punch me on the arm and whispers, "Totally called it, dude. I knew she was here." Mitchell, reveling in his victory, rocks back on his heels for a moment. But then he cannot help himself and turns back to Jeanne. "I've gotta say, though, you're not as sneaky as you thought. I knew you were here all along. So you might want to practice those covert ops skills a little more, because—"

"Stop it!" cries Medusa. "Can't you see something is still wrong with El?"

Medusa is bent over Elinor. I thought they were having a girl moment, which is why I did not intrude, but now that Medusa has spoken, it is clear that Elinor is struggling.

She became The Devil before she fell. I saw it with my own eyes. And I am put in mind of the time when Medusa told us of her encounter with the little boy—the former Dreamcatcher—in the land of the living not long ago. She said he spoke with The Devil's voice. But she made no mention of his taking on The Devil's features.

Before I can get to Elinor, Virgil leans over her. He is muttering something in a language I do not know.

"What is he doing?" I ask Mitchell.

"No idea," replies Mitchell, biting down on his lip with concern. "Alfarin, when I was trying to stop Medusa from falling, I heard... something. And then you said, 'He's gone...You have beaten him back.' What did you mean?"

I do not want to say the words aloud. Not because I am scared, but because I do not want Elinor to hear me say them. Mitchell mouths *The Devil*, and I lower my head.

Without saying it, Mitchell and I come to an understanding. I would expect no less from a friend who is akin to a twin brother, although one who is different in height, girth and body hair. I saw The Devil in Elinor, and Mitchell heard him. Neither Mitchell nor I make any attempt to get closer to Elinor. It is not cowardice that holds us back. I would plunge into the abyss time and time again for her, and I know Mitchell would put his puny body on the line for her, or any one of us, without a second thought as well. But now my mind is thinking of our domain and the trickery of The Devil.

It had never crossed my mind to question Medusa's miraculous return from The Devil's inner sanctum with our friend. I was a mess, traversing between rage and sorrow at what had happened to Elinor, and how she was changed. Yet there was also relief that Elinor was free of her torment as The Devil's Dreamcatcher.

But is this devil traveling with us truly Elinor? It is a question I have to ask. Was Team DEVIL really reunited in the heart of the library? Is this another one of The Devil's nefarious tricks, and if so, where is my princess? If this is not our beloved friend, then I will tear apart the Afterlife to find her.

And I will destroy any false apparition with my bare hands.

"I am well, Virgil," says Elinor, pushing the guide away. "I was not myself for a moment, but..."

Then she sees the blood that has stained her T-shirt.

"Alfarin, Jeanne—what happened to El? Why is she covered in blood?" asks Medusa.

"Ask the Viking, not me," replies Jeanne. "I should not have had to reveal myself to you all so soon. General Septimus said—"

"Alfarin, what happened to me?" begs Elinor. "I cannot remember."

Her voice cuts to my soul. It is full of sadness and fear. I want to believe that this is my princess. I am certain I could not be fooled by anyone else, but the thought of conversing with an imposter tears at my insides with a ragged blade.

"The peasant will struggle through the next circle," says Virgil quietly. "Her fear will not be the sort that can be held at bay by shutting one's eyes or blocking one's ears. The simple heat of the Sixth will test and pull at her very existence."

"Yours, too, Jeanne," adds Medusa.

"I am not afraid," Jeanne replies.

"This is more than fear," I say. "These are trials that seize on the very essence of our souls."

I must think. I am their leader. We are on the cusp of entering the Sixth Circle. There has to be a way to get through this. A possible solution dawns on me. "Can you take Elinor separately?" I ask Jeanne. "You have the gift of speed when you immolate. We will continue our passage on foot and will hunt for Beatrice Morrigan, but can you take her through to the other side and wait for us?"

"You think I am a common mule, with no use other than for carrying your bodies?"

I take a step toward her as Elinor struggles to stand. Even Virgil with his pious countenance has taken pity on what my princess has become. He supports one of Elinor's arms while Medusa takes the other.

"You are the Maid of Orléans, a legend through the ages," I reply. "And I ask this favor of you now, warrior to warrior. The battle to come will be bigger than anything you or I have ever witnessed or feared. Lord Septimus sent you—you, Jeanne—to watch over us for a reason. I am turning to you for aid. Elinor has absorbed the very essence of The Devil, for no other reason that she was the purest of us all. I believe that her very proximity to the entrance of the Sixth, with its heat and flame, was enough to draw The Devil out of her. I fear she will not endure the next circle because of the manner of her death."

"She was burned, but she did not perish by flame," replies Jeanne. "General Septimus told me that *you* were responsible for that."

"And in the depths of *your* torment on the pyre, did you not wish for an end to *your* suffering? For I would have done it, Jeanne. I would have put you out of your misery if I could."

Jeanne gnaws on her inner cheeks as she considers this, which makes her already thin face look almost skeletal. Her long dark hair is braided down one side. She flicks the plait over her shoulder and turns on her heels. Without another word, she erupts into a blinding light.

When the pain in my eyes has subsided and the dark splotches in my vision have dissolved, it is just me, Mitchell, Medusa and Virgil.

"That was a risk, Viking," says Virgil. "Yet a sensible one. Your woman transformed, didn't she?"

"She did."

"Transformed . . . into what?" asks Medusa.

"The fear of traveling through a circle where the Unspeakables are continually burned caused your friend to suffer a Turning," replies Virgil, beckoning us on with a gnarled hand.

"A Turning?" asks Medusa.

"You have heard it before, Medusa," I say. "In the Dreamcatcher."

"I knew it was The Devil's voice!" says Mitchell. "His laugh. I hear it all the time. It makes me feel sick."

"Are you saying Elinor spoke with The Devil's voice?" asks Medusa.

"She did not just speak with his voice," replies Virgil. "I could sense the change in our surroundings, and the smell and taste of death, unlike any other. The peasant girl must have worn his face. I wanted...to see...," he murmurs.

Mitchell mouths his three favorite letters: *W*, *T*, and *F*. Medusa mouths the words in their entirety. I mouth the Viking translation. Why would Virgil want to see The Devil? He should be thankful he could not see the horror in Elinor we just witnessed. Just when I think our guide is becoming useful, he reminds me that he is actually the most unstable of us all.

The remaining members of Team DEVIL have reached the arch of the Sixth Circle. Virgil has already passed through. The reflections of bright-orange flames dance across the black stone. Medusa keeps opening her mouth like a fish, but nothing comes out. She is lost for words.

"Look. We're nearly halfway through the nine," says Mitchell encouragingly. "We have Jeanne now, too, and while she is the Afterlife's biggest pain in the ass, she's gonna help us."

"Are you sure about that?" growls a voice from the flaming shadows.

A Skin-Walker steps toward us. He seems to materialize from the fire. His wolf pelt is bristling with a black haze. Each individual hair—a mixture of black, gray and white—is standing on end. The head of a wolf is mounted atop his own. His long, black teeth are coated with what looks to be remnants of raw meat.

"We aren't protected anymore," whispers Medusa.

Wise Medusa is right. In sparing Elinor the torment of traveling through a circle where Unspeakables are constantly roasted in flames, we have left ourselves at the mercy of the Skin-Walkers.

And mercy is not a word in the Skin-Walkers' vocabulary.

"We just want passage through," says Mitchell bravely. "Virgil is our guide. We're looking for Beatrice Morrigan, the original Dreamcatcher."

"Fools," snarls the Skin-Walker. "Do you think an old man who had blackness in his heart before he died, and who found his piety too late, can lead you to what you want? Or where you want to go?"

"Virgil showed Dante," I reply, inching myself in front of Medusa.

"Dante was but one soul, and we took payment from him in the end," replies the Skin-Walker, licking his fleshy split lips with a black tongue. "We took his eyes when it was his time. Payment in kind."

"So you want payment from us?" I ask.

"You're not getting my eyes!" exclaims Mitchell. "I might not like having pink ones, but they're still mine."

"We'll take the girl," says the Skin-Walker, leering at Medusa. He takes a step toward her and we all take two steps back. "Cupidore may even let us have a taste first."

"There's only one," whispers Mitchell, turning his back to the Skin-Walker to talk to me. "Can you take him down with your..."

Mitchell trails off. His eyes widen as he peers over my right shoulder. I know he's not breathing, but his Adam's apple is bobbing as if it has been placed in water. His black pupils have dilated so much that just a sliver of pink surrounds them.

My own senses have betrayed me. They have become so acclimated to the rotten stench of death and decay in this forsaken place that I did not notice their silent arrival.

Behind us, slinking out of the dark like the monsters of the deep, are three more Skin-Walkers. The custodians of the Circles we have already passed through.

We are surrounded.

Átján

Alfarin and Elinor

"Is Hell, or Valhalla, what ye expected it to be, Alfarin?" asked Elinor. New devices called computers had been installed in devil resources, and I was attempting to connect a mouse to the back end of one. The pesky little creature would not comply and had already bitten me twice.

"Hell is not what I expected," I replied testily, my annoyance increasing. "I do not understand why there is always so much change, for one thing. What is wrong with paper and pen for record keeping? And how is a mouse supposed to help? Surely it will just eat its way through the records."

The cursed creature had run up my arm and was taking refuge in my armpit. As a result, I was squirming as if there were ants in my pants.

"Hell is not what I expected, either," replied Elinor. "When I was living, Hell was always spoken of as a place to be feared, but I like the structure here and knowing where I am in the bigger picture."

"I understand your sentiment, Elinor," I said. "If Hell means having to work for the rest of your existence, then I have nothing to fear. Vikings are born hardworking."

"And clearly ticklish," said Elinor, smiling. "Alfarin, ye picked up the wrong kind of mouse again, didn't ye?"

I nodded, abashed. I had made a mistake in the hardware—

again. Who was the imbecile who named the hard plastic device for controlling a computer a mouse? Why, it didn't even have whiskers. Unlike the little beastie that was now gnawing a hole in my tunic...

"Lift up yer arms, Alfarin," said Elinor. "I will get it out."

I did as I was instructed. Elinor had soft hands, and her fingers were gliding over my body like feathers as she played chase with the mouse. Elinor and I had hugged, and even walked arm in arm before, but this was terrifying and glorious. A woman was actually touching me. I wanted to suck in my stomach, for I wanted her to notice my muscles, but that just made my chest pump out like I had the bosoms of a woman. Elinor was giggling and talking to the mouse like it was a child as she chased it with her delicate hands; I was so self-conscious of the contact between us I forgot there was a mouse there at all.

I was fairly sure I couldn't even remember my name.

By the time Elinor had the creature hanging by its tail, my tunic was shredded and I was heaving with hiccups.

I was also rather keen for the mouse to go back to my armpit.

"I bet ye didn't think ye would be doing this in Valhalla," said Elinor, laughing as she placed the mouse on the ground. We watched the escapee from the laboratories scuttle off into a safe, dark crevice. Elinor turned her attention to smoothing what was left of my tunic. "But do ye wish, Alfarin, just occasionally, that ye could visit Up There?"

"Up There is not a domain that plays or weighs heavily in my dead heart, Elinor," I replied. "But I am aware that there are many devils in Hell who wish to at least visit kin and friends of old."

"I would love to see my brothers and sister again," said Elinor.

"Do you think passage between the two domains will be possible one day?" I asked. "I cannot see the master of Hell agreeing to that."

"I never saw open fields or unsullied landscapes when I was alive," said Elinor wistfully. "I have seen paintings and photographs now in books, but I lived in the crowded slums. I would like to sit atop a horse one day and just gaze out toward a horizon that never ends."

"Elinor, a horse has teeth larger than my great-aunt Dagmar's," I replied, watching her as she skillfully installed and then traversed the correct computer mouse across her new desk. "Never sit astride a beast with a mouth that can swallow you whole."

"It's just a thought," said Elinor. "Ye know, I think I can take on the extra work that's on offer from the housing administration team now that I have this computer ready to go. I will be able to check names of the dead in two places now, just to make sure. Ye should learn how to use one, too, Alfarin. Apparently they have games you can play, and you love sport, I know you do."

"The only sport I need is a good fight," I replied, picking the remnants of my tunic up off the floor. "And Hunt the Mouse will be today's quest."

"Oh, be off with ye," said Elinor, smiling. "He's already beaten ye once today. Do ye really want to repeat the exercise?"

I didn't tell Elinor that I actually did.

18. Plan C

Skin-Walkers from the four circles of treachery, fraud, violence and heresy have surrounded us. Perfidious, their leader, stands several inches taller than the others, but all have an aura of hatred swirling around them that assaults the senses. Perhaps their true nature is more defined here in their dwelling. The dark auras begin to manifest in shadows of the tormented Unspeakables begging and clawing for a way out. The shadows reach up the rock walls, as if they are almost escaping, and then they are dragged back down into the dark, swirling haze that surrounds the Skin-Walkers. The smell that emanates from the Skin-Walkers is so rank it pushes down on me. It is too overpowering to be categorized as one odor. It is toxic, bitter and sickening. It is a stench beyond that of rotting death.

My first thought is the preservation of my two friends, but that is closely followed by thankfulness that Elinor is not here. She has been threatened by Skin-Walkers before. I know Jeanne will keep her safe, even if her tongue is sharp while doing so.

Four Skin-Walkers. Three members of Team DEVIL. The odds are with the sickening wolf-men. Mitchell would sacrifice himself for Medusa in a dead heartbeat, but he is weaponless. Medusa is quick-thinking, but she is what the Skin-Walkers desire because of her close connection to the evil that courses through her Unspeakable stepfather, Rory Hunter. Virgil has already walked ahead of us into the Sixth Circle, but even if he were here, he is a blind old man who has knowledge of the Circles, nothing more.

I am armed, but I cannot take on four of Hell's first creations.

"I see fear in your bloodred eyes, Viking," says Perfidious. The wolf pelt on his head opens its mouth and shudders, as if it's laughing.

"Let us go on," I reply. "We have not come here to cause trouble for you."

The lone Skin-Walker standing behind us growls. "But we welcome trouble, don't we, Visolentiae?" it says. "And doesn't this one owe you a Minotaur?"

"The Viking would be a worthy replacement, Haeresilion," snarls the Skin-Walker called Visolentiae. "So much propensity for violence in one soul...It's a wonder he escaped eternity with me, considering how many of his murderous brethren I now have the pleasure of keeping so...*entertained* down here."

A shudder rends through my spine as I sense the Skin-Walker named Haeresilion sniffing the air behind me. Mitchell's right hand is now wrapped around the strap of his backpack. He has already slipped his left arm out of it. He could use that as a weight to smack a foe, but it would only serve to delay the fight, not stop it—and Medusa has no bag at all.

Then I feel an electric pulse against my spine. My skin is damp, for it is so hot, and the moisture acts as a conductor as the charge beats against my back, reminding me that I lived once. The sensation is strange, yet familiar. The pulsing makes me think of land and sea and the blue sky.

Yes, I lived once. For sixteen winters I walked the earth and breathed the air and lived in the company of loved ones, and took comfort in the memories and legends of those who had passed on.

Then I died, surrounded by strangers. I made my foolhardy choice to enter into battle alone, and that choice resulted in my death.

The thousand years since have afforded me plenty of time to ponder my death. To turn the details over and over in my mind. To learn from the maneuvers of those people and beasts who ultimately brought about my demise. And now, surrounded, outnumbered, and overpowered as we are by doglike demons, I have to smile, for I know Elinor would have something to say about déjà vu right about now.

As the Skin-Walkers inch closer, there is some comfort in knowing that my friends and I cannot die again. Still, I think we would all prefer to avoid being torn limb from limb. And fortunately, I have the power to lead my friends away from the danger now surrounding us.

I take a step back and beckon to Mitchell and Medusa to follow in the direction Virgil was guiding us. It puts us closer to the Skin-Walker from the circle of Heresy, but I need to at least catch a glimpse of the Sixth Circle if I am to get us out of this.

Both Mitchell and I have slipped our backpacks from our shoulders. The trio of Skin-Walkers in front of us are laughing, but the sound that comes from their mouths is like no laughter I have ever heard. It is a mixture of high-pitched choking and hacking and screaming.

The heat from the Sixth Circle is now blisteringly hot, and I fear I will start to stagger. But I continue to inch the others toward the Sixth Circle.

Mitchell is level with me. *Plan B*, he mouths.

Plan C, I mouth back.

I know my friend so well now I can preempt his swearing—and the choice of words.

Pressure is building in my head. It feels as if there is something inside it, pushing to get out. I can tell that Medusa is feeling it, too, because she is shaking her wild mane of hair and rubbing at her eyes. Haeresilion of the Sixth Circle has now joined his perverse brothers in their pack. The four of them are padding across the ground toward us, their movements deliberately slow, as if they're stalking prey. With no Skin-Walker now separating us from the Sixth Circle, we could turn and run.

We would be caught in seconds.

"Septimus has so much to answer for," says Perfidious. "But I am tiring of the game. Their fear of us is not what it was when I first met them."

"You can't hurt us," says Medusa bravely. "You know Septimus has Fabulara on his side."

"That Higher's name is not one to be thrown about lightly, girl," snaps the elongated mouth of Frausneet: the one Skin-Walker who had not spoken yet. "And the Highers do not take sides. We are the original denizens of Hell. We know Fabulara's mind and what it would take to bring her and the other Highers down."

I'm picking up the pace. The passageway between the Seventh and Sixth Circles has come to an end. We have now backed up past the spiked arch that leads into the Sixth Circle. The spikes are made from sharpened rib bones. The heat and fire have increased and the color of searing flame is burning into my eyes. I know that a warrior must have peripheral vision, but I simply can't afford to take my eyes off the Skin-Walkers.

Yet.

Mitchell, Medusa and I continue to move away, but to my relief, Virgil has now rejoined us. The old man has been cantankerous and unpleasant, but he is now our Oracle, and with Elinor separated from the group, I will need him. He must get closer to us, though, for Plan C to work.

"Where did you go?" whispers Mitchell.

"Hearing the voice of … The Devil was unnerving … I wanted to be … alone."

"You picked a great moment to leave us."

"I chose an even better one to return," snaps Virgil, sniffing and grimacing.

Perfidious is growling to Visolentiae. It is not the language of dogs, but it is not a tongue I recognize, either.

I don't have much time. We are finally in the Sixth Circle. It is a cavern, filled with burning stone tombs that look like enormous ovens. Each one has an opening in the center, about five feet off the ground, that is barred. Beyond the barred window, deep in the flames, are the flailing limbs, faces, and torsos of those being burned for all eternity. I give silent thanks to the Norse gods that Jeanne and Elinor did not tarry here. The smell of burning flesh is like festering food and excrement.

"I'm gonna puke!" cries Mitchell, but he remains stoic in the sight of such horror and shouts out for Beatrice Morrigan, gagging on each syllable as he calls.

This is the smallest circle so far. Almost immediately I can see that the only movement in the circle comes from within the burning tombs. Beatrice Morrigan is not here.

And across the way, through the warped haze of the fires, I can see the exit to the passageway that will take us to the Fifth Circle.

"I say we watch them burn," calls a Skin-Walker. Three unnatural voices bark their approval.

"Virgil!" I cry. "Catch!"

My axe spins through the air toward the guide. All four Skin-Walkers immediately fall into a defensive position. Their gums retract, baring sharp fangs as their necks snap toward Virgil.

I quickly slip my hand into my backpack and pull out the Viciseometer. Mitchell has the quickest reflexes of us all, and he lunges to grab Virgil by the arm.

"Hold on!" I roar. I have no time to adjust the time and date, but that shouldn't matter. I press down on the large red button on top of the Viciseometer.

Flames that do not burn rush over us. A single scream accompanies us through the dark-gray smoke that surrounds us. This is my first time being the official bearer of the Viciseometer, and it throbs against my skin, almost burrowing into my hand. Although my eyes have been pushed far back into my head, I can still see my axe, shining like a shooting star as we are pushed through space and time.

The landing is hard, and the sudden flood of glorious color that fills my vision after the fire and brimstone of the Sixth Circle threatens to kick-start my heart. The plan worked.

"Where the Hell are we?" groans Mitchell.

"Are you okay, Medusa?" I ask. "You screamed. Did I hurt you?"

Medusa's pale-pink eyes are wide and unblinking. She purses her lips into a tight, flat line and shakes her head.

"I just wasn't expecting…we left. Holy crap, Alfarin. Where are we?"

I have brought Mitchell, Medusa and Virgil to the only place I could visualize at that moment.

Valhalla.

Not the Valhalla in Hell where my kin dwell. This is the Valhalla I saw when I was taken from my dead body in the Seventh Circle. The magnificent hall of gold is exactly the same, although the Valkyrie-harpy that tried to tempt me is no longer here.

Is my mother here?

There is a rumbling coming through the stone. The vibration of feet and hooves and wheels.

"Alfarin, where the Hell did you bring us?" asks Mitchell again. "What's the date?"

"This is the true Valhalla," I reply, looking down at the flames flickering around the Viciseometer in my hand. "I was shown a vision of it in the Seventh Circle. I knew I could get us away from the Skin-Walkers. I just needed a diversion, and my axe provided. You caught well, Virgil."

"I am impressed, Viking," says Virgil, straightening his red skullcap. "It is not often the Skin-Walkers are outmaneuvered in their own domain."

But his praise falls on deaf ears. Something is wrong. When I look down at the timepiece in my hand, the date in the Viciseometer is not the date I was expecting.

"It has been used since," I say to Medusa, holding out the Viciseometer.

"Used since what?" asks Medusa, flinching away as if the device is contaminated. "And what is that noise? It feels like an earthquake."

"To my knowledge, the last time this Viciseometer was used, it was to bring all of us back to Hell from Aotearoa. I assumed that was the date we were working with, because I did not have the time to change it back in the Sixth. And I thought that if I used that date, then some of the Skin-Walkers would be stuck in a fixed point in time and would not be able to follow us. But the date in the timepiece is different."

"So it's been used again since we gave it back," says Mitchell. "So what?"

"It is important," I reply, "because it means someone else within Hell is, or was, time-traveling. To this moment specifically. Somewhere."

"Alfarin, I don't care," replies Mitchell. "It's probably The Devil going to set off some world disaster or something. You said this was Plan C—so what's the rest of it? We have to get Eleanor and Jeanne. We can't just leave them in the Nine Circles. And we still haven't found that damned Banshee."

"That damned Banshee has a name," says Virgil, sniffing the air. "And I can smell blood. War has started."

Medusa has wandered over to one of the windows. As she does, the eagle atop the arched stonework takes flight and glides outside.

"Alfarin," calls Medusa. "You've got to see this."

The hall of Valhalla is shaking more violently now. Tiny shards of golden dust are cascading down from the ceiling of shields. The spears that form the arches are bending as the crescendo of noise from outside increases.

"What is that?" asks Mitchell as the three of us crowd around the window. "Is this a battle from your past, Alfarin?"

"No," I reply, showing him the Viciseometer. "Look at the four numbers that have been input for the year."

"We're in the future," gasps Mitchell. "Whoever is time-traveling is going into the future, although not far."

"And this is must be Ragnarök," I reply. "The battle has begun. My friends... this is the end of all days."

Nitján

Alfarin and Elinor...and Mitchell

While I was secure in my position of importance as a Viking prince in Hell, there were occasions when I doubted my devilish manhood. These occasions concerned gainful employment in Hell. For many years—in fact, ever since I had offended my father by not forcing Elinor Powell into marriage—I had washed and dried glasses in my cousin Thomason's bar. There were times when I stretched my job description, for on my watch, *washed and dried* more often than not meant *smashed and swept*. My strength was legendary—but unfortunately, so was my ineptitude when it came to handling anything delicate. Sometimes it seemed as if I could knock a glass off the counter just by looking at it. I was sure the nefarious shadows that plagued Hell aided and abetted the breakage.

And Vikings drank out of tankards anyway. Or barrels. Who was the fool who decided devils should have access to vessels made of brittle minerals?

Should I have had greater ambitions for employment? Elinor had been doing such a wonderful job in devil resources that she was asked to help out in the housing administration office a few days a week. She was an inspiration to all, including Vikings. It did not take long for her new employers to request a permanent transfer. At first, I thought Elinor would be unhappy with the change—she had wanted to move into devil resources for so long—but she welcomed it. She claimed she could seek what she was looking for more easily in housing.

I did not realize that Elinor's search was not, in fact, for family, but for another, unrelated male until the day we met Mitchell Johnson.

The housing administration department was located on the lower floors of the central business district—levels 427 to 452, to be exact. Many devils would have seen moving to a lower floor as a demotion, but not Elinor. She had a purpose, and there was a skip in her step as I walked her back to her dormitory. Her spirits were higher than I'd seen them in a long time, even though I knew her wrist ached after spending hours on end moving a plastic mouse around her desk.

Once more, I cursed the inventor of that stupid, confusing device, and wondered who he was. Probably the same fool who allowed glass into Thomason's. I would have liked to have made a "cocktail" from his bodily parts.

I was lost in my own thoughts and did not register Elinor's words at first. I came to regret my folly when I received a jab to the stomach from a pointed finger.

"Alfarin, are ye listening to me?"

"Of course."

"So what did I just say?"

"You were saying that you were glad that Swiss person won the glorious match of Wimbledon in the land of the living this year."

"No, I was not," scolded Elinor. "I was saying that I wanted to stop by the H1N1 accommodation block."

"I heard the word *won*. At least give me credit for that," I replied sheepishly.

"Wrong version of the word, Alfarin," replied Elinor, sticking her lovely little freckled nose in the air. "I said *one*, not *won*."

"I am confused."

"I mean O-N-E instead of—oh, never mind. Just make a path

to H1N1," said Elinor. "We will be here all night at this rate, and ye know ye cannot cope without dinner. I will give ye my share as a thank-you."

"Your wish is my command." And I started to swing my arms from left to right, bowling devils out of the way with ease. It was fun, and once I had momentum on my side, it took me a while to stop.

H1N1 was a new block that had been built for those devils who had died in the year 2009. The expanse of terrified white eyes going in and out of that dormitory reminded me of marshmallows... which reminded me of dessert... which reminded me of dinner.

Burgers or curry for dinner? Or fajitas or roast chicken? These were the important questions.

"Alfarin, ye are doing it again."

"No, I am not."

"What did I just say?"

"You wanted to borrow a book?"

"I said I just wanted to have a look," replied Elinor, her exasperation rising right along with my need for sustenance. "Can ye wait with me? It shouldn't be long."

"I will wait with you for eternity, my princess," I said as my stomach made a desperate noise of longing for fajitas. "But what are you looking for?"

Elinor usually blushed when I called her my princess and would affectionately call me an oaf. I had started doing so after the incident with the mouse. I had read up on words of endearment for women. I wanted to woo Elinor properly in the ways befitting a lady. But on this occasion there was no blushing and no oafing. She did not answer my question at all. Her flaming ruby eyes were transfixed on a tall, thin male with blond spiky hair and eyes that were already turning pink around the edges. He was walking into the building.

Elinor hurried after him. Although I had promised my princess to wait outside, I had no intention of leaving her to chase after some strange male alone, even if he was puny. I rushed in after her and found her in a hallway, sneaking peeks into a dormitory room. I joined her outside the doorway.

Her quarry was sitting on the edge of his bed, which he was sharing with two other devils, who were both sobbing.

He was not crying or wailing or making any desperate sound. The male looked confused. He was only wearing one sneaker. Perhaps counting to two is beyond his capability, I thought maliciously. What is so special about this new devil, and why has he captivated my Elinor in such a way?

Sensing my discomfiture, Elinor slipped her arm through mine.

"That is Mitchell Johnson," she whispered. "And he is going to be our friend."

19. A Future Foretold

"What is Ragnarök, Alfarin?" asks Mitchell.

"Ragnarök is the battle to end all battles," I reply. "Gods, Valkyrie, men, women and monsters will fall as the destruction of all worlds comes about. It is a story I have grown up hearing. It is as much a part of me as my axe, my beard and my need to box the ears of Saxon scum."

The urge to join the conflict before us is so strong I feel it physically pulling me.

"Alfarin," says Medusa sharply. "We have to go back to the Circles."

"This is my destiny," I say. I hear my voice echo in the hall, even above the din of battle, but it is detached from my soul.

"Alfarin, you can't even be sure this is Ragnarök," says Mitchell. "It could just be another fight."

"It is Ragnarök," says Virgil. "In the Seventh Circle, the Valkyrie must have tempted you with a vision and you remembered it, Viking."

The old man is standing with his head bent back, as if he's gazing up at the golden shields on the roof. Their magnificence reflects on his translucent skin, bathing it with a golden glow.

"That's insane!" exclaims Mitchell. "The Valkyries weren't even in the Seventh Circle. What Alfarin saw was a hallucination brought about by…by…anger, or witchcraft, or just sheer batshit craziness caused by the fact that he was fighting a Minotaur."

Medusa attempts to placate Mitchell by laying her hand on his arm, but I think Virgil is right. It was too real to be just a vision, and we're here now.

It was real.

"I wish you could see Valhalla, Virgil," I say.

"I do not require eyes to see," he replies, with a smile that shows off his crooked teeth and pink gums. "Sometimes the pictures in one's head are enough. And as long as they're in my head, I can enhance reality and dilute the horror. In other words, I control it, and that is all anyone wants in the end. The Devil taught me that."

"Do you know The Devil, Virgil?" asks Medusa. "Have you met?"

"A long time ago."

Virgil slowly turns his face away from the ceiling and walks to us. He seems less decrepit here, as if the halls of my fathers are healing him from the terrible effects of aging.

"Ragnarök is called that by Vikings, but it is also known by other names," says Virgil. "The coming of Kalki; the beginning of the Messianic age; the Apocalypse…"

Virgil's voice reaches me as if it is traveling through a long tunnel. I am becoming more and more detached from my surroundings. I can taste the adrenaline of fear and the sweetness of victory. Out the window, I see that the expanse of green fields I saw here before is now teeming with trebuchets, men and women dressed in armor that flashes like lightning. Black smokes rises into the sky, twisting and flailing, as if it, too, is fighting for existence. And in the distance, a large black shadow, like a cloud that is touching the ground, is creeping toward the advancing army.

The battle is taking place in the air as well. Searing balls of crimson fire shoot in arcs from the trebuchets as glimmering tornadoes, barely visible against the brilliant cornflower-blue sky twist along the ground. The targets become recognizable only when outlined by the smoke. They are human-like, with no discernible sex, flying through the atmosphere in vortexes of wind.

The shadow in the east creeps ever closer.

My mother said she left me for a higher purpose. Was Ragnarök that purpose? Is Valencia out there, waging war? Her ghost mocked me so cruelly before, but if this is where the missing piece of my dead heart resides, I still wish to know.

My heart. It weighs so heavily. How can I feel it still when it does not beat?

Then, in the distance, on a raised ledge of chalk-white rock, I see *her*. I would know that flaming red hair anywhere. It whips in the wind as she surveys the scene, and despite the horrors before her, she has never looked lovelier. Next to her is a man I normally see in pinstripes. The Roman general is dressed in body armor. Suddenly, the questions *how* and *why* are not important. All that matters is *now*.

The sweet sensation of destiny is spreading through my entire body, but as I start to allow it to envelop me, I can hear her voice talking about fate. If this is a future not yet come to pass, that means we are—or might be—successful in our current mission. It means it is possible that Elinor endures.

Elinor has always believed in fate.

I allow myself a smile. There are no pieces of my heart missing. It is whole. Completely and utterly whole. I realize, suddenly, that I no longer feel ownership of it. It belongs absolutely and unequivocally to my sweet, wise and brave princess.

This is the future—it must be. Which means this is not my time—our time—to join the battle. More must be done in order for this day to happen. I look down at the Viciseometer, pulsing with a new, excited intensity. I memorize the date.

It is not long now. I will remember. I have to remember. For this is *my* higher purpose: Ragnarök. I was destined to end my days in this place.

Medusa is still trembling beside me, unaware that the wheels in my head are spinning faster than the balls of fire being launched by the trebuchets. "I don't like this, Alfarin," she says. "We don't belong here."

"It's bad enough visiting the past, Alfarin," adds Mitchell. "But this, if this is the future, then we definitely shouldn't be here."

My friends are right, especially Mitchell. His death was caused by time travel. He saw his dead self from across the street and died because of the paradox created.

I've waited my whole existence for Ragnarök—but I can wait a little longer.

"Hold on to me," I say. "I am taking us back to the Sixth Circle. Now, listen to me carefully, for our fate is truly in our hands now. The moment we return, we must run as if The Devil himself is chasing us. Do not look back. There is every chance you will see yourselves."

"I don't understand," says Medusa. "What about El and Jeanne?"

"I am creating a paradox," I reply. I smile at Mitchell. "I am learning."

"We trust you, Alfarin," replies Mitchell, placing his arm around Medusa's waist. "Just get us away from the Skin-Walkers and back to Elinor and Jeanne."

With one last, longing look toward the soul I know so well in the distance, I input the dates that will take us back to the domain of the Skin-Walkers.

"Mitchell, what does your watch say is the current time?" I ask.

He shows me the timepiece on his wrist. I make a strategic calculation and start changing the minute hand on the Viciseometer.

"You're taking us back in time," says Medusa knowingly, watching my cumbersome movements as I manipulate the device with its fine needle.

"Not by long," I reply. "But enough to make a difference."

It is to their credit that neither Mitchell nor Medusa questions my motives or strategy. I am grateful. Both have been bearers of the Viciseometer, and their skill and dexterity with the timepiece was something I held in awe. My fingers are the size of sausages, and while they are perfect for grasping the handle of a weapon or sneaking the dregs of a tankard of ale, they are not suited to the delicacy required for inputting dates and times into an intricate time-traveling device.

Why are my fingers sweating so much? It is as if I have glands of grease secreting under my skin.

I visualize the Sixth Circle, but not the area we departed from. I picture where I wanted to be just before we left the circle. Past the flaming tombs, there was a circular platform. It was a landmark not to forget because it was edged with a line of skulls. And beyond it was the exit that I had spotted through the haze.

I see it appear in the face of the Viciseometer. I do not need to shout to the others to hold on because we are already clinging to one another. Even Virgil has accepted Medusa's hand.

Fighting the urge to take one last look at the battle outside, I press the large red button. We are swept up into a warm vortex of wind. My axe reminds me of who I am as it vibrates in my hand. A Viking. A man. A devil. Mitchell's comforting arm is around my shoulders. It has been strange to use this device without Elinor beside me. In all our time travel, I had become used to the smell of her hair tickling my nose. Apple and mint.

We land together on the skull platform. My friends and Virgil have not forgotten my words, and we run for the passageway that will lead us to the Fifth Circle. We pass two columns made of black stone and bloodstained skulls. Only when we are through do Mitchell and Medusa stop running and whip their heads around, searching.

"Where are Elinor and Jeanne?" cries Mitchell. "They aren't here."

"If my calculations are correct..." I start counting with my fingers in the air.

I get to twelve before a streak of golden light rushes past us. Jeanne and Elinor appear.

"Alfarin!" cries Elinor. She throws herself into my arms and buries her head in my chest, and I want to roar with happiness that my Elinor is safe and herself once more. "How are ye here? We only just left ye!"

The Viciseometer is still in my hand. Elinor gazes at it reverently. I only have eyes for her.

"Ye time-traveled?"

"Four of the Skin-Walkers surrounded us the second Jeanne took you through the Sixth," says Mitchell. "Which means they're still back there. We should hurry."

"But we have Elinor with us now," I say. "Which means they will not attempt to take us again—not while we stay together. They fear her."

"Can someone please explain what we just did?" cries Medusa. "Am I in another paradox?"

"You are—but you will not disappear, Medusa," I reply. "I created a loop in time. One that bypasses most of the Sixth Circle for me, you, Mitchell and Virgil. I took us to the other destination to give us time to come here, just a few moments ahead of our other selves."

"So we're back at the beginning of the Sixth Circle just about to disappear in front of the Skin-Walkers right now, but the loop in time has brought us here, via Valhalla?" asks Medusa, her face screwed up in concentration.

I nod.

"That was genius quick thinking, Alfarin," says Mitchell, slapping my back. "You have paradoxes *owned*. Now, are you going to tell us about that battle, or do we not want to know?"

"What battle?" asks Jeanne immediately.

"Ye time-traveled to Valhalla, Alfarin?" inquires Elinor. "The one back in Hell?"

"These questions are to be answered another time," I reply. I slip the Viciseometer into my pocket. "We must stay on mission. The Banshee is here somewhere, and we must find her. But Jeanne, I am glad to have you standing by my side. I have seen the future. We must put our trust in Lord Septimus."

––––––

Yes, I have seen the future, and I am thankful for it. For in that glimpse, I have seen Elinor, and if that future comes to pass, that means that she not only survives our search for the Banshee, but she becomes a warrior.

A Valkyrie.

Tuttugu

Alfarin, Elinor and Mitchell

"Go and speak to him, Alfarin," urged Elinor.

I folded my arms across my chest—a chest that was far more impressive than that of the puny-looking specimen across from us—and scowled.

"I will not," I replied.

"Please, Alfarin."

"If I am not enough devil for you, Elinor, then I will accept the slight to my character, albeit with bad grace," I said. "But I will not invite another man to take my place. I have my honor and my pride. And my plate of pie and gravy—which is getting cold while we have this nonsensical conversation."

"But he looks so alone," said Elinor sadly. "I thought he came in here with someone . . . a girl . . . but I must have been wrong."

Elinor looked confused. She did that a lot, but then, so did I. Ever since the new millennium, our memories had become slightly foggy around the edges. It was as if we were seeing things through a veil. We discussed our symptoms at length, and I even went so far as to ask my father, King Hlif, about it.

My father said Thomason's beer did that to everyone, but since Elinor and I rarely drank, my father's words did little to ease my discomfiture that somehow, something in my immortal existence had changed. And I did not know what it was.

The male we were following around to and fro was Mitchell Johnson. He had recently been hired as The Devil's intern, and he worked on the very first level of the central business district in Hell.

Level 1 or level 666—I did not care for these details. With his short blond hair, he looked like an elongated nail brush. His body seemed so feeble that I was sure I would meet more resistance running my axe through a toothpick.

Jealousy was not an impressive emotion. I did know this. And I did not like it in myself. Jealousy made Vikings weak—and I was becoming insanely jealous of the attention Elinor Powell was showing Mitchell Johnson. Her obsession was from a distance, but what would happen once they started to speak? Mitchell Johnson would surely fall under her Valkyrie-like spell, too.

So I kept the blade of my axe better sharpened than usual.

———

All that changed one evening as I was walking Elinor home from the housing administration office. The crush in the corridors of Hell was unbearable. Something had happened to cause panic, and devils were getting trampled and crushed. It was occurring more and more as rumors of a passage out of the Underworld spread faster than the sickness we came down with after Cousin Odd licked all the glasses at Thomason's.

Elinor tried to keep hold of my arm in the melee, but we were torn asunder by the sheer number of devils. I saw her being pushed closer and closer to the balcony of level 180, where the kitchens were. Fate was already working against us. We could not remember why we had gravitated toward that level, and it was here that the stampede had started.

My axe was already pressed against my chest; I could not move anything except my head and my mouth. The latter was yelling for someone to help Elinor as she started to rise above the crowd. So many were being trampled that those closest to the edge were being pushed upward by the pressure.

Then a hand appeared from nowhere and grabbed Elinor's wrist from the back of her neck. She was too scared to cry out. I saw her red eyes widen, and then she disappeared from view and my frantic voice became lost on the wave of thousands more.

It was many hours before I found her. She was with Mitchell Johnson, and he was trying to get her to eat strawberry cheesecake. He looked up as I approached. Fear flashed across his face at the sight of my axe, but I was so relieved at seeing Elinor safe and well that I no longer wanted to crush his nose with my fist. In fact, I wanted to crush him in a bear hug of gratitude.

"She's all right," said Mitchell Johnson in a voice that had an American accent. "Which is more than can be said for some of the others. I didn't know dead bodies could be that flexible. But Elinor's been checked over by the healers and given a clean bill of health—uh, it is Elinor, isn't it?"

"Mitchell saved me, Alfarin," said Elinor. "I thought I was going over the edge, but he was there. It was fate."

I wasn't entirely pleased about it, but I knew my duty as a Viking. "I am forever in your debt, Master Johnson," I replied, going down on one knee. "From this day forth, my axe will be your willing accomplice, ever ready to hack the fingers from the unworthy hand of those who mistake you for a washing-up utensil."

"What the—"

"It is okay, Mitchell," said Elinor. "Alfarin is the best friend a devil could have. And thank ye for the cheesecake."

"Don't mention it," replied Mitchell, continuing to look at my axe nervously. "I don't know who makes the cheesecakes in the kitchens, but they're the best. Septimus swears by them. He's always getting me to come down here and get one for him. It's just lucky I was here when you were. Or unlucky, if you count the poor bastards who went over the edge."

"Would you like to join us for dinner, Master Johnson?" I asked.

"It's the least I can do to thank you for saving my princess from plummeting into the abyss."

Mitchell smiled. I was pleased that he was not fawning over Elinor like some lovestruck fool, but was instead caring for her in a way that a brother might.

"That'd be cool," replied Mitchell. "If you don't mind, Elinor?"

"Ye absolutely must," said Elinor. "I insist."

"Pizza or Chinese?" asked Mitchell. "Or what about Indian?"

"My ironclad constitution could take a hot curry right now," I replied. "Or what about meat pie…or noodles…or a good hog roast?"

"Pancakes and eggs…or triple cheeseburger and fries…," said Mitchell.

"Not another boy obsessed with his stomach!" cried Elinor as Mitchell and I started to walk away.

As we stepped over the clothes and other belongings that had been abandoned in the stampede, I asked, "Do you have a lady friend, Master Johnson? We could happily accommodate her in our plans tonight, too."

"Nah," replied Mitchell. "No one…no one special." But his face was screwed up with the same quizzical look that Elinor and I saw on each other's faces more and more often. Then Mitchell smiled. "And forget this Master Johnson stuff. It's Mitchell Johnson, four syllables and nothing more."

A fellowship had been born in death.

20. The Way Out

"Alfarin, what will we find in the Fifth Circle?" asks Mitchell as we continue our journey to find The Devil's Banshee.

"The Fifth is for those who committed heinous acts in anger," I reply.

"Heinous acts in anger…," Mitchell repeats from the rear of our group. "And how, exactly, is that different from the circle for the violent?"

"Those with a predisposition to violence enjoy it," replies Virgil. "The Unspeakables in the Seventh Circle still have that propensity in their black hearts. The Unspeakables in the Fifth are different. For them, anger or wrathfulness is an emotion that wanes after the moment has passed. They may even feel remorse for the actions that come as a result of their anger. But no matter what, if their rage leads to the death of another, then the Fifth Circle is where they will forever dwell. For instance, many of your so-called *keepers of the peace* reside here in eternal suffering."

"*So-called* keepers of the peace?" asks Elinor.

"You mean like the people who carry out the death penalty?" says Mitchell. "They're angry because a life has been taken, and so they do the exact same thing, but they can hide behind the law?"

"Indeed," replies Virgil.

"Does that mean Jeanne will find her tormentors here?" asks Medusa.

"No, my murderers were in the last circle," replies Jeanne. "I was burned foremost for my beliefs, and in anger second."

"Jeez, even in this place there's administration and hierarchy," says Mitchell. "So how are the Unspeakables who killed in anger punished, Virgil?"

"Here you will find the never-ending swamp of the River Styx," replies our guide. "The Unspeakables are contained within its murky, poisonous depths. We will have to cross the swamp by boat."

"Like in the movies?" asks Mitchell, and he stops walking the second he voices his question. "Oh, sorry, I forget sometimes that you guys didn't die at the same time as me. You wouldn't have seen it represented in the movies. But there are a lot of them."

"Were you ever going to reveal yourself to us?" I ask Jeanne as we continue to walk along a narrow tunnel lined with flaming torches ensconced in openmouthed skulls.

"General Septimus instructed me to assist only if it appeared your team was in peril," she replies in her thick French accent. "I am, after all, supposed to be locked up, and revealing myself, even in the Nine Circles, puts me at risk of The Devil's further wrath."

"But how did you know where we were?" asks Medusa. "We didn't exactly enter the Circles in a traditional way."

"Indeed. I was not expecting your guide to conjure up another entrance in order to escape the Skin-Walkers. I was not aware he could do that. It was fortuitous that I had not gone on to the true entrance, but was listening in as General Septimus led you to Virgil. I watched you enter through the stone. And I followed."

"Are you Lord Septimus's spy?" I ask. "Mitchell has long believed that he has an angel working for him."

"I am no spy," snaps Jeanne. "Although I now know who General Septimus's eyes in Heaven belonged to. I am here for self-preservation and the return of my rightful place only."

"So who is the spy?" asks Mitchell.

"That is for General Septimus to reveal, not I."

"But you believe Lord Septimus will get you back Up There?" I ask.

"No, Viking," replies Jeanne. "This *is* the way back to Heaven for me."

"Maid of Orléans," says Virgil with a sigh. "You should not have told them that."

"This is a way to *Up There?*" exclaims Mitchell. "Are you kidding me? So Up There is the same as Dante's Paradise? I would have thought Paradise would at least have food."

"This is a route that few know of, and even fewer use," replies Virgil. "Only the bravest—and most foolish—even attempt it."

"So, in return for helping us endure the Nine Circles," I say to Jeanne, "Lord Septimus told you of another path to return to Up There. Why have you not just left us and gone on alone?"

"I am no devil," replies Jeanne. I know she speaks the truth, which is why I do not have the heart to inform her that her milky-white eyes have acquired the tiniest hint of pink. "I am not a monster to be locked up in Down There's asylum, either," she adds, glaring at me. "I did not leave you because I believed General Septimus would make good on his promise to help me. But I knew that if he heard that I failed you…"

Jeanne trails off. Is that a brief flash of fear I see in her pale-blush eyes? She is not scared of The Devil or even the Skin-Walkers. She is fearful of Lord Septimus. What did he say to her?

"But Up There banished you, Jeanne," says Medusa. "How do you know they won't just return you the second you go back? Assuming you even do make it back?"

"I have to at least try," replies the French warrior.

"Then we will help ye," says Elinor quietly. "We know ye do not like us—"

"—and the feeling is mutual," mutters Mitchell, and Medusa elbows him in the ribs.

"—but we admire ye. And ye saved me back there," continues Elinor. "We will help her, won't we, Alfarin?"

"We will," I say distractedly. As the tunnel ahead ahead widens and opens into the Fifth Circle, I find it is not the flailing bodies thrashing about in the expansive swamp I focus on, but rather, a sight in my mind's eye: a green field, teeming with warriors and blood.

How does this scene from the future come to pass? Does it, in fact, come to pass? I want in my heart to believe it does, but I have to wonder, where are Mitchell, Medusa and I in that future? I look around and see that Mitchell and Medusa are now walking so close together they could be sewn into the same cloth. Suddenly, I wish more than anything that I could see how this ends for Team DEVIL. Not just our quest to find Beatrice Morrigan, but our existence. For there has to be an end—it was foretold in the tale of Ragnarök. The dead not worthy of existing simply cease to be.

An analogy comes to mind. The Highers are the chess masters, and we are all pawns being positioned for their entertainment.

A cold, harsh laugh, like a pickaxe scratching across ice, blows through the tunnel. No one cries out in alarm—we are all becoming desensitized to the sights and sounds of horror now—but the hairs on the back of my neck buzz with static and my beard tingles in a way that is unpleasant. Bile rises in my throat.

Fabulara isn't here—I can't smell her, for one thing—but she can hear me, and she wants us—me—to know she is listening.

The Fifth Circle spreads out before us. We stand in a line on the edge of the murky brown swamp. It appears to go on forever into the distance. Twisted hands and feet splash about in the depths as soundless bodies writhe to escape. I can see no beasts keeping them at bay, but when an Unspeakable appears to be on the verge of escaping the brown water and climbing out onto glistening black rock, something in the depths drags the tormented one back down. It is yet another realm filled with cyclical suffering.

"How do we get across?" asks Elinor, slipping her hand into mine in an easy intimacy that I welcome after the trials our friendship has recently suffered.

"On that," I reply, pointing to a smoky dark-gray shadow that is inching its way toward us across the brown sludge.

As it gets closer, the vessel and its pilot become clearer. The vessel itself is wooden, like a normal rowing boat, but without oars or embellishment, save for a single skull fixed to the front like a grotesque figurehead. The muscular man punting it through the swamp with a single pole is naked, save for a tattered and torn red cloak around his neck. His tanned skin glistens with sweat.

"Oh my!" exclaims Elinor, blushing. "Can we not pass him some of yer spare pants, Alfarin?"

"Virgil," calls the man in a deep baritone voice. "It has been many years, old man. I was beginning to believe you had begged for your eyes back and gotten released from your fate."

"Phlegyas," replies Virgil. "I am as likely to be released from my bonds as you are from yours."

"We aren't all going to fit into that boat," whispers Mitchell, jerking his head back the way we came. "And we have company in the shadows."

I turn around and can see the black, distorted haze of the Skin-Walkers moving back down the tunnel. Elinor the Dream-catcher is our defense, but Mitchell is right, we will need to make the journey across the Styx in two groups. Elinor cannot be split in two, meaning one group is going to be left defenseless.

As if she is reading my mind, Jeanne crosses her arms and scowls at me.

"Do not even think to ask," she says. "I cannot turn it on and off at will. Only if one or more of you is in grave peril am I able to immolate."

"Yet you took Elinor?" I say.

Jeanne looks away. I see her mouth tremble.

No. Jeanne's mouth does not quiver; she is mouthing a single word.

Fire.

Jeanne immolated not because Elinor was in grave peril, but to help her avoid her worst nightmare. The French warrior has empathy in that hard soul of hers. Which means I do not believe her when she says she can only immolate if one or more of us is in grave peril.

I want to call her out on it, but I hold back. Warriors are also strategists. I want Jeanne on our side. This is a risk with the Skin-Walkers stalking us through the Circles, but the Seventh Circle has taught me to control my anger.

I will take some good out of this wretched place if I can.

"You can try to hide it, Jeanne, but I know you care about us," says Medusa quietly. She must have seen Jeanne mouth the word, too.

"Do not flatter yourself," replies Jeanne, but at this, Medusa gives herself a little private smile. I think she understands Jeanne's troubles better than anyone, and the Maid of Orléans is less harsh with Medusa than with the rest of us.

"There are six of you," says the naked man called Phlegyas. "For payment, I will take three at a time to the other side."

"And how much gold do you require?" I ask, hoping that Mitchell and Medusa packed money as well as rope. From their confident demeanor, I am happy to assume they did.

The naked man cocks his head to the side and sniffs at the air. I am reminded of Virgil, although I do not believe the ferryman is blind, for his eyes are the deepest of red.

"I do not need gold," replies Phlegyas. "For what would I spend it on?"

"Then what is your price?" I say. "Quickly, man. We do not have time to tarry on the shore of such a forsaken place. We must cross to the other side."

"I sense you have something more precious than gold, Viking," says Phlegyas, raising an eyebrow with knowing intent.

My immediate thought goes to Elinor. She is not my possession, but I will not allow anyone to take her. My countenance must have reflected my thoughts, because Phlegyas smiles at me. He knows exactly what I was thinking.

"No, Viking," he says, shaking his head. "You have a greater jewel on your person than even that lovely creature holding fast to you. To ferry you across the Styx, I want that timepiece you carry. I want the Viciseometer."

Tuttugu ok Ein

Alfarin, Elinor and Mitchell

A new friendship was born. While my adoration of Elinor continued to grow, I was the first to admit that having another male in our friendship group was healthy. It was good to talk blood, sport and women.

And Mitchell did me a favor, possessing as he did the silhouette of a spoon. Next to him, my girth was even more impressive.

Mitchell introduced me to a game called soccer. Eleven players would kick a ball up and down until a goal was scored by placing it in a net. We procured a full team from my brethren and the males in Mitchell's dormitory who were not jabbering wrecks. I found it exhausting, even though there were few places to run around unhindered in Hell. I discovered I performed best in the position of goalie. Few could get a ball past me and my hands—and the fact that my axe often deflated the balls meant we were unbeaten for the season.

To reciprocate this manly bonding time that Mitchell offered me, I introduced him to a game called Hunt the Heathen Saxons and Watch Them Choke on Their Entrails. If I had not seen my new friend devour several hamburgers, his reaction to the game would have given me cause to believe he was vegetarian. Mitchell certainly had a bad case of swooning around thick dead blood.

And Saxon blood was very thick—just like their skulls.

Mitchell became like a brother to me, but it was clear he was lonely. He had died after being hit by a bus: a large metal beast that was used in the modern world for transporting people too lazy to march or row to their intended destination. Time and time again, Elinor and I tried to find him a woman, and there was no shortage of applicants. Mitchell was widely regarded by female devils as handsome, in an unconventional way that did not involve facial hair. The buxom wench Patricia Lloyd could barely keep her hands off Mitchell whenever the three of us ventured into the library. After a while, Mitchell stopped coming with us.

Mitchell's disconsolation in this regard came to the fore one night at the burger bar. He had procured a camera—an inanimate object that could capture a single moment in a frozen image—from Lord Septimus. Elinor was fascinated by it and was directing me and Mitchell to create scenes that made her laugh. We were only too happy to oblige, for Elinor's laugh was like music: another area where the talented Mitchell excelled.

"Place yer arms around each other," called Elinor as a huge plate of fries was delivered to our table.

"No wonder I can't get a girlfriend," muttered Mitchell. "I swear devils in here think the three of us are in some kind of ménage à trois."

"That sounds like a dessert," I replied. "I would like to try it."

Mitchell started choking; I think he had a fry lodged in his throat. I slapped his back so hard that his face was propelled into the plate. When he pulled himself back up, a fry was stuck up each nostril. Then I laughed so hard, my control over my bladder almost forsook me. Mitchell retaliated by placing fries up *my* nose.

Elinor passed the camera to another devil and joined us at the table.

"I want to record this moment," she announced, throwing her

arms around me. "And Alfarin"—she glared at me—"it is customary to say 'pardon me' when ye expel gas."

"That was not me," I replied indignantly. "It was Mitchell."

"It wasn't me, either," he said. "I thought it was Elinor."

We laughed for the camera, but I could not help noticing that Mitchell had raised his fingers to his shoulders in the same way I had in order to grasp Elinor's hands.

Mitchell's long fingers found nothing but air.

The flash fired and Mitchell took the camera from the other devil, nodding his thanks. He sat with it a moment and then stood. "I'll get these printed for you guys," he said sadly.

Our friend trudged out of the burger bar, looking around for someone who wasn't there.

"We need to find him a girl, Alfarin," said Elinor. "It is breaking my dead heart to see Mitchell so alone. And we should be a foursome. Three seems so..."

"Uneven," I replied.

Elinor was right. More than ever, I was convinced that Mitchell needed a woman. One who was strong and opinionated. And one who could bring out the best in him. For I had learned firsthand that I was my worthiest self when I had a partner in crime who was better than I.

21. Anger Unleashed

Phlegyas's eyes remind me of Lord Septimus's. Whereas Virgil's blind eyes are like creamy milk, and the bottomless black eyes of the Skin-Walkers reflect the darkness of their souls, Phlegyas's shine with a red fire. It is not as hot in this circle as others we have passed through, but he has clearly been in the depths of this place for many thousands of years. His face is lined, but not wrinkled. If I had to estimate his age of passing into the Underworld, I would have said around forty years, but his toned, undamaged body hints at his good fortune in life.

"You cannot have the Viciseometer," I reply. I keep my voice as flat as possible, and I do not blink, as I do not wish to break eye contact with the ferryman of the River Styx. I do not believe he means us harm or is being deliberately obtuse. Phlegyas wants a chance to escape, as Mitchell once did, and I can empathize with that.

I have to wonder how he knows I have a Viciseometer hidden on my person. He cannot have seen us use it, and the timepiece has no obvious way of showing itself.

"If you do not give me the Viciseometer, then I cannot take you across," says the ferryman. There is pity in his countenance and weariness, too. Phlegyas pushes his pole into the brown water and starts to punt the boat away.

"Wait," calls Elinor. "Please don't leave us. Is there something else we could give ye?"

"It is the Viciseometer or nothing," replies Phlegyas.

"How does he even know about it?" mutters Mitchell, turning his back to the river.

"When your senses have been assaulted with the very worst for as long as mine have," replies Phlegyas, "they also become extra-attuned to that which can ease suffering. I have sensed the presence of the Viciseometer before in this circle." He smiles. "I can also hear it whistling and see the sparks emanating from your pocket."

Mitchell leans in to me. "Alfarin, what are we going to do?"

"The Geryon would be really handy right now," says Medusa. "He could take us over, one by one."

With eyes narrowed like a haughty feline, Mitchell slowly and deliberately engages Jeanne. Her response is as expected.

"I cannot fly you across," she snaps. "So cease with your unsubtle requests. Do you think I am lying?"

"You've been able to immolate at will to keep ahead of us to this point," replies Mitchell angrily. "So yeah, I think you're lying."

"I have been able to keep ahead of you because that was my command from General Septimus," replies Jeanne. "I saved the peasant sibling to Johnny because that was also part of my task. I am more skilled in immolation than any of you because it is not just rage that ignites it. I am a soldier, and I can separate my emotions of anger and compliance."

"In other words, you're a robot," snaps Mitchell.

I try to block out their bickering. Their fighting is pointless, and I cannot waste time observing it. We have to cross the River Styx to get to the Fourth Circle. We have come so far. I will not be beaten by the request of a naked man who rides in a boat all day.

"Virgil, how do we cross?" I ask the old man. "I will not give away the Viciseometer. As soon as we have found The Devil's

Banshee we will need it to travel back to Lord Septimus and The Devil."

"Phlegyas wishes to leave," replies Virgil. "So give him options."

Phlegyas is watching our conversation closely, although his flaming red eyes are being drawn to the increasingly hostile confrontation still taking place between Mitchell and Jeanne. We are in the Fifth Circle, the dwelling of those who killed in fury. Mitchell does not have the capability for murder in his soul, but he is a powder keg of anger. He showed that when we traveled back to Washington to revisit his death, and he was the first of us to immolate back in the land of the living. This circle could be a danger to him. He has had only four years of death, and I do not begrudge him his anger at the unfairness of his passing. Seventeen years old for a modern devil is different than it is for those of us who had to become men when we were but children.

I want to help Mitchell through the trauma of this circle, but I need to manage the passage of all of Team DEVIL. My father, King Hlif, has made leadership look easy, almost fun. For me, it is harder. What options can I give Phlegyas? I could strike him down and take the boat by force, but he is not our enemy. I want to continue to show my friends, and especially Elinor, that I am becoming more than just an axe-wielding man-mountain of strength.

The answer is obvious once it comes to me.

"Travel on with us," I say. "Phlegyas, ferry Team DEVIL, Virgil and Jeanne across the river and continue through this hope-forsaken world with us. We have but a few circles to go before we reach Paradise. Somewhere here we believe we will find our quarry, the Banshee named Beatrice Morrigan. Then I will personally see you to the place of your choosing with the Viciseometer."

Phlegyas strokes his curly gray beard and juts his jaw slightly to the right.

"I have been the ferryman here for many millennia," he replies. "The few who have crossed this way have never invited me to join them. I was cursed to remain here. By inviting me, you are also offering protection from that which will come after me?"

"You have my word," I reply.

Mitchell and Jeanne are now nose to nose, and I can see that Medusa and Elinor are trying to pull them apart. Their abuse of each other is causing sprinkles of rock to cascade down upon us as their shouting reverberates around the circle.

"You have my word!" I repeat over the din. "I cannot give you the Viciseometer, but I will offer assistance if you help us—and as you can hear, that is now becoming more urgent."

"You are a witless fool who blindly follows General Septimus without question!" Jeanne screams at Mitchell.

"*Me* follow Septimus blindly?" yells Mitchell. "Look who's talking! I wasn't the one who went into the Circles of Hell at his bidding without any backup."

"I knew what I was doing. I have been listening to you, intern. You know nothing about this place."

"What makes you such an expert? I've been dead for four freaking years, you witch! Most devils who died in my year are still total wrecks. Do I know everything? No! Am I affected by all this? Yes! But I deal with this crap my own way, and at least my mental state never got so bad that I was carted off to Hell's lunatic asylum!"

Mitchell is starting to hit below the belt, and Medusa sends me an anguished look.

"Alfarin!" she cries. "He's starting to get hot. Hurry."

Medusa has both of her arms around Mitchell's chest, but she cannot pull him away from the confrontation with Jeanne.

"I am an expert in *all* matters because I listen and learn, fool!" screams Jeanne.

"I will follow you, Viking," says Phlegyas, thankfully realizing just how important it is that we now leave this circle. "If you give me your word, not as a devil, but as a Viking."

Virgil snorts. I know he is remembering my short-lived—albeit deliberate—lies and treachery in the Ninth Circle. I did what I had to do then, and I do it now.

"You have my word, Phlegyas," I say. "As a Viking prince. Now take Elinor, Jeanne and Medusa first. Mitchell, Virgil and I will cross second."

"Do not double-cross me, Viking," says Phlegyas. "There is a reason I was placed in this Circle of Hell."

"There's no way Up There is going to take you back, Jeanne!" cries Mitchell. "You know that, don't you? The angels don't want you anymore!"

"And have you ever considered the possibility that the reason General Septimus keeps sending you out on dangerous missions is because he wants to be rid of you?" screams Jeanne. "Even your own *mother* replaced you!"

"*Alfarin!*" screams Medusa.

The explosion that follows Jeanne's insult catapults me through the air. I land with a thick splash in the foulness of the River Styx, and I am immediately pulled under its surface by the Unspeakables whom I have joined in torment.

Tuttugu ok Tveir

Alfarin, Elinor and Mitchell

The attention some women paid to their appearance—even in Hell—baffled me and Mitchell. I had a standard uniform and never deviated from it. I favored a loose tunic over my upper body and a loose pair of shorts over my lower body. My abhorrence of constricting garments ruled supreme. In life, I wore furs for warmth and leather armor for battle. In Hell, I had no need for either.

Mitchell favored long pants and T-shirts with messages printed on them. He wore a red T-shirt with an image of Che Guevara on it a lot, but I don't think that was a personal favorite; he wore it often because he could not be bothered to change. My friend did not mourn its loss when I accidentally used it to mop up spilled lemonade in his dormitory one day. Mitchell and I were of the same mind: clothes existed to stop ketchup from getting on our skin.

Elinor's clothes were simple but pretty. She favored loose-fitting white dresses. On her feet she wore cotton or satin slippers. She made no sound when she walked, which drew less attention to her. Mitchell favored sneakers, while I chose sturdy leather boots lined with fur. The smell emanating from my feet wasn't pleasant, even I would admit that, but my footwear served a purpose, which was to effectively kick devils out of the way when I was trying to get somewhere.

Everything should have a purpose, even the cloth we wore.

When it came to garments, one thing that Elinor and Mitchell had in common was their love of pockets. This also baffled me. I did not like being constrained and weighted down. Heavy items kept in pockets also had an unfortunate habit of clacking against my manliest parts. And if you find that funny, see how well you can walk when your glorious man bits have been assaulted by a hard metal object.

Or a hard rubber object.

Or any kind of object.

Mitchell liked many pockets in his long trousers because he said he needed his cell phone, wallet and comb on him at all times.

"You never know where you'll end up one day," he said as I met him after work. He had emptied his pockets onto the ground in a search for gum.

"Hell," I replied, without irony.

A deep laugh resonated from the accounting chamber that Mitchell had just exited. The great Lord Septimus appeared in the doorway. He threw a packet of gum at me, but I was not prepared and it flew over the edge of the level 1 balcony.

"Take it from one warrior to another, Prince Alfarin," said Lord Septimus in his drawling accent. "Never underestimate the power that something small can wield. You would not be able to hide that magnificent axe of yours easily, but a pocket could conceal an equally powerful weapon."

"Pockets are for old ladies to keep their mint sweets and false teeth in," I replied. "Not for fearsome Vikings. Vikings do not have anything to hide or contain. This is also why we do not like to wear underpants."

"Too much information, dude," said Mitchell.

But my response to Lord Septimus had been bravado. For when a general offers advice, warrior to warrior, you listen.

So in that moment I swore a secret oath to myself, to ensure that all my shorts had at least one pocket concealed within—just in case I ever had the need to conceal a small, powerful weapon.

22. Mitchell's Woe

The filth of the swamp quickly fills my mouth. I know I am yelling, but I cannot hear my own voice over the screams of those Unspeakables being tormented beside me in the depths of the River Styx. The cacophony of their high-pitched agony is not real, I know this. The Unspeakables here are like the others in the Circles of Hell, tongueless and unable to communicate by voice. Yet their agony and hopelessness have manifested themselves into something that can speak.

And whatever it is, it's coming for me.

My skin is being flagellated. I cannot see by what—I will not see by what—for I must not open my eyes to the horror into which I have been thrown. Jeanne's taunt about Mitchell's mother set off an immolation. Devils are not supposed to be able to do that in Hell, but my friend and I have now both done it within the depths of the Nine Circles. I reached my own immolation by experiencing something so difficult to attain, and yet so pure, it took me beyond pain. Beyond hate and anger. It took me to the abode of the gods. My immolation took me to the true Valhalla. I can only hope that Mitchell is in the same kind of Paradise, for I cannot help him now.

The writhing bodies around me are pulling me farther and farther down, and the weight of my backpack is not helping. My axe is lost. I must get to the surface or I will never break free.

Panic is threatening to engulf me as fast as I was engulfed by this infernal river. I clench my teeth and try to refocus. I am blind and my hearing is compromised. I have nothing but rudimentary swimming skills. I manage to pull the dead weight off my back, and I feel the backpack slide down my legs. I had foreseen that both books I started this journey with would not finish the quest. I hope that is all that is lost. The Viciseometer is in the concealed pocket of my shorts. It is the first time I have ever placed an object in there, but after the need to use it in the previous circle, I must be able to get to it quickly.

That unusual action gives me hope that hope is perhaps not willing to forsake us yet.

I start to pull myself up through the swamp. Jagged teeth bite at my skin. The Unspeakables are already lost souls, I tell myself as I push and punch them away. I am not theirs to claim, and I will not share their torment.

My arms and shoulders are screaming in pain as I fight against the depths of the River Styx. Now I have no sense of which way is up or down. The screaming and crying are relentless, but I find there is no empathy for these dead in my soul. They are here because they forfeited the right to decency in life.

A hard object hits me in the face. Instinctively I cry out, and immediately swallow some of the swamp, which burns my throat and stomach. The hard object, thin and round, slams into my shoulder again. I push it away, but it falls on me a third time.

I open my eyes for the first time, and amongst the bloodied, twisted limbs of the Unspeakables, I see a pole. I grab hold of it, pushing away the fingerless stumps of those around me who are also trying to find a way out.

Phlegyas, Virgil and Mitchell are in the boat. Mitchell is bright red with weeping burned skin. The pain he is in must be immense, but he joins the others in heaving me into the boat. My ears are still ringing from the screams beneath the river, and Mitchell's cries of agony join the chorus.

"Where are the girls?" I splutter. I gag as the remnants of the River Styx are expelled from my stomach into the boat.

"Your women are still on yonder shore," replies Phlegyas.

"Are they hurt?"

"They are dead," replies Virgil matter-of-factly. "But they endured the fire of your immolation," he adds, turning to Mitchell. "And their chief concern was for you boys, Viking."

"That girl...," groans Mitchell. "I swear, Alfarin...I'm gonna take your axe to her...."

He trails off and slams his flat palm onto the bottom of the boat three times. I think he is trying to release his pain.

"We must remove your friend from this circle with haste," says Phlegyas. "This was his bane."

"Where's my axe?" I ask. "Does anyone have it?"

"The girl with flowing red hair found it," says Phlegyas. "You still have the Viciseometer?"

I feel my pocket and nod. My clothes are filthy and torn. I smell like a roasting hog that's been basted in shit. Phlegyas continues to punt across the river, but our passage is smooth, as if an invisible tide is keeping the Unspeakables in the Styx away from us. Mitchell raises his left hand and forms a blistered fist. I bump it gently with mine.

"I'm sorry," he moans. "I'll be all right in a minute...or ten."

"You continue to surprise me, my friend," I say. "We have both now beaten one of the conventions of Hell in that immolation should not be possible. Lord Septimus's faith in us was correct. We are exceptional."

"It wasn't the taunt about my mother...replacing me...that made me explode," groans Mitchell. "I saw my brother behind Jeanne. The vision was so clear...I could have sworn...it was...it was as if he was already in Hell."

Mitchell's pink eyes are bloodshot and bruises are forming below. I know what he is thinking, and I know he dares not say it aloud for fear of it coming to pass.

Has The Devil already chosen a new Dreamcatcher in the few

days that have passed since we commenced this quest? The master of Hell is evil, but he is also strategic. He will have a Plan B, too, just in case we do not return with Elinor. Mitchell's brother, M.J., will become the next Dreamcatcher if we fail. We have not discussed this since we spoke of our own Plan B before we had even entered the domain of the Skin-Walkers. Yet I admit that I have barely given the fate of that little boy a second thought since.

Now I will find the thought hard to remove.

"We still have time, my friend," I say, mustering up as much encouragement in my voice as I can. I am more than a leader, I am a friend. Mitchell needs me as the latter right now more than anything.

"But we're no closer to finding Beatrice—"

"Mitchell," I interrupt, gripping his hand in mine. "We will not fail. We are almost through the Fifth. She was not on the shore we departed, and we will search the approaching shore before we leave this circle. If we do not locate her there, there are only four more circles remaining. We *will* find her."

"He will need to rest," says Phlegyas, maneuvering the boat to the platform. "I can find us somewhere to do so."

"Is it safe?" I ask.

"We're in the Nine Circles of Hell, man," says Mitchell, gritting his teeth. "Nowhere is safe."

Mitchell and I wait and watch as Phlegyas maneuvers the boat back across the River Styx to ferry across Elinor, Medusa and Jeanne. It is the longest wait of my existence. When they arrive safely, Elinor gravitates immediately to me and Medusa falls into Mitchell.

"Are you hurt, my princess?" I ask. There is a whiff of burned hair around her, but other than that and extra-red cheeks, Elinor appears unharmed. My axe is blackened, but it's nothing a good cleaning cannot fix.

"I am fine, Alfarin." Elinor hands me my axe. "But look at poor Mitchell. And we have little water left to lessen the pain of the burns."

"This is your fault," snaps Medusa, turning on Jeanne. "What the Hell is wrong with y—"

But Medusa stops speaking, for Jeanne is crying.

"Your friend, the damaged one," urges Phlegyas. "Take him. We cannot rest here. We must leave. Once the Skin-Walker Iratol notices my disappearance, it will be to the detriment of us all."

"Iratol will join with the others in tracking us," I say. "But if we stay together, we have the means to stop them from attacking us. Trust me. I gave you my word as a Viking prince."

Medusa and Phlegyas take hold of Mitchell. He towers over both of them, even with his head bent forward in pain.

"Is he still coming with us?" whispers Elinor, jerking her head toward Phlegyas.

"Yes," I reply. "It was the only way safe passage could be guaranteed. I would have been left to thrash about in the river for the rest of eternity if he had not come for me."

"I know," says Elinor. "And I am very glad, very glad indeed, but . . . but Alfarin, do ye think ye could get him to wear some clothes?"

"I will wrap my cloak around my waist if it makes you feel more comfortable, child," says Phlegyas. "I have had no need for clothes for many millennia."

"We can see that," mutters Medusa, turning her face away.

"Can't ye give him your spare set of clothes?" asks Elinor.

"I could," I reply, sniffing my armpit. "But I will have to change myself. I cannot go on smelling like something has died in my pants."

"Something *is* dead in your pants," calls Mitchell in a high voice. "You!"

The laughter that escapes his lips is a cross between a cat being castrated and a wolf's howl.

"Pain is making that one hysterical," says Virgil. "If we cannot let him rest in this place, then let us move on. We must not tarry."

Team DEVIL has two bags of supplies left. Medusa's was lost to the Unspeakables in the Eighth Circle; mine has just now been lost to the depths of the River Styx. Elinor has food and water in her bag; Mitchell has a change of clothes that might be a fit for him, but with my girth, definitely not for me.

"The smell might get better as ye dry out, Alfarin," suggests Elinor. She throws Phlegyas a T-shirt and a pair of Mitchell's pants with more pockets than any devil could possibly need. "I am begging ye, Mr. Phlegyas sir, please cover yerself up."

"Don't think I'm going to forgive you for what you did to him," says Medusa through her teeth as Jeanne stands up and starts to follow Virgil.

"You have no idea what I have suffered," replies Jeanne. The tears are gone, replaced by a haughtiness that stretches her skin across her cheekbones and makes her appear even gaunter than before. "You have not seen war or conflict, or the anger and violence of man."

"I've seen more of it than I will ever share with you," says Medusa. "But if you stopped the self-pity for a few minutes, you'd see the good in people, too. What you did to Mitchell, what you drove him to, was unforgivable."

"I do not seek his forgiveness—"

"We need to get out of this circle before anger consumes all of you," says Virgil. "Death in the young always brings out the worst, for you are all still, at heart, emotional adolescents...."

This man knows nothing of our collective suffering, yet for once, each member of Team DEVIL remains silent. We are all facing our darkest fears in this vile place. The Seventh Circle was nearly my undoing, and Elinor would have met her doom in the Sixth, had Jeanne not spirited her away. Mitchell will make it out of the Fifth, but only just, which leaves only Medusa to face her fate. I believe The Devil was right when he said it was the Second Circle. The place where her stepfather exists in perpetual torment.

But that is still two circles away. I turn my attention to the here and now. We must search this shore for the Banshee. And if we do not find her, we enter the Fourth. The circle of greed.

Team DEVIL remains as tight a foursome as ever, but our procession through the Nine Circles is ever-expanding. Virgil, Jeanne and now the clothed Phlegyas accompany us. In fact, the ferryman is leading us, with Virgil at his heels, through another rock tunnel, but this one has a slightly higher roof, at least three feet beyond the head of Mitchell, who is the tallest in the group. We saw no sign of Beatrice Morrigan on the opposite shore of the River Styx, and we have been hurrying through this tunnel ever since we gave up the search.

In the torchlight, I can see small, stubby stalactites reaching down. Unlike usual rock formations, they are moving.

"Oh, my mother in Hell!" exclaims Medusa, looking up. "Are they what I think they are?"

Elinor cries out and ducks. Mitchell groans and then gags. There is no food in his stomach to regurgitate.

The objects moving from the roof are the amputated fingers of the Unspeakables in the Fifth Circle. I saw the stumps on the hands that groped me and tried to grab a way out of the River Styx, but what had happened to their digits did not register.

We come to a small circular area. It even has stone seats. A perverse civility in the midst of grotesque horror.

"Here. Here is the place where you can eat, drink and rest," says Phlegyas, running his fingers through his long, straggly hair.

We all take several long gulps of the water that Elinor and Mitchell have in their backpacks, but not one of us eats. Mitchell is unable because of his burns, and the rest of us have no stomach for food.

I take the Viciseometer out of my stained shorts. I know Phlegyas is eyeing it, but I position my axe between my knees and allow the blade to gently scrape along the burnished gold casing. It's a tuneless warning. The Viciseometer is mine, and I don't need to be in the Fifth Circle to rage against anyone who tries to take it from us. For the Viciseometer will be our ultimate salvation. It is the only way we are ever getting out of here. And I will protect it with everything I have.

Tuttugu ok Prir

Alfarin, Elinor and Mitchell

"**What do ye miss most about being alive?**" asked Elinor one day, setting down her sewing needle. The three of us were sitting on Mitchell's bed. Elinor was trying to teach Mitchell and me to repair our own clothes. We had pricked ourselves so many times that there was more dead blood on Mitchell's mattress than remained in our bodies.

"I miss feeling the sun on my face and the wind in my hair," I replied.

"Alfarin, that's the kind of thing a girl would say," teased Mitchell. His face was screwed up in concentration as he attempted to stitch a hole in one of his T-shirts.

"And what do you miss most, O Epitome of Testosterone?" I asked testily. I had given up trying to darn my socks. Holes were healthy. It allowed skin to breathe...figuratively.

"I miss my mom mending my clothes, is what I miss," growled Mitchell. "This is hopeless, Elinor. How do girls do this without turning themselves into pincushions?"

"We practice and do not give up as easily as silly boys," replied Elinor. "And ye must know that plenty of the manliest men can wield a needle and thread, Mitchell." She pats his arm to distract him from his frustration. "Now, be serious with my question. Ye must miss more than just yer mother mending yer clothes."

Mitchell put down his needlework. "Elinor, I've been dead for just over a year. I miss *everything*. My friends, my folks, my music, my books...I miss the weather. I miss breathing. I'd like to walk five yards without being crushed. I want to go online and plan a vacation. I want to be able get a passport so I can go *on* the freaking vacation. I'd like to prick my finger on a needle and bleed normal blood, not this gross lumpy stuff that's in me now. I miss my bed. I miss kissing girls who have a pulse..."

Mitchell trailed off. "Sorry," he mumbled. "That was greedy, wasn't it—and insensitive."

"A little," I replied, wondering what it would be like to kiss a certain girl without a pulse who was sitting just inches from me at that moment.

"Septimus is always telling me how stoic I am, but I'm not. I'm just better at keeping it bottled up," said Mitchell. "I'm being an ass, Elinor. Ignore me. This is just...hard."

"Oh, Mitchell," said Elinor. "Most of the dead take decades to come to terms with not living. Ye are doing brilliantly, and just think, ye already have an amazing job with Mr. Septimus. He would not have given ye that job if he didn't think ye were special. And it's okay to miss things about living. That is not being greedy. True greed is being selfish. Desiring things for wealth, or power or food."

"Food," Mitchell and I groaned together. We banged fists: a custom that Mitchell brought with him from the year 2009, along with the words *dude*, *WTF* and *awesomesauce*.

"Oh, for Up There's sake," snapped Elinor, quickly emerging from her sympathetic reverie. "I am going to make *food* a cussword for ye two."

———

The three of us left Mitchell's dormitory and the sewing to find sustenance. I had pushed my holey socks into Mitchell's pillowcase when he wasn't looking. I was marking his territory, like a true friend.

"Can you imagine if the Highers had taken food away from us?"

asked Mitchell. "I know many devils want to be angels, but I've heard rumors that they don't eat, or sleep."

"That is not a fate I wish to even contemplate," I replied.

"Fate. Another F-word," Mitchell said to Elinor jokingly. "We're amassing quite the *fabulous* collection. Would you like us to add more?"

Elinor then let rip with several more F-words. None of which she knew before Mitchell joined us.

He was becoming quite the bad influence on her.

And I liked it.

23. The Fourth Circle

"The Fourth Circle is the domain of the Skin-Walker named Cupidiar," says Virgil. "It is the final place of those who murdered for greed."

"Cupidiar?" questions Medusa immediately. "But isn't there another Skin-Walker called Cupidore?"

Virgil rubs his colorless eyes with his thumb and forefinger. He massages so deeply into the sockets, I can see his eyeballs move behind his lids. It's not a pleasant sight, as when he removes his thumb, blood leaks from the corner of his eyes.

"Cupidiar is the twin of the Skin-Walker who resides in the Second Circle," replies Virgil. He cannot see the shocked look on Medusa's face, but her tone of voice was enough to betray her worry. In our recent quest to find the Devil's Dreamcatcher, our encounters with the Skin-Walkers were never pleasant. But nobody suffered in their presence like Medusa—and especially around Cupidore, who took an extra-disgusting interest in our friend. Her connection to one of his victims, and her understandable fear, made her a feast of emotions for the Skin-Walkers to feed on, and there is no reason to believe they don't still want her for their own. To be so close in this circle to the Skin-Walker she fears the most will be a terrible burden for our friend.

Mitchell rubs Medusa's back but flinches with pain as he moves.

His skin is now peeling in thick flakes. It will take him longer to recover after the immolation without cold water to take the heat out of the burns.

I wish I could absorb the mental and physical pain of Team DEVIL. If there were a way, I would in a dead heartbeat.

I still remember that pulse in my chest. There have been times recently when I have imagined I actually have it. Perhaps that is because our adventures of late have made me feel more alive than any battle I faced before my passing.

"Ye have even more devils here to protect ye now, M," says Elinor, pressing a water bottle into Virgil's hands.

"Yeah," mumbles Mitchell. "Jeanne is really—"

I give Mitchell a swift nudge with my hand, but he is clearly still in so much pain that my touch barely registers. Jeanne is someone who has to be treated differently, and mocking and alienating her could be to the detriment of all. Of course I am angry with her for what she said to Mitchell, but we must stay united and strong. There will be plenty of time for Mitchell to exact verbal revenge on the Maid of Orléans when this is over, and we are getting nearer to that moment with every stride.

"In Dante's book," says Elinor, changing the subject, "the dead in the Fourth are condemned to push boulders uphill for the rest of eternity. We will not find fire or filth in this next one, will we, Virgil?"

"Well, that'll be a nice change," says Mitchell. "An easy circle for once. Go Team DEVIL."

"I would not say it is going to be easy," replies Virgil, standing up. "Now, if the immolating fool among you can walk, we should be on our way."

Phlegyas's eyes have stopped flickering to my pocket, where the Viciseometer is softly vibrating against my thigh. Instead, he is now watching Elinor. His expression is unreadable. Phlegyas does not seem to possess the reflex to breathe that most devils retain, and this makes his tanned face appear almost statue-like.

"You have kindness in your soul," says Phlegyas to Elinor, and my princess blushes. "It radiates out of you. I am surprised the other immortal domain did not try to claim you for its own."

"Mr. Phlegyas," replies Elinor. "I have worked in administration in Hell for many, many years now. If there is one thing I have learned, it is that there is no reasoning behind who goes to Hell and who goes Up There. It is down to the whim of the Grim Reaper at the HalfWay House on the day ye arrive. And their whims seem to gravitate downward."

"So you are happy with your fate?" asks Phlegyas. His tone is polite, but his line of questioning has brought forth an unhappy throb of anxiety in my chest. A slight one, but it is a warning nonetheless. I do not like where this conversation is heading.

"I...*am* happy," says Elinor, and at her response, Medusa and I immediately swap looks. The hesitation in Elinor's voice belies the words from her mouth. The truth is, she *was* happy. But The Devil destroyed that happiness, simply because she was the best of us all.

The hatred for him that I had barely managed to conceal back in Hell bubbles in my chest once more. From the day new devils arrive in Hell, we all hear rumors of The Devil's twisted nature. But my kin and I had always dismissed them as propaganda. Instilling fear is an effective method of crowd control, and Hell was good at disseminating fear among the masses.

But now I have seen his nefarious ways myself. The Devil's despotic character cannot be allowed to endure. Mitchell is correct in his bluntness: The Devil is insane, and all of Hell is in danger. Lord Septimus sees this. I think he has seen this for many millennia. The Highers created two domains of Afterlife for those who died in our world, but, like any territory with a ruler, the realms of the Afterlife are only as stable as those who govern them. If Ragnarök really is coming, then I will do everything I can to ensure it is the end of days for the unhinged master of Hell as well.

The fingers groping down from the ceiling are dwindling. We are closing in on the Fourth Circle. We can hear loud thudding noises and feel vibrations in the rock beneath our feet.

"How are you to proceed through this circle?" calls Phlegyas. He looks so strange in Mitchell's cargo pants, like a terra-cotta figurine in the wrong landscape.

"The same way we have made passage through all the circles so far," I reply. "We walk."

"Well, technically we've jumped, climbed, flown and time-traveled, and you've swum through one of the circles," says Mitchell; his voice is already less cracked and gravelly than it was a few moments ago. "Walking through a circle will actually be a novelty."

"You need to form a tight line and follow me," replies Virgil. "Do not allow yourself to be caught between boulders. At best you will be crushed. At worst, you will disintegrate into ash."

"So the Unspeakables aren't pushing the rocks in pits?" asks Medusa.

"They are not," replies the guide.

"Does that mean we have to walk amongst them?" cries Elinor. "But we've been separated from them so far!"

"See for yourself," replies Virgil.

We have arrived at a wide expanse of space in the rock, easily the length and height of a longship. Before us is a circular landscape that confuses my senses. Men and women, as far as the eye can see, are pushing huge black boulders with their chests. Not one single rock is spherical, making their labor even harder. The ground appears flat, but the Unspeakables are moving their legs as if they are ascending, with thighs straining and knees bent. It is the closest we have come to so many of the Unspeakables so far, my unintended swim notwithstanding, and the sight is unnerving. For once they appear as people, albeit shaven and bloodied. Collars of inverted spikes pierce their skin at the neck, causing thick blood to slowly ooze down their purple-bruised bodies. All have their hands manacled behind their backs. Firelight is coming from holes in the ground and rock walls, but every few seconds it is extinguished as a black shadow moves across it.

And standing on the largest boulder of all, which is being slowly pushed by two Unspeakables, is the Skin-Walker Cupidiar. The head on his wolf pelt has already caught sight of us, and it slides its long black tongue over its bared fangs. Slowly, the Skin-Walker turns his own head toward us and smiles. He is far enough away for Elinor to be of no consequence to him, but close enough to cause Medusa to tremble in fear.

Elinor immediately goes to comfort Medusa. As long as she stays close to us, I do not believe we are in danger from the Skin-Walker in this circle, or any others who are tracking us in the darkness.

But the knowledge that I am using my princess as a shield is the cause of much anguish to my dead heart. *I* should be protecting *her*, not the other way around.

"Virgil," I call. "You said you would lead us."

"Stay behind me and follow in this order," commands Virgil. "Peasant girl first, then Phlegyas." Both immediately step in behind our guide. "Then the one who smells of burning flesh." Mitchell and Jeanne both move to stand in line and collide.

"I think he means Jeanne," says Medusa, taking Mitchell's hands and pouring some water over his fingertips.

"We shouldn't waste it," whispers Mitchell, resting his forehead on the top of Medusa's snakelike hair.

"I'm not," she whispers back.

Their intimacy is so natural, and I feel ashamed for watching. Mitchell brings out the best in our lady friends. He claims to be clueless around them, but he does not give himself enough credit. He has taught Elinor to be tougher, without losing her gentleness, and in the short time Medusa has been in our company, Mitchell has drawn out her fearlessness and pragmatism. I wonder what the two of them were like before the paradox Medusa joined us. I wish I could remember more. To know that some of my timeline has been wiped out and refreshed is unnerving. But I realize that since our last trip to the land of the living, the ghosts of previous memories have been bothering me less and less. Perhaps that is because it feels as if the new Medusa has always been in our midst.

Virgil looks back at her. "The snake-haired girl should walk behind the girl who smells of burning flesh. Someone needs to keep those two separate." He points, only a fraction askew because of his blindness, at Mitchell and Jeanne. Neither argues with him, and Medusa takes her place in line. "Viking, you and your weapon should follow last," says Virgil.

I do not like being separated from Elinor by everyone else. Neither do I like the fact that she is sandwiched between Virgil and Phlegyas. Yet I must place my trust in our guide, for that was Lord Septimus's will.

We begin wending our way through the toiling Unspeakables. The smell of their sweat and blood is rank in this circle, but the heat is bearable, perhaps only a slight increase over what we are accustomed to in Hell. The Unspeakables see us, and a few of the closer ones snap their jaws as they push the huge boulders with their chests. I can hear Mitchell muttering, "They are not like us...they are not like us...," and soon that chant becomes our anthem as we progress through the Fourth Circle, surrounded by evil. We cannot afford to feel compassion or empathy for these tortured souls. They are here because they murdered for greed.

"Keep looking and calling for Beatrice Morrigan!" I command. "She is not an Unspeakable; she will not be pushing a rock if she is here."

Medusa is the first to make accidental contact with a boulder after trying to dodge another. She screams as the blackened rock scrapes along her arm. A large gash appears in her skin, which bubbles at the edges.

"I warned you to be cautious!" Virgil chides from the front of the line. "The Unspeakables' skin becomes hardened to the torment. Your delicate hide cannot take it."

"The boulders are sharp and toxic," I call out.

"Of course they are," mutters Mitchell. "Sharp *and* toxic. My favorite combination."

With my axe at the ready, I keep one eye on Mitchell, who is in front of me, and another on Cupidiar the Skin-Walker. He has leapt off his boulder and is now slowly stalking through the circle, sniffing the air, with his gaze firmly fixed on Medusa.

"Keep together and follow Virgil," I call out, trying to motivate my friends, as a bowman would motivate the crew of a longship. "One foot in front of the other. Concentrate on the movement of the boulders and nothing else. We are closing in on our destination." I call out for Beatrice Morrigan, but there is no reply, and every movement in my line of sight is from a tortured Unspeakable. Once again, I see no place for a Banshee—or anyone else—to conceal herself, and I am disappointed to conclude that our quarry does not lie in this circle.

Suddenly, Cupidiar slashes at an Unspeakable in front of him. The cursed one falls to the ground, and his boulder immediately rolls over his prostrate body. The crunch of bones ignites my gag reflex.

At the sound, Virgil freezes. "Take cover!" he cries.

No, it was never going to be as easy as simply walking through.

As I look around for something, anything, to shield my friends from whatever is coming, everything goes black, and the sound of howling wolves fills the air.

Tuttugu ok Fjórir

Alfarin, Elinor and Mitchell

Elinor, Mitchell and I had become great friends. And while our threesome from different times was uneven in number and sex, there was a comfortable familiarity among us that was pleasurable in its ease. Mitchell was accepted quickly by my kin; they found him amusing. His closeness to Lord Septimus was also a matter of intrigue. A job as The Devil's intern was a coveted position. Many in Hell could not understand how such a new devil could slip into such a role so quickly.

"I think young Mitchell Johnson is being trained for a task," said my father brother, Magnus. "There is no doubt he has taken to death like a warrior."

"He has not taken to death, Magnus," replied Elinor. "Mitchell just keeps his feelings about it hidden better than most. Ouch, these damn things are hotter than Hell!"

She was trying out a device called a straightening iron on my father brother's hair. It was not going well. Magnus's hair had not been washed in over one thousand years. Elinor had already soldered a fork and a set of false set of teeth into Magnus's follicles, but it was an accident. She couldn't have known they were in there—and how long they had been there was any Viking's guess.

"I don't believe it," said Magnus. "Mitchell Johnson has taken to death better than many with ten times his number of years in the

Underworld. That shows ability to take orders and perform them without thinking, without second-guessing. He is being trained as a soldier by Lord Septimus. Mark my words."

"Soldiers *do* think," said Elinor, pulling a moldy piece of bread from Magnus's hair. "I know many soldiers in Hell. They think too much, if truth be told."

"Men are either leaders or followers," I said.

"And what about women?" replied Elinor testily. My father brother winced as the smell of burning hair wafted through Valhalla.

"I was not slighting your sex," I said quickly. "The Valkyries are as fearsome as any Viking. You would make a wonderful Valkyrie, Elinor."

My princess beamed. I had said the correct words.

"I can follow orders, too," she said. "I just need to know the reason for them."

"Even if you disagreed with the order?" asked Magnus. "Would you follow through then?"

"The greater good is what matters in the end," said Elinor. "Take yer hair, Magnus. I have followed yer orders and straightened it, even if I did think it was a bad idea. I thought we would burn down Hell, for a start. But look at the end result." Elinor held up a mirror for Magnus. "Ye are looking fabulous for the Masquerade Ball tonight."

I could not contain my mirth. With his long, pointed face and his golden hair now straighter than the flat side of a knife, Father Brother Magnus looked like an Afghan hound. Mitchell picked an unfortunate moment to walk into the hall. He strode in, took one look at Magnus, burst out laughing and strode right out again.

"You need to get your friend in line, Alfarin," growled Magnus. "And I double my original offer of ten barrels of mead if you take my place tonight."

"Not a chance in Hell or Valhalla, Father Brother," I replied. "I am a leader, not a soldier, and I do not follow orders or take bribes.

Also, I have already suffered a Masquerade Ball. Third Cousin Magna is all yours tonight."

Magnus stormed off, cursing the Allfather at his predicament. Laughing, Elinor and I joined Mitchell in the dark corridor outside the Viking hall.

"I would follow ye into battle, Alfarin," said Elinor. "Ye know that, don't ye?"

"I would never ask you to do anything you didn't want," I replied.

"I'll follow you, too, Alfarin," replies Mitchell. "And not only because you know the directions to every place to eat in Hell with your eyes closed."

My friends did not realize how much their words meant to me. Could I already be a leader of men and women? Was I ready for that responsibility? Leadership was not just about orders. It also involved making hard decisions. Lord Septimus certainly thought so.

Lately, the Roman general seemed to be turning up wherever I happened to be: Thomason's, the library ... why, he was even in the next toilet stall on level 666 one evening.

I often found it difficult to do my business with harp music playing over the speakers, but trying to do it with the most powerful servant in Hell next to me was many times worse.

"I heard you managed to get out of taking your sweet cousin Magna to the Masquerade Ball this year," said Lord Septimus as he washed his hands.

"I have done my duty in that regard once in the Afterlife," I replied. "And that was quite enough."

"And what if your proposed partner had been Miss Powell?" asked Lord Septimus with a smile.

"I would do anything Elinor asked of me, including dressing up like a penguin and dancing like one."

Lord Septimus smoothed his hands over his glistening black scalp and looked at me seriously.

"And what if Miss Powell were to ask my intern to accompany her? The three of you have become very close."

"Then I would respect her decision…and incapacitate Mitchell a few hours beforehand," I replied jokingly, although I was unsure where Lord Septimus was heading with this conversation.

"Three is such an uneven number," said Lord Septimus. "Four has always been my favorite."

"I would have thought six hundred and sixty-six was your favorite, Lord Septimus," I replied. "I would certainly never allow The Devil to hear you favor any other."

Lord Septimus laughed. He had a great laugh. A warrior's laugh: sonorous and true.

"No, I suppose I ought to keep my fondness for the number four under wraps," he said. Then he turned serious again. "A true friend will always have your back, Prince Alfarin," he said. "Decisions involving the fate of friends are always the hardest ones of all."

"I was only joking," I replied, thinking he was referring to my crack about incapacitating Mitchell. "I would never hurt my friend."

But Lord Septimus only grew graver. He placed his hands on my shoulders. He was several inches taller than I, and although I was far broader, there were few who could make me feel as small as Lord Septimus did in that moment.

"You are a warrior, Prince Alfarin. As am I. And I have sacrificed men—friends—on the battlefield before. They haunt me in my nightmares and my existence in this Afterlife. One day you may have to decide whether to leave a friend behind. Think on this carefully. For I would rather have one true friend beside me in battle than ten who are only interested in saving their own skin."

"Lord Septimus, I really was only joking about incapacitating Mitchell."

"One last thing, Prince Alfarin," replied the great Roman, ignoring my protestations. "You are a fine figure of a Viking, but it is easy for corporeal souls to get complacent in the Afterlife. Learn how to run. I see a lot of running in your future."

With a final pat on the shoulder, Lord Septimus left me in the toilets. Three other devils in open stalls stood openmouthed—one had actually pissed his pants—as The Devil's right-hand man swept from level 666.

"What was all that about?" asked the devil with the wet trousers.

"I think Lord Septimus needs to find his sense of humor," I replied. "Or I need to learn to tell better jokes."

And I also needed to learn how to run. Apparently.

24. Following Orders

When I come to in the darkness, the first emotion that registers is pain. A distinct stabbing pulse emanates from my head. My chest constricts and my throat tightens. I do not need to breathe, and there are many moments when I do not even register the instinct, but I do now, for it feels as if my entire upper body has been compressed by a heavy weight, and the desire to fill it with air is strong.

"Medusa! Medusa...talk to me...please, say something...Virgil...help me...she's not moving!"

Mitchell's cries are anguished, and my pain is eclipsed by a new sensation: fear.

"Elinor, Mitchell, Medusa!" I cry. "Where are you? Call to me!"

The darkness is impenetrable. A suffocating mass with no end and no beginning. I try to get a sense of myself. I know my body is bent; sloping, really. I am lying prostrate, but over something spherical. My arms and legs are draped over the rounded edges, as if I am a sacrificial offering. I must be on a boulder, yet my skin is unharmed.

The wolves are still howling, but the sound is muffled. Something solid is now blocking the sickening, desperate noise from reaching us.

"*Elinor!*" I cry. My throat and mouth are filled with dust and small rock particles. I choke and cough as I shout her name over and over again.

But my princess does not reply.

"Mitchell, where are you?" I shout.

"Here, with Medusa, and Virgil...I think."

"Where is *here*?" Our voices are echoing around us in the darkness. I cannot tell which direction Mitchell's is coming from.

"I don't know where I am, Alfarin!" shouts Mitchell. "I can see jack shit! I only know I'm with Medusa because of the hair."

"Virgil is with you, though?"

"I think so!" shouts Mitchell; he breaks off to cough. The sound is so violent and phlegmy, I fear he is hacking up the lining of his useless lungs. "I can feel his robes. He's moving a little now."

"Is Elinor with you?"

"No, but she was near Virgil when the roof came down, so she's probably—*arrgghhhhh!*"

I have heard men scream before. It is a falsehood to believe they do not. Fear and pain and the understanding of impending death will reduce the voices of even the bravest of men to the most primal of sounds. It is that which is now expelling from my friend's mouth. A base cry of fear that has been inherited through the ages. It is joined by howling that no longer sounds muffled. It is a solitary howl that speaks joy and pleasure at others' pain.

And I cannot help Mitchell, for I know not where he is in this crushing darkness.

"*Arrgghhhhh!*"

"Mitchell! Mitchell...what is it? Make another sound...I will come to you...."

But my friend falls silent, too.

"Jeanne...Phlegyas..."

"I am here, Viking," groans a feeble French voice. It is weak, but close.

I roll off the boulder and feel my left shoulder pop. Pain judders through my body again. A dislocation. I had many while I was alive, and several in death, too. Supporting my elbow with my other hand, I slam my dislocated arm into a rock and push upward and rotate at the same time. A hand grabs my calf as the welcome sensation of the ball joint slipping back into the shoulder socket warms my body.

"Use the Viciseometer for light," groans Jeanne. I realize it is her hand on my leg.

I plunge my hand into my pocket and pull out the timepiece. The red circular face immediately lights up with miniature flames. I feel the heat spreading across my bloodied palm toward my wrist. The light is enough to illuminate the space around me.

Jeanne is propped up in a sitting position. Blood is oozing from a cut above her eye, and a nasty flap of skin is hanging down from her brow.

"I think the roof came down" is all she manages to say before she closes her eyes and leans her head back against the rock.

"I know," I gasp.

Elinor…Mitchell…Medusa…I must find my friends. I hold the Viciseometer aloft like a torch and take in what is left of the Fourth Circle. It is a mass of brand-new rock from the roof of the cave, but there is movement from beneath the ground. Feet, shoulders and heads are starting to appear as tortured monsters crawl out of the dirt.

"Viking, over here," calls a voice. It is Phlegyas, and he is propping up Elinor. They do not appear to be hurt, just shocked.

I pick up Jeanne and gently drape her over my undamaged shoulder. She offers no resistance and is as light as a roll of cloth.

"We must find Mitchell and Medusa!" I cry. "He screamed out and then fell silent. The Unspeakables that were buried are starting to climb out of the ground. We must hurry."

"They were not buried," calls Virgil. In the light of the Viciseometer I spot our guide. He stands up and falls back against a boulder. "The Fourth Circle is constantly remaking itself. When one Unspeakable falls, they all fall and are sucked into the ground, from which they must free themselves without the use of their bound hands. New rock boulders will drop from the cave roof, and this is what they must push."

"Cupidiar must have been bored with their efficiency," says Phlegyas. "Either that or he wished to bring down the roof on us. He struck that Unspeakable with deliberate intent."

"Virgil, where is Mitchell?" I cry. "Where is Medusa?"

"The girl is here," calls Virgil. "I've just found her. She is not moving. I heard the boy calling to you earlier, but now he is silent and I cannot feel his presence in the air."

Elinor and Phlegyas tread a path toward me and Jeanne. The Maid of Orléans is moaning softly.

"We need to find Mitchell!" cries Elinor, taking my face in her warm hands. "And then we need to get out of here. The Unspeakables are coming through the ground. I don't want them near me. They are evil. I fear they might trigger another attack on my soul from The Devil."

"Viking, you must get moving. Come fetch the girl with snake hair from me and take everyone in that direction." The blind guide points away to my right. "Stay together," he orders. "If you need to use the new boulders for stability as you walk, you can touch them. They have not yet absorbed the toxicity of the Unspeakables. But they will not stay safe for long. Once the Unspeakables break through the surface and start to move, the rocks will be as dangerous and toxic as before. Go now! I will find the boy."

"He cannot find Mitchell!" cries Elinor. "He is blind, Alfarin. We have to stay!"

But the bodies of the Unspeakables are progressing ever faster out of the ground.

"Phlegyas, stay close to Elinor," I say. "We will carry Medusa and Jeanne out of the Fourth Circle."

"*What about Mitchell?*" screams Elinor. "*Ye cannot leave him.*"

I am trying to stay calm and collected. A Viking's intuition is one of the strongest tools we have, and I know that Virgil is right. Also, I am a leader. And I must do what is right for the majority.

My heart may not beat, but I know it works all the same...for I feel it breaking.

We make our way to Virgil. His red robes are torn, and where the fabric is shredded, dark blood, so thick it looks like tar, is oozing over wrinkled skin. Medusa is lying by his feet. She could be sleeping.

"I will find the boy," says Virgil. "You must trust me. Head for the Third Circle. Cupidiar brought down his domain for a reason. With the peasant girl you have a Dreamcatcher to protect you from the Skin-Walkers, but once the Unspeakables start pushing the new rock, it will become too dangerous for you to move within this circle. You can see already that their stones are much larger than what they were pushing before. The smaller boulders you saw earlier were the result of their wearing the rock down. Go—now!"

"I am not leaving without Mitchell," sobs Elinor. "We have to find him."

"He is not here!" retorts Virgil angrily. "He has been taken. Only I can find him."

"The mission," groans Jeanne. "We must not...deviate..."

"Elinor, Phlegyas, carry Medusa out of this circle," I say. "I will light the way with the Viciseometer and carry Jeanne. We will regroup in the tunnel between this circle and the Third."

"I am not leaving!" cries Elinor.

"Yes, you are!" I shout back. "Phlegyas, pick up Medusa. Elinor, protect those of us remaining."

"Ye cannot order me around."

"Yes, I can!" I roar. "I am the leader of this quest and you will do as I command!"

Elinor opens her mouth and closes it. Her beautiful red eyes are swimming with tears. My soul is splintering into a thousand pieces, and I know that because of what I am now telling her to do, Elinor will not help me put them back together.

I grab Virgil's robes in my anger, but my hold loosens as he places his gnarled fingers on either side of my face.

"I am not what I appear, Viking," he whispers. "I will find the boy. Do not wait for me. Go on to the Third. You will already know it is the circle where gluttony is punished."

A piercing howl shrieks through the cave once more, and I whip my head in its direction. Part of me begs to hear another scream from Mitchell, for then at least I would know he is here, but there is nothing.

I turn back to Virgil.

"Find my friend, I beg of you."

And I leave Mitchell behind.

Tuttugu ok Fimm

Alfarin and Mitchell

"A boys' night out" was how Mitchell described the evening of entertainment ahead of us. Elinor had agreed to sit out so Mitchell and I could partake in the male-only bonding rituals of our respective times. She had even volunteered for an extra shift at the housing department to take her mind off the fact that she would be bereft by my absence.

At least that was what she told me as she skipped away with a beaming smile on her beautiful face.

"This is exactly the kind of thing I would be doing if I were living," said Mitchell as we wound our way through the mass of devils, all ambling about without any thought to their destination. "Birds, booze and something else beginning with *b* that will come to me."

"There are no such winged creatures in Hell," I replied, confused as to why Mitchell's evening of merriment would involve feathers.

"Not that kind of bird, Alfarin," said Mitchell. "*Bird* is an English word for chicks—girls."

"But you are American, my friend," I said. I was starting to think Mitchell had been hit on the head by an overly large accounting book. He was making little sense.

"I know!" exclaimed Mitchell. "I was trying to be...what's that word? Elinor would know. Oh, *alliterative*. But it doesn't matter. The point is, tonight we are going to be players in the field of love. I'm sick of being alone. I want a girlfriend."

And you will continue to be alone if you say you are a "player in the field of love," I thought, but I kept my musings to myself. It was good to see Mitchell excited, and any female would be fortunate to win his heart. He was a fine example of manhood, if you discounted his weedy body, his inability to wield a weapon heavier than a pencil and his penchant for saying the letters W, T and F.

Seeing as Mitchell was my closest male friend, I decided to embrace his enthusiasm and use of modern language. I slapped my arm around his shoulders, helped him up again when his knees buckled and said, "So, tonight I am your wingman?"

"Yes!" hollered Mitchell. "That's exactly it. You're my wingman. Your job is to make the girls think I'm awesome."

"But you *are* awesome," I said. "You can play music like Beethoven himself. You know how to cuss in five languages. I have seen you throw a grapefruit at a Saxon head from a distance most Vikings can only dream of and hit your mark. And you can place four hamburgers in your mouth at the same time. Mitchell, these are fine qualities that any woman would be quick to embrace. Now, look around. Which woman would you like me to approach about your awesomeness?"

We were in a new arena for entertainment in Hell called a nightclub. There was music, although the thumping beat was already making my head hurt. Devils were moving, although they were so packed together I could not tell if they were swaying to the music or trying to get out.

"Hi, Mitchell," said a female voice.

Success already, I thought. Mitchell really was a magnet for pretty girls. Erin Fanshawe was a devil I had been introduced to only recently because of her fascination with my friend. Like Patricia Lloyd, she was buxom and had a habit of turning up wherever Mitchell went. Her long dark hair and dark-pink eyes were an attractive quality. As was the sweater she was wearing, with elaborate peacock feathers stitched to the front. An exhibition of the mating ritual in birds. This was what Mitchell must have meant when he mentioned the winged creatures. It was time to be the wingman.

"Hi, Erin," mumbled Mitchell. He appeared to be looking at her chest, and he was already clutching at his throat. These were good signs. He wished to ravish her, I thought.

"Erin," I said, slapping my chest with my fist. "My awesome friend wishes to copulate with you. I will stand guard with my axe while you 'get busy,' as they say in modern times."

"Oh, Mitchell," gushed Erin.

And she jumped him.

Their exhibition was confusing but energetic. Mitchell turned red, then purple. Instead of murmuring sweet exclamations, he started gasping and yelling that he couldn't breathe. You are dead, I thought. Of course you cannot breathe. Erin was smothering him in kisses, then screaming at him as he tried to fight her off, then punching his chest as he tried to crawl away.

"She is such a moron!" exclaimed a female voice. "Mitchell is allergic to feathers. He's having an anaphylactic reaction. Get her away from him, Alfarin. She's trying to do CPR. If Erin had a brain cell, it would die of loneliness."

I looked around for the source of the situation, but while there were devils watching the increasingly desperate spectacle, no one was close enough to have spoken with such clarity. The hair on my neck stood on end as Elinor's words about déjà vu inevitably flitted through my head. There was no time to ponder the origin and owner of the ghostly voice, however, for no matter what time or place it came from, her words were correct: Mitchell was in trouble.

My friend was not a willing partner in the match. He was still trying to escape. This was what he really meant by *wingman*. Mitchell did not require someone to find him a woman. He needed a friend to help him run away if things went wrong.

I picked Mitchell up, threw him over my shoulder, saved his reputation by announcing to the watching throng that he had swooned in the sight of such beauty and took him straight to Hell's medical wing for a shot.

Yes, I was the perfect wingman, and I would always be there for my friend.

25. Leave No Man Behind

Leave no man behind. That ethos has been around a lot longer than modern man realizes. It does not have its origins in the American military. It is a code that for many years went unwritten and unspoken and was passed through the ages among warriors of many tribes. That is because a group of soldiers becomes a family. They are brethren. No instinct in any human is as strong as the desire to live, yet death is the one state guaranteed in one's existence. There is no stopping it, especially in battle. So you watch out for one another and protect one another, because one day your life might depend on it. And that breeds a trust among soldiers. A bond.

I was never left behind. My death came about because I wandered off. Yet as I saw with my own dead eyes, my clan came back for me.

Even in death I was not forsaken.

As I power through the darkness—with Jeanne bouncing over one shoulder and the tiny flames from the Viciseometer illuminating the way—I continually repeat the words, "I had no choice, I had no choice." It's the only way I can try to reconcile my actions with the aching in my soul.

But my soul is dead, and my heart feels useless once more. I had a choice. And any words I mutter now cannot change the decision I have just made.

I left Mitchell behind.

Phlegyas is carrying Medusa in his arms. Her eyes have not opened. Elinor is stumbling over rocks and the emerging heads and shoulders of the buried Unspeakables. Her grief is beyond words, and even her tears look like drops of blood in the feeble firelight.

I have left a blind man to find my friend.

Phlegyas reaches the connecting tunnel between the Fourth and Third Circles first. Elinor trips and skids her way through next. Jeanne is moving with more energy now, and the second I stop, she slips down my shoulder.

"I can walk, Viking," she says in a hushed voice. The French maiden catches me by surprise when she adds, "Thank you."

Leave no man behind. The phrase continues to echo in my head.

"Viking, we must go on to the Third," says Phlegyas urgently. He has taken a water bottle from the last backpack we have: Elinor's. He is pouring some into Medusa's mouth. Her lips are trembling, and her translucent eyelids have movement behind them at last. Jeanne surprises me once more and drops to her knees next to Medusa. She takes the water bottle from Phlegyas.

"I will do that," she says.

Leave no man behind.

What happened to Mitchell? One moment he was talking to me, and the next he was screaming in pain. High-pitched and primal. Did an Unspeakable hurt him, or a Skin-Walker? Was he crushed by a boulder?

I hold the Viciseometer aloft. My shoulder aches in protest, but I merely raise the timepiece higher, daring the pain to consume me. I deserve it.

You think this journey will bring out the best in you, Viking. But it could also bring out the worst. In all of you. Friend will betray friend.

Love will be unfaithful to love. It is inevitable. All of your masks will slip and you each will be revealed for who you really are....

Virgil's words. Prophetic to the last syllable.

Leave no man behind.

"Elinor."

My princess does not turn around. Her hands are splayed across the rock; her forehead is pushing into the stone.

"Elinor."

I gently place my hand on her back; she does not move. I stroke her hair, as I have done on many occasions. Still she cannot face me. I can see the pink outline of the scar on the back of her neck. The very neatness of it makes my stomach shrink. My blade was her savior and foe that day in 1666. There are times when I am so connected to my axe, I barely notice that it is there. When I was carrying Jeanne, it became an extension of my arm, almost weightless. A part of me.

I know what I must do. I will leave a piece of my wretched body with Elinor, and then perhaps she will find it in her loving soul to forgive me.

My lips gently kiss her scar. It is so brief, I cannot tell if the fleeting touch even registers, but she must feel the weight of the Viciseometer slip into her back pocket, and the handle of my axe come to rest against her leg.

"I am delegating leadership to you. You need to save yourself—and M.J.," I whisper. "Do this for Mitchell. Carry on through the Third. I will see you on the other side, my princess."

I will see you on the other side, my princess. The last words the living Elinor ever heard. And they were uttered by me.

Elinor turns around, and I absorb the look of love on her face as she cries out.

"Alfarin, don't ye leave me!"

Leave no man behind.

Mitchell Johnson is not just a man. He is my friend.

And I will not leave him.

I plunge back into the darkness of the Fourth Circle. I have no light. I have no weapon. I have no protection whatsoever, except the bond of friendship I have with Mitchell Johnson, The Devil's intern and a brother to me in every way.

My boots connect with objects hard and soft. Momentum is my friend, and I let it guide me through the darkness to the spot where I think the guide was left behind.

"Virgil, Virgil!" I cry. "It is I, Prince Alfarin, son of Hlif, son of Dobin! I have come to aid you!"

"Viking, go back!" cries a voice, aged and decrepit.

My head whips to my left. That is the direction of the old man's voice. He said his other senses had become more attuned because of his blindness. I must not be afraid. I must forget that I cannot see and instead embrace what senses I have left.

An Unspeakable grabs at my body. They are moving clear of their confinement. My fist responds. The connection is glorious. A release of pain and hurt and anger and regret.

I push past rock and tortured skin. "Call to me again, Virgil!" I roar.

"To your right!" cries Virgil.

Virgil cannot see me, but I place my trust in him. I change direction in the darkness and run straight into a large rock that is already being moved. My hands sear with pain, but the sensation is brief. The rocks have yet to absorb the full toxicity of those who killed for personal gain. But I can tell, even in the darkness, that the circle has already started up again its relentless loop of suffering, and it won't be long before all of the newly fallen rock is being pushed by the Unspeakables.

"To your right again," calls Virgil, even closer now. "Hold out your hands, Viking. I will do the same. I can feel your...your..."

"Feel my what?"

The old man and I collide and crash to the ground. A rumbling and groaning to my left kicks my instincts into high gear, and I roll over as fast as lightning. A rock and the shuffling feet of an Unspeakable breeze past my head where I am lying on the ground.

"And they dared call me insane," says Virgil. "You've come back for him, haven't you."

"I have. Now, where is Mitchell?"

"Cupidiar took him. I thought I was close enough to protect the boy…"

"You are brave, Virgil, but no match for a Skin-Walker."

A dim light is inching through the cavern, pale orange, like the early-morning sun. I can see that more Unspeakables are now out of the ground.

"Where would Cupidiar have taken Mitchell?" I ask.

"Into the ground," replies Virgil. "We will have to follow."

"How?"

"Trust me," says Virgil again, but in the dim light, I suddenly sense that this is not the same unpleasant old man who was so easy to fool as we entered the Ninth Circle. Virgil is softer in face and warmer in countenance. His hands remain at his side as he weaves a path through the fallen boulders, sniffing the air and leaning to his right with his head bent as he listens to the shadows.

"A leap of faith," says Virgil suddenly, coming to an expanse of dark sand that is moving, as if an Unspeakable is about to break through.

"Why are you helping me?" I ask warily. "You don't even like Mitchell."

Virgil ponders the question, but his opaque eyes stare directly into mine as he does. Is that a flash of another color I see behind the foamy white? The shadows are starting to play tricks on me.

"I have felt nothing but pain and anger and hatred for so long," he replies quietly. "But your company has started to awaken in me another emotion that has no place in the Nine Circles of Hell. This feeling is most disconcerting…" He trails off.

"What feeling is that?"

"Love," says Virgil simply. "Now jump."

Tuttugu ok Sex

Alfarin, Elinor and Mitchell

Mitchell had procured cell phones for Elinor and me from Lord Septimus. She loved hers, while I found them a pain in the posterior. Why were the buttons so small? Were they designed for ants? I would wager their inventor was the same fool who created the computer mouse. I made a mental note to find out his or her name, for when he or she arrived in Hell, I would give him or her a piece of my mind and a close-up of my axe. Then that person would know the meaning of pain in the posterior, for I would shove my cell phone where the sun no longer shined.

Although I despised cell phones and made my feelings widely known, Mitchell was forever sending me texts:

> **starbanners** @ 8. new girl serving behind counter. hot!
> library NOW. patty has me cornered—help!
> thomasons @ 7. something 2 ask u.

———

Elinor and I arrived at Thomason's to meet with Mitchell, but the all-too-familiar and unpleasant sensation of being in a strange moment in time, like déjà vu, that we all felt had meant that Mitchell and Elinor had an argument and she left us. I led Mitchell down a dark corridor. I wanted to afford him the chance to explain before he apologized. Yet Mitchell was vexed. He was biting his nails, and he had lost one of those feminine bracelets he always wore: an olive bead one that Elinor liked . . . I think.

"This wasn't how it was supposed to happen," muttered Mitchell.

"How what was supposed to happen?"

The smell of piss was everywhere; Cousin Odd had been marking his territory again.

"I'm leaving, Alfarin," said Mitchell. "I'm leaving now."

"Leaving what?"

"I'm leaving Hell. I can't explain everything here, but I'm going to ask you to trust me, Alfarin. I'm asking you to come with me."

"No one can leave Hell, my friend."

"I've found a way."

I crossed my arms and leaned back against the damp stone. Big mistake. My tunic was going to require bleaching. Cousin Odd could spray like a water cannon if he had had enough mead.

"Then when do we leave?" I replied. Mitchell looked as if he was going to kiss me with relief. As first kisses go, it would be memorable, for all the wrong reasons, including the smell.

"You'll really come with me?"

"The gods would curse me if I allowed you to undertake this on your own, my friend. How much time do I have?"

We continued to converse. Mitchell did not divulge his plan, but he did not need to. I told him I would follow him into any battle.

Mitchell was my friend, my brother. I would never allow him to go somewhere dangerous by himself. He needed me.

As I needed him.

26. A Leap of Faith

A leap of faith. A jump into the unknown for my friends. That is an act I would perform without question. The old man takes my hand, and for a beat in time his fingers are not gnarled and rough, but slim and soft.

"Jump!" cries Virgil.

I do not have to be told thrice. With a roar I leap into the moving sand.

Immediately, burning particles cover my body. I have kept my eyes closed, not in fear, but for preservation. Any body part I leave exposed is an open invitation to the unknown evil in this place to attack. While Virgil's blindness makes the rest of his senses far more acute than mine, I want to preserve the one ability I have, if it means saving Mitchell.

We land quickly and with a soft, squelching sound. Sticky liquid rises around my feet. The rock-hewn chamber we have arrived in is well lit with blazing torches that look like human heads.

Virgil sniffs the air, which is ripe with the metallic stench of meat and blood.

"Your friend is this way," he says, pointing. "Listen—he is not far. And he is still capable of making noise. That is a good sign. It means the Skin-Walker has not yet removed it to join the others."

"Removed what?" I ask.

"Look at what we are treading upon," replies Virgil.

Long slabs of meat. Some thicker than others. They look like grotesque purple slugs, engorged with blood.

Tongues.

And they are still moving.

"What is this devilry?" I exclaim as a rush of sickness and bile combines in a bitter flow through my gullet.

"The fate of your friend if we do not reach him."

I have left my weapon with Elinor—I do not need it. It is not anger that spurs me to run through the shallow sea of flesh; it is love. Mitchell is not Cupidiar's to defile and torture.

And I will tear the Skin-Walker limb from limb if he even tries.

———————

I find Mitchell in the next cavern, upside down and spread-eagled across a stone wheel that has five spindles carved into it. His body is tied with ropes and his mouth gagged. He is desperately trying to break free of his bonds. I can see blood smeared across his bare chest. Judging from the deep lacerations, the blood is clearly his. My friend has not fully recovered from the burns of his immolation, and his skin is still a sunburned pink.

His pain becomes my next motivator. No one with such love in his heart—for his brother, his family, his friends—should suffer such torment.

The Skin-Walker has heard my arrival, I am sure of it, but Cupidiar is either too stupid or too vain to acknowledge my presence in his torture chamber. The beast is standing by a large flaming urn. In his hands are two long implements; he is heating them in the fire.

Then Virgil steps into the cave.

"Free your friend," he whispers. "I will deal with the Skin-Walker."

Cupidiar swirls around. The wolf pelt on his back arches its back and the snarling mouth on top of the Skin-Walker's head growls and bares bloody teeth. A chewed piece of tongue falls from its mouth. It thumps onto the ground with a crackling sizzle and disintegrates into blackened ash.

"The boy is mine," snarls Cupidiar. "He was a trespasser."

The implements in his hand are a pair of tongs and a long knife. Both are blazing white with the heat.

"The boy is not yours!" I cry. "He is ours. And I am claiming him back."

"Touch him and it will be your tongue I feed to my wolf next," snarls Cupidiar. "I am not an enemy to make, Viking."

"Neither am I," I reply, flexing my fingers. "I am Alfarin, son of Hlif, son of Dobin. I am one quarter of Team DEVIL, a confidant of Lord Septimus, the bane of The Devil, and Mitchell Johnson's wingman. And you are about to understand the meaning of Hell."

I run at the beast. He is quick, far quicker than me, and I slam into the rock wall as he sidesteps me. Yet while I am cumbersome in weight, I have the reflexes of a cat, as any warrior should, and these do not desert me. Pain does not even register as I swing my body clockwise and my fist connects with razor-sharp teeth. Instinctively I grab a handful of coarse fur and pull my quarry toward me. My flesh burns as Cupidiar's burning knife connects with my forearm.

"Fool!" cries Cupidiar. "I will hack your body into pieces and leave only your eyes intact, so they can watch as I feed your friend's tongue to my wolf!"

Suddenly the Skin-Walker crumples to the ground and howls in misery.

Virgil has his hands on either side of the Skin-Walker's face.

"When will you listen to me!" Virgil roars at me. "I said free your friend and I would deal with the Skin-Walker!"

I do not understand how an elderly, feeble being such as Virgil can have such power to make a Skin-Walker cower, but I run to Mitchell with Cupidiar's blade and hack through his bonds. I cannot help myself, and as I tug the gag from his mouth, I check to see if his tongue is still in place.

"Ge-*hoff*, Atharin," chokes Mitchell as I wiggle his tongue around. "Ith's slill there."

I embrace my friend like I have never hugged any Viking, man or devil before.

"I knew you'd come for me," he whispers, clutching at the back of my tunic.

"No friend gets left behind."

I have something in my eye. Something big and terrifying and very, very wet. So does Mitchell. We wipe our eyes with the backs of our hands, suddenly more interested in the decor of the torture chamber than in looking at each other.

"Are you ready to listen, Viking?" calls Virgil. He still has the cowering Skin-Walker between his hands. I can see ghostly swirls of red and white mist floating around his fingers, which are definitely no longer gnarled and decrepit. The Skin-Walker is jerking and whimpering in misery.

"I am," I call back.

"When I release Cupidiar, we must run. You and your friend must not leave me behind. Do you understand? You must follow my directions to the letter."

"We understand," I reply.

"Virgil isn't any ordinary guide, is he?" mumbles Mitchell.

"No, he isn't," I reply. "Indeed, I no longer believe he is a guide at all."

"*Run!*"

Tuttugu ok Sjau

Alfarin, Elinor and Mitchell

Team DEVIL was born in Hell and named at the HalfWay House. The Grim Reapers treated the dead as names on a piece of paper, but my friends and I had the last word. With the Viciseometer that Mitchell had procured from Lord Septimus's office in our possession, we traveled through time to the moment of our deaths. Mitchell wanted to stop his demise; Elinor wanted to ensure that hers happened—not because she wanted to die, but because she wanted to choose the path of least suffering; and my death was one I simply wanted to witness. And Medusa...

Even now, we will never truly understand what we did to Medusa, but when she eventually came into our existence and we learned of her experiences both on earth and in Hell, the facts of her life and death were a constant reminder that time is not something to take for granted.

Time is a movable state and should be treated with respect.

———

I knew watching my death would be hard on my friends, but it was Mitchell who was most affected by what we saw that day. I found the peace that I had not known I craved until the moment I saw my father carrying my lifeless body, wrapped in a red shroud, to the shoreline. Respect and honor were mine. I watched from a copse of trees, with my friends at my side. In the state Mitchell called a paradox, I knew that while my body burned, my corporeal soul had arrived at Valhalla. Yet it was also present to witness the scene. It made me think of the shadows in Hell. What were those shadows that followed me, really? Were they just manifestations of darkness, or were they actually more Alfarins, waiting, watching?

A universe of shadowy Alfarins... what a glorious thought.

27. Question Time

Heat.

Relief.

Fire.

Fear.

Blood.

Questions.

Flesh.

Screaming. Howling. Screaming. Howling. Heat. Relief. Fire. Fear. Blood. Questions. Flesh.

My mind has stopped working and I have become a slave to single words.

Mitchell. Virgil. Mitchell. Virgil.

Medusa.

Elinor. Elinor. Elinor.

Am I holding Virgil, or is he holding me? Our hands are entwined—not like lovers, but like captive and captor. Desperate, clinging.

Do. Not. Let. Go. Do. Not. Let. Go. Do. Not. Let. Go.

Our blind guide is running with me and Mitchell trailing behind him, clutching his hands like strings attached to a kite. He is leading us away from the Skin-Walker he overpowered so effortlessly.

Who is this devil, really? A charlatan, a fraudster? Lord Septimus knew who Virgil was, but the most powerful servant in Hell has been tricked once by a mind more devious than his.

Perhaps The Devil has an equal in deviousness. If Virgil is that equal, he would be wise to keep his trickster ways hidden from the master of Hell. Virgil is not what I thought.

"Can you guide us back to Medusa and Elinor?" gasps Mitchell. He is struggling, but still his concern is for our friends. Mitchell is all heart, even in the depths of permanent torment.

"I must take you to the Third Circle," calls Virgil. "Passage through the Nine Circles is your only option now, and it has been since the beginning. You know this. Death cannot be cheated, especially if you want something from it."

"Alfarin, will the girls be there, waiting?" asks Mitchell.

"I do not know," I reply. "I left Elinor, Medusa, Jeanne and Phlegyas in the connecting tunnel. My last words to Elinor were to continue without me—us. I left her the Viciseometer and my axe."

"You came looking for me without your axe?"

"Yes."

If Mitchell could read my mind, he would see more in my answer than one word. He would see that I said good-bye to Elinor, not knowing if I would endure in this existence. For as she turned to me and begged me not to leave her, I did not just see the loveliness in her face, but I saw her once more on the fields of battle, alongside Lord Septimus.

And in my chest I felt the loneliness of my own impending doom, and also that of Mitchell.

For we were not in that vision from Valhalla.

I left Elinor my axe not for protection in the Circles of Hell, but for protection on the fields of Ragnarök. Time has permitted me to see her future. I am yet to be afforded the honor of seeing my own.

It still has to be earned.

Running blind, Virgil leads us on through a path of flesh and blood. It drips from the roof, it slides down the rugged walls. My boots squelch through the tortured castoffs of Unspeakables left unable to scream.

Yet I can hear them with every step.

It is hard to not think of the sheer amount of evil that has walked the land of the living when you are treading on its remains, yet as the ground becomes firmer and the walls begin to glisten in the firelight with crystals instead of blood, it becomes easier to think of the good in mankind above the horror. Billions and billions of dead souls must have transferred through the HalfWay House. Good, decent, hard-working souls. Numbers that far outweigh the number of Unspeakables in the Circles of Hell. Some are sorted into Up There, most arrive in Hell. The destination is irrelevant in the end. Death comes to all, but fate is in one's hands. Not even the businesslike Grim Reapers can strip the dead of that.

I just wish there were a way to show the living this, for when one is on one's deathbed, one will only have regret for what one has *not* done.

"Do you not think the living deserve to exist without the knowledge of what is to come?" asks Virgil suddenly, breaking the claustrophobic silence that has cocooned us since we escaped Cupidiar. "Knowledge of an unending Afterlife filled with toil and hardship would not be welcomed by most."

"I think devils who have the power to see into another's thoughts should mind their own hearth first," I retort. Virgil's question has made me uneasy, as he has suddenly reminded me of The Devil, who gave me the impression back in the accounting chamber that he, too, could read my thoughts. Virgil has no right to intrude into any part of my death, least of all my mind.

"What are you really thinking, Viking?" asks Virgil, slowing to a halt at a fork in the tunnel.

"I want to know who you are," I reply.

"An answer for a question."

"Riddles?" asks Mitchell incredulously as he gingerly touches the deep lacerations across his chest. "Really? Oh, this is fantastic. Our girlfriends are in who knows what kind of Hell right now, with only a naked ferryman and a psychotic witch for company, but screw that, let's play a game! Hey, as long as we're at it, I think I have Monopoly hidden in my boxers! We could ask the Skin-Walkers to join in! I think Perfidious should be the banker, don't you? He seems like a fair guy. And instead of jail, we're sent to a Circle of Hell!"

"Pain has been known to make my friend hysterical," I say. "Is there anything we can do to quicken his healing?"

"Hysteria makes him hysterical," replies Virgil, pointing to the left side of the fork in the tunnel. "Trust me, I know. It is not far to the Third Circle. I can smell the excess of gluttony. It is rank. Now will you indulge me?"

"Ask," I reply.

"I am fascinated by your devotion to this quest. You have come all this way, and you may still have far to go, to find The Devil's Banshee. Yet she clearly does not want to be found. You of all devils know the pain of love. Why not leave her be? Does The Devil even miss his original Dreamcatcher?"

"That's *two* questions, Virgil," Mitchell says menacingly.

"I have only the words of Lord Septimus to fall back on," I say. "But he told us that The Devil loved Beatrice Morrigan very much."

"Septimus would know, of course," replies Virgil. "He, too, was married once, but unhappily. Sometimes it is one's own unhappiness in a relationship that shines a brighter light on true love in others."

"My turn," I say. "Who are you?"

"You know who I am. I am Virgil, guide to the foolish, the brave and the lovelorn."

"I do not believe you."

"My turn," says Virgil, ignoring my statement. "How long was the girl you pine for a Dreamcatcher?"

"Days, weeks. I do not know," I say. "What I do know is that it was a continuous horror from which she could not escape."

Mitchell is pulling on my arm. His entire body is turned back to face the way we have just come.

"Alfarin, we're being followed," he whispers. "The shadows."

"It will be the Skin-Walkers," says Virgil. "There are six trailing you at the moment."

"You were able to beat back Cupidiar," I say. "Can you teach us how?"

Virgil laughs, but it is more the hacking, phlegmy bark of an old man than an expression of humor.

"It is not something that can be taught! It is a gift, if you choose to look at it that way. A gift that is—"

"The girls aren't here," says Mitchell, looking around frantically. "Where the Hell are the girls?"

We have come to an entrance, but one that is far smaller than any we've seen so far. It is a set of bars, packed tightly together. Human teeth are fused to the black metal like miniature gravestones.

"Your traveling companions will have gone on ahead," says Virgil.

"What *exactly* do we find in the Third Circle, Virgil?" I ask.

"The Unspeakables here are those who murdered for addiction and want," replies the old man. "They lie sightless in the vile slush of their making, victims to the ceaseless icy rain."

"Rain?" asks Mitchell. "In Hell? Golly gee, this is quite the field trip we're having, isn't it, Alfarin? The Devil should run tours. He could call it Seasons of Sin. I'll sell tickets from the accounting office—help pay the bills."

"*Hysteria,*" I whisper to Virgil. The old man simply does not know what to make of Mitchell. His mouth is gaping as it tries to form the words that do not do my friend's twisted humor justice.

"The ice rain might heal his burns from the immolation," says Virgil eventually. "I do not think there is a cure for such madness, though. I certainly never found it."

Virgil pushes the bars and we step through into yet another cave.

There is light, but it is not from fire. The temperature plummets as scenes like colorful rainbow-filled shadows play out over the walls, as if they are being projected from within the rock. They are glimpses of the living world left behind: blue waves crashing against the shore, children playing with jump ropes, couples kissing, a table filled with food, blood, blood, a knife slashing down on exposed skin, blood...

"I hate this! Get us the Hell out of here, Virgil!" cries Mitchell.

A rumble, like thunder, causes the three of us to turn our heads upward. A crack appears in the roof of the cave.

"Hold on!" cries Virgil. Suddenly, thousands upon thousands of small white balls, with just a blob of color in their centers, cascade down on top of us. My first instinct is to grab Mitchell; his first instinct is to grab me. We both snatch for Virgil as another crack, this time in the wall, appears in front of us.

We slide through the opening, spinning and turning on an avalanche of human eyeballs to the Third Circle of Hell.

Tuttugu ok Átta

Alfarin and Elinor

After we had visited my death, I knew I needed time to be alone. Mitchell had decided that our home base in the land of the living would be the opulent palace known as the Plaza Hotel in New York. Pleasant as it was, it was not a place to clear my head. So I ventured outside and walked amongst the gleaming metal beasts called cars to the great green park across the way.

I knew I was being watched, by the living and the dead. Those with beating hearts were obvious about it; I could see their eyes widen as I stopped traffic with the mere manliness of my figure as I strode to the park. The dead were but rumors on the biting wind, yet I sensed their presence all the same. I did not know it then, but I was picking up on the faintest trace of Skin-Walkers, who in another timeline had been stalking Team DEVIL because of Medusa, right here in New York City. Her participation in this adventure to the land of the living had been erased in a paradox, but the evil of the Skin-Walkers permeated all timelines. Medusa was not with Elinor and Mitchell back at the Plaza while I took my walk on this day, and yet she had been—once. And so had the Skin-Walkers...who left an indelible trace of wickedness wherever they went.

I still wrestle with the complexities and consequences of this paradox.

Fortunately for me, one constant that not even time could

change was Elinor. She had followed me out of the hotel. We sat on a bench in silence at first, if one could call it silence. There was so much noise and color around us, even in the dead of night. How did the living in that city ever sleep?

"My death should be next, Alfarin," said Elinor suddenly. "And ye must promise me ye will do exactly as I ask of ye when we are there."

"I will not let you down," I replied.

"I know. And I will never let ye down, either," she said, resting her head on my shoulder. "I have waited for so long, but I am not scared. This is fate and meant to be." She shivered. "Come. It is starting to rain, and I am still so cold. Can we go back?"

I stood up and offered Elinor my hand, but at that moment, three people appeared out of the darkness and blocked our path. A male, a female and a child who was adult in height and yet had the pustulant skin pox of an adolescent. The adult male and female wore thick-rimmed glasses; he also had two cameras around his neck, while she was carrying a tome titled *The Rough Guide to New York City.*

Elinor and I were about to be accosted by that which dead New Yorkers still bemoaned in the Afterlife.

Tourists.

"Take a picture, mate?" asked the older male in an accent I recognized as English.

They wanted a picture of me mating? I was not happy about this question, but before I could refuse, the woman pushed the pox-ridden adolescent toward me and grabbed my arm, looping hers through, although her fingers spent too much time groping my biceps for comfort. Then the other started clicking away with one of the contraptions called a camera.

The female then seemed very interested in my broad shoulders, as she kept putting her arm across them.

The silent adolescent looked as if he wanted a one-way ticket to Hell via a hole in the earth.

Elinor stood with her hands on her hips and did not know what to say when they pressed green paper with numbers on it into her hands. Professing their thanks, the man and the woman stumbled away, dragging the boy-man with them.

"Ye are going to end up on the Internet, Alfarin!" hissed Elinor. "I have heard all about it. There is a new thing called a meme. Mark my words, there will be pictures of ye with the words *Keep calm and hug a Viking* written underneath."

I puffed up my chest in delight. This was a grand journey indeed. I had witnessed my death, seen my body burned with ritual honor, and been accosted by Internet tribesfolk who paid for the privilege.

"Do you think there is enough money there to buy a bucket of chicken?" I asked.

Judging by the tight line Elinor's mouth had created, there might have been, but I wasn't about to get it.

28. Cerberus

It is almost impossible to stand. The ground is wet and slippery, as if covered in a film of decaying leaves. The eyeballs roll to the sides of the passageways and are swallowed by holes in the rock floor.

I help Virgil to stand. A thin layer of white mucus clings to his red robes. The skullcap remains atop his thinning hair, but he flattens the cloth down to secure it. Mitchell is bent forward, holding his knees. He is gagging, but my friend has no food in his stomach to retch up. I tug a long string of eyeball membrane from Mitchell's spiky blond hair.

I never believed I would see the day when our appetites were vanquished, but it has finally happened. My throat is parched, but I do not think I could stomach a drink or a meal right now without regurgitating them. There is no food left that would not remind me of the horrors I have seen in these circles.

"The Third Circle is the domain of the Skin-Walker named Gulapale," says Virgil. "The Unspeakables here lie in the rain, continually beaten down by the ice and hail that fall from above. As in the Ninth, you will have to take care as to where you tread, but remember, the Unspeakables are not encased here. If a hand grabs your leg, they will take you down. And if you value your sight..."

The blind guide trails off. To lose one's vision must be a dreadful torment. To never see beauty, even in Hell, is a fate I would not like to endure.

"Three more circles," says Mitchell. "But we have to find Medusa before the Second Circle, Alfarin. We can't let her face Cupidore and whatever is left of her stepfather alone."

"We will find them, and Beatrice Morrigan," I say confidently. "But we must hurry. How are your burns and lacerations, my friend? Even in this weak light, I can see the healing. You are strong."

"I've felt worse," replies Mitchell. "I can't remember when, but it'll come to me."

The three of us walk toward a gauzy, shimmering curtain. A pale sheen, like moonlight, illuminates it. There are several animal noises echoing beyond. Distinct growls, different in pitch and length, get louder the closer we get to the curtain.

The smell is atrocious and relentless in its assault on my nostrils. A mixture of rotting fish and excrement. Even the outhouses in my Viking village did not have a stench like this.

"Will we have to pass Cerberus?" I ask Virgil.

"You will," replies the old man. "Yet with luck, the others may have done most of the work in that regard."

"What do you mean?" I ask, stopping. "The others will have done what work?"

I am learned—I know of Cerberus. A three-headed beast of a dog who was the offspring of the monsters Echidna and Typhon. His job is to prevent the dead from leaving the circle—

"Enough," says Mitchell, interrupting my thoughts. "We don't have time for a Q and A session, or for strategizing. We've gotten this far. Can we just go on instinct from now on? Our plans always go to shit anyway."

We step through the shimmering apparition—it is ice-cold rain. My skin protests as the sensation of a thousand needles pricks my skin. But Mitchell, already battle-scarred and damaged, does not stop walking. His eyes are keen and alert.

"Lead us through, Mitchell," I call. "Virgil, you tell Mitchell the way, and I will bring up the rear."

Pathetic figures are curled up in balls on the ground. Brown slush from the falling hail laps at their flayed skin. They barely move as Mitchell traverses a path toward the sound of the growls, which are getting more ferocious with every step we take. The Unspeakables have dark, bloody pits where their eyes once were. Virgil said this was the circle for those who murdered for addiction and want. Their eyes are removed as punishment for coveting. This Circle of Hell has order amidst its chaos—a structured evil.

"Alfarin," calls Mitchell. "I think I can hear shouting."

"Do not wander away from me," says Virgil. "Gulapale is the most animalistic of the Skin-Walkers. He will not toy with his prey like Cupidiar. You will be pinned to the ground and your eyes devoured before you have time to scream."

I have yet to understand why Virgil is immune to the Skin-Walkers, but for the moment, I am content simply with using his power to our advantage. For with every step we take, we get closer to Beatrice Morrigan. And when we find her, I will not entertain a conversation with her. The circles have tested me to my limits, but I have seen us through and led Team DEVIL almost to the end. If the Banshee will not come back with us, I will just take her. Even if it's by the hair, I will take her. That creature is returning to The Devil whether she wants to or not.

Virgil is making a strange noise, snuffling like a forest animal. I think it is muffled laughter. Our guide is insane, that much is clear. Yet he has been faithful to the cause, and I owe him a great debt for assisting in the rescue of Mitchell.

The Unspeakables continue to shudder on the ground. I am soaked through, and my limbs are becoming heavy and wooden with the cold. The icy rain is relentless and falls like hail on steel. Mitchell leads on with purpose; his pale body looks like white marble in the rain.

Then a large black creature comes into focus through the torrents. And at its feet—at first appearing like stick figures—are four souls I recognize. They are dodging and weaving with their arms flailing, and it seems almost as if they are throwing things at the beast.

"Do not leave my side!" shouts Virgil, preempting my desire to run to Elinor, Medusa, Jeanne and Phlegyas. It is just as well he cried the warning, for a split second later, a Skin-Walker lands in front of us on all fours like a stalking wolf.

Gulapale has darker, redder skin than the other Skin-Walkers. It also has a sickly green tinge to it. It is akin to the special shade of unstable rust that used to affect Viking iron if it was not cared for with respect. His limbs are longer than those of the other Skin-Walkers, but his body is squat. The growl that emanates from his chest is canyon-deep. As he crouches, his sharp blackened nails scrape against the ground, gouging lines that look like the scars slashed across Mitchell's chest.

"Cross my path, Virgil," he snarls, again with the same inhuman, animalistic voice as the other Skin-Walkers. "I dare you."

Virgil does not reply, but he accepts the challenge with a step toward the monster. Gulapale immediately yelps and jumps backward, like an injured animal.

"Stay close to me and join your friends," says Virgil, not taking his white eyes from Gulapale's direction. "Phlegyas has told them how to get past the beast with three heads. We must blind it with mud."

I look to Mitchell for one of his utterances of wit, but my friend has a steely countenance. I know it well. His hysteria has ebbed. And his humor will not return until he is reunited with Medusa.

"Three heads, seven of us," I say. "I like those odds."

Gulape is snarling and spitting, but he does not come near us. As we get closer to the three-headed dog, Cerberus, I can see the others clearly now. My soul soars. Elinor, her long red hair darkened by the vile rain, is issuing orders like a true leader. To my surprise, Jeanne is following. Phlegyas is throwing handful after handful of dark-green filth at the beast's eyes. Medusa is the least active of the four, but it is good to see her on her feet.

Then she turns and sees Mitchell.

"No—Medusa, stay there!" cries my friend, throwing out his hand as a visual warning in case she cannot hear. "Don't leave Elinor."

The others stop throwing mud and turn, too. Huge smiles betray their relief. Even Phlegyas grins. Jeanne...well, Jeanne always looks as if she has gas trapped in her intestinal tract, but I am not offended by the lack of an outward display of pleasure at our return.

"Do not stop!" cries the Maid of Orléans. "The beast can devour three of us with one snap, and I do not intend for it to be my head it chews on."

With thoughts like twin brothers, Mitchell and I flank Virgil, lift him clean off the floor and run. Ahead, I see my axe and the last backpack lying on the ground. Brown slush has covered the blade, and I can see an Unspeakable inching his fingers toward it. The evildoer is blind, but my weapon is like a magnet, drawing him closer.

I step on the Unspeakable's fingers and tread them into the ground.

"My axe is not for the likes of you to covet!" I snarl. I pick it up and start swinging at the mud surrounding us, loosening huge chunks for the others to throw.

Cerberus is a beast the size of three men. Red eyes—watery and filled with pus—dart in all directions as we throw more mud to blind it.

"Mitchell and Medusa!" I cry. "Aim for the head on the right. Jeanne and Phlegyas, your quarry is the center. Elinor..."

"Yes?"

"You are with me?"

I did not mean for it to come out as a question, but my voice rose at the end nonetheless.

"Always," replies my princess.

"Virgil, sniff out the exit!" I shout. "*Now throw like our deaths depend on it!*"

Cerberus twists and ducks, his sharp teeth snapping, but the beast is soon edging backward into the cavern. His four paws crush countless Unspeakables as layer upon layer of mud coats his eyeballs. From the corner of my eye I can see Virgil feeling a path across the rock wall.

"Virgil," I call. "When you have the way out, shout for us. We will all come running at once."

Seconds later the old man cries out and we all splash through the slush toward him. At the last moment, Mitchell ducks back, grabs the last remaining backpack and only just makes it into the corridor with his head intact as Cerberus's central mouth snaps a yard above him.

Medusa punches Mitchell on the arm; then she throws her arms around him and buries her face in his neck. For once he is not smothered in hair. The icy rain has flattened Medusa's wild curls.

"Ye saved him," says Elinor, collapsing against me. "Ye saved Mitchell."

"I could not have done so without Virgil," I reply. "But never doubt me, Elinor. I told you once that I would never let you down, and whilst I cannot die trying, I have an eternity to show you."

Team DEVIL is through the Third Circle. Just two remain, but for Medusa, the terror to come could prove the hardest of all.

Tuttugu ok Níu

Alfarin

Death was not peaceful. Death was not natural. And the taste of fear that coated the tongues of those who had a drawn-out death lingered for centuries in the Afterlife. Broken bodies were mended by Grim Reapers at the HalfWay House, but death memories could not be erased—unless there was a paradox, and few got to experience that.

Elinor's death could have been worse. It was a statement I made to myself over and over again after witnessing the event—and participating in it.

Elinor had always said she died in the Great Fire of London, and so that is where we time-traveled next. I felt prepared. But to actually witness her demise was horrifying. Imagine burning with no escape. Smelling your own flesh roasting. Feeling your pulverized internal organs failing. When Mitchell and I found her, she was experiencing all that and more. Who in Hell would own such a death? And how could I refuse my princess when she begged me to end her agony?

I know I did the right thing. But I found the day of her passing very hard to exist with. It was not the flash of my blade or the blood that followed that haunted me, though those images would be seared in my memory forever. Rather, it was the screams that plagued me. Hell was full of shrieking devils, yet the screams of the living that I heard all around me on Elinor's deathday were far worse. Perhaps they stayed with me because they howled with more than just pain. There was also the noise of the knowledge of impending death—and the fear that what was to come was far worse than their current suffering.

I never told Elinor or Mitchell of the nightmares that haunted me after that day in 1666. And they were always the same.

Darkness and screams.

————

Lord Septimus found me one evening walking the corridors of Hell. As much as I loved my friends, occasionally I needed my own company. Of course, one was never truly alone in Hell. There were always devils around, and even the solitude of the library was inhabited by shadows. But strangers and shadows would not wonder at what was going on in my head.

"Out walking again, Prince Alfarin?" Lord Septimus's question startled me. I had been deep in thought and looked up to find I'd unwittingly made my way into the central business district. I could not explain why, and I hoped I was not in trouble.

"I could not sleep, Lord Septimus," I replied. "I apologize if I disturbed you."

"There are nights when I do not even attempt to sleep," said Lord Septimus. "May I accompany you for a stretch, Prince Alfarin?"

I nodded, and he smiled. "Truth be told, I find I can hear myself think much better when I'm out in the open." He led me onto an express elevator, and after a brief, hurtling journey, the doors opened to reveal the level 1 corridor.

"This way," said Lord Septimus, stepping off and striding down the hall. I followed, and when he disappeared around a corner, I discovered he'd stepped onto the balcony that looked down on the six hundred and sixty-six floors below us. He beckoned for me to join him at the cast-iron railing.

The sight was magnificent. And of course, I thought of Elinor, and wished she could see the constellations of torches with me, from this high up.

Lord Septimus was quiet for several moments. Then he turned to me. "I cannot differentiate between the screams of the living and the screams of the dead when I sleep," he said softly. "Perhaps I should have been an angel and had that ability taken away from me for eternity." He laughed, but his mirth was heavy with sarcasm.

"You hear screaming, too, when you have a nightmare?" I asked.

"Always."

"Who?"

Lord Septimus's flaming red eyes flickered back to the corridor. Across the hall from the balcony was the massive door that led to the accounting chamber—and within that, The Devil's Oval Office.

"Helping those we care about escape torment is honorable, Prince Alfarin," said Lord Septimus. "Yet sometimes our best intentions have unforeseen consequences."

"I killed Elinor Powell," I said quietly.

"I know."

"Who did you kill?" I asked, my voice barely a whisper.

"I was a Roman general in life, and am The Devil's number one servant in Hell," replied Lord Septimus. "I have so much blood on my hands I could fill a river."

My midnight stroll was not having the calming effect I desired. I had an iron-clad stomach, but Lord Septimus was making me irritable, and suddenly the great height was making me nauseous.

"I should head back to my dormitory," I said, eager to get away. "It was...interesting talking to you, as always, Lord Septimus."

"Never run from the screams of your nightmares, Prince Alfarin," called Lord Septimus as I reached the elevator. "They are there to remind us we were once human, for good and bad. Screams are the sound of our conscience. They are the voice of pain, but also love."

29. The Second Circle

"We should take more rest, water and food," I say. "At least for those who can stomach it."

Mitchell collapses to the ground of the connecting tunnel between the Third and Second Circles and doesn't move. Terrified exhaustion claims Elinor and Medusa, too. Jeanne offers to take first watch, and Phlegyas offers to keep her company. Virgil's blind eyes are open, but he appears to have gone into a trance.

I sleep and have a nightmare of blood and screams.

When I awaken, Medusa and Elinor are keeping watch. My princess has found a flintlike rock and is sharpening my blade. I watch the graceful, hypnotic sweep of her arm as it moves down and away, igniting the silver edge with sparks of white fire. One by one, the others start to stir. Our journey through the Nine Circles has taken us at least three days and nights by my calculation. We cannot afford to lose more time.

"We have but one true circle of torment to travel through, and then we reach Limbo," I say as Jeanne stretches. "One more circle, and then this horror will be over."

"Except we haven't found any trace of Beatrice Morrigan yet," whispers Medusa. Mitchell passes her a half-empty bottle of water.

No. A half-full bottle of water. A glass must always be half full.

"But we're getting closer, M," says Elinor. "And that's what matters."

"What do you think The Devil is doing right now?" asks Mitchell, turning to me and keeping his voice low. "How long have we been in here, Alfarin? I'm so tired, I can't think straight. What if he's taken my brother already? When that Skin-Walker had me, that's what he kept saying."

"He was feasting on your fear, my friend," I reply. "The Skin-Walkers can take us individually. If they had held me captive, they would have attempted to scare me as well. But do not forget just how deceitful they are. Lying is second nature to them. For now, I do not believe The Devil has taken M.J."

I thump Mitchell on the back for encouragement. But privately, I must admit that the more evil I witness in this vile place, the more I start to believe that we may be too late. The Skin-Walkers are not creatures of their word. Why should the master of Hell be? The Devil could have sent Grim Reapers out to find a new child to be his Dreamcatcher the second we left through the reception area's doors. The majority of devils in Hell are true of soul, and only ended up there because of a random, bureaucratic choice, nothing more. But the realm's despotic ruler is a different matter altogether. Very little about him seems random anymore.

"Are ye ready, M?" asks Elinor, placing her arm around Medusa's shoulders. The newest member of Team DEVIL is wilting before my eyes. She is slight of build anyway, but her entire frame appears to be shrinking into itself.

"The Second Circle is for those who murdered for lust," says Medusa. Her tone is monotonous, as if she is reading from a textbook. "They are blown back and forth by a violent storm."

"Cupidore is the Skin-Walker with governance over this next place," adds Virgil. "And it is the largest and most heinous of all. For unlike the other Circles of Hell, it is not just the final dwelling of those who murdered. Those who robbed the innocence and virtue of man, woman and child also end up here, even if those victims continued to live after their torment. There are more victims, and therefore more perpetrators to bring here."

"Rory Hunter is in here," says Medusa.

Mitchell steps forward and takes her hand.

"Alfarin has his axe, Medusa," he says. "And I have my fists. If that bastard comes anywhere near you, there'll be nothing left of him. I promise you."

And I believe him. To destroy another in battle is a warrior's bane and glory. It is a feat that results in terrifying nightmares and magnificent dreams. Mitchell arrived in Hell a very different soul than the devil who stands before me today. Hell has made Mitchell Johnson into a devil who is to be cherished and also feared.

For now, when it counts, he will step up first to take and deal the blow.

"How are we to proceed through this circle?" asks Jeanne. She and Phlegyas are standing side by side, waiting for orders. Neither appears to be afraid, but that is not necessarily a good state of mind. Fear keeps the mind alert and senses primed.

"How violent is the storm in this circle?" I ask Virgil.

"It is one of the nine," replies Virgil, rubbing his eyes.

"That does not answer my question," I say.

"I think that's Virgil's poetic way of saying on a sliding scale of craptitude, we're in for a dumping," says Mitchell.

Even the corners of Jeanne's mouth raise a fraction. The end is so close. We cannot fail now. Optimism and hope must be our allies—finally.

"'But to that Second Circle of sad Hell, / Where in the gust, the whirlwind, and the flaw / Of rain and hail-stones, lovers need not tell / Their sorrows—pale were the sweet lips I saw, / Pale were the lips I kiss'd, and fair the form / I floated with, about that melancholy storm,'" recites Elinor.

"I know it…I know it…," I say, stroking my beard. "That is Keats, is it not?"

"Ten points to Alfarin," says Elinor. She turns to Jeanne, who has quickly lost the rumor of a smile. "Alfarin and I quizzed each other on poetry one Valentine's Day. Keats has always been my favorite."

"And nothing says *I love you* more than a passionate quickie in the Circles of Hell," mutters Mitchell. "I think this place has finally addled Elinor's brain."

"I never thought the day would arrive when I agreed with Mitchell Johnson, but I do," replies Jeanne. "Forget your poetry points, Viking. Tell us how we are to proceed. Beatrice Morrigan is still our goal, and she remains out of sight."

"If Keats is correct," I say, ignoring Jeanne, "we can expect whirlwinds, rain and hail. We need to stay in close formation, all seven of us. If someone is taken by the wind, then the other six can act as anchors. Virgil is to lead the procession once more to guide us through the circle. We will follow in pairs. Jeanne, you and Mitchell next. Medusa and Phlegyas to take the fourth and fifth places, followed by Elinor and me at the rear."

"Boy, girl, boy, girl," says Jeanne sarcastically. "How quaint."

"Strategic," says Phlegyas. "Males are naturally heavier and stronger than most females. That isn't a slight to your abilities or bravery or character, Maid of Orléans. It is simple fact."

"Are you ready, child?" asks Virgil to Medusa.

"Beatrice Morrigan…Beatrice Morrigan…," says Medusa, shaking out her limbs as if preparing for a race. "Let's go."

Virgil takes us on a short walk, but it comes to a dead end. We do not question his guidance. Instead, we wait patiently for him as his gnarled fingers trace circular patterns over the rock wall.

It starts to shake. Fragments of stone fall from the roof.

"Help me to push!" cries Virgil.

Phlegyas, Jeanne and I step forward, and the four of us press our heels into the ground and propel a door of sorts away from us. It does not come away in one clean square or rectangular shape. The edges are jagged and sharp. It is more of a lightning bolt than a door, but it is an entrance nonetheless.

And the moment it opens onto the Second Circle, Jeanne is sucked through by a vortex of wind.

I grab her ankle, but I, too, am lifted off the ground. Phlegyas holds on to my waist as Mitchell and Medusa rush forward to assist. Elinor swaps places with Mitchell and he jumps up, wraps his arms around Jeanne's body and drags her downward.

The whirlwind passes and we fall into a heap on the ground.

"Thank you," says Jeanne quietly, pushing herself up. "Your strategy worked, Viking. That is wind like I have never felt before. It was like hands, furiously tearing me away from the ground."

"Hail and rain we can deal with," says Virgil. "But you will have to keep a sharp eye on the wind funnels as they pass through the circle. The angel is correct. The storm is a tempest of hatred and anger. It wants to claim you."

My eyes adjust to our new surroundings. The elements are harsh in here, and I have to keep one hand over my face to see just a few steps ahead.

"Keep to the edge, Virgil," I call. "Even if it takes longer to circumnavigate the perimeter, it will be safer."

We start our slow procession through the Second. I can hear the howls of Skin-Walkers behind us, and the lone howl of the one hidden by the storm in this circle. I could help Medusa with supportive words from here—even though Elinor and Phlegyas are between us—but I do not. She has Mitchell. Medusa is not a devil to be smothered.

Unspeakables loom to our left like trees bent double by the wind. Their feet are encased by the stony ground, but their legs and backs are exposed to the viciousness of the elements. It should not be possible for bones to bend like theirs do, but this is not a realm that plays by the normal rules of nature. As we get closer, I can hear their bones shattering as they try to right themselves after the passage of the tornado. Each Unspeakable has its mouth open in a relentless scream of agony, but, like the Unspeakables in every circle, with no tongues to form the noise, they cannot voice their pain.

The worst of the worst are punished here, but for the first time, an Unspeakable has an actual face and a name.

Rory Hunter. The Unspeakable who was allowed by The Devil to escape the Circles of Hell with The Devil's Dreamcatcher in tow. Rory Hunter thought he was smart, but The Devil manipulated him like a marionette. The master of Hell tricked him into wielding the Dreamcatcher to let loose a terrible virus on angels to test its efficiency.

And his four victims just happened to be the members of Team ANGEL—with Team DEVIL thrown into the mix just for fun.

There is so much for which I will never forgive The Devil, and Operation H, the name he gave his experiment, is one of them. My anger toward Rory Hunter, for all he did to Medusa in life, and for all he did to her—and us—in death, burns just as hotly, even though he was recaptured by the Skin-Walkers and returned to his rightful place here, in the Second Circle of Hell.

A thought suddenly occurs to me. I lean forward as we continue to trudge through the hail and rain.

"Elinor, move forward and swap places with Jeanne," I say.

"Why?"

"Because it is not just Medusa we need to watch out for in this circle."

My princess does not question me further; she just does as I ask. I pick up the pace and fill the gap she creates when she passes the others to the front of the group. I can only just make out her form in the blur of precipitation.

Suddenly Jeanne breaks free from the singular formation. I hear Medusa scream out, and our friend quickly follows the Maid of Orléans.

"Stop them!" cries Virgil, but we do not have to be told. Elinor, Mitchell and I are already running after the two girls. We catch Medusa quickly, but Jeanne is gone. A quick burst of light is all that remains before it dissolves on the wind.

"Jeanne has gone after Rory Hunter. She blames him for her predicament!" I yell as hail the size of golf balls beats down against our exposed skin. Mitchell's naked torso is already pockmarked with huge red welts. Medusa wraps her arms around him to try to protect his body with hers, but the hail is getting larger. We cannot stay here.

"Did she immolate?" shouts Mitchell.

Medusa nods. The wind is getting so violent my tongue is being pulled from my mouth. I can feel the pressure pushing out my eyeballs.

"We cannot leave Jeanne!" yells Elinor.

"Another wind funnel!" cries Phlegyas. "To our left!"

Elinor's feet are whipped away from beneath her and she is dragged into the vortex. I slam my axe into the ground and push Mitchell and Medusa down onto the handle.

"Hold on!" I cry as I hurl myself into the storm.

I am immediately thrown around like a rag doll, with no sense of up or down, left or right. The violence of the screams contained within shatters my eardrums, but a sickening sixth sense tells me that these are not the cries of the tortured Unspeakables, but are instead the voices of their living victims.

And one voice is pleading above them all.

I can hear the abuse of the living Melissa Pallister within the wind funnel.

Prir Tigir

Alfarin, Elinor and Mitchell

Mitchell Johnson was seventeen years old when he died. One year older than I was when I met my end, and two years younger than Elinor. He could never remember why he ran out in front of that bus on the eighteenth of July in 2009, but it was a decision he wanted to change—right up until the moment he time-traveled back to that day and saw the event unfold from a different perspective.

After visiting Elinor's death, we had used the Viciseometer to go to the busy American city of Washington, DC, on Mitchell's death-day. By this point, Team DEVIL was having problems. Our journey seemed strange, and fuzzy somehow, and our group of three felt an absence among us. Later on, we would discover that our befuddled brains were trying to cope with a hole that had been ripped into our timeline and our memories. Our friend Medusa Pallister, whom we had yet to meet, had been amongst us on this journey—but had disappeared from our midst in a paradox.

We did not know any of this at the time, of course, and the true consequences of that paradox were about to be revealed to us.

Elinor and I tried to stop Mitchell from changing his death, but the decision in the end was his alone. I watched my friend walking toward his living self with the intention of alerting him to the oncoming bus. Elinor was sobbing on my shoulder. The Mitchell we knew and loved in Hell was about to disappear. In a strange sense, death was coming to one who was already dead. It was a reversal of the natural order.

As I watched, I realized that the living Mitchell was the one who didn't seem real to me. *He* was the shadow, not the dead, corporeal soul closing in on him. And he seemed so oblivious to the fact that he was living.

Then the living Mitchell glanced up and saw his dead self across the street, just as the Greyhound bus approached.

My death was the result of my own naïveté. Elinor's happened because of her selflessness. She put her two little brothers' lives before her own.

But Mitchell's death was caused by…*him*. The living Mitchell saw the dead Mitchell and, shocked at the sight of his own soul, ran out into the road to get a better look—and just like that, he was crushed. And now that the moment had been fixed in time by the Viciseometer, it could never be undone.

That was the moment when I first sensed that something far more powerful than Team DEVIL was steering us down a path from which we could not deviate.

A final, final fate.

We were puppets. And we had no clue who was holding the strings.

30. Weapons of War

The ghost of Melissa Pallister is in my head. She is begging Rory Hunter not to hurt her. Begging him to think of her mother. There is no cessation to this terrified voice of a child who had her soul torn from her heart while she was living.

And it makes me angrier than ever before.

How dare Unspeakables take what is not theirs to own? A life, a soul, a heart, a body. Melissa Pallister was an innocent, and she was violated by someone who should have wanted to do nothing more than protect her.

The heat of rage is burning in my chest. I can sense it spreading through the congealed dead blood in my useless veins. Awakening every inch of me that once lived.

But I am not the only one starting to immolate in the vortex, for my princess can hear the voice, too, and it tortures her just as much as it pains me.

Elinor and I explode into a firestorm of flame and smoke. Elinor never tried to learn how to control immolation as I did on the shores of Lake Pukaki, and the force of her explosion propels us both out of the tornado and through the wide expanse of the Second Circle. The icy rain and hail help to keep fire from blistering my skin, but the pain I still feel is exquisite agony.

We drop to the ground, knocking over Unspeakables like

skittles. Their brittle, wind-whipped bodies continue to bend and snap. I reach for Elinor and fall back. The trauma of immolation has morphed her features into the face of The Devil once more. Her black eyes are bleeding bloodred tears and she is laughing with maniacal energy.

"Beatrice!" screams The Devil Elinor. "My Beatrice. Come home to me!"

Virgil and Phlegyas are running through the rain toward us. At first, I think the ferryman is dragging the guide by his tattered red robes, but Virgil is several steps ahead of Phlegyas, and it is our newest companion who is being led by the blind man.

"The girl speaks with the voice of The Devil!" cries Phlegyas. "How can that be?"

"Beatrice...I know you can hear me!" cries The Devil Elinor, convulsing on the ground. "Long have I searched for you. Come home! Your place is at my side!"

Virgil is hit on the head by a large hailstone. He collapses to his knees and crawls along the mud toward Elinor. The bones of an Unspeakable some ten steps away from us crackle as another vortex of wind hurtles toward us. I cannot see or hear Mitchell and Medusa. They are unprotected in this tempest, as is Jeanne—wherever she is now.

The Devil's face fades away and Elinor is returned to us once more. Hail assaults her burned, smoking body. I am no longer registering my own pain from immolation. I need to gather my warriors and get us the Hell out of here.

The funnel of wind veers to the right. It pulls at Phlegyas's legs, but I throw myself down on Elinor, Virgil and the ferryman all at once, and all three are spared from the passing tornado. Completely sodden, I am heavy enough to anchor them to the ground.

At this point, I have no sense of where we are or how deep we have been taken into the circle. There is no torchlight here—it would be snuffed out in seconds by the rain—but there is a kind of natural light, like a late-afternoon sun, that hides everything on the far periphery but affords me clear tunnel vision to see what is directly ahead.

"We must find Mitchell, Medusa and Jeanne!" I cry. "Virgil, use your senses. Jeanne has immolated. Can you smell her flesh? Mitchell and Medusa may be calling for help. Can you hear their cries?"

"I can hear M," chokes Elinor.

"That is not *our* Medusa!" I cry. "That is the stolen echo of the living Melissa Pallister, and is the reason we immolated, Elinor. You must force the voice from your head."

But Elinor shakes her head. Her soaking-wet hair is caked in mud and is singed and broken from the fire.

"It is M, our M!" she yells, pulling herself up. "See?"

Elinor is pointing to a long, swirling shadow moving across the ground that has two fires lit within it, at least fifty feet in the air.

Mitchell and Medusa. And like Elinor and me, both have immolated. The Second Circle of Hell has managed to create weapons out of all of us.

"Follow it!" I cry. "And hold on to one another."

The fires continue to blaze, each equally bright. Mitchell has already immolated once in this monstrous place, but this is the first time in the Circles of Hell for Medusa. Team DEVIL is now truly an army of warriors, and our weapons come from the very hearts that no longer beat.

Phlegyas stumbles on a length of wood lying on the ground and pulls Elinor down with him. Virgil and I slide into a pile of hailstones and send them scuttling in all directions. An Unspeakable is lying on the ground with its arms and legs bent at unnatural angles. Flesh hangs from its body where it has been flagellated by the elements. It twitches, rises and then snaps back up as if it has been inflated. I was hoping never to see this scum again, but even in his wretched state, I recognize him. The Unspeakable is Rory Hunter. My gag reflex is strong and the acidic taste of bile rises and falls in my throat.

Our eyes meet. For a split second, the agony and fear in his eyes give way to familiarity as he recognizes me. But I do not allow myself to wonder what is going through his mind as he sees us here. I will not waste any more time on this miserable wretch of a soul. Rory Hunter defiled an innocent girl. He shattered her to her core. And in so doing, he also defiled the gift he was given to lead an honorable, productive life. For so many reasons, he deserves this eternal agony.

I turn away for the last time, glad that Medusa is high above us and unable to see the disgusting creature at my back.

"Your axe, Viking," says Phlegyas, handing me my blade. The handle is scoured with the scraping of fingernails. A torn nail is embedded in the wood. It is too large to be Medusa's. It must be Mitchell's.

"They're falling!" cries Elinor. "Look, the fires in the wind funnel are dimming. M and Mitchell are dropping. Quick."

The four of us find our feet and run toward the descending Mitchell and Medusa. They are falling through the funnel in slow motion, buffeted by the winds of Hell. We reach Mitchell first as the vortex dissipates around them—his pink eyes are rolling in their sockets—but like mine, his skin is not as cindered as Elinor's.

Medusa is a mess. Her entire body is smoldering with gray smoke as the rain beats down upon what is left of the heat within. The mass of hair is missing in chunks, and her skin is as red as blood.

I pull Mitchell to his feet; he leans forward and puts his hands on his knees.

"I heard her," he gasps, fighting for the breath he no longer needs. "I could hear Medusa...I mean the living Melissa."

"So did we," I reply, pulling off my tunic. Elinor and I work together to manipulate Mitchell's arms and head through the sleeves and neckline. I have little to offer him, but the cloth from my back may ease the suffering of his skin, just a little.

Mitchell stands up, and my tunic slips right down over his skinny shoulders and lands in a puddle of mud at his feet.

"We need to find Jeanne," says Elinor, gently patting Mitchell on the back before picking up my tunic and passing it back to me. "We need to get to her before any of us immolate again. I could not bear to hear…"

She trails off and wipes her bloodied face. It is Virgil who comforts her, and I am glad. I need to lead my friends and companions out of this holding place of evil. The time for embraces will be when this is over.

"Jeanne is unprotected in this circle because she is not with a Dreamcatcher like Elinor," I say. "It sickens me to say it, but I fear our best hope of finding her is to listen for the howling of the wolves. Cupidore is already here, and the other seven were following us. If they can attack her in formation, they will."

"Ignore the Unspeakables, they cannot harm us," says Phlegyas, joining Mitchell to pull Medusa to her feet. "Not even the one you fear the most."

"I don't fear him," mutters Medusa. "I hate him."

"Medusa, do you wish for Virgil to take you to the exit?" I ask. "The Skin-Walkers do not seem able to touch him. We will stay with Elinor for protection, will search for Beatrice Morrigan and will find Jeanne and meet with you."

"We stay together, Alfarin," she snaps, wincing with pain. "I am not afraid of Rory Hunter, not anymore."

Mitchell shakes his head at me; his wretched, bruised-looking eyes are narrowed in warning. *Do not push it* is the silent command.

"He will not come for you in this vile place, Medusa," I say quietly. "For I have seen him, and his punishment is fitting."

"We stay *together*," repeats Medusa. I nod my acquiescence.

"Virgil, you have the keenest hearing of us all," I say. "Lead us toward the Skin-Walkers."

"They will outnumber us, Viking," says Virgil. "If this group is torn asunder by another funnel of wind—"

"*Do it!*" I roar. "We are not leaving this circle until we have Jeanne d'Arc amongst us!"

I do not order the formation, but Virgil leads and the rest of us walk behind him, holding on to the person in front and the one behind. We stay close, calling for Jeanne and Beatrice Morrigan. Our heads whip back and forth in the rain as funnels of wind bear down on us.

The snarling of wolves is being carried on the wind.

"What if Jeanne's immolated out of here?" calls Mitchell. "We could be going down a dead end."

"She wouldn't have left us," shouts Medusa. "Jeanne's a warrior who follows orders. Septimus told her to protect—"

Medusa suddenly stops. At first I fear another tornado is crossing our path, but then I see our quarry. Jeanne is running. A faint golden nimbus surrounds her, and her speed is greater than that of any devil I know, but it is not an angel's immolation.

Fear has dampened her anger.

She is being chased. Three Skin-Walkers are on her tail. They do not run like wolves on all fours, but are loping on two legs with their long arms trailing toward the ground. Their heads are bent so it appears the wolf heads are the ones desperate for the feast.

That means there are another five Skin-Walkers close by.

I have seen diversions before; in life I instigated them myself when marauding with my Viking brethren.

Jeanne is being chased into a trap.

Prir Tigir Ein

Alfarin, Elinor, Mitchell and Medusa

Team Devil was completed the day Mitchell Johnson introduced us to Medusa Pallister—again. Of course, we did not know this was a second meeting. Not at the time.

She had been hired as a second intern in the accounting office, to work alongside Mitchell. Clearly, my friend was quite taken by this intriguing girl with her wild curls.

Elinor would call it fate. Mitchell would call it good luck. Medusa later discovered it was a paradox.

I silently called it the actions of a master tactician, manipulating time itself.

Lord Septimus was not a devil to be crossed.

By anyone.

31. Perfidius's Threat

The stubbornness of angels. Why didn't Jeanne stay with us? I know better than anyone the folly of leaving one's brethren in the midst of battle. We cannot reach her in time. Even without her weapon of flight, I would not be able to outrun her and the Skin-Walkers. My strength is my greatest gift, but even though my reflexes are quick, I am no distance athlete.

And I cannot split our remaining group up and ask Mitchell and Phlegyas to go after her, because then they will be left unprotected without Elinor and Virgil.

Team DEVIL screams as we watch Jeanne being overpowered like a gazelle. One Skin-Walker jumps for her neck; another leaps for her back. She is down in seconds.

Medusa pulls Mitchell toward her and kisses him hard on the mouth.

"This is Rory's fault!" she cries, pushing him away. "I have to make this right."

"Medusa!" yells Mitchell. "*What the Hell?*"

We all cry out as Medusa breaks free from the formation and dives into a vortex of wind that is winding a path to where Jeanne is trapped and about to be mauled. Elinor and Mitchell are hollering Medusa's name, but it is the pleading voice of Melissa Pallister we hear being carried by the wind as a ball of flame erupts in the center of the funnel.

"Why would she do that?" gasps Virgil. "I do not understand…"

I pull him around and grasp his face in my hands; his skin is soft like butter. Virgil's eyes are no longer foamy white in color; they are jet-black.

"You can see!" I exclaim. "How?"

"Forget Virgil!" shouts Mitchell. "We have to get to Medusa and Jeanne before the Skin-Walkers destroy them both!"

The three Skin-Walkers that were chasing Jeanne have been joined by the other five, but they are so preoccupied with getting Jeanne, they have not noticed the tornado gathering strength beside them. A fireball is dropping from the funnel, but the flames are being wrapped around the tendrils of wind, and at least ten feet of the twister is now encased in flames.

Such bravery. Such sacrifice. The firestorm that is Medusa is about to land directly on the eight Skin-Walkers.

Cupidore and Perfidius are the only two Skin-Walkers to jump out of the way in time. The other six are sucked into its midst and carried away. Their howls of pain and surprise reverberate around the Second Circle of Hell. The ground shakes and the intensity of the hail and rain increases. Ice coats my hair and beard. My tunic is in shreds, and I realize, for the first time, that everyone's clothes are in tatters.

But on we run toward Medusa and Jeanne. Both are lying in crumpled bloody heaps on the ground next to an Unspeakable who is clawing at the ground toward Medusa. Safe from the inferno of fire are Cupidore and Perfidious, who are returning for Medusa as well as Jeanne now. The rest of their pack is forgotten in their bloodlust.

I take my axe in both hands and run. With momentum as my ally, I plow through the frozen Unspeakables. Mitchell and Phlegyas are charging at my side, both of them roaring like kings in battle. Elinor and Virgil follow just a few steps behind. Both are crying out with the same voice. I am so shocked to hear it that I nearly stumble.

It cannot be.

For them to be crying out in the same voice can mean only one thing.

Finally I understand who Virgil truly is.

For I have heard that cry before.

It was the warning alarm we heard back in Hell when we were trying to make our escape—the one that sounded during the riot.

And it means that not only is my Elinor liberated, but M.J. will be safe.

My blade slices into Cupidore just as he is lowering his head and extending his wolfish tongue to lick Medusa's neck. He flies through the air with his entrails exposed. The inevitable flashback to my death does not weaken my resolve. Perfidious spits and snarls as we circle him, but the advantage is ours once more.

"You dare enter our domain and attack us," growls the leader of the Skin-Walkers, standing to his full impressive height. "This will not go unpunished. You have opened the door to an existence of never-ending fear and pain, Viking."

"Mitchell, carry Medusa," I order. "Phlegyas, take Jeanne. Virgil, get us out of here."

"Give me the Viciseometer," says the guide. "I am now able to see us into the final circle."

I pass the vibrating red timepiece to Virgil. It illuminates with a red glow that is like a ball of fire. Elinor helps Phlegyas to pick up Jeanne. The French angel's thick dead blood has been diluted by the relentless rain, and it runs in a river down their bare arms. She moans softly; her eyes are open. Medusa is also awake, but her groans are louder. Mitchell has her cradled in his arms.

"Do not change the times," I say to Virgil. "You must imagine the place we are to travel to. That will then transfer into the face of the watch."

"I know how to use this," says Virgil with a small smile. "I have used it many a time before."

I catch a glimpse of the Viciseometer as a sea of locations from Virgil's mind flashes across its face. For an instant, it settles on an ornate chamber decorated with bloodred drapes that frame a massive bed. A stone dais lies at the foot. Virgil and I lock eyes as the Viciseometer's face finally settles on what I know is the next circle.

"I will come for you first, Viking," snarls Perfidious. I turn from Virgil to find that the wolf-man's body is twitching with submissive pain at being so close to Elinor and Virgil. But the Skin-Walker is not backing down. "If it takes a thousand years, I will have you. You will not be protected forever by a vessel of The Devil's dreams. Before the end of days you will make a mistake, and I will take out your throat and drag you into the mouths of the beast in the Ninth."

"And Bót will be waiting for you," I reply, kissing the bloody blade of my axe, my sins finally atoned for. "Now, Virgil!"

The wind is warm as we are sucked through time to the final circle. The end is close.

And we have The Devil's Banshee.

Prir Tigir Treir

Alfarin, Elinor, Mitchell and Medusa

The Devil's Dreamcatcher was a weapon: the finest any realm would ever know. We discovered this on our journey with Medusa back to the land of the living, where we hunted down an escaped Unspeakable, her stepfather.

We learned firsthand the power of the Dreamcatcher he had in his possession. It was terrifying in its greatness.

But do you wish to know the downside to the finest weapons of war?

They aren't exclusive to one side.

32. Limbo

The Banshee has been Virgil all along, but in disguise. Whether she is keeping up this charade by choice or force, I do not know. What I do know is that one false move now could jeopardize everything we have fought so hard for. I believe that something in Team DEVIL has been drawing the Banshee out, and the longer she is in our company, the clearer her true self will become.

If I am not mistaken, that *something* is love. Lord Septimus told us that The Devil loved Beatrice Morrigan very much. Unless he took her to be his wife by force, and I have not been told he did, then I must assume that feeling was reciprocated.

But the Banshee has been in the Circles of Hell for a long time. And after spending centuries in a place of such doom, it stands to reason that all sense of love that resided in her soul has been long forgotten. This realm of evil, this chaos, has become *her* death. In coming here, Team DEVIL has reminded her what it is like to love, and we must continue to do that in order for her to be completely unmasked.

Mitchell is holding on to Medusa as if *his* death depends on it. Her skin is slowly returning to normal after her second immolation, but it is the damage inside I am most worried about. I thought seeing Rory Hunter would be the worst scenario she would face in that

Second Circle, but his physical form was just the vessel of evil. The real horror for Medusa was hearing her own voice, remembering.

Reliving.

Jeanne is being cared for by Elinor and Phlegyas. They are tearing up pieces of cloth from Virgil's red robes by hand and are wrapping the strips around Jeanne's torn skin, but she is so badly hurt that I can tell she needs to be healed properly by those who can mend the bodies of the dead.

Time is not on our side.

Time is never on our side, even when we think we have the means to control it sitting in a hidden pocket.

I place my hand on the guide's shoulder.

"Is this the final circle for us... Virgil?"

"A short walk, and then we will be in the fields of the castle in the First Circle of Hell," he replies, turning to stare at me. "That is my dwelling. It has been my dwelling for many years now. So many years I had... forgotten..."

His eyes are still as black as ink. This is good. What is hiding within is not withdrawing from me.

"I will need the Viciseometer back," I say, holding out my hand. "I made an oath to Phlegyas."

"We haven't found Beatrice Morrigan yet," says Mitchell, rocking Medusa. She is clutching at his arm with clawed fingers. "Alfarin... remember Elinor and M.J. We're running out of time."

"But we are through the worst," says Elinor. "We are so close."

I want to tell them. I want to give them hope, especially Mitchell, who is in a world of internal pain over his brother, but I cannot. Subtlety is not a state that comes easy to me, but I must at least try, using the skills that Elinor and Lord Septimus have been teaching me over the centuries.

Beatrice Morrigan is still hidden deep within Virgil. I must ease the Banshee to the surface gently.

"Virgil, please... lead us through the final circle," I coax. "We would never have come this far without your guidance. We will forever be in your debt."

"Remember, there is still a Skin-Walker here," replies the guide. "He is the watchman for those who are waiting."

"Waiting for what?" asks Mitchell.

"A second chance."

"At what?" I reply.

"At life," replies Virgil. "This is a place where evil breeds evil. Those who occupy the First Circle are the seeds of the evil yet to come."

"*What?*" cries Mitchell. "You mean they're just sitting around, waiting to be reincarnated?"

"In a manner of speaking," replies Virgil. "Do you think the Skin-Walkers want a cessation of pure evil on earth? Of course not. You know yourselves that Heaven and Hell are not split into good and bad. The Afterlife is not that simple. Not that black-and-white. The dead are simply divided up. But the arena of hate that is the Nine Circles needs to be replenished in order for the Skin-Walkers to feed. And so the Unspeakables in the First Circle are held back from their fate in the other eight circles so they may go back and breed more evil. *Lasciate ogne speranza, voi ch'intrate.* Remember those words I first spoke to you? 'Abandon all hope, ye who enter here.' Hope is left at the entrance to the First, but the First is where it all starts."

"Then take us away from true evil and toward hope," I say. "For it is that which we have all been clinging to all along, even you... Virgil. We never abandoned hope. If we had, we never would have entered the Ninth. I still have hope."

"Hope?" echoes the guide, his eyes glistening like small pools of oil. "I lost mine a long time ago."

"What did you hope for?" I ask.

Virgil stares into the distance. "I hoped for *hope*," he replies. "My existence had become too...noisy. Too colorful. Too...dramatic. I longed for peace."

"So you came into the Nine Circles of Hell to find it?" mutters Mitchell. "You're nuts."

"Maybe we can help you get hope back," I say, a little more earnestly. "If you want it."

Medusa is attempting to stand. Her legs are wobbly, like a newborn deer's.

"Your eyes, Virgil!" she exclaims, coughing up blood into her hand. "They aren't white anymore. Can you *see*?"

"For the first time in a long while," replies Virgil.

And Medusa smiles. It transforms her face, giving it light and color and health.

"Phlegyas and I will carry Jeanne," calls Elinor. "But we must get her to the healers in Hell before too long, Alfarin."

"No!" cries the Maid of Orléans. "I am going home. I am going back to—" Her French accent is lost in a growl that escapes from her shredded throat as she calls out. Blood oozes from her neck, and she clamps her hand down on the wound. It seeps between her long fingers like jam between pieces of bread.

"Viking," says Phlegyas. "The Skin-Walkers will come for me in the end. My escape from Hell is only temporary. But before I am returned to my place at the River Styx, I wish to see my home. When we are through the First Circle, take me to Delphi in Greece. I wish to atone for my crimes in life before I am brought back here."

"No, Phlegyas!" cries Elinor. "We can keep ye safe."

"Sweet child," says Phlegyas, laughing. "I wish to see blue skies and mountains once more. You have given me a chance to do that. Yet fate is not our friend. We all have a path, and to be the ferryman of the Fifth Circle is mine." He turns to Virgil. "When we get the chance to go home, old man, we should take it. Yes?"

"Alfarin," pleads Mitchell. "My brother."

"Virgil," I say. "Please lead us."

"I do not need to," replies the guide. "Continue walking through this tunnel, and it will bring us into the First Circle. The stone arch is where you must go."

He hands me the Viciseometer. I wait for the others to start the last procession, and I change the time on the milky-white face of the time-piece. Lord Septimus will expect us to be waiting back in the accounting office when he arrives.

I will not let him down. But I am not going back without The Devil's Banshee.

"How long was the peasant girl a vessel for The Devil's dreams?" asks Virgil.

"Too long for her, not long enough for him," I reply.

"She will never be the same. You know that."

"Yes."

"You know who I am, don't you, Viking?"

"Yes."

"Will you take me back by force?"

"I will not need to," I reply. "It was told that you left to find your-self in the Circles of Hell—the one place where The Devil could not, or would not, find you, and yet the one place where you were safe because of what you are. But you have hidden in plain sight, taking on the guise of Virgil, and tempting men like Dante with visions of a Paradise that does not exist."

"What is your point, Viking?"

"My friends and I have remained true to ourselves in this Hell. For better and worse. We have seen the worst in each other, and the very best. We did not need to find ourselves, and I believe you now see that, too. Innocent children are being taken because you left, Beatrice Morrigan. And in all this time, did you find yourself? No, you did not. You have taken on a false identity. This shell you wear is not yours; it is a mask. Peace may never be yours in the way I own the word, but you could do the right thing still. Come back with us. Phlegyas is right: we all have a fate in death. Mine is still to come, for I have seen it in a vision. Your fate is to be The Devil's true Dreamcatcher—the one being who can wield any control over the master of Hell."

We have been led into a green field. Not a bright, lush meadow with light and life, but a dark, shadowy field that is the color of dusty wine bottles. To our left is a black stone castle, just visible under a false starless sky that has been created for this circle. Shadows swirl around it like a heat haze. To our right is a black stone arch. The words *lasciate ogne speranza, voi ch'intrate* read backward, hollowed out of the rock from the entrance on the other side.

And Elinor, Mitchell, Medusa, Phlegyas and a bloodied Jeanne are standing in a semicircle, facing Virgil and me with open mouths. They all heard our conversation, and now they know we have had the Banshee with us all this time.

"Which is to be *your* path, Beatrice?" I ask gently, easing out her identity like a splinter embedded in skin. "Will you go left, to the castle of Unspeakables waiting in Limbo, or turn right, and come with us in the direction of hope?"

"You think hope is as easy as walking that path over there, Viking?" asks Virgil bitterly. "You think *love* is easy? You know nothing of the pain of either. I love The Devil, but to exist with him is to love his hate. And there was no end to it. I lost hope because I could see the end of both of us. But there wasn't a moment when I didn't ache for him. Hope and love are ruled by pain, and I was hurting so much, I lost who I was."

"Don't speak to me as if I know nothing of love," I reply. "My body is that of a man who saw no more than sixteen winters, but my soul is a thousand summers strong. Love is the reason I am here. The reason any of us are here."

"Come back to me."

Mitchell, Medusa, Phlegyas and even Jeanne all fall back in horror. Sickening cold sweeps through my body like a wave as Elinor speaks with The Devil's voice once more. Virgil shudders next to me, stretching out an arm toward my princess.

Elinor disappears as The Devil takes over her entire body. Her ragged clothes, torn and bloodied by what she has suffered in the Circles of Hell, morph into a black three-piece suit. With his black hair slicked back and the perfectly groomed goatee curled into a neat C, The Devil looks as if he's out for a walk in the park.

I try to stay calm. My fingers dig into the handle of my axe. To see Elinor completely possessed in body and soul is almost too much to bear, but this is my final test. It is obvious to me now. The Devil is the only one who can persuade Beatrice Morrigan to return to him.

And if he fails, we are all doomed.

Prir Tigir Prir
Alfarin

Anyone who knows me, Prince Alfarin, son of Hlif, son of Dobin, understands that like any Viking, I glory in the promise of Ragnarök, and all the sweat, tears and bloodshed it foreshadows.

But what I have never admitted to anyone is that I have a nagging question about the battle, and it terrifies me.

When the war is over and the victors proclaimed, what happens to the souls *after* the end of all days? I have grown very fond of this existence in the Afterlife.

And I do not want it to end.

Yet as in all great tomes throughout history, The End is approaching.

For all of us.

33. Ragnarök

"Walk away," says Phlegyas, taking my arm.

"No."

"We have to make it through the arch," he replies, pulling a little harder.

"I'm not leaving Elinor."

Virgil is starting to disappear. At first into shadow. Then slowly his red robes become torn black silk. The red skullcap is replaced by long black hair, flailing in a wind that doesn't exist.

But most striking is the way his haggard, lined face has morphed into the visage of a woman. It is pale and angular, with black oval eyes and high cheekbones.

"Come back to me, my Beatrice," implores The Devil.

"Where is El?" whispers Medusa frantically. "Where did she go? He's just projecting himself through her... isn't he?"

"We must leave," says Jeanne, backing away. "I cannot go back. I will not go back Down There."

She stumbles. The grass of the meadow crackles as she falls. Phlegyas pulls her up. Jeanne's hands are cut with delicate slashes.

"The grass," she says. "It is sharp."

"Alfarin," calls Mitchell urgently. "What do we do?"

"I'm not leaving Elinor."

This doesn't feel right. I'm supposed to do something else, but

I don't know what. We have been guided all this time by the very object we were searching for, but Virgil is gone. I can no longer turn to him for counsel or enlightenment.

The Devil and the Banshee are just staring at each other; their hands are outstretched, but neither is moving. They are both in limbo. Too afraid to get closer for fear of pushing the other away.

Limbo is a period of waiting. But for how long? Elinor cannot be the physical vessel for The Devil for any extended time, I am sure of it. To draw out his toxic dreams as his Dreamcatcher is a state no normal devil could endure for long, but to have this psychotic manifestation possess a body without resolution will almost certainly be intolerable—and impossible.

"It hurts to love you," says Beatrice softly.

"It hurts to be apart from you," replies The Devil. "We are so much stronger together. I see that now. Please don't leave me again."

I want The Devil and Beatrice Morrigan to forgive each other, even if they cannot forget, but both are proud. I know they will stay in this prison-like state for all eternity to avoid humiliation and further pain.

Lord Septimus told me I must see this through to the end. The very end.

My death occurred because I did not listen to orders.

I will not allow the destruction of Elinor because I failed to listen for a second time. This is my quest, my journey, and maybe the end of my days.

My personal Ragnarök.

"Mitchell," I call. "I am to stay here. I will not leave Elinor, but you will soon be unprotected without the power of a Dreamcatcher. Run to the other side of the arch and regain all of the hope that was once abandoned. Take everyone back to the time I have already placed in this." I throw Mitchell the Viciseometer. "Tell Lord Septimus I am seeing this quest through to the very end. However long it takes. He will understand."

Mitchell catches the Viciseometer with one hand; he doesn't even look at it. His pale-pink eyes do not leave mine. His face is stricken with grief.

"Don't ask me to leave you, Alfarin!" he cries. "You didn't leave me."

"We are in Limbo, and the longer we stay here, the harder it will be for all of us to pull away!" I cry. "Now go."

"I am not…going back…into the darkness!" cries Jeanne.

"Can you get over yourself for more than five seconds?" yells Mitchell. "There are worse things happening here!"

"I will not—"

"You selfish, self-absorbed—"

The Maid of Orléans immolates into brilliant white light that illuminates the entire circle. But it isn't the flashing streak we have become used to. It is a slow burn, and as Jeanne flies away like a projectile that has lost momentum, her dead blood falls from her wounds like red rain.

"Delphi, Viking," says Phlegyas. "You gave me your word."

"We'll take you there," says Medusa. "Mitchell, El can't hold out for long. There'll be nothing left of her if The Devil stays in her. We need to get back to Septimus. He'll know what to do."

But Mitchell and I exchange a look, unseen by Medusa, that speaks of understanding the mind of The Devil's accountant. Medusa wants to believe that Lord Septimus will never abandon us, but we know different. It would not be abandonment through indifference or even a lack of love, but through his duties as a leader. As with any great commander, the bigger picture is what is important to Lord Septimus. He will not come for me or Elinor. We are on our own.

A strange noise is expelling from Beatrice Morrigan. A continuous low-pitched hum. The Devil smiles, and for just a second, I see Elinor's sweet mouth. She is still in there—holding on.

"*Go!*" I shout to Mitchell, Medusa and Phlegyas. "The

Skin-Walkers will be able to attack the second you are out of the range of protection from Elinor and Beatrice."

"You're my brother, Alfarin!" cries Mitchell, and he slaps his bare chest with his fist: a Viking gesture of comradeship. "Never, ever forget that!"

Mitchell grabs Medusa's hand, and together with Phlegyas, they sprint toward the arch. Seconds later, a pack of wolves descends the steps of the castle and runs across the dark-green grass of the meadow. Flecks of blood spurt into the air as they try to catch my friends. The Skin-Walkers do not notice their skin being flagellated by the shards of sharp grass. Indeed, they seem to revel in the pain. Their mouths are open; black tongues loll at the sides of their bloodstained teeth.

Mitchell, Medusa and Phlegyas pass through the arch and disappear into a flash of flame.

They are safe.

The exhilaration of seeing my friends to freedom from danger quickly fades. A weariness is starting to overcome me. I step toward The Devil and Beatrice Morrigan. My axe feels heavy and unnatural in my hands. I need to end this stalemate quickly, but my mind feels sluggish.

"Here is where you'll find yourself, Beatrice. At your husband's side. You can...move forward...together...," I say, but my voice—a deep booming timbre that has been my constant companion in life and death—has been replaced by a wooden slur that makes me sound drunk and foolish. Time is slowing down and dragging out my very soul.

And the low-pitched hum is getting louder. The noise is still continuous, but it is becoming more of a pained cry.

"I have missed your song, my love," says The Devil. "I have heard only crying for so long. Sing it to me now."

"Hold on, Elinor," I call in the same elongated drawl. "I will not forsake you! We are so close to the end. You have endured so much. And Mitchell and Medusa are safe."

Beatrice Morrigan throws back her head and starts to scream. It is a relentless, terrible cry of pain and suffering. The dark grass beneath her bare feet blackens and shrinks down into the earth. The ground is vibrating and cracking. A circle of death starts spreading out, with the restored Banshee at the epicenter. As it reaches my feet, the toes of my boots blacken and crumble. I only just jump back in time before the rot sets in to my corporeal dead soul.

She is destroying the landscape around her, and by default, because they are in it, The Devil and Elinor are next in her path.

I have one choice left, because running away is not an option.

Lasciate ogne speranza, voi ch'intrate. These are words that will haunt you all for the rest of your existence. Limbo, lust, gluttony, greed, anger, heresy, violence, fraud and treachery. You will see, taste, smell, hear and feel the evil of man, and you will find yourself wanting, Viking.

Virgil's words, but he was wrong, for I am not haunted. I go to my eternal doom knowing that I have witnessed the very worst in death, and far from my being found wanting, the final choice was mine and mine alone. My existence will end in satisfaction.

I get to The Devil just as the toxic scream of the Banshee reaches him. I wrap my arms around his waist and close my eyes. He starts to struggle against me. I am ending The Devil's state of limbo, and he is scared. His strength is unworldly. Someone so thin should not have his hardiness. But I hold on, fighting against the intensity of his fervor for violence. And then, at last, with an almighty bellow from the depths of my soul, I push The Devil into the open arms of his wife.

"Go to her and give me back my princess. For I have not forsaken hope."

My existence goes black. I am falling. My soul is dissolving. The Banshee screams in the darkness. No light. No…nothing. Then I see the ghosts of my past one more time. Their powder-white spirits are coiling in the darkness like smoke. Valencia moves through the black expanse of death like a mermaid through water. Her long hair floats around her face, caressing the darkness. She stretches out a slender hand, but as much as I feel an ache for the mother I have never known, the love I have for Elinor pulls me back.

Pain.

Then comes the pain of a soul splintering as the ghosts dissolve into wisps of nothing. Of course there would be pain at the end of days. Only a fool would have hoped otherwise.

I am rising. My soul is no longer dissolving. The Banshee continues to scream in the darkness. But a pale light, reddish in color, filters through my eyelids. There is wind on my face.

And still, pain.

Sharps claws are digging into my shoulders. I open my eyes and a familiar face bends down to smile at me.

"You have friends in high places, Viking," says the Geryon, the bestial part-human, part-reptile from the Eighth Circle.

"Elinor," I gasp.

"I am here, Alfarin," calls my princess. She is holding on to the Geryon's other front claw, restored to her full, perfect beauty once more. We are high above the First Circle of Hell, but the entire landscape is imploding into a bubbling mass that looks like a gigantic mud pool. Fumaroles of black mist begin to emerge from it.

I cannot see either The Devil or the Banshee, but I can still hear her terrible scream. It vibrates into my very bones.

Elinor reaches for my hand, and we cling to each other as the First Circle of Hell starts to disappear below us. The Geryon flies us over the arch where I saw Mitchell, Medusa and Phlegyas use the Viciseometer. And there, standing on a patch of dwindling ground, is someone I recognize.

"General Septimus," says the beast, touching down. "You have but seconds."

"I have time in my hands," says the most important servant in Hell. His red eyes blaze with more than just fire. "Prince Alfarin, Miss Powell—if you would take my arm."

"Come with us, Geryon!" I say. "You cannot stay here."

"I will see you both again," says the Geryon. "For the end of days is coming, and with it, the shadow." His long neck bows to us all, and then, as the ground starts to crack and move, he takes flight.

I swear to the Norse god Forseti that the Geryon calls out "Ragnarök" as he flies into the black dust of the imploding First Circle.

Lord Septimus presses down on the large red button at the top of the Viciseometer. My body is still not mine to command. The heaviness of time is beached within my very essence. I can smell blood and sweat. The taste of smoke and fear coats my tongue.

We land in the accounting chamber. My manly legs cannot support my body and I drop to the ground, smashing my knees into the hard stone floor.

Two other bodies collide with mine and Elinor's, knocking us completely over, but exhaustion claims every inch of me before I can identify them. I sink into the ground as if I am made of soft butter.

I am not the same devil that left this place, but I did what I should have done in life.

I stayed.

When I awaken, I am in a room that I have visited once before during my one thousand years of death. Bright white light hurts my eyes, and it takes an age to focus on the sights and sounds now assaulting my senses.

It is the same room, lined with screens and telephones, where we were taken for interrogation after Rory Hunter escaped Hell with The Devil's Dreamcatcher. I have been placed in a corner, atop a thin mattress. I am wearing a clean black tunic that drops to my knees. My legs and feet are bare. The golden hair that keeps my legs warm at night has been shaved away, and several bandages are wrapped around wounds that throb with pain. The veins that still hold my dead blood within are engorged like dark-purple worms.

None of this concerns me. What worries me is that I cannot find Bót.

There are many devils in this room. Some are sitting down, leafing through papers. Others are talking into phones. Several are crowded around the largest screen of all. Lord Septimus is among them.

Only, at first I do not recognize him, for he is not dressed in the sharp tailored suits for which he is known so well.

Instead, he is outfitted in full battle armor: a dark-brown leather cuirass with thick, studded strips falling in a fringe at the front. Beneath that, Lord Septimus is wearing a simple white tunic edged in gold thread. In a scabbard attached to his belt is a sword. It does not fit fully into the scabbard. The sword is bent.

"Lord Septimus."

He turns and smiles. His teeth are as white as the spotlights in the room.

"Have some water, Prince Alfarin," says Lord Septimus, pouring me a glass. I drink it in three gulps. I am handed another—and another.

"I will have food brought to you as well," continues Lord Septimus. "You have been out for the count for a long time."

"Where is Elinor?" I ask, looking around. "Where is she? And where are Mitchell and Medusa? And—and where is—"

"They are all here," replies Lord Septimus. "And so is this," he says, smiling. From under my mattress he draws Bót and hands it to me. For the first time since I awakened, I feel more like myself.

"Walk with me, if you can, Prince Alfarin," says Lord Septimus. "I have a great deal to tell you."

I allow the general to guide me out of the room. He has always struck me as a tall man. He towers above me and most other devils. But now, in his battle uniform, he appears even larger.

Any thought that he was taking me to the accounting chamber on level 1 disappears the moment we set foot in the central business district of Hell. It has been transformed. Large fires are blazing on every floor, which no longer hold offices and places of work for devils, as the walls have been torn down. The noise of steel grinding into rock vibrates in my ears. Flaming sparks and glistening sweat combine to light up the entire cavern.

"What has happened here?" I cry. "Where is the order of death? It has been replaced by chaos."

"You and Miss Powell were in Limbo with The Devil and the Banshee for just minutes in your time," says Lord Septimus. "But time in Limbo extends toward the infinite, where a minute becomes a week for those existing in the true Underworld. Your selflessness was a gift, Prince Alfarin. Your sacrifice and readiness to see your quest through to the end gave me the opportunity to officially set in motion what I have been intending to do for a long while."

"I do not understand."

"It was thanks to your efforts in the Nine Circles that The Devil was persuaded to leave Hell, Prince Alfarin," says Lord Septimus. "The Devil took a risk and lost. He knew that if he ever left Hell for the Nine Circles and ended up in Limbo, he could be trapped there, which is why he never went looking for Beatrice, much as he longed for her. I can only assume that his connection to Miss Powell alerted him to Beatrice's location. But the Banshee's whereabouts would have remained a mystery to him for all eternity if you hadn't worked so diligently to ease Beatrice out of her shell. Once she was unmasked and named, he could not stay away—even if she was in the one place he feared most. And when he left to possess Miss Powell and confront Beatrice, I made my move."

"*Alfarin!*"

So many voices cry out my name, but it is the sweet soprano of my beloved English peasant girl that pulls me forward.

Elinor, Mitchell, Medusa, Johnny and Angela are running along the corridor. I lumber toward them like a three-legged bull elephant.

"Ye are awake at last!" cries Elinor. "Ye have been asleep for so long. I wanted to wake ye, but Mr. Septimus has kept ye close to him."

"Good to see you, man!" cries Mitchell, hugging me. Either he is stronger, or I am weaker. I cannot have that. I must eat meat. Now.

"Oh, Alfarin," says Medusa. "It's here. It's happening!"

"What?" I croak. Even Johnny has more strength than I as he slaps me on the back, and I feel my legs buckle. This simply will not do. Elinor's brother is akin to a stick insect with red hair. Did I leave my manliness back in the Circles of Hell? If so, I need to be taken back there so I can retrieve it right now.

Only Angela appears wary. She hugs me briefly, but once done, she starts to bite on her nails and doesn't stop. Her eyes are now pale pink. How long have I been sleeping?

I must look like a witless weakling, for Team DEVIL and the two members of Team ANGEL step back and look to Lord Septimus.

"Do you want us to bring Alfarin up to speed, boss?" asks Mitchell. "Or do you want to?"

"As always, I trust in Team DEVIL," replies Lord Septimus. "I do not have as much time as Prince Alfarin deserves, for I am awaiting a communiqué from Private Owen Jones. He has been on another reconnaissance to the battlefield, although there is still no sign of Mademoiselle d'Arc."

"Battlefield?" I ask.

"We'll get to that," says Mitchell. "First, how about a meat feast pizza?"

"*Wait!*" I pull back from Mitchell and Elinor, who have each taken one of my arms. "Did we do it? Did we save M.J. and the other children? Does The Devil have Beatrice Morrigan back as his Dreamcatcher?"

"We are assuming he does," replies Elinor. "But The Devil is no longer the master of Hell, Alfarin."

"*What?*"

"There's been a coup d'etat," says Johnny. "The peasants are revolting."

"Speak for yourself, Mr. Powell," replies Lord Septimus. "I have never been a peasant, and in my deathday clothes, I am certainly not revolting. In fact, I understand I am regarded as quite dashing. By the way, Miss Powell, there will be a debriefing in my office in three hours."

"And I will be there," replies Elinor.

"Even in a skirt Septimus looks cool," mutters Mitchell. "There's no hope for me, standing next to him."

"Hope for what?" exclaims Medusa, elbowing Mitchell in the ribs. "Who are you trying to impress, huh?"

"Absolutely no one," replies Mitchell, planting a lingering kiss on the crown of Medusa's head. "I've got you, and that's more than I can handle."

"Are you two...?" I find I cannot finish the question, I am so surprised and delighted.

"Poor Alfarin," says Elinor, sweeping my long hair away from my face. It has grown several inches since we began our quest. "Ye have missed even more than I, even though I was in Limbo with ye for so long. But then, ye have always liked yer sleep. Yes, Mitchell and Medusa are courting. And Mr. Septimus has started an uprising. And The Devil is amassing his own army. And I... and I..."

"And El is the most important one of us all," says Medusa proudly. "I think it's safe to say that The Devil's former right-hand man has gotten himself his *own* right-hand man. I mean, woman."

"He has?" I ask, looking at my princess and Lord Septimus in wonderment.

"Yup," Medusa replies, putting her arm around Elinor's shoulder. "Since she's seen The Devil's dreams and nightmares, she knows what he's planning to do."

"Which is what?"

"We are going to war, Prince Alfarin," replies Lord Septimus. "The end of days for Up There and Hell is upon us."

"Ragnarök," I say, when I can find my voice. I clutch Bót in my hand, and suddenly I feel strong. "I am ready, Lord Septimus."

This is what my fate has finally brought me to.

———————

I am a Viking.

A man.

A devil.

Alfarin, son of Hlif, son of Dobin, that is me. And I have started the apocalypse.